"A five-year-old mystery and the best kind of love ⟶ ⟶re of Sarina Bowen's twisty new thriller *The Five Year Lie*, which explores one woman's race toward the truth after receiving a text from her deceased ex. But this is more than just a twisty thriller. *The Five Year Lie* explores themes of loyalty and family, motherhood, and the tragedy of having to say goodbye too soon. I devoured this book in one day, and I guarantee you will too."

—Julie Clark, *New York Times* bestselling author of *The Last Flight* and *The Lies I Tell*

"An expertly woven story of love, revenge, and murder. In a world where so many books feel so similar—this was a refreshingly unique read and an addictive blend of love and mystery that I couldn't put down. This is storytelling at its finest, and I can't recommend this book enough."

—A. R. Torre, *New York Times* bestselling author of *Every Last Secret*

"Sarina Bowen is always an auto-buy for me, and this is the kind of book that's sure to stay with you. You can't go wrong!"

—Ally Carter, *New York Times* bestselling author of *The Blonde Identity*

"With tension that grabs you from the first page, characters that draw you in, and the romance of a life time. You won't be able to look away."

—Kylie Scott, *New York Times* bestselling author of *Lick: A Stage Dive Novel*

"Buckle up! *The Five Year Lie* is a twisty, roller-coaster tale of love and suspicion, revenge and murder. The cameras in our homes are supposed to watch for strangers but we never think they might be tracking us. Sarina Bowen layers on the suspense in this crackling story of passion and betrayal."

—Joanna Schaffhausen, author of *Gone for Good*

THE FIVE YEAR LIE

THE FIVE YEAR LIE

SARINA BOWEN

HARPER

NEW YORK · LONDON · TORONTO · SYDNEY

HARPER

HarperCollins books may be purchased for educational, business, or sales promotional use. For information, please email the Special Markets Department at SPsales@harpercollins.com.

FIRST EDITION

Designed by Jen Overstreet

Library of Congress Cataloging-in-Publication Data has been applied for.

ISBN 978-0-06-328060-1 (pbk.)

24 25 26 27 28 LBC 5 4 3 2 1

For Lauren Blakely. Thank you for being amazing.

PROLOGUE

"Soap and water," the woman says, watching her son wash his hands in the grimy bus station sink. She catches herself hoping he won't touch anything on his way out of the bathroom. A month ago, this sort of garden-variety worry was the only kind she had in her life.

It isn't anymore.

"Dry your hands on your jeans," she says when he's done.

Her son looks up at her in confusion. In all four of his years on this earth, that was never the plan. There's always a towel. And dinner at the table, and clean pajamas at nighttime.

"It's okay," she whispers, even though nothing is okay. She swipes his hands on her own jeans and then clamps one of his damp hands into hers. "Stay close." She nudges the bathroom door open with a knee—because germs are still bad even when you're running for your life—and guides him back into the busy terminal.

She makes a beeline for Bay 24. She's thirtyish with light brown hair that skims her shoulders as she moves. Her clothes are well cut, because she comes from money. But her expression is pinched with anxiety.

"We'll wait here," she says, lifting him onto the last available seat on the end of a bench. "Hold on tight to your shark."

The boy clutches his stuffed toy and asks, "Can we get on the bus now?"

"Soon," she says, hoping it isn't a lie.

So far, she's sold this trip to him as an adventure. You can't tell a four-year-old that you're running scared. That you know too much, and that others who knew too much have already been killed for it.

This bus trip is her best chance at anonymity. She plants herself in front of his small body, and avoids eye contact with anyone but him.

It's possible that she and her child have already been reported missing.

A hundred yards away, in the security office, a stocky guard drinks a cup of Dunkin' coffee in front of a bank of monitors. With one finger on the smudged keyboard, he flips from camera to camera.

In Bay 16, he spots a man pacing erratically and talking to himself. The other passengers are clumped together on the other end of the platform, giving him space. Mick'll have to deal with that dude before his dinner break.

He pokes the arrow key again and flips to the next set of images. He's got forty-eight feeds to monitor, but only two eyes. So he devotes exactly 1.8 seconds to the camera focused on Bay 24.

His gaze snags on the woman and the little boy right away. He sees her anxiety. She's fidgety, but so are a lot of people. And single moms aren't exactly on top of his list of problems. Not unless they get pickpocketed.

He flicks to the next group of monitors, already forgetting her.

Out in Bay 24, the loudspeaker crackles to life. The young woman straightens up as they announce her bus. Her nervous fingers move instinctively to the pocket where she's tucked two tickets issued to names that don't match her own.

The little boy slides off the bench, and they both turn toward the security camera.

In the olden days—like 2015—unmonitored surveillance cameras were stupid creatures, with the unblinking gaze of a toddler in need of a nap. But times have changed. The overworked security guard isn't the only one watching.

The camera in Bay 24 feeds its images to the cloud, where a piece of AI software triangulates each face in its focal range. All those eyes and noses and scowls. More data for its endlessly hungry maw. The system sees it all.

And now it sees her, too.

Even as the young woman shuffles toward the door, breathing diesel fumes, the software is measuring the geometry of her face. On a distant, humming server, the precise distance between her intelligent brown eyes is compared against the angle of her wry mouth. In a fraction of a second, the configuration is charted and checked against the database.

A match is made.

The location noted.

A few more electrons smash together, and a message pings across the ether, lighting up a distant phone.

Subject identified.

1

ARIEL

"Oh, Ariel! Have you signed up for the picnic yet?" This question is lobbed at me even before I can extract my son from his bike seat.

Even so, I take my sweet time removing Buzz's helmet and hoisting him down to the ground. When I finally turn around and acknowledge Maddy—one of the preschool's pushiest PTO mothers—she offers me a clipboard with a dangling pen disguised as a daisy.

Reluctantly, I take it from her. GRADUATION DAY PICNIC SIGN-UP SHEET! it reads. PLEASE TAKE ONE SLOT FOR YOU, AND ONE SLOT FOR YOUR PARTNER!

That's a lot of exclamation points for a Monday morning. The list of jobs is numbered from one to thirty-six. That's two for each of the eighteen kids in Buzz's class. The choices range from baking two dozen cookies to running the sack race.

The whole thing makes me feel salty. First of all—since when do preschoolers *graduate*? And then there's the careful use of the word *partner*. Some of Buzz's classmates have two mommies or two daddies. So that was thoughtful—but only up to a point.

"What if I don't have a partner?" I ask Maddy. "Am I still supposed to take two slots?"

"Oh." Her smile fades by one or two notches, and her eyes reflect genuine puzzlement, as if the existence of single mothers has never occurred to her. "Just do the best you can."

So I scan the list. The easiest options—napkins, compostable paper plates, and drinking water—have already been nabbed. I scribble my name beside the request for ten watermelons and a chef's knife to cut them up. Then I note the date—three weeks from now. Somebody's an overachiever. I hand back the clipboard.

She glances at it, and I brace myself to hear her say something about my half-hearted volunteerism. "Pro tip," she says instead. "You can use folded cardboard to make a guard for the knife. That's how I avoid slicing the lining of my bag." She pats the Tory Burch tote under her arm and smiles.

"Good idea," I say with the closest thing I can muster to a smile. Then I take Buzz's hand and walk him into the old brick building.

In Buzz's classroom, several children are already ransacking the dress-up box, pulling out velvet cloaks and outlandish hats. Buzz pastes himself to my thigh, though, and doesn't move to join them. He always takes a couple of minutes to warm up to the chaos of preschool.

"He's a quiet child," my mother, Imogen, always says. "Watchful."

Just like his father, I'm always tempted to add. But I never talk about Buzz's dad.

Buzz likes school, though, so I just ruffle his hair and wait him out. And sure enough, after he watches the action for a minute, his grip on my hand loosens.

His teacher—the wise and kind Miss Betty—approaches us. "Good morning, Buzz. I have some new hats to try on today. And I got the sand table out this morning. See?" She points toward a quiet corner of the room.

My son's eyes shift to the sand table, and he drops my hand.

I lean over and plant a kiss on his sweet-smelling head. "See you after lunch."

He flashes me a quick smile before heading over to the sand table.

"There we go," Betty says. "Good weekend?"

"Absolutely. We helped my mother with some gardening. There was lots of whistling. Sorry." Buzz is the only kid in his preschool class who can whistle, and he does it constantly. Sometimes it's tuneful. Sometimes it's not.

Betty's eyes crinkle in the corners when she smiles. "I don't think he even knows when he's doing it," she says. "And there are worse habits. Enjoy the day."

I take one more glance at my child. He's already holding a tiny rake and smoothing the sand, his lips pursed in a whistle.

Sometimes when I look at him, I just ache.

After drop-off, I pedal slowly toward the office. It's a warm spring day, and let's be honest—no one is going to fire me from my lowly job in the family empire for being a couple minutes late.

Seagulls screech overhead as I navigate the twisty brick streets. I never imagined I'd live in New England forever. I always assumed I'd be off making art in Dublin or Prague. Or at least Brooklyn.

Then life happened. Namely Buzz. But there are worse places than Portland, Maine, especially with ample babysitting and a free place to live.

My setup is just about as cushy as a single mother could ever expect. I work part-time for my family's tech company. That paycheck, combined with my trust fund, keeps me flush with enough cash to afford all the things that privileged four-year-olds enjoy— private preschool, day camps in the summer, and trips to the children's museum.

It also allows me to spend three afternoons a week pursuing my real passion in the studio—creating blown glass.

Even as I walk my bike into the office building, my mind shifts to a series of flasks I've been making. Their sides are flattened and blocky. Like the facets of jewels. I'm experimenting with an ombré effect, where the bottom of the vessel is made from colored glass that slowly gives way to clear at the neck . . .

"Careful, Ariel."

I lift my head and find Hester, my uncle's assistant, right in my path. She's an attractive middle-aged woman with a sleek gray pixie cut and a noticeable addiction to wrap dresses.

She's also grumpy as hell. My uncle and I are both a little afraid of her. "Sorry," I say quickly.

Scowling, she trots up the open stairway to the second floor, which is the nerve center of Chime Co.

It takes me a moment to lock my bike to the rack under the stairs before I follow her up to the second floor, where I step into a vast office space that's already mostly full of computer programmers, managers and support staff.

This is Chime Co., the largest tech company in Maine and the number two manufacturer of doorbell cameras in the country. Years ago, my father and his brother founded the company in my uncle's basement. But now there are hundreds of employees—so many that Uncle Ray just bought the office building so that we could expand to two more floors.

I'm the office manager. My hours are flexible, and the work isn't very taxing. I don't mind it, but I'll never be Chime Co.'s employee of the month, either.

Case in point—the conference room is already filling up with programmers for the Monday meeting, but there's no way I'm going in there without coffee. So I head for the coffee counter on the far wall.

Skilled programmers are always in short supply, and must be wooed by perks like good coffee and snacks. The job of stocking these goodies falls to me, which means the coffee is *excellent*, and there's a bevy of complements in the mini fridge, including hipster choices like oat milk and flavored creams.

I make myself a latte before heading into the meeting. The only open seat in the conference room is next to Hester, who gives me a fresh scowl as I sit down.

In return, I beam at her. She hates that.

At the head of the table, my uncle is already opening the meeting. Without breaking his cadence, he nods hello to me, his expression friendly, in spite of my tardiness.

It's a cushy job. I'll own my privilege.

I dig into my shoulder bag for my planner and a pen. Usually the content of these meetings has little to do with me, but we're in the middle of an office move, so I have to at least feign attention.

Then, as one of the programmers launches into a lengthy update, my phone chimes loudly with a text.

Oops.

I could ignore it and pretend that intrusion came from someone else's phone. As one does. But I never ignore texts when Buzz is at school. Emergencies are rare, but there was a stomach bug last year and—even worse—a head lice incident this fall.

Lord in heaven, let it not be lice again.

Under Hester's judgmental gaze, I pull out my phone and check the message.

But it's not the school. In fact, the name on the screen stops me in my tracks.

Drew Miller.

I blink. But when my vision clears, his picture is still there—a photo I took of the two of us at sunset in Fort Allen Park. And when I read the text message, I stop breathing.

> Drew: There's trouble. I need to see you. Meet me in one hour under the candelabra tree. Don't tell anyone where you're going.

That message would rattle me coming from anyone. But coming from Drew, it's heart-stopping.

Because Drew Miller, the only man I ever loved, and the father of my child, is dead.

2

FIVE YEARS AGO, JUNE

The girl across the aisle looks up suddenly, forcing Drew to flick his eyes back onto his own monitor.

Way to be smooth, he chides himself.

He drags his eyes back to his work. He's struggling to concentrate on the lines of code on his screen, and for all the wrong reasons.

People-watching is part of his mission at Chime Co. He needs to learn every single thing about the way this place works. He wants all the office gossip. And he needs to understand how deeply the feud between the two founders runs.

Staring at the boss's daughter is not part of the plan. It's just that Ariel Cafferty is so damn distracting.

The cursor blinks expectantly on his screen, but he can still see her out of his peripheral vision as she bends toward her sketchbook again, her brow creased in concentration as her pencil meets the page.

He edits the last command he's written and waits for the compiler to update. Ariel twirls a lock of her hair around a finger, and he holds back a sigh.

He's not above chatting up a girl for information. But what would *this* girl know? Probably nothing. The whisper network says she's just filling in while the office manager is out on maternity leave. And only because her daddy makes her.

Still, she probably lived with that asshole for most of her life. There could be something there. Maybe she knows why her father and her uncle hate each other so much.

Unbidden, his glance finds her again. That keeps happening. Partly because she's ridiculously attractive, with shiny hair in a rich shade of brown and eyes that flash like she knows a secret. She's wearing a sleeveless dress that shows off tanned shoulders. If she were any other girl, he'd like to test their smoothness under his palms.

The really fascinating thing about her, though, is her obvious disdain for this whole place, and particularly for her father. It's fair to say that she's the only one in this room—besides Drew—who isn't afraid of that man.

If she *were* afraid, she wouldn't take those long lunches. And she wouldn't answer the phone with an expression that implies its existence offends her. And she definitely wouldn't sit there sketching at her desk, the pencil case propped open in front of her.

Maybe he'll ask her out for drinks. Just once. So he can find out what she knows.

As he watches, she taps a blue pencil against her lip, eyeing her work with a critical stare.

From this angle, he can't see the drawing. But he's not about to invent a trip to the espresso machine or the men's room just to look. Even if the curiosity is burning him up inside.

Absolutely not.

Nope.

"It's not you," a low voice says from nearby.

It takes Drew a beat to realize which guy at an adjacent work-space is speaking to him. "Sorry?"

"She's not drawing *you*," his neighbor continues without look-ing up. The guy's name is Zain, and he's barely said ten words since Drew started this job. "There are cameras all over this room, by the way. If you spend a lot of time staring at her, somebody will notice."

Well, fuck. "Good tip. Much appreciated."

Zain is silent for another long beat. "She draws glass," he con-tinues eventually. "If you're so curious."

"Glass," he repeats like a dummy. "Like, things you drink out of?"

Zain smirks. He's a thirtyish guy with a thin face, outrageous eyebrows and wildly curling hair. And his skin has the pallor of someone who never goes outdoors.

He doesn't fit the Chime Co. mold. At all. The office favors a frat boy vibe that Drew has been trying to mirror—clean-shaven faces, nice shirts and foul mouths.

"She's an artisan," Zain adds. "Think vases and candleholders. Some of it is pretty great."

"Oh. Cool," he says in a voice that betrays no interest. But his traitorous eyes go right back to their new favorite place as he tries to fit this information into the impression he's formed.

For starters, she's the heir to a fortune. Chime Co. grew its revenue by over a hundred percent last year. More than a million customers are panting to pay a few hundred dollars for a premium doorbell camera. There's big money in deterring thieves from stealing your gluten-free meal kits off your front porch.

And this girl only cares about *glass*, a technology that probably hasn't changed much in a thousand years?

Huh.

"Incoming," Zain mumbles, dropping his chin and typing like a madman.

After a couple of years in combat situations, Drew has excellent instincts. He drops his gaze just as the big boss himself rounds the aisle and crosses in front of him, blocking out the view of Ariel.

That should make it easier to concentrate. Except Drew is blatantly eavesdropping as he scrolls through his block of code again.

Edward Cafferty doesn't open with a friendly greeting for his daughter. Instead, he growls a question at her in exactly the same tone that makes the programming managers quake. "Where are the presentations?"

"In the conference room," Ariel says immediately. She doesn't add *you dickhead* to the answer. But it's implied. "Ten copies. Stapled."

Out of the corner of his eye, Drew sees her holding up a yellow note card—the same kind her father uses for everything, often dropping them onto the team leaders' desks like a surly mailman.

Drew has only been here a couple of weeks, and he's already seen a flurry of those yellow cards. There's no greeting on them, either. Just a job request, with a deadline at the bottom.

Version push 3:30p. Meeting 4:15p.

There are office jokes about the yellow cards—like maybe the boss uses them at home with his wife. *Dinner 7p. Missionary sex 9:45p.*

Now Edward Cafferty folds his arms like a general addressing the troops. "And the coffee service? The client will be here any second."

There is a loud silence, and Drew thinks, *Uh-oh.*

"Coffee service?" Ariel repeats quietly.

"Coffee, tea, pastries and a fruit platter," he sputters. "We order the same way for every damn presentation."

Her defiant attitude is gone now, probably because she's seen this show before, and she doesn't like how it ends. This is only Drew's second week of working here, and he already knows the boss is about to blow a gasket.

"It wasn't on the card," she says softly.

Edward Cafferty drops his voice, but it doesn't make him any less threatening. "I gave you this instruction on *Monday*."

"Well, shit," she says, and Drew *almost* laughs. But he wouldn't want to draw attention. Ariel rises from her chair. "I'll go find something now."

Remarkably, she slips past her father without the volcanic eruption that Drew is expecting. Possibly because of time constraints—the client's arrival is imminent, and maybe it's not a good look for the CEO to throw a tantrum just now.

Sure enough, he's all smiles a few moments later when a team of visiting cops is ushered past the programming staff and into the glassed-in conference room. And he smiles again when Ariel opens the glass door twenty minutes later, carrying a box of coffee from Dunkin' and a waxy bag of cookies from the bakery down the block.

It's a crocodile's smile, though. Drew knows the type.

So does Ariel, apparently. She doesn't go back to sketching afterward. She puts away her brightly colored pencils and makes herself busy with a stack of receipts and a grim look on her face.

Drew puts his head down and goes back to work on his code. He has plenty to do, plenty to learn. He's given himself ninety days to accomplish his personal mission at Chime Co. And fourteen of them are already gone.

The client meeting ends right around five. Drew notices that

Ariel doesn't even look up as her father escorts his clients to the door. There's a round of hand-shaking before the visitors depart.

But she must sense what's coming.

The minute they leave, Edward storms right back to her desk and plants himself in front of her again. "What the fuck, Ariel? What the actual fuck? Your solution to a huge mistake is a box of coffee from *Dunkin' Donuts*?"

Drew actually holds his breath, wondering if she'll say something flip.

"Apologies," she says stiffly. She tilts her chin up and looks him right in the eye, though, refusing to cower.

Edward hates that. So he gets louder. "This job is so easy a goddamn *monkey* could do it! But you never apply yourself. This business is responsible for every comfort you have in the world. That client could grow our revenue ten percent." He sweeps an arm out, indicating the room. "We could provide jobs for five or ten more people. Is it too much to ask that you put away your toys and do your fucking job?"

"No, sir," she says crisply. "It won't happen again."

"It *better* not. Now get your ass into that conference room and clean it. There are cookie crumbs everywhere."

Drew can almost hear the sound of her jaw clenching. But she doesn't argue. "Consider it done."

The boss begins to turn away from his daughter, and Drew sees her exhale.

But then he whips back around again. "And you *clearly* need to spend more of my fucking money on some decent clothes. You're dressed like a slutty teenager."

After a long beat, the boss finally storms off. His office door slams shut a few seconds later.

Ariel lifts her head suddenly, and a dozen programmers quickly look away.

Drew's head is already down, though. He's tapping code into his keyboard, as if oblivious. But the word *slutty* is still ringing in his ears.

Jesus. Who says that to his own kid?

He doesn't glance at her again until she walks toward the conference room. Only then does he dare lift his gaze. The yellow dress she's wearing is sleeveless, but simple in design. It's not too short, either—just short enough to show off the tattoo on her calf—a profusion of sunflowers. If anything, the dress is preppy, and would look boring on someone else.

But it makes Ariel look like the only flower in a drab place.

Cleaning that conference room should only take ten minutes. But she makes it last forty. And it works for her, because her dad is gone when she emerges. And everyone else is funneling toward the doors.

Except for Drew. He waits, which is a dumb thing to do. But he does it anyway.

And Ariel only scowls at him for it. "Are you about done? I'm supposed to tell the cleaning crew they can come in. There's nobody here to impress anymore. So you can run along now."

"Oh, I'm done all right." He stands up, taking her in. "I'll bet you've had enough, too. That was barbaric."

Her eyes dip. "That was nothing new. Just his fun little way of showing love." She picks up her pocketbook. "Get gone. It's Friday. Time for brewskis and smack talk with the other code monkeys."

"I think I missed my window. They're probably three drinks in already." He really *should* be chatting them up, and not Ariel. But here he is anyway, following her to the door. "I'll walk you out."

"You don't have to be nice to me," she says. "It won't do you any favors with the boss. Try putting on kneepads and kissing his ass directly."

His own laugh surprises him. "That is *not* on my to-do list. He needs a lesson in manners. A man shouldn't speak to anyone that way, let alone his own child."

"I'm not a child," she grumbles. "And to be honest, I was a hellacious teenager. We all have our flaws."

"Still." He follows her down the stairs, where she pushes the front door open. He takes his first breath of salty, summer air. "It's not right—"

"Look," she says, stopping on the sidewalk. "You're very charming, and not bad to look at. And I know he's a prick. But I don't really want to treat it with talk therapy, you know? It's Friday night, for fuck's sake."

He blinks, and then smiles. "What's your favorite medicine, then?"

"Vodka. Seafood. Live music. Smoking a bowl." She lifts her chin, turning the suggestion into a dare.

Christ, he's playing with fire. This might be the dumbest idea he's ever had, or the best one. It could really go either way. "I'm good for those first three things," he says, leaning against the brick wall like he owns the place and bringing out his best smile. "But pot makes me broody." Not to mention that doing drugs with the boss's daughter is the worst idea ever. "So what's your favorite watering hole?"

It's her turn to blink. As if she can't believe he'd go there. "You followed me out here to console me, huh? Or did you hear the word *slutty* and decide to look for your opening?"

Well, ouch. He'd imagined he was smoother than that. "See, I don't think that dress actually qualifies as slutty. You'd have to try harder. I don't know if you really have what it takes."

She barks out a shocked laugh and then turns her smile away from him, as if it's something private she's not willing to share.

It makes no sense, but he actually has to restrain himself from kissing her right then and there. But he controls himself, at least for now.

And then he takes her out for vodka tonics, fried clams and live music.

3

ARIEL

When I finally remember to breathe, I look more closely at the message on my phone. The time stamp is fresh. And when I scroll up, I find the last texts I ever sent to Drew, dated almost five years ago.

There's not much here. When Drew and I were together, I was still on my parents' phone plan. Since my father's day job was essentially spying on people, I never knew who might have access to my texts. So Drew and I used to call each other instead.

What I wouldn't give to hear his voice right now. Just one more time.

After my father's sudden death, though, I texted Drew directly. The last frantic messages in our thread are all from me. I begged him to call.

He didn't, though. He left me instead. And then he died a few months later.

It was a traumatic time in my life. And I'd never expected to see his name pop up on my phone again. It makes no sense at all.

Scrolling back down, I read the new message several more times.

> Drew: There's trouble. I need to see you. Meet me in one hour under the candelabra tree. Don't tell anyone where you're going.

It's baffling. Dead men don't send texts. Yet I keep looking down at the screen, willing another message to come through. But nothing does.

I *know* Drew isn't on his way to the park to meet me. Of course he isn't. But I suddenly know I'm going to go there anyway.

Someone sent me that text. Maybe it's a sick prank. Or maybe someone else has Drew's number now—someone who likes the candelabra tree in Deering Oaks Park.

With a thumping heart, I tap Drew's avatar, bringing up his contact information. My finger hovers above the *call* button. Then I remember I'm in the middle of a meeting.

But not for long.

I grab my bag off my lap and hoist it onto my shoulder. But the jerky motion takes up too much space in tight quarters, and my elbow clips my coffee cup on the conference table. Over it goes.

"Shit!" I hiss as my latte begins to spread in a caramel-colored pool across the walnut surface.

Several things happen at once. Hester jerks back from the table with a noise of outrage as the spill runs in her direction. From my other side, a pale hand shoots out to grab the offending cup and right it.

Heads turn. The room falls silent.

"Sorry," I mutter a couple of times. Now I'm digging in my bag for napkins and hurling them at the table, trying to stanch the bleeding.

The guy who's trying to help me—a scrawny programmer named Zain—shoots me curious looks while we both try to contain the damage.

"Sorry," I say again. "Two seconds and I'll be out of your way."

I jam my phone in my pocket and then gather the sodden napkins in both hands.

With a dozen pairs of eyes following me, I traipse out of the room.

My uncle actually follows me to the doorway. "You okay, Ariel?"

"Yup," I say with a jerky nod. "Just, uh, forgot about an appointment. Dentist."

"Huh, okay. See you later?"

"Of course."

The door shuts behind me again as I drop the whole mess into a wastebasket. My pulse is racing, and I'm sticky with coffee.

But I open my phone again and dial Drew's old number. As if I hadn't done that same thing a hundred times after he disappeared.

The circular photo grows in size as my phone initiates the call. And while it tries to connect, I study the photo. He's in profile, his lips pressed to my cheekbone. His eyes are closed, as if he loves me too much to think about anything else.

As if he's not going to ghost me a few weeks after this photo is taken.

But then he did.

I hold the phone to my ear and hear a tinny ring. Then a recorded voice says, "There is no mailbox set up for this number. Please try your call again later."

I end the call, still confused. My mind whirling.

This morning's text doesn't make a lick of sense. And yet I know I have to go look for him anyway. I can't not go.

I exit the building not ten minutes after I arrived. Back on my bike, I make a beeline to the north, toward Deering Oaks Park.

These days I live in the carriage house behind the Victorian mansion where I grew up. But the summer I met Drew, I had my own place near the park, and we used to meet under the tree and go for long bike rides together. Or sometimes we'd just wander along the paths, holding hands and swapping gossip.

Our relationship was—and still is—my biggest secret. My father was a controlling man, and actively hostile toward every boyfriend of mine he ever met. So Drew and I had to keep our dalliances quiet. As a Chime Co. employee, it would have complicated his life, not to mention mine.

I was twenty-four that summer, and I already knew I'd never please my father. So we snuck around. It wasn't even difficult. Drew had a small apartment on an unfashionable street near the university, where my parents wouldn't deign to go. And I was sharing an apartment with a high school friend in Parkside, out of their sight lines.

Pedaling toward the park with the wind in my face, I feel like a time traveler. Five years ago I was still a carefree artist in training, working for my dad that summer just to get him off my back. I spent all my other waking hours at the glass-blowing studio. I didn't have a boyfriend, and I wasn't interested in dating.

Until I met Drew, that is. And fell fast and hard into the kind of love where you fall asleep dreaming about him and wake up looking for him. Every time he smiled at me, I knew I'd found my other half.

Or so I thought. I had no idea how badly I could be hurt. And if someone had tried to caution me, I wouldn't have listened.

Even Drew warned me against getting too attached. That first night we went to dinner, I asked him if he was new to Portland.

"Just passing through, to be honest," he said. "I needed this job, but I probably won't stay long."

"Why?" I heard myself ask, while we sipped vodka tonics at a dockside clam shack, under cheap string lights at an open-air table.

"Maybe this isn't something I should tell the boss's daughter." His blue eyes flashed as he gave me a guilty smile.

"Really? Because my dad and I are so close?"

He snorted. "No, but it's going to sound ungrateful. I got a medical discharge from the army, and I needed a job. Pretty glad your father hired me even though my programming is rusty."

"But now you've realized he's not your dream boss?"

Drew lifted his broody eyes, giving me a view of his strong neck while he contemplated the night sky. "It's not that. I just don't think I'm cut out for corporate work. I can't make a whole career of it, because I don't believe in the product."

"Too invasive?" I asked. Because if you work at Chime Co. for more than ten minutes, you realize how many thousands of hours of surveillance the company captures.

"Too *pointlessly* invasive," he said. "The product creates a culture of fear. Like if you don't put these cameras all over your neighborhood, you'll never be safe."

I changed the subject after that. His plan to leave Chime Co. bothered me, and I didn't really want to examine why. From minute one, I'd fought my attraction to him. Preppy computer programmers really weren't my type. In theory.

Yet it took me a single hour to fall headlong into his crooked smile. After the bar closed, we walked along the docks, and he took my hand in a lazy way that asked for nothing in return. He tipped his head back and whistled along with the Steve Miller tune a cover band was playing two docks over.

His confidence was at least as attractive to me as his strong jaw. He had a quiet brand of swagger and a thick scar on his cheek under one eye. It was the kind of flaw that only served to bring his perfections into higher relief.

He wasn't at all like I expected. He told me about his years in the army, and I asked if he'd had a girlfriend waiting at home. I was still looking for the fatal flaw.

What can I say? I've always had trust issues.

But he laughed and pulled out his phone to show me a picture. "Yeah, here's my one true love."

I braced myself, but the picture on the screen was . . . "Is that a German shepherd?"

"That's right. Her name's Coby. She turned out to have a lousy nose for explosives, so I adopted her overseas. Now my buddies are taking care of her in North Carolina. But one day I'm going to win her back."

A hot army vet who loves dogs? It was hard to believe he was real. And by midnight—when he finally kissed me on the moonlit pier—I would have followed him anywhere.

I was young and full of the rawest kind of hope. When he captured my face in two broad hands, I already felt sorry for all the people who didn't know it was possible to fall in love in a single night. They hadn't looked into his clear, bright eyes. They hadn't felt this deep tug in the belly on the first kiss.

It was magic. Three months of magic. And even knowing what I know now, I'd jump off the same cliff a second time. No question.

Plus, I got Buzz out of it. He's the best thing in my life.

There's a long traffic light at Forest Avenue. I stop, my foot on the ground, my heart thumping against my rib cage. Most of me knows that Drew isn't waiting under that tree. He left me, and then he died. I'm still angry about the first thing, if not the second.

But the park is just out of view. For another whole minute, anything is possible. I love him with the darkest, greediest part of my heart, and I'd shave several years off my own life just to see him one more time.

As long as the light stays red, a tiny piece of me can believe he's there waiting.

It takes an eternity, but the light finally changes. I push forward, coasting through the intersection on shaky knees. I pedal slowly onto High Street, and the candelabra tree comes into view before I'm ready.

From this vantage point, there is no one visible beneath it. Still, the tree is so broad that an adult could easily be concealed by its powerful trunk.

I slow down, dragging my gaze off the tree, scanning the park for any familiar faces. *Somebody* sent me that text. Somebody asked me to meet him here.

But there are very few pedestrians this morning. I spot a homeless man shuffling toward the rose circle. And there's a young woman in workout clothes walking a poodle. She doesn't spare me a glance.

I dismount, and then walk my bike the final ten yards down the path, around the giant tree.

There's nobody on the far side at all. Just an empty circle of wood chips beneath the tree. My eyes get suddenly hot and teary. I lay my bike down in the grass, and I walk underneath the canopy alone. I sit down on the ground, which is hard beneath my seat. And I pull out my phone and stare at the text again. I type into the text box.

Ariel: Drew?

Then, feeling foolish, I hit the button to send it. Not five seconds later, a red warning appears beside my text.

Undelivered. Try again?

I do. But the result is the same.

4

I sit in the park for two hours as the temperature climbs, until my limbs are stiff and I'm so parched I could cry.

Nobody approaches me. And now that I've done its bidding, my phone has gone silent.

Two hours is plenty of time to go down the rabbit hole of my life, though. And I don't like what I find there.

When Drew left me, he did it in a cowardly way. It was the week my father died of an overdose of painkillers. That week is a blur. We were all so shocked. The funeral was several hours of Chime Co. employees hugging me and shaking their heads in disbelief.

But Drew didn't turn up for the service. The only thing I remember clearly from that day is sitting in the church pew, my head swiveling around like a bobblehead doll trying to find him.

He wasn't in the church, though. And for three days, he hadn't answered any of my texts. I couldn't understand it. Now that my father was gone, it didn't matter who saw us together.

It wasn't until the following Monday when I made it back to the office. And there it was—a message to my work email address, for fuck's sake. It was the only email Drew ever sent me, and it had arrived on the morning of my father's funeral. He'd probably sent it during the service, knowing I wouldn't see it right away.

Ariel, I'm truly sorry. But this thing between us got
awfully heavy awfully fast. And it's time for me to move
on. I'll never forget you.
—D.

It's that last line that really gutted me. *I'll never forget you.* As
if that's reassuring, when I'd sailed way past the never-forget-you
zone on the first kiss.

He broke me, and that was *before* I realized I was pregnant.

I spent the next several months trying to process Drew's betrayal, while also trying to mourn a man who was cruel to me my
whole life. I didn't cry for my father, but I cried for Drew like I'd
cry for a lost limb.

Meanwhile, my mother was also a mess. My father made her
life hell, but there was no joy in his sudden passing. She was also the
executor of his will, which meant lots of meetings and phone calls
and a stack of death certificates that she and Ray had to FedEx in a
hundred directions.

Without my uncle, it would have all been worse. Ray had to
wear a lot of hats after my father's death. He helped my mother untangle all the probate stuff. He was there when we needed him most.

And when I finally realized I was pregnant, Ray was the first
one I told. Because it felt like a dress rehearsal for telling my mom.
And because he'd always been kinder to me than my father. Not the
type to take this sort of news by screaming at me for being an idiot.

"Oh, Ariel," he'd said instead. "That's amazing. And I've always
thought *Ray* made a nice baby name for either a boy or a girl."

I'd let out a laugh that ended up as a sob.

Ray is the only hugger in my family, so he'd pulled me into his
arms. "Is it rude of me to ask who the father is? If you need me to

brandish a shotgun, I'll need to check Reddit for some instructions first."

I was ready with my lie because I was so ashamed of getting pregnant by a man who was no longer taking my calls. "It was some tourist I met on Memorial Day weekend. I don't even know his last name."

"Did you get a phone number?"

I shook my head. Looking distraught had been easy, because I was.

And here I am again, doing another rotation through my personal pain cycle. Loving Drew, and then losing him again in the space of a morning. And for what?

When I finally get back onto my bike, I feel emotionally drained. Although nothing has changed. My life is the same as it was when I got up today.

Except for one inexplicable text.

Someone has to have sent it. But I can't think of who, let alone why. And I already know I'm going to drive myself half-crazy trying.

I don't even bother going back to work. I ride over to the glass studio instead and lock my bike to the old hitching post outside the storefront.

Larri is the manager of the studio, as well as my friend and mentor. When I walk in, she looks up in surprise from the glass she's rolling on the marver.

Even so, I don't explain why I'm early. "Need an extra pair of hands? I have a couple hours."

She blinks behind her protective goggles. "Yeah. Sure. Suit up. And change the music. This song is shit."

Ten minutes later we've found our groove together. Each time I step on the floor pedal, opening the pneumatic door to the furnace,

I feel calmer. The blast of heat from the 2,000-degree chamber is the closest I get these days to a lover's embrace.

Collecting a few ounces of molten glass on the end of my pipe, I pass it to the end of Larri's. While she spins the piece, I reach up and snip off the glass at a place she indicates with barely a grunt. After seven years of working together, we're like dance partners who already know each other's rhythms.

Right after college, I'd joined the studio as her apprentice. She's barely older than me, but she's had twice as much studio time, and some of her work still makes my jaw drop.

Today she looks grumpy, though. But don't we all.

"Something bothering you? Or are you just working on your hot-and-broody vibe?"

Larri can't even manage a smile. "Had the *worst* fight with Tara this morning. Can't decide if I'm the asshole or not."

"What happened?"

She purses her lips. "We were at the coffee shop together, and I saw her phone light up with a doorbell alert. So I picked it up to see who was at our place."

I'm deeply familiar with those snapshots. They are my family's contribution to the way doorbell cameras work. "Okay, so?"

"The photo was her dealer."

I suck in a breath. "Oh *shit*."

"Yeah."

We work in silence for a moment while I take that in. Larri and Tara have been on-again, off-again since high school, I think. But Tara is a recovering addict, so they've been through hell together. "What did he want? Does Tara know?"

"*She*," Larri corrects. "A chick can be a drug dealer, too, you sexist bitch."

I snort.

"Tara claims she hasn't seen her in years and has no idea why she'd knock on our door."

"But you don't believe her."

Larri scowls. "I don't know what to think. She *swears* it was out of the blue. She handed me her phone to read through her messages, and I had to scroll through literally years of her texts to find the name. So it *looks* like they haven't been talking at all. Unless . . ."

Goose bumps rise up on my arms. "Unless what?"

Larri reaches for the tweezers to shape her piece, which is turning into a slender, footed goblet. "What if they've been using some other app? Maybe this was just a slipup."

"Well . . ." My head swims with confusion. I'm the last person who should be giving out advice today. "Does Tara *seem* okay to you? Is she doing all right?"

"I thought so," Larri says. "But that's the thing about living with an addict. You second-guess every little thing. You're always waiting for the next disaster. Addicts lie. You're supposed to say—the *addiction* lies. But sometimes it doesn't matter who's betrayed you, right? I don't even know how to talk to her about this. I was, like, thirty seconds from packing up my stuff and leaving forever. I have loved her since the ninth grade. But I don't think I can go through this again."

"So you came here to melt some glass instead?"

"Yeah. Hit me." She nods at the furnace.

I step on the pedal and feel the devil's breath on my bare arms.

"When are you going to go gay for me, Ariel? All our problems will be solved."

I roll my eyes.

"No, hear me out—you've been pining for years over some guy

you never even introduced me to. What a waste, right? We could be having a torrid affair."

It's the perfect opening to tell her about my own outrageous morning. And about Drew. She doesn't even know his name.

But I don't say a word. Trusting people has always been hard for me. And after Drew left, it got twice as hard. So I pass her another few ounces of glass and wipe my forehead with my arm. "We already get sweaty together, Larissa. The magic is gone for me."

She laughs. We keep on working. And neither of us touches our phones.

My mother picked up Buzz from school at noon, as she usually does, so I catch up with them a few hours later at the playground. Mom is eager to run off for a massage appointment, which spares me from having to discuss my day.

Buzz isn't ready to leave, so I indulge him by pushing his swing until my arms are like jelly. And for the rest of the evening, I'm basically an absentee parent. I feed him frozen pizza, and I cut bathtime short because I can't make cheerful conversation like a normal human.

My mind is like the washing machine on spin cycle, tumbling around and around with the same questions. *Who sent me the text? What is happening?*

Why did Drew leave me? Why do I have to think about this again?

And then there's the text itself. *There's trouble. I need to see you. Don't tell anyone where you're going.* It's so ominous.

Drew never said anything like that to me. Not once.

After a terrible night's sleep, I text my mother the next morning, asking her to take Buzz to school so I can go to work early.

Ariel: I have to make up for yesterday. I forgot about a
dentist appt.

Lying makes me feel like a heel. But after five years of secrecy,
I'm good at it now.

She appears five minutes later, because she's an early riser and
I live in her backyard. Well, hers and soon maybe Ray's too. About
three years after my father's death, she and Ray became a couple.

I'd bet a lot of money that people in the office gossip about it.
But I really don't care, as long as she's happy.

"How was the dentist?" she asks as I toss my keys and my phone
into my bag.

"Uneventful. No cavities."

"Grandma!" Buzz interrupts my lies by tearing down the stairs
toward us.

"Careful on the stairs," my mother and I say in unison.

Since the moment I announced that I was pregnant with a
stranger's child—and that I'd be raising the baby—my mother has
been supportive. And even if I sometimes feel like a bird who failed
to fledge from the nest, it's pretty handy to live ten paces from
Grandma, with free babysitting, too.

I kiss my boy goodbye and head to work on my bike. I want a
few minutes alone with the employee directory before the office
fills with programmers and salespeople.

But when I arrive in the office, I'm not the only occupant. Zain
is hunched over his keyboard at the desk beside mine.

"You're early," he says as I take my seat.

"You're observant."

He stops typing and lifts his messy head. "Is that a joke?"

"Yes, it is." It doesn't work to be flip with Zain. He isn't very good at taking social cues. "Thank you for helping me yesterday when I spilled coffee everywhere."

"Welcome," he mutters, going right back to work.

I boot up my computer and then poise my hands on the keyboard, gathering the courage to look Drew up in the corporate directory. I haven't done that for years.

But when I type *Drew Miller* into the search bar, the screen comes back blank, with **No results.**

My breath catches. Right after he left, when I was so hurt and confused, I used to pull up his employee photo and stare at it, wondering where he'd gone, and whether he'd come back.

But now he's just gone. Again.

"Zain," I say quietly. He probably knows everything about how our database works.

"Yes?" He stops typing.

"Before your time, we had an employee named Drew Miller, and—"

"It wasn't before my time," he says curtly. "I used to sit over there." He points to another section of the bullpen. Chime Co. has grown fivefold in the last few years. "His desk was near mine. You just never noticed me until Ray moved me over here."

"Oh." *Whoops.* "Sorry."

He shrugs. "You weren't the only one. Drew Miller was friendly, though. Asked a lot of questions. Never hid my favorite coffee cup."

I sit back. "That's a thing?"

He shrugs again. Then he leans over to stare at my screen. "They deleted him from the directory?"

"Apparently." I clear my throat. "We were, um, friends."

"*Friends.*" A frozen smirk appears on his face. "Is that what you called it?"

Surprise makes me snappish. "You know what? Never mind." I push back my chair, preparing to go make myself a cup of coffee.

"Hold up. Sorry," he says. "I knew it was a secret."

I glance around, but we're still alone. "What do you mean you *knew?*"

"I used to see you two on the weekends at the Holy Donut."

That was one of our favorite spots.

". . . But you ignored each other at work. Like, completely."

This is also true. We never made eye contact in this room. Because people talk, and the office is full of cameras. "Yeah, my father was . . ."

". . . A dickweed?" Zain suggests. "No kidding. And I don't judge, Ariel. I just liked knowing a secret that nobody else knew."

I blow out a panicky breath, wondering if Zain could be toying with me. Because *someone* is. That text didn't drop out of the sky.

Was this his idea of a sick joke?

"What happened to Drew, anyway?" Zain asks. "He just disappeared."

Wouldn't we all like to know. "He moved away."

"Was he fired?"

"No," I say curtly. I clear my throat and point at my computer monitor. "Do we delete everyone who quits?"

He chews his lip for a moment. "I doubt it. I mean, it makes sense to remove old employees from the company directory. But nobody is truly erased from the database, because we record everyone's activity in the database, and we keep it forever."

I know this already, because you can't work here without hearing the warnings. Every keystroke is logged. Every line of code. Every email. Chime Co. stores a lot of private consumer data, and there are strict rules about how it's handled. The only way to prove that we haven't misplaced customer data is to keep very accurate logs of everyone who touches it.

Regardless, the company gets sued at least once a year.

And my father wondered why I was so disinterested in the family business.

"Check this out," Zain says, tapping on his own keyboard.

I lean over to see his monitor, where he's pulled up the entry for another ex-employee of the firm. Bryan Zarkey stares out at me from the screen, with his name, his log-in handle and his termination date.

"Remember this guy?" Zain asks. "He was the cybersecurity guru before me."

"Sure. He quit around the same time as Drew." I remember having to clean out his desk, which was full of granola bar wrappers.

"He's still in the directory," Zain points out.

"Okay, that's weird."

Zain shrugs. "You could ask the HR contractor about Drew. They probably have a whole file on him."

"I guess." But what are they going to say? Even if there was a reason why Drew has been deleted, it's not like they'd share his file. That's probably illegal. And what would I give as a reason for asking?

Zain's glance darts in my direction before zapping away again. "How badly do you need to look him up? Is this because of Buzz?"

My stomach dives. *This* is why I never talk about Drew. Anyone who knew we were dating could guess who Buzz's father was. And that's between me and Buzz. And Drew. "That's private," I say stiffly.

"You're right." He winces. "That's a shitty question. Sorry to pry."

He isn't the first to ask pointed questions, of course. But I never talk about Drew.

Someday I'll tell Buzz the real story—that I loved his father with my whole heart, and he abandoned me. And then he died. But he's too young to hear about it.

I never even told my family, even though Mom and Ray would have been cool about it. But what's the point now? I spent my pregnancy frantically searching for Drew. I scoured Facebook and LinkedIn. I searched his name with every phrase I could think of—*programmer, army, Portland. Blue eyes.* I even called a few Andrew Millers whose photos weren't available on the internet.

No match. And then one awful day I found Drew's obituary, and I finally stopped searching, and started mourning.

All I've told Buzz is that his father died before he was born. My mother assumes that's just a myth I've invented for my little boy. She doesn't know that it has the benefit of being true.

And if Zain knows so much about me and Drew, did he decide to pull a prank on me?

After a moment's hesitation, I decide to test him. "Look," I whisper to Zain. "Let me show you something." I pull out my phone, which offers more privacy than a company computer. And I google *Drew Miller obituary Fayetteville Daily News.*

It comes up right away, and I hand the phone to Zain.

Reading the headline, he sucks in a breath. "Christ. He *died*? In a motorcycle accident?"

"Right," I say in a level voice. I could recite the short obituary from memory by now. *Army veteran Drew Miller, 30, was laid to rest yesterday at Cedarwood Cemetery after dying in a tragic motorcycle accident on Tuesday. Drew was raised in Maine and studied at the University of Massachusetts before achieving the rank of lieutenant in the US Army.*

After his discharge, he worked as a data engineer for a Fayetteville military contractor. He loved motorcycle riding and hiking. Left to cherish his memory are his army teammates and his beloved dog, Coby.

"God, I'm sorry," Zain says, aiming this apology somewhere near my cheekbone while handing back my phone.

He looks genuinely remorseful, too. Which is curious.

Just in time, I notice that Uncle Ray is striding down our row. I tab guiltily away from the employee directory on my screen and look up at him with a plastic smile. "Morning."

"Morning. Teeth okay?" He puts a hand on my shoulder.

"No cavities."

"Well done." He winks, his eyes the same shade of brown as mine, and my father's before me. We also share the same brown hair, although Ray's is graying at the temples, just like my father's had.

But the resemblance stops there. Where my father was rigid and terse, Ray is upbeat and chipper. My father looked the part of the CEO in immaculately pressed clothes. Whereas Ray's shirt will be untucked by lunchtime.

More crucially, Ray has an air of kindness that my father never had a single day in his life.

Now Ray's watch lets out a loud beep, and he squints at it. "Ooh. Hester says I have a call in ten minutes. Later, guys."

As I exhale, I notice that Zain is doing a perfect interpretation of Programmer Working Diligently. His long fingers fly over the keyboard. And I just watch him for a moment, hoping he won't betray my secrets.

Zain is a strange bird. I've heard that he's highly skilled, and highly paid. But he has one of the least interesting jobs in the whole room—cybersecurity.

Most of the code monkeys my uncle hires would rather work on feature development, or video optimization. Those are the sexy jobs.

But somebody has to do the boring work. And that's Zain, apparently.

My job fits the same niche, too. Dull but necessary. Five years later, I'm working the exact same job as I was when I met Drew.

I wonder what he'd say about that.

I wonder if he cared about me enough to even have an opinion.

Someone in this room has an opinion about me, though. Someone wanted to startle me. I swivel my chair slowly around and scan the collection of programmers and support staff who are trickling into the building for another workday.

There's a lot of nerd power in this room. If anyone could hack my texts with a message from a dead man, he probably works here at Chime Co.

But who?

5

On most weekday afternoons, my mother picks Buzz up from pre-school so that I can have a hot date with molten glass. Tuesday, I put in three hours of studio time before grabbing some takeout for dinner on my way to pick up my boy.

As I open the kitchen door of my mother's house, I hear Buzz squeal with delight. My heart lifts as I walk through the mudroom and into the kitchen.

He's standing on a chair in front of the sink, my uncle Ray next to him.

"Give it a little more vinegar, Buzzy," Ray says. "It will erupt again."

"Vinegar is stinky," Buzz complains. But then he pours some more of it onto what must be a "volcano" they've built in the sink. And Buzz lets out another whoop of joy.

They both look happy, but the kitchen counter is trashed. There's baking soda spilled on the counter, and some kind of food coloring, too.

I take in the scene for a long moment, and it's like traveling to an alternate universe. My father would never have tolerated this kind of chaos in his house. From the time I was small, I knew that leaving a buttery knife on the countertop would result in a stony rebuke.

But Ray is completely unconcerned by the mess.

"Mama!" Buzz says, turning around to find me lurking in the doorway. "Look!"

I circle the kitchen island to stand behind him. There's a sludgy red mess in the sink, still fizzing. "Fun, Buzzy. How many times did you make the volcano blow?"

"Pretty sure we lost count," Ray says with a chuckle. He's wearing a faded T-shirt reading HACKATHON 2018, which now has food coloring splotched across the chest.

"Did you get noodles?" Buzz asks, eyeing the bag of Chinese food in my hand.

"You bet. Are you ready to clean up so we can go home and eat them?"

He jumps off the chair with a louder thump than a forty-pound human ought to be capable of.

But nobody yells. Ray doesn't even flinch.

"Wait, wash your hands in the bathroom," Ray says instead. "With soap, to get the food coloring off."

"Okay, Raybo."

Raybo. That's a new one. I right a fallen box of baking soda and grab a sponge to wipe up the counter.

"Ariel, I need to tell you something," Ray says, his voice low.

His serious tone makes my pulse skitter. I drop the sponge. "What is it?"

His expression softens. "Christ, it's nothing bad. This afternoon I took your mother out to lunch and asked her to marry me. And she said yes."

"Oh."

Oh.

It takes me a long beat to rearrange my dizzied thoughts and think up an appropriate response. We've officially become the weirdest family in Portland. "C-congratulations," I finally stutter.

He actually laughs. "Ariel, honey. Thank you. But you don't have to do that."

"Do what?"

"Hold back." He shakes his head slowly, his expression tender. "I know we're not an ordinary family. It doesn't bother me to acknowledge it. And whatever *Hamlet* joke you just made in your head, I'm here for it."

I feel a spark of irritation. There are reasons why I'm not a sharer. Good ones. And I learned that habit right in this very house. "I feel fine about the marriage," I insist. "You and Mom have been a thing for a while." And this doesn't even make the top ten shocking things I've had to think about today. "Where is she, anyway?"

"She had a little appointment," Ray says. His eyes flick toward the door. "Dr. Benti."

"Oh," I say slowly. Dr. Benti is Mom's psychiatrist. "Everything okay?"

"Yes," he says quietly. "Your mother assured me she's fine."

So it's normal for the newly engaged to request an emergency psych appointment with their shrink?

I almost say that out loud. Almost. But therapy has been good to me, so there's no reason for my cynicism. And the back door opens suddenly.

My mother calls out a cheerful hello. "Buzzy, are you still here? I brought you something."

"Grandma!" He scurries into the kitchen and around the island. "What is it?"

I grab the sponge and continue cleaning baking soda off the

counter. My mother enters the kitchen a moment later, beaming. "Here's my Buzzy bee! I stopped for cupcakes on my way home. I'll send some of them home with you."

"Cupcakes!" Buzz yells, and I hold back a sigh. Icing makes him hyper. They'd better be mini cupcakes.

"Hey, doll," Ray says, crossing the room to kiss her, while I pretend not to notice.

It's just hitting me that there will be a wedding. Not a huge one—my mother will keep it small. She's very proper, and she abhors ostentatiousness. I once heard her say that elaborate second weddings are gauche.

But still. I'll have to smile big and pretend to believe in happily-ever-afters. As if those were real.

When I glance at my mother, she's standing closer to Ray than usual. Her hand is on his chest, and her smile is wide. "How was your afternoon?" she asks him softly.

"Well, there were several volcanic eruptions in the kitchen," he says with mock gravity.

"Oh my," she replies with twinkling eyes.

"They went BOOM!" Buzz says, and he follows it up with an exaggerated sound effect.

"You don't say," my mother says indulgently as Ray ruffles his hair.

At least I know Ray won't treat my mother like a servant. He won't punish her with angry silences or critique her outfits. Once, in this very kitchen, my mother dared to get annoyed at my father for eating a deviled egg off the carefully arranged tray she made for Easter dinner.

I was eight or nine. Old enough to freeze like a frightened deer when I saw the anger in his eyes at her complaint.

Just to prove who was boss, he swept the whole platter off the countertop. It landed with a terrifying crash, sending crockery and bits of egg in every direction, before he stormed out.

Mom and I were left standing here, frozen, our Easter dresses dotted with yolk and ceramic shards, like shrapnel. And it was Ray who strode in a few minutes later with a broom and a soft voice. "Stand still, ladies. Let me get the worst of this so nobody steps in it, okay?"

We didn't discuss it then, and we don't really discuss it now. My mother discovered therapy under the guise of "grief counseling" after my father's death. And good for her.

But if I look hard enough, I can still see the ghost of my scared young self in the corners of this kitchen.

Mom is in the mood to celebrate, though. She pulls a clamshell cupcake holder out of her shopping bag and steps over to the countertop to open it. "How was the afternoon? What did I miss?"

"Ariel and I had a little chat," Ray says, giving me a smile.

"Oh," my mother says softly. She glances up at me, a vulnerable expression on her face.

I force my mouth into a smile that's far more placid than the past forty-eight hours deserve.

When she smiles back at me, her obvious happiness makes me feel like a heel. If she can be a blushing bride at fifty-eight, I guess I can keep my brittleness to myself.

"Hey—funny story," my uncle is saying now. "And I'm pretty glad we don't run a cell phone company."

"What's that?" my mother asks, putting a full-sized cupcake into a Tupperware container for Buzz.

Maybe I can convince him to save half of it for tomorrow.

"I got a text yesterday morning from the Bagel Tree." Ray swipes a drop of icing from the cupcake container and licks it theatrically off his finger. I can hear him winding up to tell a story. ". . . They said my smoked salmon and fried egg sandwich was ready. But I hadn't ordered anything, so the text didn't make any sense. I called over there, and they were just as confused as I was!"

My gaze snaps upward as I realize what he's saying. "Wait. They . . . didn't send the text?"

"Oh, they did." Ray laughs. "Five years ago! But I didn't figure that out until I heard a story on the radio—thousands of people got outdated texts yesterday. Isn't that crazy?"

"Five *years*?" I gasp.

"It was on the news!" he says with a hoot, oblivious to my distress.

"Wait, what?" My mother stops her work on the cupcakes and stares up at him. "What did you say about your text?"

Ray starts his story over again. He loves to tell stories.

But my mind is already spinning. And my limbs are suddenly cold—as if someone has drained all the warmth from my body.

". . . A cell tower went out of service, somehow, and a bunch of texts never went through. Then yesterday all the old texts were delivered at once. Nobody knew that could happen."

I finally remember to breathe. But it doesn't help much. Five years ago *when*? I still have only half the story.

My mother is staring at Ray, too. "That is wild."

"Isn't it?" He chuckles. "Here, Buzzy. Take this from Grandma before your mother decides it's too much sugar." He passes Buzz the sealed Tupperware. "What do you tell Grandma?"

"Thank you!" Buzz yells.

I stumble through saying good night to my mother and thanking Ray for entertaining Buzz with volcanoes. Then I usher Buzz down the driveway and into our little home.

Stepping through our door means walking right into the tiny

kitchen. It's open to a cozy little living room that holds exactly one love seat and a single upholstered chair. Upstairs is more roomy, because the space extends above the garage.

But I don't head up there now. I put the noodles down on the counter and reach into the cabinet for two plates.

"Not too much broccoli," Buzz says.

"Okay," I reply automatically, because my mind is still blown. On autopilot, I make a plate of food for Buzz, and a small plate for myself.

We sit down at the table, and I break a family rule and pull out my phone. When I google *text messages delivered five years late*, a newly posted radio story comes up immediately. "I'm going to play the news for a minute, okay?"

Buzz nods and tries to twirl a lo mein noodle on his fork.

I press *play*, and the familiar host, with her light Maine accent, begins to report the story.

"More than thirty thousand cell phone customers in York and Cumberland counties received confusing texts yesterday morning after an excavator hit a defunct cell phone tower that's been out of service nearly five years.

"Both of Maine's largest mobile carriers disclaimed responsibility, blaming a third party tower vendor for the service failure. But nonetheless, both are investigating the outage. One Verizon analyst reports that all the erroneous texts seem to have been sent within the same one-hour window on the morning of August sixteenth, 2017."

I drop my fork with a clatter, and Buzz looks up at me, confused.

With a tap, I halt the news story, which was almost finished anyway. Then I pick up my fork in an attempt to behave normally.

But it's no use. I couldn't eat another bite if I tried. August sixteenth is a date that I could never forget. It's the morning my father died.

It's also just a few hours after the last time Drew spoke to me. Or so I thought.

There's trouble. I need to see you.

It's not a prank. Drew wrote that wild, urgent text.

He wanted me to meet him. But I didn't show up.

What the hell happened that day? I have no idea.

And I'm terrified that I never will.

6

Our bedtime ritual seems to last forever.

After the usual pajama and teeth parade, I get into Buzz's bed with him to read. I campaign for a couple chapters of *The Tale of Despereaux*, but he has other plans.

"Too scary. How 'bout Frog and Toad? The one with the cookies."

"Sure," I agree, even though I've read this book a thousand times already. Larri gave it to us for Buzz's third birthday, and he took to it like a fruit fly on a bunch of overripe bananas. Occasionally I "lose" this book on a high shelf just to give myself a break.

Now I get the book and flip to the cookie story, where Frog and Toad will inevitably work out their problems before anything gets too dire. Buzz likes that.

"Buzz is not a risk-taker," Ray said once. When I bristled, my uncle just smiled. "When he learns to drive someday, you'll be happy about it."

Two stories later, I hug Buzz good night. His hair tickles my face as I kiss his soft cheek. "Good night, baby."

"I'm not a baby," he says. But then he grins, because this is our little routine.

"But you'll always be *my* baby," I point out. That's my punch line.

I shut out the light, and then I sit there on the edge of the bed for a lingering moment. I stroke Buzz's hair and tell him that I'll see him in the morning.

Sometimes he tries to prolong my stay by asking me questions that I'll feel obligated to answer. Sometimes they're doozies. "How did the dinosaurs end up underground when they died?" Or "Why doesn't Grandma like corn on the cob?" Those are both stumpers. One because I never studied paleontology, and two because, seriously, it's corn on the cob.

And once in a while he'll ask, "Why don't I have a daddy?"

That question is the worst. I always answer the same way—that he died. And that not everyone gets to have two parents in their lives, but Buzz has lots of people who love him.

Yada yada yada.

But I know it's not enough. His friends all have daddies. And I can't believe that after years of therapy during my early twenties, most of it dealing with what my therapist and I called my *parental abandonment issues*, that I am destined to pass on to my son—wait for it—parental abandonment issues.

Go me.

Buzz doesn't hit me with any impossible questions tonight, though. He relaxes against the pillows as I kiss him one more time and then leave, closing his door *almost* all the way. He likes it to stay open a crack.

He's cautious. Like his mama.

I head down to the kitchen and rinse our dinner plates in the sink. The sound of Buzz whistling to himself floats down the stairs.

Before he could whistle, he used to buzz his lips, like a raspberry sound, but quieter. I thought it was a phase, but my mother pointed out to him that since "buzz" was his name, maybe that was his special sound.

He buzzed constantly for months after that, and my mother was tickled.

I've never told anyone where his name came from, though. Not a soul. It's an inside joke between me and the father he'll never meet.

The second night I spent with Drew was the night I noticed his tattoo. He'd left the lights on, and we were lying there, coming down from a sexual high. Drew's gentle hands stroked my back, and a hum of joy rose inside my chest.

Even when we had our clothes on, I felt elated to be near him. I tried to hide it, though. I was afraid what Drew would do if he knew how much I liked him. It's like I already knew I'd scare him off eventually.

It was hard work holding that in and not blowing my cover. So instead of lying there in his bed gushing about this wild connection I felt whenever he smiled at me, I went with humor instead. "Do you *really* have a tattoo of Buzz Lightyear on your shoulder? What are you, twelve?"

He chuckled, and I felt the vibration against my fluttering chest. "That was my army nickname. Buzz."

"Really? Why?"

"Well, I have this buddy named Woody."

I laughed, letting some of the joy bubble out of me. "Was he a cowboy?"

"No." Drew propped himself up on one elbow, and I was briefly distracted by how attractive he was. All warm skin and smooth muscle. He was smiling again, which made me almost dizzy. "Woody is a grumpy hick from the Midwest. But we had a lot in common. We're both nerds. Both had a rough upbringing. So we spent a lot of time together."

"And that's why they called you Buzz?"

"That and we managed to get left behind once—like in the movie."

I tugged the sheet up over my chest and turned to face him. "You fell out of a moving van?"

"Nah. It was a training mission, and we were fiddling with the radio. We missed our commanding officer's signal." Drew rolled his blue eyes at the memory. "It was mortifying to discover that the team moved out without us. They had to double back, because you never leave a man behind. Then our opponents won the mission, and Woody and I had to scrub toilets for weeks."

His smile told me that was actually a good memory, though, not a disaster. So I asked another question, craving more of his history, more confidences. Just more of Drew. Maybe if I kept him talking, he'd never leave me. "Where is Woody now?"

"In one of the smallest towns in Michigan. There's a hundred and forty-two people. He says I can make it a hundred and forty-three anytime I want."

"Sounds kind of quiet," I whispered, tracing his Buzz Lightyear tattoo with my fingertip, just to have a reason to touch him.

"Not as fun as this. That's for damn sure." He leaned in to kiss me again.

Memories are such strange things. After he left, I spent a lot of time cataloging everything he ever said to me. Every compliment, every joke, every evasive answer.

At the time I didn't even notice how little I knew about his past. But now I keep sifting through these memories, searching for clues to who he was.

I put the last dish in the dishwasher and close the door.

When I was four months pregnant, the obstetrician told me I was having a boy. Right away I knew I'd call him Buzz. It was such an easy decision—my little boy and I were left behind, too. Just like the toys in the story.

You'd have to believe in miracles to think that I'd ever see Drew again. Yet I went to the candelabra tree anyway. The perfect fool.

Upstairs, the whistling trails off. I put our leftovers in the refrigerator, and then I pull out a bottle of pink wine that wasn't opened the last time Larri came over.

I don't usually drink alone. It's a little rule I made for myself, because I'm often lonely. It would be way too easy to get into the habit of sipping wine every night in front of the TV.

But tonight I twist the top right off and pour myself a full glass.

And then I almost drop the bottle when someone knocks on my door. I whip my head around to see who it is.

Sorry! Zain mouths from the other side of the little square windowpane.

Heart pounding, I open the door. "What are you doing here?" It's not the most polite question I've ever asked. But I wouldn't have thought Zain even knew where to find me.

He looks over his shoulder at the main house. "Can I come in? I'm probably on, like, seven different Chime Co. cameras right now."

"You're not," I say, opening the door wider to let him step inside. "Mine is disabled."

"Really?" He smirks as he closes the door behind himself. "Why?"

A memory—my father screaming into my cell phone one September night when I was fifteen. He caught me on camera, leaving for a party that he'd forbidden me to go to after I dropped out of a computer programming class without telling him. *Get back here, you ungrateful little bitch.*

I became sneakier after that incident. But that's beside the point. ". . . For the same reason you're eager to get out of the driveway. I don't want my home to become a surveillance state." That's how it had felt growing up as Edward's daughter. He was always watching me, waiting for me to make another mistake. I've always associated the cameras with his personality.

Zain shakes his head, that smirk still playing on his lips. "But Chime Co. saves lives. That better be true, or else I'm spending seventy hours a week on a scam."

"How'd you find me anyway?"

He shrugs. "Hackers never reveal their secrets."

"Want some pink wine?"

"Yes, ma'am."

I pour him some, setting both our glasses on the kitchen counter. The couch seems too cozy for a chat with a man I don't really know. "So . . . why the visit?"

"Well . . ." He fidgets with his wineglass. "I pulled a tape and looked it over for you. Found some weird data, and didn't really want to talk about it in the office."

"Okay . . . a tape?"

Zain's chuckle is an awkward staccato sound. "That's what we call them, although it's not really on *tape*. It's a digital log of entries to the database. And it's stored on these." He pulls a gray, oblong thing out of his backpack. It looks like an external hard drive, without the cord. I've seen them before in my uncle's office.

Now I stare at the thing. "Are you supposed to carry those around?"

"Heck no. So don't tell anyone," he says, a crease appearing on his forehead. "Do you want to know what I found in Drew's HR file or not?"

"You know I do." I take a gulp of wine.

Zain's expression animates as he begins to explain. "The tape keeps a coded record of every change to the database and a record of whose log-in made it. This one includes Drew's hire date. So I scanned it for new log-ins, and I found the day they created his." He pulls a sticky note out of his pocket. "Drew was employee number 311. And I found every keystroke Ray's assistant made when she set up his file." He pulls a laptop out of his backpack and sets it on my countertop.

"That's not a Chime Co. machine, is it?"

Zain gives me an eye roll. "Did you seriously just ask me that?"

"Sorry."

"Not an amateur here, Ariel. This is my own machine, and it's an air gap. It's never been connected to the internet."

"Oh." I wince. "That makes good sense."

"Every system has vulnerabilities. But this is as secure as it gets. Let me boot 'er up." He turns on the machine and taps in his password.

I look away to be polite. "Did you hear anything on the news about the text message thing that happened yesterday? With all the delayed texts?"

"Sure did," he says as the screen blinks to life. "Got one from my mom asking me to bring home some half-and-half. Except she switched to almond milk a while back."

"You live with your mom?" I ask.

His eyes narrow. "Don't judge. You live in your mom's backyard. Hey—did you get one of those delayed texts?"

"Yup." I take a careful sip of wine. "From Drew."

His eyes widen. "Oh, *shit*. That's why you were thinking about him again?"

I nod.

"Wow. And you spent a whole day thinking a dead man texted you?"

"That's right," I choke out. It's strangely humiliating to say it out loud. "The text wasn't about milk, either. He wanted to meet me. He had something to tell me."

"Holy shit. Show me."

I pull my phone out of my pocket. On the lock screen I find a text from Larri.

> Larri: Guess what? That doorbell text Tara got was five years old! I'm such an asshole. LOL!

At least one of us feels better.

I open up the thread from Drew and show it to Zain, who squints at it. "Yeah, okay. That could mess with someone's head. Any idea what was wrong?"

Slowly, I shake my head. When Zain hands the phone back, I read the rogue text one more time. Rationally, I know it's just pixels of light illuminating a glass screen. Electrons dancing a jig they learned five years ago. It isn't real.

But my stupid heart still hasn't gotten the latest upgrade. It's Ariel 1.0 who's staring down at the screen. His face is *right there*.

"Okay," Zain says, moving on already. "Look at this—I dumped the keylog off the tape and into a text file and wrote a widget to make it play like a movie in real time. This is everything Ray's assistant typed into Drew's personnel file. Watch." He taps a key, and the words begin to appear in a column on the screen.

FIRST: Drew

MI: E

LAST: Miller

"Wow. That's a little eerie." It's like we're watching an invisible person fill out a form.

More data appears, including his Social Security number, and I scan every bit. I didn't know his middle initial before, so that's something. His home address is the same apartment where I used to visit him, on Exeter Street. His education and military service are also familiar.

I notice he leaves the emergency contact information blank. Not that it's a surprise—Drew had already told me he was alone in the world. "At least we have his Social Security number? Is there anything I could learn from that?"

"Oh, you sweet summer child," Zain says with a laugh. "I have a buddy who can do a *lot* with a social. Date of birth. Place of birth. Criminal record. Parking tickets. It's not free, though. Should I ask him for a quote?"

I hesitate. But only for a second. "Yeah. Do it." It's madness to obsess over a dead man. But maybe I'll glean a few details that Buzz will someday want to know.

"There's one more thing I need to show you." He makes his fingers into a tent and stares at them. "I just think it's weird."

"What?"

He puts his hands to the keyboard again. "Pull out your phone? I need to see the obituary again."

"Sure?" The browser tab is still open from when I showed him earlier. All I have to do is set it on the counter.

He types rapidly for a moment on the laptop, and then Drew's familiar face appears on the screen. "See that? His ID photo, uploaded on the same date as this HR file was done. It has the same plain background as mine."

"Yeah, okay?"

Zain points at my phone. "The obituary photo is identical. Why would that be?"

"Because it's a decent photo?"

Zain tilts his head and looks at his own screen again. "But, like, which of his army buddies in North Carolina had a copy of it? And how'd they get it?"

My heart skips a beat inside my chest. "That's a good question." I can't believe I didn't notice it before. Then again—that obituary shook my world. I was too busy crying to wonder about the photo.

"I just think it's strange," he says. "I wonder if the newspaper would tell you who sent in the obituary?"

"Doubt it," I stammer, while my head explodes for the tenth time in two days.

"You could check," he says.

I could. But it would probably lead to nothing. And I don't see why Zain cares. "Why do you want me to? Why did you come here?"

His eyebrows crowd together aggressively. "Because you were curious about him, and so was I. Thought you might want that data. Seems like you don't have a lot left of him."

This is a hundred percent accurate, but I still don't understand his interest in the matter. "Just . . . don't talk to anyone about this, okay?"

He frowns down into his wineglass. "I didn't miss the whole deep, dark secret thing. Not an idiot, here."

"Sorry," I say quietly. "I'm having a very strange week."

"Mama?"

I whirl around and spot Buzz at the top of the stairs, his red pj's bright against the polished wood. "Hi, baby." I set my wine down and I slide off the stool. "It's bedtime."

"I know," he says. But he doesn't move.

"I'll go," Zain says. He snaps his computer closed. "That's all I had for you."

It was plenty, though. "I do appreciate it."

"Yeah. 'Course." He jams the computer into the bag and heads for the door. "Sorry to wake up your kid."

"No . . . Thank you for, um . . ."

He flashes me a frozen smirk and lets himself out.

I walk Buzz back up to bed. Again. This time I lie down beside him in the dark. My heart rate is still charging along, and I wonder if I'll ever feel calm again.

"Who was that man?" Buzz asks.

"My friend from work." I rub his small back.

"He's nice?"

I hesitate a half second, because I don't know what to think of Zain at all. "Yes," I say, and maybe it's even true. "He shares all his toys in the sandbox."

Buzz smiles in the dark. And I lie there beside him until he falls back to sleep, his eyelashes fluttering softly.

I don't remember ever feeling as innocent as he looks right now. Before I learned how dangerous it is to love someone.

7

FIVE YEARS AGO, JUNE

Two or three times each day, when he walks onto the second floor of Chime Co., Drew passes a photo of Edward and Ray Cafferty installing the very first doorbell camera on Edward's front door, while their late father—a retired cop—looks on.

Company lore—and a dozen business magazine profiles—chart Edward's journey from law enforcement to technology CEO. He didn't start as a beat cop like his dad, though. He got dual degrees in criminal justice and management, with an emphasis on crime stats.

Meanwhile Ray—the family tinkerer—had gone to MIT to become an engineer. He had a work-study job in campus security, though, and he wanted to do his homework on shift. So he rigged up a camera that would alert him whenever someone passed by.

Eventually Ray showed the camera to his older brother, who saw the potential right away. "Hey, can you put a doorbell on it?" Edward famously asked. "I heard that's going to be big."

That's how Chime Co. was born, a marriage of Ray's fine engineering and Edward's ruthless business acumen. Ten years later, they've already sold millions of cameras on five continents. And they have hundreds of contractors and employees.

And Drew is one of them. Although he hates himself a little every time he meets a deadline. His coding skills are improving at a rapid rate. It's nice to know that his college degree wasn't a complete waste of time. But he'd rather burn this company to the ground than contribute to its success—even in a small way.

It's Friday afternoon again, which marks his third week at the company. And he's exhausted. Before coming to Portland, Drew had been warned by a half dozen healthcare providers at the VA that the transition to civilian life is always hard.

They weren't kidding. So far it's hell. It shouldn't be this hard to sit in an ergonomic office chair and write code. But by Friday his injured knee is as stiff as a crowbar.

Nobody likes a whiner, though, and all the people who care about him are either far away or dead. So he doesn't complain. Instead, he puts two Advil into his pocket. Then he pulls a box of Girl Scout cookies out of his backpack. Thin Mints today. He bought three different boxes last week from his landlord's granddaughter.

Trying not to limp, he crosses the open-plan office to the kitchenette and selects a coffee pod to drop into the machine. After swallowing the pain pills with a nip of water, he puts a mug beneath the spout and presses the button.

Then he opens the cookies, taking one for himself and placing the rest of the plastic sleeve on the counter, as if in invitation.

By Drew's count it only takes seven seconds for a young programmer named Trevor to decide it's time for a coffee break. Trevor is a twenty-three-year-old who talks of nothing but the Patriots. Drew can picture him a year or two ago, wearing his baseball cap backward on a frat house lawn somewhere.

"You'll help me with these cookies, right?" Drew asks as his coffee finishes brewing. "I like supporting the Girl Scout troop, but I don't want to get a gut."

"If you insist," Trevor says, already reaching for a cookie.

Sometimes trust can be purchased cheaply.

"Looks like they're setting up for another one of those Friday meetings," Drew says, parking his hip against the countertop and taking a sip of his coffee. "What goes on in there? Besides snacks and better coffee than we're getting."

Drew is careful not to look at Ariel when he says this. But he's relieved to see that she's already procured an urn of the good stuff for the conference room, plus several high-end catering trays.

And this time her father grunted his approval instead of losing his shit.

"Every Friday it's a different police force," Trevor says, reaching for another cookie. "Cops love Chime Co. They'd put a camera on every house if they could."

"Makes the neighborhood safer," Drew says, because that's the party line at Chime Co. Even if the truth is far more complicated. "But why bother rolling out the red carpet for law enforcement? I thought the genius of Chime Co. was selling cameras right to consumers." This, according to the internet, is what made the company grow so fast. Security cameras used to be marketed to gas stations and liquor stores. Now everyone wants to turn their home into a mini surveillance state.

"Yeah, it was Edward's idea to go direct to consumers," Trevor says. "He got the idea when a friend of his got mugged. A pregnant lady. Got pushed down in her own driveway. Lost the baby. They never caught the guy."

"Oof," Drew says, even if Edward strikes him as the least sympathetic man in Maine.

"That story always gets trotted out in the Friday meetings with cops. They get a boner off this idea—that with a Chime Co. camera, your arrest rates could go way up. So they want Chime Co. to sell as many cameras as they can. It makes their job easier. Plus, police departments get perks and incentives when they sign up with us."

"Incentives," Drew says carefully. "Like what? Free donuts?"

Trevor dumps a sugar packet into his coffee. "The police force offers a special discount on Chime Co. cameras to every house in the precinct. It's great advertising. And each installation means an ongoing subscription fee."

"Nice racket," Drew says.

"Yeah, and the force earns points for each camera they push."

"Like frequent-flier miles?" Drew asks.

"Exactly like that," Trevor agrees. "They use the points to get camera equipment of their own. They can put it wherever—like public parks and bus stops. Anywhere crime happens."

"Uh-huh. I get it. Better than donuts." Fewer calories, plus a side order of invasion of privacy.

"Yeah, and when the department signs on to the partnership program, they also get a map of all the cameras in their jurisdiction. Helps them access private footage."

Drew's neck tingles, even as he keeps his tone nonchalant. "A map. How does that work?"

"Every camera has a serial number," Trevor says through cookie crumbs. "If the police own the cameras, they can see 'em anytime, yeah? But the private ones they can't see on demand."

"Unless they get a warrant," Drew supplies.

"Yeah, but that's not the only way. The police can request the footage from anyone's doorbell camera. There's a function in the app for that. It's quicker than a warrant. Most civilians just hand over the footage with one tap."

Drew nudges the cookies toward Trevor. "So how does the cop know who to ask?"

"That's why the partner program matters. If a police force is signed up with us, they see a real-time map of every camera in the neighborhood."

"Handy," Drew says quickly. "And that's not a privacy concern?"

"People can opt out," Trevor says with a shrug. "But most of them don't bother."

Drew takes a sip of his coffee because he can't think of anything nice to say.

"Thanks for the cookies. I should probably get back to it." Trevor takes one more cookie for the road.

But Drew snaps his fingers, as if an idea has just come to him. "Hey, can I ask you a question? I'm working on a new feature for the app, and I can't remember how the control stack links up to the client record. Can you remind me?"

"Sure, dude." He makes a loose gesture for Drew to follow him.

Drew is right on his heels as Trevor reaches his desk and nudges the mouse to wake up his screen.

Chime Co. terminals lock after a three-minute hiatus, so the log-in screen appears on Trevor's monitor. Drew watches very carefully as Trevor inputs his password.

He watches far less carefully as Trevor explains the bit of code he'd asked about. And then he goes back to his own desk and gets busy with the work he's being paid to do.

Friday afternoon drags on, and Drew has to bargain with himself not to stare at Ariel, even though she's right in his field of vision. And even though she's worn low-cut tops to work every single day this week.

He knows her fashion choices aren't for his benefit. They're a blatant *fuck you* to her father.

Drew appreciates her sense of humor almost as much as he appreciates the view.

When five o'clock finally comes, Zain stands up from his desk chair and stretches. "Want food?" he asks. "Thinking of running out to the deli before it closes. Then I'm going to put in a couple more hours."

"No thanks," Drew says, trying not to feel disappointed. With Zain hanging around, the night won't end the same as last week—when Drew found an excuse to treat Ariel to dinner, before spending the best three or four hours of his year making her laugh.

Then he kissed her good night, and that kiss lasted half an hour.

Terrible idea, though. What had he been thinking?

Zain walks out, and Drew writes another line of code. His goal is to be an average employee in every way. Average productivity. Average hours spent at his desk. Average khaki pants. When he moves on from this job, nobody will be able to remember much about him. *Drew? Nice guy. Kinda average.*

That's the plan, anyway. It's the best one he's got.

Ariel passes by his desk in a swish of lemon shampoo and attitude. She doesn't even glance at him as she turns the corner in front of his desk, heading for the door on tanned legs that he shouldn't be noticing.

At the last second, though, a Post-it note flutters from her hand and onto his desk. If he weren't so damn aware of her, he might have missed it.

Like a good spy, he waits until she's gone to pick up the note and read it. *Code monkey—Oxbow beer garden 7p. Good music tonight.* It's accompanied by a sketch of a monkey flashing the sign of the devil. The drawing is probably one inch square, but it contains more life than anything else in this whole fucking room.

He should just stand her up. That would send a message, and prevent him from doing anything really dumb.

Also, he shouldn't spend the money. Portland is more expensive than he's used to. He's burning through his savings. And he's promised himself that he will donate every fucking penny Chime Co. pays him to the youth center where he played hoops after school as a teen.

But the note is burning a hole in his psyche. He looks at the code on his screen and tries to remember why it's important. Or even what he was going to do next.

Later, he'll think of this as the minute it all went to hell. When he made the choice to tuck that sticky note carefully into his wallet, instead of dropping it into the trash and getting back to work.

But his heart has already followed Ariel to the beer garden, where he'll spend the evening memorizing the shape of her smile when she laughs.

8

ARIEL

"Ariel?"

"Hmm?" I look up quickly to find my uncle standing over my desk.

Hell. I drop my phone onto the blotter—facedown so he can't see the browser where I've been searching for the phone number for Cedarwood Cemetery in Fayetteville, North Carolina.

"Hester informs me that the Medford police force is coming in for a four o'clock meeting. Maybe you could rustle up some coffee and cookies?" He wiggles his eyebrows playfully, then glances at his smart watch. "We still have three hours, but Hester has already reminded me twice. It's like she knows me or something."

"Right," I say quickly. "I've got you covered."

"Good deal." He knocks twice on the surface of my desk. "There's a presentation as well. Hester was going to print it, but we seem to be out of copy paper."

Crap. I meant to order it yesterday. "Forward the file to me." I rise from my desk so fast that the chair scoots out behind me. I've never been the most dedicated employee of Chime Co. But this week I'm an outright disaster. "I'll run out and get a couple reams to tide us over until our delivery from W.B. Mason's."

"Thanks, darlin'," he says. "You okay? You look tired."

"Too much Netflix," I say with a tight smile. "Send me that presentation."

He heads back to his office, and I grab my pocketbook and shove my phone inside.

"Yo. Ariel." This low-voiced greeting comes from Zain, who is also typing at warp speed while staring fixedly at his monitor. "I've got news. Meet me in the line at Sisters Deli in twenty minutes."

A wave of nervous energy rolls through my chest. "Got it," I mutter. Then I head outside.

When I walk into the deli with my two reams of copy paper, Zain is already lurking inside the door. He peels himself off the wall and joins me at the back of the line. "Hey. My buddy got some preliminary information on that Social Security number. It's pretty interesting."

An unfamiliar woman seated at a table to our right looks up when he says this, her gaze curious.

Zain levels her with a stare, his dramatic eyebrows bunching together. "Maybe mind your own business?"

Her gaze drops to the table. Then she actually picks up her coffee cup and leaves the deli.

"I have that effect on a lot of women," he says dryly.

"What did he say?" I press.

"The preliminary check was just a verification—to see if the number was real. That part is actually public information. We could have looked it up ourselves if we'd known."

"Okay. But what did it reveal?"

"The social is real, and it was issued in Maine. But in 1963."

My first thought is—*that's impossible*. But then I realize it isn't. And the copy paper in my arms starts to slip.

Zain grabs both reams from me, and I'm too upset to argue. "So our *Drew* was legally a . . . sixtyish-year-old man?"

"Actually, older," he says in a low voice. "It used to be that nobody got their Social Security number until they got their first job. So that person is probably over seventy now."

"Okay," I say with forced calm. "So Drew, if that was even his real name, was using someone else's . . ." I swallow hard.

"Identity," Zain says quietly.

"But *why*?" Zain just shakes his head. I'm sure he's already wondered the same thing. I just need a moment to catch up. "Unless the bad social is just a typo?"

"Probably not. If an employee provides a name that doesn't match up to the right Social Security number, it will get flagged by the system. So it's likely that the real Andrew Miller was given that number in 1963."

"So then how did he take a job as that guy, with that birth date?"

Zain shrugs. "Hard to say. But remember that your dad used a subcontractor for HR. Drew would have interviewed in our offices when he got hired. Then he would have filled out all the paperwork, which got sent to the off-site HR company."

"Oh." I think I see where this is going. "So if all the documents matched up, the HR worker might not spot the mistake."

"It's just a theory," Zain says.

The line moves, and I automatically take two steps forward. But my mind is bounding around like a scared rabbit. Who the hell was Drew Miller, if he wasn't Drew Miller?

"My buddy will do more work on it if you like. The fee is two hundred bucks."

Such a small amount of money, really, for something likely to blow my mind. "I'm good for it." And angry, as well as desperately curious. He left me, which was bad enough. But he also lied to me right from day one?

For years now I've been carrying around the golden memories of our time together. Even if only for a short time, he was the best person in my life. I thought he was worthy of my love, and that all my sadness had a purpose.

Now I want to howl like a banshee, right here in the deli.

"It's one thing to know for sure that he lied," Zain says thoughtfully, oblivious to my anguish. "But the harder question is why."

"Yeah. Sure," I mutter. "I'd *love* to know that."

Or maybe I really wouldn't. If Drew was a cheat and a liar, I'll have to carry that with me, too. And navigate Buzz's future questions about his father.

"Did you call the cemetery?" Zain asks. "I saw you googling it on your phone."

"Not yet."

"Could be interesting," he says. "Now there's *two* Drew Millers."

"What do you mean?"

"Who's buried in North Carolina? That's what I'd want to know."

"Seriously. Who *was* that guy?" I take a panicked, shuddering breath.

"Hey," Zain whispers. "This is a lot, right? Do you want me to just drop it?"

"No," I say immediately. "I hate liars."

"Okay." He pauses. "I have some more ideas. After my buddy does his research, we can try to find the real Andrew Miller. Although we don't actually know if they knew each other."

"You said your friend traces people for a living. Can I pay him to keep digging? Beyond the Social Security number?"

"If necessary. But first you have to order something for lunch. And cookies for your uncle."

Sure enough, it's our turn at the counter. I stare up at the menu board with unseeing eyes.

"You like the Greek wrap, right?" Zain prompts.

"Um, yes?" Although I don't know how he knows that.

"Two Greek wraps, please. And the lady needs a few more things."

I stumble through my bakery order and then follow Zain back to work. Even with two reams of paper and a deli bag, he holds the door open for me. "Ladies first."

"Thank you," I say, looking him directly in the eye. "I owe you."

"No problem. Besides, you just bought lunch."

I muddle through the next couple of hours somehow. By four o'clock, the presentations are printed and collated, and there are cookies and coffee at the ready in the conference room.

"Thanks, Ariel," my uncle says before he goes into the meeting. "You're a lifesaver."

I'm not, and it's weird to be praised for the same half-assed work that my father used to berate me for. But I've got bigger problems right now.

The moment the conference room door closes on my uncle, I'm back at my desk, tossing my belongings into my bag. "I'm out of here. Thanks again for all your help today," I tell Zain.

"We'll get to the bottom of it," he mumbles.

I don't know whether I'm more afraid that he's right, or that he's wrong.

Either way, I leave the building. Walking slowly up Congress

Street, I pull out my phone and call the *Fayetteville Daily News*, asking for the obituary editor.

The woman who answers has a pleasant Southern drawl. But she isn't helpful when I ask her who placed Drew's obituary.

"Apologies, ma'am. I'm sorry for your loss, but I cannot divulge any information about the deceased's loved ones. If you feel we've made an error in the obituary, you can write us a letter and we'll consider a retraction."

"I just want to thank them," I try.

"Ma'am, I'm truly sorry."

So that was pointless. My next call is to the cemetery in North Carolina. I get their answering machine, and I leave a message asking for help locating Drew's grave.

Then I buy a piece of salmon to roast for dinner and pick up Buzz from his Grandma's backyard, where he's whistling on the swing set that Ray installed for him last summer.

The tune cuts off mid-whistle when he sees me.

"Mama!" he shrieks, leaping off the swing. "Did you know that dinosaurs had feathers? Just like a bird. And nobody knows what color. They didn't have green scales like a lizard. Some books are wrong."

Before I can get a word in, he's done a complete circle around my body and then he asks me if he can have a Popsicle. "I'm going to turn my tongue purple and then take a picture with your phone."

"It's good to have goals," I say, waving hello to my mother in the kitchen window. "You can have it after dinner, though. I'm making fish with rice and corn."

"Can I put the rice in the rice cooker?" He gallops toward our door.

"Absolutely."

I follow him inside. The minute I close the door, he starts whistling again. He presses the button that pops the top of the rice cooker up, and when it makes a playful series of beeps, he laughs.

This is what you missed out on, Drew. Or whatever your name was. Whatever you were up to, I hope it was worth it.

By eight thirty, I'm slumped into the corner of my tiny sofa, clutching a wineglass.

I have no idea what's the proper response to finding out that you fell in love with some kind of con man. So I've defaulted to staring at the TV and drinking wine.

There's a polite tap on my door, and even from this oblique angle I can make out the silver halo of my mother's hair through the misted glass.

Hell.

I hide my glass on the floor between the sofa and the wall. Then I get up to open the door.

She enters on a breeze of Jo Malone fragrance and . . . tequila?

"I made margaritas!" she announces.

"Margaritas," I echo, my gaze dropping to the ceramic pitcher in her hand. It says PARTY TIME in a bright script, and it's decorated with cheerful lemon wedges. I've never seen it before in my life. "So you did."

"Take this," she says, passing me the pitcher. "I have to go back for the glasses."

I stand in my open doorway like a dummy, the pitcher freezing my hands, as she dashes back to her own kitchen. She returns a moment later with a pair of giant margarita glasses—the kind you'd see at a beach resort. There's salt on the rims, along with perfect lime wheels.

"This is . . . a surprise," I manage to say. I've never seen my mother sip anything stronger than a glass of wine with dinner. My father didn't approve of women drinking. I wonder if she's ever *had* a margarita.

Who is this woman?

"I'm still capable of surprises." She gives me an arch look as she sets the glasses down on the counter. There's also a canvas shopping bag over her arm. From the bag she extracts a brand-new Moleskine notebook with the plastic wrapper still on it, followed by a wooden bowl with two wells—one filled with chips, and one filled with salsa. "We have a wedding to plan, Ariel. I need your help. It has to be perfect."

"Why?" I say before I can think better of it. But *why* is the theme for this week. *Why* did I get a text from a dead man? Why was he lying to me?

And so on.

"You make a good point," my mother says cheerfully, pouring margaritas into both giant glasses. They're frozen margaritas, too. I guess my mother's Vitamix learned a few new tricks tonight. "The wedding *doesn't* have to be perfect. I don't need to be perfect for Ray. Or for anyone else."

You can practically hear her therapist's voice in there. *Nice work, Dr. Benti.*

". . . But I'd *like* to throw a nice party. I thought we could brainstorm."

"Okay, but weddings aren't exactly my specialty." I carry both glasses over to the sofa.

She follows me with the chips and the notebook and settles herself into the little armchair. She pins me with a gaze that's much sharper than she ever would have used on my father. "Then you can drink a margarita and fake it for an hour, Ariel. I'm asking nicely."

I take a gulp of frozen margarita and wonder if aliens have swapped her body for someone else's. We don't do this. We don't bond over drinks and share our deepest desires. For the first twenty-five years of my life, we had nothing in common except shared animosity toward my father, and often each other.

She wanted me to be a good girl, so that he'd shut up.

I wanted her to grow a pair and tell him where to get off.

But then he was gone. And after Buzz was born, things got easier between us. We finally had common interests—baby clothes, toys and all the cute things Buzz says and does.

A wedding, though? "All right. What's your plan?"

She sips from her giant margarita with the daintiness of Queen Elizabeth from her teacup. "This won't be an ordinary wedding. Second weddings can be so gauche."

I guess she's still in there after all. "So no church, then? And no big white dress." I lean over the bowl of chips and start eating them as if it's my job.

"Definitely not." She unwraps the notebook and pulls a fountain pen out of her pocket. She opens to the first page and starts writing. "I want a casual setting. Forty or so guests. Fifty—tops. Close friends only."

"Casual setting—like the country club?"

She shakes her head. "Anywhere but there. That's where your father and I had our reception."

"*Oh.* Shit. Okay, not there. Too much like *Hamlet.*"

She laughs, and then our eyes meet over the rims of our respective margarita glasses. "This is weird," she says. "I know it is. But I'm going to hold my head up high. Just like you do, darling."

"What?" I take another sip. The margarita is superb. But that's not a surprise. My mother doesn't do anything half-assed. She probably studied seventeen recipes before making this one.

"You always just do your thing and you don't care what anyone thinks," she says, setting her glass down on my coffee table. "You have a lot of backbone and you never, ever blink. I have always admired that about you."

Whoa. I shove a chip into my mouth and chew, because I am afraid of what I'll say to her. My mother's lack of a backbone when it came to my father made my childhood treacherous. Mom isn't the only one who ever went to therapy. My college psychologist explained to me that taking my bedroom door off the hinges and smashing my phone with a cast-iron pan were abusive behaviors, and that my mother could have protected me from that.

You're angry at her and mistrustful of others for a reason, she said.

Not that now is the right moment to say so. "Thank you," I say instead. "So how do you want this wedding to look?"

"I want a brief ceremony, followed immediately by amazing food," she says. "But maybe it's a daytime event. Live music, but no dancing."

It sounds to me like she already has a plan. But I'll play along. "What are you going to wear?"

She takes a chip delicately between two fingers and frowns. "That will be tricky. It has to nod at tradition without looking like I'm trying too hard to be a young woman. Maybe a dress in a champagne color."

"Or white but casual," I suggest. "A pantsuit?"

"Maybe," she says. "It will depend on the venue, and the time of day."

"I'll google some spots," I say gamely. I pull out my phone and look up *wedding venues Portland Maine*. My screen fills with a million results.

There's an entire industry for this. Of course there is. I start scrolling through the results—scene after scene of seaside altars, beautiful flowers, elegant table settings.

It's all very lovely, but it leaves me cold. I know with a bone-deep certainty that a wedding is something I will never plan for myself. Since Drew blew in and out of my life, I've never had the urge to put myself out there again.

Besides—single moms aren't exactly what thirtyish-year-old guys are looking for. And that's fine. I don't want a guy. I only wanted *one* guy. And he didn't want me back.

He didn't even tell me his real name.

9

The next morning, I pour myself into my office chair and take a deep gulp of coffee. My head is throbbing.

"You okay?" Zain asks without looking away from his screen.

"I will be. My mother got me drunk."

His hands freeze on the keyboard. "You told her about . . . ?"

"*No*," I say firmly. "It's still in the vault. And that won't change."

He actually turns to look at me. "Did you google any seventy-year-old Andrew Millers yet?"

A tremor shimmies through my chest. "No. Did you?"

"No, but I spent half the night combing through the rest of that tape I showed you."

"Is that why you look exhausted?" There are purple smudges beneath his eyes.

"It's nothing coffee can't fix." He turns back to his work.

I watch his fingers fly over the keyboard again. "Why are you helping me with this? What's in it for you?"

"Nothing. But it's the most interesting thing that's happened to me in years." He stops typing. "Sorry. Was that a shitty thing to say? It's happening to you, not me. But it's still interesting. I don't get why he needed to lie. He was smart. He was confident. He didn't say really awkward things all day long, like some people."

He flinches after he says that last thing, and for the hundredth time I try to decide whether Zain is honestly creepy, or if he's just awkward and I'm a heartless asshole with trust issues.

Meanwhile, Drew's motivations are the ones I'm supposed to be litigating. "Maybe he wasn't qualified for his job," I suggest. "People lie on résumés all the time, right? Colleges they didn't really go to. Jobs they didn't really hold."

Zain tips his head back and forth as if considering the idea. "But Drew didn't show up with a stacked résumé. He went to UMass, not Harvard. People lie about military service, I suppose. But Ray would've only cared about which programming languages he knew anyway. We were kind of desperate for warm bodies back then."

"I was pretty desperate for his warm body, too," I mutter.

Zain's face promptly turns the color of a tomato. "Even if he wanted to inflate his credentials, that's no reason to use someone else's name. That's just asking to get caught."

"Fair point. You worked with him, though. Do you think he inflated his credentials?"

Zain drops his eyes to the keyboard. "He wasn't the best programmer I ever worked with. Wasn't the worst, either. He was slow, and he asked a lot of questions. He wasn't dumb, though. Just rusty. He knew his OOP languages but said he hadn't used them much in the army. Wait." Zain looks up. "What if he wasn't even *in* the army?"

"He was," I say, automatically defending him, before realizing that nothing he ever told me is reliable. "I think so, anyway. He had all the tattoos. And, uh, a lot of war wounds."

Zain's hands go still on the keyboard. "Really?"

"Extensive," I say quietly. "Take my word for it." And even as I say it, I feel a weird tightness in my chest. Drew trusted me enough to show me his scars. I can still picture his wary face that first night when he stripped off his clothes. Like he'd never been more naked in his life.

But I didn't recoil. It was just the opposite—I stepped into his personal space and kissed him like the end of the world was nigh. And he clung to me like he was drowning and I was the lifeboat.

That was real, damn it. Maybe the rest of it was all lies. But that night meant something.

"Interesting," Zain says, scrubbing his forehead. "That's bad-ass. What were the tattoos? Was his unit number on there somewhere?"

"Probably?" I uncap my coffee and take a gulp. "There was an eagle and a star. But I wasn't exactly focusing on his, uh, metadata, Zain."

"Fair." He snickers. "What else did he tell you about himself? He asked a *lot* of questions—but he never seemed to answer any."

"Um . . ." I search my memory for anything related to his past. "He didn't give me a lot of detail. He said he'd had a difficult childhood. That he grew up in foster care, which was pretty awful until he was a teenager. Then they placed him with a great guy. An army vet who helped Drew apply to college and the ROTC program."

"And where was that?"

"Somewhere upstate. Not Portland." Zain probably thinks I'm the dumbest person alive. "I'm not sure where. I didn't press him for details. But I should have."

He shrugs. "Some people never talk about their shitty pasts."

"Right," I agree, although it's more than that. I'm not a sharer, either. I didn't want to tell Drew all my ugly moments—like the breakdown I had in college that finally led me to therapy.

He didn't mind that I kept the darkest crevices of my heart private, and I extended the same courtesy.

That's how you end up dating a con man, I guess. Live and learn.

"What else did he tell you?" Zain asks.

"Well . . ." It's going to be a short list. "That he went to college in Massachusetts, like it says on his résumé." But I suppose that could have been invented, too. "He got his injuries in Syria. He was working in army intelligence, supporting a unit that disposes of explosives, but somebody missed one." That must be true? He got injured somehow. "He drank his coffee black. He liked German shepherds and paperback thrillers. He was into motorcycles and wanted to buy one."

Zain cringes.

"His best friend from the army went by Woody, which probably isn't *his* real name, either."

"Not helpful," Zain mutters.

But how convenient. It's so obvious now how little I knew about Drew. "He liked maple donuts, and yet he still had six-pack abs. He was really good in bed."

Zain snorts with laughter while turning bright red.

"We're running out of things I knew about him. Don't judge."

"Hey, I'm not." He clears his throat. "Do you have any pictures of him? There are some new toys out there for finding faces on the internet."

"Only one." I pull out my phone and open up my photos. "Drew said he didn't like to have his picture posted on social media. He made me promise. It's the only paranoid thing he ever said to me. But that's not a red flag, huh?" I roll my eyes at my own stupidity.

"Nah, I'm kinda with him on that," Zain says. "You can't work for this company and not understand that your right to privacy is under threat. In this building we've got *millions* of people's faces on our company servers. If you had free rein, and you wanted to spy on somebody, you could follow them around from camera to camera. Social media is the same, except public."

"But you'd only care about that if you had something to hide." I pass him my phone, showing him the picture of Drew's text avatar.

He looks at the photo and shakes his head. "A profile shot, and his eyes are closed." He returns my phone and starts to say something else, but then stops himself when Brendan, the programmer who sits on Zain's other side, picks that moment to show up.

"Morning, crew! Zain, you look like shit. Did you have a wild night?" The guy cackles. "Pick up some girls? Dance the night away?"

"Something like that," Zain mumbles.

Brendan drops his wallet and phone on the desk and heads for the coffee maker, slapping guys on the shoulder as he goes.

"How about Becky's for lunch?" Zain asks under his breath. "I still have to show you what else I found last night."

"Wait. Anything good?" I ask, my pulse quickening.

He hesitates. "Interesting, but not illuminating."

"Fine. Becky's. Early, so we can get a table." *And because I'm dying inside.*

"You know it."

10

FIVE YEARS AGO, JUNE

It's late on a Wednesday afternoon, and the senior programmer is keeping tabs on the Cafferty brothers as they yell at each other across the bullpen. There's a glass wall and twenty feet or so of distance between him and the co-owners of Chime Co. So he can't hear what they're fighting about.

It doesn't matter, though. This is common. This time they're in Ray's messy office, standing on opposite sides of the big oak desk, like bookends, as if to put as much distance as possible between themselves.

They've quarreled—loudly and frequently—ever since he started working here. They fight about the hardware design, the manufacturing costs and the software. They fight about the branding and the timeline of new releases.

Different topics every time, but the fight is really always about the same thing—power. Whose dick is bigger. Who's really in charge.

After they emerge, they'll probably fire off conflicting emails to him. And then he'll lose a precious hour of technical work just trying to reconcile their petty arguments.

It's the same shit every month. It never changes.

Only one thing is different today—their audience. Most programmers know to keep their heads down and avoid the drama. Nobody wants to get caught in the cross fire. Edward, particularly, is a colossal dick when he gets angry.

That new guy, though, isn't worried. Drew Miller has wandered over to the copier right outside Ray's door. He's puttering around with the machine, rearranging his document on the glass, and slowly refilling the paper in the tray.

What he's *really* doing is eavesdropping. It's so fucking obvious. Programmers don't have any use for the copier. Paper is for losers.

And Drew is a nosy fucker. The guy asks too many questions. He seems almost systematic about it, with everyone in the room getting a turn on the other end of his "aw shucks" routine.

There's something off about him. There really is.

Ray's office door flies open, and Edward storms out. He walks ten paces, enters his own pristine office and slams the door before lowering himself carefully into his egotistically large leather chair.

None of the longtime programmers looks up.

Coincidentally, Drew Miller is done with his copy machine project. He walks through the room, whistling a little.

When he passes Ariel Cafferty, he doesn't glance at her. No eye contact. That makes Drew Miller the only man in this room who *doesn't* look at Ariel. This behavior is new, too. His first week here, he was just like the rest of the guys. Couldn't take his eyes off her.

Which can only mean one thing—they're banging, and they don't want anyone else to guess. Or they want to bang, and they just haven't gotten around to it yet.

Isn't that rich? The spoiled princess giving it up for the army stud. Drew is one of those guys who gets by on his good looks and strong handshake. He's some kind of battlefield veteran, too. Edward Cafferty has a hard-on for tough guys and uniforms, so he probably ate that shit up during the interview.

As Drew passes her desk, heading for the coffee station, Ariel keeps her head down. But the moment he clears her airspace, she lifts her gaze and admires his ass.

She is a stupid, stuck-up bitch. Always has been. This little charade is so obvious to anyone who cares to notice. Which, to be fair, isn't many people. Chime Co. is populated by surprisingly clueless humans.

A lot happens around here that nobody sees.

The programmer picks up his mug, rises from his chair and follows Drew toward the coffee. Ignoring the other man, he rinses out his cup and spins the rack of coffee pods. All the slots are empty, except for the decaf, which is still full, of course.

It's Ariel who's supposed to keep this thing stocked. But she doesn't bother. So he grabs an unopened box of coffee pods out of the cabinet, rips the top off and grabs one.

"Oh, awesome," Drew Miller says. "You mind if I . . . ?"

"Go ahead." He trains his eyes on the clipboard under Drew's arm, aiming to see what the hell the kid was photocopying.

But Drew, that sneaky fucker, has clipped the pages onto the board upside down. Who does that? Someone who's up to no good, that's who.

"Nice mug," Drew says as they fire up side-by-side coffee machines. "I think you got the best one."

"Thanks." The mug says BINARY IS AS EASY AS 1, 10, 11. It's his favorite because of the shape, not the cheap joke on the front. And if Drew wants to pull him into a conversation, he's gonna have to do better.

Drew smiles, then asks a real question. "Why do you think they fight like that? Does it happen a lot?"

"Do you have a brother?"

Drew's smile fades. He shakes his head.

"Yeah, neither do I. So I guess I wouldn't know." And now his phone beeps, so he pulls it out of his pocket. "Excuse me. I'd better answer this."

Drew waves him off with another white-toothed smile.

He grabs his coffee and reads the message on his way back to his desk. It's arrived via an encrypted chat. From TheBoss to Brainz.

He's Brainz in this scenario, of course.

TheBoss: How's our project today? Any hiccups?
  Brainz: Humming along. No new bugs.
TheBoss: Excellent work. BTW I hear there's going to be good
             weather for fishing this weekend. Don't make any
             plans for Saturday.
  Brainz: Sounds good. You know I love fishing.

He pockets his phone and gets back to work.

11

ARIEL

Becky's Diner is a Portland institution. It opens at the crack of dawn, early enough to serve the lobstermen who come in after dropping their traps. By the time normal people are ready to eat, there's a long line for tables or a seat at the counter.

Zain and I hit it at eleven thirty, before the lunch rush. We snag an outdoor table up on their back deck and order fat club sandwiches.

"And coffee, please," Zain says. "Keep it coming."

"You look like you could do a face-plant on the table," I tell him.

"Well, that's flattering." He stretches his arms overhead and rotates his neck. "Every programmer does all-nighters sometimes. It's the nature of the beast. And I need to put the tape back on the shelf before anyone gets suspicious."

"What did you find?" I demand.

He rubs his forehead. "I used to think Drew was just a slow programmer. But he had some time-consuming hobbies." He chuckles. "Our boy was a busy man during his three months at Chime Co."

"Doing what?"

"Well, it's weird. When I first looked at everything under Drew's log-in, it was pretty boring stuff. He did his job. Nothing fishy. *Yet.*"

Zain's voice betrays his excitement, though. It's like listening to one of Uncle Ray's stories—you have to sit back and let him tell it.

"Then I realized I should search by terminal ID as well as log-in."

"Terminal ID?" I ask.

"Yeah—every computer in the office has a unique ID. Most people log in from a home computer, too, so that makes two terminals. So I matched Drew's log-ins to his terminals. And guess what? Lots of people got logged in on his computer."

My head swims. "You mean—he sat at his desk and logged in as other people?"

"Yes!" he says, smacking the table. "As *four* other people. What a sneaky fucker he was. And he did this early in the morning or late in the afternoon. Sometimes at lunch. Can you guess why that is?"

I shake my head.

His face lights up. "Because he sat near *me*. He must have worried that I'd notice. Or he didn't want to chance it."

"Because you are so observant that it's honestly creepy?"

He snorts.

But I'm not really joking. "Drew was good at reading people. He read me easily enough, didn't he?" *Lonely girl. Daddy issues. Willing to put out for snarky soldiers with blue eyes.*

Won't ask too many questions.

Zain flashes his awkward smile. "Don't be so hard on yourself. I didn't ever guess he was a spy, either."

"A *spy*." My stomach bottoms out. "For *who*?"

"I have no idea. But why else would he steal passwords and poke around the network? You can check my work, by the way. I printed a copy of everything he did. It's in your bottom desk drawer."

"Thanks." But it's a struggle to square this sneaky Drew with the one I thought I knew. Either I'm very stupid, or love made me blind. Because I never got that vibe off him. The Drew I knew wasn't quite so complicated. He liked hanging out with me. He liked to be outdoors. And he really liked taking me to bed.

Nope. I just can't see it. "So what was he looking at while posing as other people?"

Zain leans his pointy elbows on the table. "At first, he spent hours just figuring out how all the databases fit together. Then he started digging into the way camera IDs work. He seemed particularly interested in how we code police department cameras versus private ones."

"What does that tell you?"

He shakes his head. "Not much. He opened some of the police department files and looked at the feeds, which is absolutely a violation of company policy. But he seemed to be poking around randomly. He didn't view the videos for any length of time, either. Just a few seconds. It wasn't, like, stalkery stuff."

Yikes. At any given time, Chime Co. stores millions of hours of video. I don't understand the tech involved, which is probably why I picture it like a vast honeycomb—millions of circular glass lens eyeballs on millions of houses, each one containing the live image of another front porch in another town.

Or, in the case of the police cameras, on another public lamppost. But either way, watching videos for fun is the kind of thing that would get a guy fired. "Is that all he did?"

"No." He waits for the waitress to plunk a mug of coffee down in front of him before continuing. "After that, he started looking at the PriSys. That means—"

"—Private Request System," I finish. It's a way for law enforcement to ask private citizens to share their doorbell camera footage with police. They get a notification in the app, followed by a little message:

> Dear homeowner, we are investigating suspicious activity on your block between the hours of two and four a.m. last Monday. If you consent to sharing your camera's footage during those hours, please tap the CONSENT TO SHARE button.

"Of course I know what that is," I remind Zain. "It 'changed the shape of police work' if you believe the *Wall Street Journal*. My father printed out the article, highlighted that passage and hung it on his office wall."

Zain chuckles. "I don't think you're stupid, Ariel. But you've always told people you didn't really know much about the business. It's, like, a point of pride. So I'm not going to assume you know the jargon."

"Okay, that's fair," I grumble. "I'm sure the entire programming staff thought of me as a spoiled brat. They probably still do. Whatever."

"Nah." He reaches for the cream and dumps it into his coffee. "They just think you're hot."

I ignore that. "So what do you think Drew was doing? Vandalism? Espionage? Stealing corporate secrets?"

"Hard to say at this point. And the tape ends a few weeks after his arrival. I'll have to swipe another one to keep looking. Or . . ." He eyes me over the rim of his coffee mug.

"Or?"

"You could steal it," he says. "They're on the shelf in Ray's office. You're in and out of there a lot more often than I am."

I hesitate. But only for a second. "Sure. Tell me how to find the right one."

"Easy peasy. They're sequentially numbered." He glances around the patio before fishing the tape he'd stolen out of his pocket and passing it to me. "When I took this one, I nudged the end of the row so that it wasn't obvious that one was missing. All you have to do is slide the next one out and push this one into the empty slot."

"Okay. Sure." I stow the tape in my bag, feeling a weird rush of adrenaline. Digging into Drew's lies won't make them less real. But I know I'm not going to be able to walk away. "This feels like looking over Drew's shoulder."

"Five years later, but yeah. Isn't it fun?"

"Sure, sure. The way playing with live grenades is fun."

He laughs. "It's fun for me because it's not my life. I just get to play private investigator."

The waitress puts two big sandwiches down on the table in front of us, and we pause our conversation just long enough to thank her.

Then I pick up my sandwich, suddenly hungry. "You'd make a good private investigator."

"Yeah, up until the minute I came face-to-face with a bad guy. He'd just snap me in half."

I try not to laugh.

I fail.

12

FIVE YEARS AGO, JUNE

"Welcome to the warrant desk. I'm Evan."

When Evan holds out a hand, Drew shakes it. It's a Friday afternoon, and they're standing one floor above Drew's usual desk.

"I really appreciate you volunteering for this shift. I usually take the Friday night myself, but my niece is having her dance recital, and my sister says I'm an asshole if I don't show up."

"Hey, it's no problem. We've all been there." *And you have no idea how eager I was to volunteer.*

"Take a seat, and let's do this." Evan rubs his hands together. He's a tanned white guy in his twenties with an easy demeanor. "There are two ways for police to access Chime Co. cameras. The easy way is to request footage from consumers who use the app."

"Right. PriSys. And most people say yes." Drew's been researching this since his chat with Trevor. Police make over a thousand requests each day, and eighty-two percent of their requests for footage are granted.

"Sometimes people say no, though. Or sometimes police don't want to tip off the neighbors. That's when they get a warrant instead. The cop fills out an affidavit and submits it to a judge. If the judge signs off on it, that request ends up here." He pats the monitor. "Our job is to review each one to make sure it's complete."

"Huh. So how did you get this job?"

Evan parks his hip against the desk. "I work in marketing as a law enforcement liaison, but I'm also the warrant desk manager."

No conflict of interest there. Jesus.

"Handling law enforcement requests is a pain. But with great power comes great responsibility." Evan smirks. "This year we're on pace to get twelve hundred warrants and court orders—the highest number yet. We're staffed until eight p.m. every night. Friday is the busiest day of the week, so you'll get three or four in the next couple of hours. Make yourself comfortable."

Drew glances around the upstairs office space. It's Chime Co.'s version of Siberia. This is where the bookkeepers and other support staff sit—the people who don't work on the product itself. There are ugly file boxes stacked up against one wall.

It says a lot about how they view the warrant desk.

"All right," Drew says in a bored voice. "How do you know when there's a new request?"

"You don't have to stare at the screen, if that's what you mean." He waves a hand at the monitor. "The notification makes a loud sound, and a new request will show up at the top, in bold type. We don't allow anyone to call in their warrants. If someone happens to call, you need to insist that they put it into the system. That's part of our compliance process."

"Got it," he says, giving Evan a serious nod.

"First, you read the camera ID off the search warrant and type it into this field." Evan leans over Drew's shoulder to show him the form. "That's how you grab the right video for the police."

Drew has a million questions. More than Evan could ever imagine. But he restrains himself to the most relevant ones. "How can I be sure that the camera ID is correct? I don't want to hand over the wrong home's footage."

"Once you input the ID number, the address where the camera is registered will appear on the next screen. Compare that address to the one on the search warrant. If they match, then you don't have to worry."

"What if they *don't* match?" he asks carefully.

Evan taps the form on the screen. "Explain right here what the problem is. And then refuse the request. It's better to be safe than sorry. We take our customers' privacy seriously."

Sure you do, pal.

"If you have any questions, you can text me. If I don't see it, you can call Ray Cafferty. Here's his number." Evan drops the COO's business card on the desk. "If we ever screw something up, the warrant won't be admissible in court. So let's not do that."

"Yessir."

Evan grins. "Before I go, you need to identify yourself for the camera. Do you have your ID on you?"

"Sure." He unclips it from his belt.

"Look up and show it to the camera. It's up there—on the ceiling."

Drew spins around and spots the camera's dark, insect-like eye. He holds the ID toward the lens for a moment.

"That's fine," Evan says. "The camera is tightly focused on the keyboard and the screen. If there's ever a lawsuit over passing footage to law enforcement, there's a record of your actions, okay? So don't stand up and lean over the monitor—it blocks the camera's view. We save the video *forever*, in case there is ever a question about the integrity of our process."

"Got it."

"Cool. Then I'm out of here." Evan checks his watch. "Don't leave before eight fifteen. That's just past the deadline for West Coast law enforcement to put their warrants through. You'll probably see some action in the next hour."

"No problem. Have a fun night."

The guy barks out a laugh. "Sure, pal. Dance recitals are totally my jam." He gives Drew a wave and then departs.

Drew glances around again. The accountants have gone home. He's the only one left on this level. He picks up the thick business card, where Evan has scrawled a mobile number beneath the embossed ink.

Now he has the COO's private number, which could be useful. Ray is a bit of a mystery. The guy is charming. Always telling a story. But his warmth has an oily quality to it. He's too earnest. Too eager to be everyone's best buddy.

Maybe it's a birth order thing—a psychological reaction to wading through life as Edward Cafferty's brother. That man would as soon cut you as smile at you.

Drew turns his attention to the warrant system. As a dress rehearsal, he opens up a new validation. When the form comes up, he types in a random ten-digit camera ID.

An address pops up immediately. It's for a camera in Winston-Salem, North Carolina. But it says **DEACTIVATED** in red letters beside the address.

Interesting.

He tries another number, just three digits off from the first, and gets a camera in Claremont, California. But then the elevator doors on the far wall part. Drew closes the record and looks up to see who's coming.

It's Ariel, with a plastic bag in one hand, a six-pack of beer in the other and a catlike smile on her face.

The sight of her face makes his pulse jump. It shouldn't, but it does. "Hey, girl. You lost?"

"Hey, soldier. I heard the new guy got stuck with the worst job in the building." She stops on the other side of the desk. "And I owe you dinner."

"Well, I accept." He didn't think he'd see her tonight. In fact, when he volunteered for this gig, he assumed it ruined his chances of hanging out with her for the third Friday in a row.

That should have been a good thing. He's still trying to stay away from Ariel.

So why does he feel like this is the most important moment of his week?

Just then, the law enforcement system chimes loudly with a real request.

Ariel sets the beer on the next desk over, out of the camera's view. Then she stands at a distance behind him and peers at the screen. "Looks like you've got a warrant there. Better get on that. I'll open the beers."

"Uh, right."

He sits down and opens the request. It's from a police department in Beaumont, California. They want to see ninety minutes of camera footage dated three days ago. There's a pdf attached with the camera ID number, signed by a judge. *The Honorable Jorge Booth.*

All right then.

Drew types the ID number of the camera into the search window. Out pops an address on Palm Avenue. He checks the warrant and finds that the addresses match perfectly.

Then he types the first several letters of the judge's name into another field, and the system suggests JORGE BOOTH, 9TH CIRCUIT.

All the details match. But he double-checks every single one just in case.

"It's a match. Hit the button." Ariel pulls a container out of the plastic bag, and suddenly he can smell cumin and chilis. "I got us Mexican food."

And that's the nudge he needs to hit *submit*. One click and *boom*. Done. He's just turned someone's private video over to law enforcement, against their wishes, and in less time than it takes to order a burrito.

"Why did you volunteer for this, anyway?" Ariel asks, covering the desk with food containers. "I've done this job, and it's a snooze."

Now, there's a question he can't answer truthfully. *I'm a snoop, and I need to know how private video ends up in stalkers' hands.* "I would have thought this job was perfect for you," he says instead. "Lots of extra time to spend with that sketch pad."

"True. So what's your excuse?"

"The new guy has to do his bit."

"But I thought you didn't care about this job." She's dishing rice onto two plates, and the scent of it makes his stomach growl.

"Well, I don't." And that's the honest truth. "But someone had to pull this shift. And I assumed you'd be with your family tonight anyway."

She looks up with surprise. "Why? Because of my dad's knee surgery? Do you want chicken or pork or both?"

"Whatever you're dishing out, I'm eating." That seems to be his whole philosophy with Ariel. There isn't anything she can do that he doesn't want more of.

She heaps several different items onto a plate, adds a generous dollop of guacamole and passes it to him. "I did send a bag of take-out food to my parents' house. And I'm sure my mother is grateful. She's stuck at home with his grumpy ass for a whole week. No—a whole *life*. But that is her choice."

He has nothing nice to say, so he takes a bite instead.

"My father put off this surgery for two years, because he thought he could just command his knee to stop hurting. The doctor finally refused to refill his pain meds if he didn't just get it done. He doesn't want me hanging around offering him tea and soup, though. He knows I'd probably poison everything."

He snorts with laughter.

"Besides, he wasn't the kind of dad who gave a damn when I got sick." She shrugs. "How'd you get that scar on your cheek? It looks recent. Still has that new-scar shine."

The abrupt change of topic startles him enough that he gives her the truth. "Shrapnel. From an IED last year."

"Damn." Her lips quirk up in the corners. "You probably don't mind my asking, right? Most guys would have to admit they got stoned and jumped off the garage when they were sixteen."

"Oh, I have that scar, too," he says. "But it's on my ass."

After she stops laughing, she opens two beers, and the next hour and a half flies by. He tells her a little about his time in the army. It feels damn good to tell her something about himself that's actually true.

Lying to his employers at Chime Co. isn't very hard. His work here is important. But lying to Ariel feels like a real betrayal. "Thanks for dinner. You know I appreciate it."

"You're welcome." Her gaze crashes into his, and nobody blinks for a second.

He didn't mean to see her again tonight. Or last Friday, for that matter, when they sat talking in a beer garden until they closed the place down. They ended the night hard-core making out against the front door of her little apartment building.

He prided himself on walking away instead of inviting himself upstairs. But it's doubtful he'll find the strength to walk away one more time.

She licks her lips, and his judgment slides a little further down its rocky slope toward doom.

Ariel finally looks away and begins tossing their plates into a plastic bag. "Let's discuss our entertainment options. I don't like any of the bands that are playing tonight."

"Movies, then? Darts? Bowling?"

"You *bowl*?" Her pretty brown eyes widen. "I might need to see that."

"My best friend grew up in a town with nothing but a lumberyard and a bowling alley. And he's crazy competitive, so I had to learn just to show him up. Bet you can't beat me."

"Bet I can," she argues immediately. "But I have a better idea. You're not dressed for it, but I think it won't matter."

He looks down at his dress shirt and chinos. "I need a tie for whatever you have in mind?"

"No way." She laughs. "I just don't want you to ruin that nice shirt."

"I have my gym bag downstairs. But where are we going?"

She shrugs mischievously. "Guess you'll find out when you get there. A T-shirt would be good—but only if it's cotton. No synthetics. Closed shoes, too. No flip-flops."

"What about my studded leather pants? Too much?"

"You do you, soldier." She looks at the time. "You're off duty in twenty minutes. Two forty-five Commercial Street. And bring the rest of the beer."

"Will do."

His smile doesn't fall until after she's gone.

The warrant system dings with one more request right before quitting time.

He patiently taps all the information into the system, triple-checking every detail.

And the whole thing takes three minutes. Still quicker than ordering a burrito.

An hour later he's standing in Ariel's glassblowing studio. And it's suddenly obvious how deeply he's into this girl.

She's wearing Carhartt overalls. Her hair has been pulled into a messy bun. Her feet are covered by the ugliest work boots he's ever seen. And she's issuing instructions like machine-gun fire. "Turn it. Faster. Blow! Harder."

She drops to a crouch in front of him, long limbs glistening with sweat from the 1,200-degree furnace. Her grimace is focused on the misshapen blob of glass on the end of his five-foot pipe, and her safety goggles make her look like a bug.

Yet she is impossibly lovely. There is nothing sexier than a girl who can make beautiful objects from fire and glass. And then make you look like a fool when you try to do the same.

"*Harder*," she demands. "One more good push."

"I bet you say that to all the guys." He puts his mouth on the pipe and tries once more to force air into the glass at the end. His cheeks might burst right off his face.

"Good!" she says suddenly. "Now heat it and swing it."

He immediately turns toward another raging fire, this one

covered by a sheet of metal except for a six-inch circle in the center. "I can't believe you really call this thing a 'glory hole,'" he says with a chuckle.

"You already owe a dollar to the dick joke jar," she says.

"The . . . what?"

She points at a handblown jar on one of the studio's cluttered surfaces. There's a sharpied sign taped to the front: DICK JOKES $1 PER OFFENSE. "We've heard them all before, soldier. And spin that faster, or it will droop."

"Yes ma'am. Wouldn't want it to *droop*." He spins the blob of glass on the end of the pipe and falls, if possible, a little further for her.

"Now we're going to shape the mouth," she says, and he bites back yet another inappropriate comment.

God, the things he wants from her mouth.

But there's no time for daydreaming. Ariel attaches a metal rod to the opposite end of his work. Then she uses an ordinary metal file dipped in water to cleanly break the blow pipe off his glass object. Like magic.

She hands the piece back to him on the metal pole. It looks like a lumpy little shot glass now. "Back to the glory hole. Then we shape the neck."

Fifteen sweaty minutes later, she's helped him use an oversized set of tweezers to bully the rim of the tiny cup into shape. Using more of her trickery, Ariel breaks the piece off the rod and then uses an honest-to-god flamethrower to smooth out the bottom.

With the fire in her hand and a frown on her face, she looks like an avenging angel. His heart can't take it.

When she's finally satisfied, she grabs the tiny cup with a flame-proof glove and opens the door of the annealing oven, where finished pieces rest. She sets his piece down beside the one she dashed off to instruct him, and he howls with laugher.

"What?"

"*Look* at them." He can't stop laughing. One cup is smooth and symmetrical, curved to fit into the hand. Like a frozen teardrop. It's the kind of thing a fine restaurant would produce if you order a shot of twenty-five-year-old whiskey.

The other is a thick-sided, misshapen disaster. A lump of glass with a volcanic hole in it.

Ariel removes her safety goggles with a smile. "Everyone starts somewhere. Now find me some ice cream. I'm desperate."

They're too sweaty for a real restaurant. So dessert is two milk-shakes from the Duckfat take-out window, sipped at a picnic table.

"Show me some of your real work," he demands as they trade milkshakes for a taste test. Hers is banana cheesecake, and his is strawberry. "I want to see what a professional can do."

"Is this, like, *Hey, baby, show me your sketches*?" she asks, handing back his milkshake. The cup is considerably lighter than it was a minute ago.

"Maybe," he says, his voice husky. "I think I have a competence fetish."

Her laugh is joyful as she pulls out her phone. "I'm still an ap-prentice. But these are my current obsession—I'm making goblets. The shape is sort of medieval."

He basically moans when he sees the photo—three beautiful glasses with broad tops that taper elegantly to a decorative base and a flared foot. The shape is historic, but the clear glass lends them a contemporary vibe. And they're nearly identical. "How long does it take you to make these?"

"On a good day I can produce two or three. Each one of those sections of the base is another trip to the furnace. And most of my studio time is spent assisting Larri. She blows light fixtures for sale—that's her bread and butter. For fun she makes elaborate bongs."

"Artists are a good time," he says, knocking her elbow with his.

"You know it. My father can't figure out why I'd want to 'waste my life'"—her fingers are air quotes—"in the studio, when I could learn to be just like him. He expends a lot of energy trying to think up ways to motivate me."

"You're plenty motivated," he says. "How many hours have you spent making glass?"

"Thousands? Nobody ever said trust funds weren't handy." She props her hand on the picnic table and meets his gaze. Her hair is escaping its confines, and there's a smudge of ice cream on her overalls. But all he can see is her bright, intelligent smile.

He's never spent any time with rich girls. He assumed that privilege made people shallow. But she's just the opposite—unflinching and unapologetic. And utterly addictive.

And still a terrible idea. She can't help him do what he came to Portland to do. She can only get in the way.

That doesn't explain why he leans in and kisses her right there. She tastes like strawberry ice cream and bad decisions.

They leave a few minutes later, hands locked together, pace slow. Neither one of them names a destination, and yet they pass her neighborhood and head toward his little apartment building on Exeter Street.

When they reach his block, it's the final frontier. He stops in front of his building. "Are you coming inside?" he asks. "Or should I call you an Uber?"

"If I'm going home, you're coming with me," she says. "And my roommate will play embarrassingly loud music for us to overhear."

They're standing so close together. Practically nose to nose. "That's a habit of hers?" he asks, buying time to make this decision.

"It's just payback," she whispers. "I like to blast Marvin Gaye's 'Let's Get it On' when her boyfriend comes over."

He laughs, and they end up tongue-tangled again, right there on the front stoop, until a pair of dog walkers applauds for them as they pass by on the sidewalk.

"Christ," he breathes, his body on fire. He fishes his keys out of his pocket. "There's, uh, one more thing you need to know about me. This isn't my worst scar." He taps his face, right on the spot where the shrapnel went in.

"So? Everyone knows that chicks dig scars."

"Yeah, well." He takes a big breath and tries to slow his racing heart. "The other scar is the kind you need to be prepared for." He lifts his left shoe off the ground, balancing on his right. And with far more nonchalance than he feels, he tugs the pant leg up so she can see the prosthesis where his calf should be. "I lost part of my leg."

She lifts wide eyes to his. "Holy fuck, soldier. I had no idea."

The next few seconds seem to last forever. The guys at Walter Reed coached him to expect a certain amount of shocked rejection. Or—worse—pity.

If this is about to get weird, he just hopes it's over quickly.

"Look." Ariel puts a hand in the center of his tightening chest. "I'm sure there's some exact right thing I'm supposed to say right now. And maybe I can come up with it later. But first you need to take me inside and finish what you started."

He blinks. Then he blinks again.

She takes the keys out of his hand, climbs the three steps up to his door, finds the right key for the outer door and opens it. "You coming or what?"

That shocks him into action. He follows her into the vestibule and reclaims his keys so he can open the second door. "If you're sure."

"Enough with the talking," she scoffs. "We just went over this."

He opens his apartment door, tows her inside, and then shuts her up with another kiss.

After that, nobody says more than *Oh God* all night long.

13

ARIEL

After lunch with Zain, I prepare an excuse to sneak into Ray's office—a printed update on our office move that I can leave on his desk.

But he seems glued to his office chair. There's a meeting with the head of marketing, followed by several phone calls. Hester brings him a late lunch from the Bagel Tree, too, while I wait impatiently for my chance.

Eventually, I watch him answer a call on his mobile phone and then wander out toward the coffee counter on the opposite side of the bullpen.

I glance at Hester, who sits outside Ray's office. She's on the phone, too. I'm not going to get another chance as good as this one. So I slip the tape Zain filched into the dark green folder with Ray's report. Rising from my chair with a straight back and my head held high, I stride into his office.

It takes me a sweaty ten seconds to eye the tapes lined up on the shelf, identifying the next one in the order. I tug it out and slip mine into its place. Then I drop the report onto Ray's desk and stride out again, the tape casually pinned by my thumb against the folder.

When I step out of Ray's office, I find that he's nearly upon me. His phone is still pressed to his ear, and he raises his eyebrows at me, as if asking if I need something.

I give him a smile and go back to my desk.

My heart is pounding, though. I used to be an excellent sneak, and I *never* got nervous. In high school I knew how to climb out of my bedroom window without the security camera—a Chime Co. prototype—alerting anyone. All I had to do was cut through the neighbor's backyard.

I had no guilt, and I was never afraid.

The circumstances were different, though—I'd hated my father, and I didn't respect his rules. It's not like that with Ray. I don't enjoy lying to him, even if I have my reasons.

With a guilty shiver, I drop the tape into Zain's backpack, which is sitting on the floor between us, unzipped.

"Good work," he says without looking away from his screen.

"Thanks," I mutter. But I'm already second-guessing myself. Zain just made me complicit in his little escapade, and I'm not even sure why I went along with it. If Drew was a thief or a corporate spy, why do I need to be mixed up in it?

What if his leaving was a blessing, not a curse? That's not a question I'm used to asking myself.

I go back to my spreadsheets, but my head is in a dark place. What I need is an hour or two in the glass studio.

Before I leave, I open my bottom desk drawer, looking for the printout that Zain left me. I'm not prepared for what I find there. His file is as thick as a dictionary. "Are you serious right now?" I mutter as I pull it onto my lap and flip it open to the middle.

It's barely decipherable. Each entry is a date and timestamp, a log-in and terminal number and a bunch of commands. My head hurts just looking at it.

Still, I jam it into my bag and leave the office behind, without a word to anyone.

Larri doesn't even look startled when I walk in early again. I suit up and get to work on a prototype for a whiskey decanter, while she's trying to shape a delicate glass bubble that's meant to form the centerpiece of a chandelier she's building for a commission.

But it's tricky work, and her attempts keep landing on the floor.

The third time I hear the telltale crack, followed by curses, I set down the pipe I'm cleaning and grab a dustpan to scoop the biggest shards off the concrete. "You need help with that thing?"

"No. Don't worry about me. I'll get over my snit in a second." She guzzles from a beat-up metal water bottle with Portland Pride stickers all over it. "It's been a shit week. Tara isn't speaking to me at the moment. She's still mad."

"Wait, why?" I demand. "Because of that text? It was an honest mistake."

"You weren't there." Larri removes her goggles and wipes her forehead with her sleeve. "When I thought she was using, I said some ugly things. I told her I was done. I was willing to abandon her over a misunderstanding. She's not over it."

"Well, shit. I'm sorry."

She gives me a grimace. "That's not even the worst part. Right after our fight, she texted the dealer to demand that she never knock on our door again."

My stomach drops. "Oh *no*."

"Oh yes. The bitch turned up the next day and threatened Tara. Said if she ever talked about their business together, she'd kill us both."

"God! I'm *so* sorry." And here I thought I was the only one having a rough week.

She shakes her head. "So now she's freaked out, and *still* mad at me. I honestly don't know if we can get past this. I *was* ready to walk, and she sees it as a huge betrayal. All the hard work she's done staying clean for years. Because I didn't believe her when she defended herself. That fucking text blew up my life."

"Tell me about it," I mutter.

"Hang on, did you get one of those texts, too? From who?"

I swallow hard. "An old friend."

She chucks her pipe into the warmer and turns toward me. "What kind of old friend are we talking about?" She squints, and I can see her doing the mental math. "Do you mean Buzz's daddy?"

I've held this in for so many years now that I feel like a dam about to burst. I nod.

Larri whistles. "Holy shit. Really? And you let me just blather on about my drama without *mentioning* it?"

"I've been upset."

She laughs. "You don't do upset like normal people. You realize that, yeah? Most people overshare and overeat."

"Pink wine seems to be my drug of choice."

"Jesus Christ. Jesus Christ." She wanders over to the bench and sits down. "You got a text from a man who abandoned you five years ago. What did it *say*?"

"That he wanted to meet me. But I *knew* it was bogus, Larissa. He's dead, okay? That's why I don't talk about him. There's no point."

She's staring at me again. "He's *dead*? You're sure?"

"That's right." Except for the new, nagging feeling in my gut that just won't go away.

She whistles again. "So who was this guy? All I know is that he messed with your head and that you didn't want anyone to know you were together. How come I never met him?"

"He's just a guy." I take my pipe out of the warmer and blow a puff of air through it to make sure it's not blocked. "You never met him because you and Tara were having a really rough summer. I barely saw you."

"Ah. Five summers ago? Yeah, things were . . ." She gives a mock shiver. "Terribad."

"Also, I was working more or less full-time for my dad, remember? That's where I met him—at the office. But he split after three months."

"And then he *died*? I always wondered why you didn't hunt his ass down and make him pay child support. I figured maybe he was bad news."

"No," I say quickly. Defending him is still my natural impulse. "He died right before Buzz was born. Motorcycle accident. He never knew he had a kid."

"Honey, I'm sorry. Still not sure why you never talk about him."

Because it hurts. "Because I wanted it to be Buzz's story to hear first. And also there's no point. Are we going to blow some glass today or what?" I carry my pipe over to the furnace and step on the pedal to open the door.

The furnace breathes its heat onto my skin, like a friendly dragon from one of Buzz's picture books.

I leave the studio at four thirty and start walking. But my feet don't seem to want to turn toward home. After twenty minutes, I find myself on Exeter Street, where Drew lived.

Standing in front of the little three-story building, though, I wish I hadn't come. Someone has hung purple curtains and an anime decal in the window of his old apartment. It just looks wrong.

This isn't the first time I've stood here on the sidewalk staring up at his abandoned window. I did this during my pregnancy, while I was hormonal and baffled by Drew's leaving. I even called the landlord—his phone number was visible on a note inside the vestibule—to ask whether Drew had left anything behind for me.

No dice, though. And the landlord wouldn't even tell me exactly when Drew had left. He actually hung up on me when I pressed him for details.

On a whim, I climb the three steps up to the door and peer inside the vestibule once again. The same business card is still hanging above the mailboxes. The ink on the phone number is fading, but it's still legible.

I pull out my phone and call the landlord again.

"This is Bert," he says. "How can I help you?"

"Bert, I'm standing outside your rental property on Exeter. Five years ago I called to ask you if a man named Drew Miller had left anything behind in his apartment for me. He left suddenly."

He grunts his assent. "I remember him. And you, too."

"Well, he's dead now. His son turned four years old in March, without ever meeting his father. We still know nothing about his departure from Portland. If he left anything behind—like a forwarding address—we deserve to know."

He is silent for a few seconds. "He's really dead?"

"I'll show you his obituary."

He sighs. "I have a box of his things in my basement."

My heart leaps into my mouth. "You do?"

"Let me find it. I'll be there in ten."

The next ten minutes are the longest of my life. At last, a slender Black man with salt-and-pepper hair comes around the corner clutching a file box. Bert gives me a wary glance before he approaches. He stops a few feet short and balances the box on his hip. "Drew Miller is really gone? What a waste."

"Do you want to see that obituary?" I pull out my phone.

He seems to consider the question. "Show me your boy instead. I love kids."

Well, that's easy. I open my phone and the first photo in the gallery is a shot I took of Buzz in the park last week. He's got his foot on a soccer ball and he's smiling into the camera.

Bert's expression softens as he admires Buzz's photo. Then he sighs. "Shame about Drew. Liked that kid. Always polite. Never late with the rent—until the day he split. Sent me a text to apologize. Pain in my ass—I had to haul all his stuff out of there. Not like there was a lot of it. Still, pissed me off."

I eye the box. It takes physical effort not to jerk it out of his hands. "I'm sorry."

He looks down at the carton. "I donated his clothes and his kitchen things. But there's some stuff in here I thought he might come back for. Suppose I could give it to you. Five years is a long time to hold on to them. Guy's not coming back, is he?"

"No, he isn't," I say quickly.

"All right," he grunts. "Here you go, then. Best of luck to you and your kid."

I can't hold back any longer. I reach for the box, and he passes it into my hands. It's heavier than I expected. "Thank you. It means a lot to me."

He nods, shoves his hands into his pockets and then disappears around the back of Drew's old building.

I grip the handles of the file box and start off down the street. It's a twenty-minute walk home. But I only make it around the next corner before I pause to brace the box on my hip and nudge open the lid with my thumb.

The first things I see are gold buttons on dark blue fabric. It's the dress uniform that used to hang in Drew's closet. The bulky material covers up whatever else is in there.

I hoist the box and shamelessly plunge my nose down into the fabric, inhaling deeply. But all I get is a musty basement smell. There's none of the spicy aftershave and clean cotton T-shirt scent of Drew.

Chastened, I force myself to nudge the box closed and then carry it home as quickly as I can, stashing it in my bedroom just as Buzz and my mother arrive in the kitchen downstairs.

"Mama!" he yells up the stairs. "I'm home from Grandmaaaaaaa's!"

I pull the bedroom door shut and hurry down to meet them.

I'm all out of pink wine. But as soon as I'm sure Buzz is asleep, I make a cup of Raspberry Zinger tea and then carry it up to my bedroom. I pull the curtains, turn on the overhead light and lift the box onto my bedspread.

When I lift the lid, those shiny gold buttons look up at me again. I rest my hand on the heavy fabric of the jacket and make myself pause.

This is the last moment when anything is possible. For one more second I can still believe that the box is full of answers. I might find a diary explaining everything. A heartfelt goodbye letter with my name on it. An apology. An explanation.

That's a lot to ask of this box.

After a deep breath, I lift the jacket out and give it a shake. It's heavy, and wrinkled from spending years folded up. I spread it carefully on the bed. It still looks snappy, with a couple of medals pinned above the pocket. Someday I'll give this to Buzz. I'll have it cleaned, and I'll hang it in his closet. He can invent worshipful fantasies about his hero dad, and I won't contradict a single one of them.

Even if I can't figure out why he left me *and* the uniform behind.

The uniform trousers make up the next layer in the box. I lift those out and set them aside. Beneath that I find three books. Two of them are expensive-looking computer programming texts. But there's also a hardcover copy of *The Hobbit*. I open the cover, and find an inscription.

With love always
        —E

Hell. I don't know who E is. And I'm not sure I want to. But I guess I'll be reading *The Hobbit* to Buzz when he gets a little older.

Beneath the books I find a small wooden picture frame, upside down. When I turn it over, my heart flips at the familiar sight.

The photo is just a four-by-six snapshot. But it's the only piece of decor that Drew had on the wall of his tiny apartment—a view of the peaked roofline of a house against a blue sky. The house is dark red, and the clapboards have that slightly uneven look of a century-old New England home. But they've been recently painted. And centered in that peak is a circular plaque. It's white, with eight painted hands forming a circle. The hands are carefully rendered in different skin tones, each one clasping the wrist of its neighbor.

When I asked Drew about this picture, he told me that this was a shot of his foster father's house. "One of the younger kids painted that plaque, and I helped him hang it. I took the photo to make the kid happy. But then I kept it because that's the only real home I ever had."

It's another little piece of Drew. I'm going to hang it up, too.

I set that aside and reach back into the box. There's a little leather tray where Drew used to put his change when he emptied his pockets at night. There's a tin for storing shaving soap. Drew bought it at a Portland shop one Saturday when we were out wandering after breakfast.

When I open it up, the cake of shaving soap is dried up, but the scent still clobbers me. Sandalwood and lemon. I hold it in both hands and slowly inhale, until tears spring into the corners of my eyes.

I read once that scent is the strongest trigger of memory. I don't know if that's true, but for a shining moment Drew seems so close again.

But it sort of backfires when I exhale. Once again I'm very much alone, sitting on a bed with a dead man's things that haven't been touched in years. Nothing says *dead and gone* like leaving your shaving soap behind for someone to sniff and cry over.

Get a grip, Ariel, I tell myself. *If he left us without a backward glance, he wasn't worth it.*

I put everything down on the bed and pick up my teacup. I don't know why I expected Drew's possessions to make sense of his life. If anything, I'm more confused than I was this morning. Why did he leave these things behind at all? Why was he in such a hurry to clear out of Portland that he couldn't be bothered to take his shaving soap, and his favorite photo?

I thought he left town to get rid of me. And maybe he did. But the haste gives me pause.

The box is almost empty now. The last thing inside is a cigar box I recognize. It sat on his desk, but I never knew what was inside.

I lift the lid and find a mishmash of objects, some of which Bert might have tossed into the box when he cleaned the apartment. There's a steel ballpoint pen. There's Drew's razor—a heavy thing that screams quality.

The box is cluttered by a bunch of paper receipts. Their ink is faded, but one of them is from Holy Donut. I recognize the barely-there logo.

When I push the receipts aside I find some foreign coins. Silver with a gold ring around the edge, and a script I can't read. There are eagles on them.

Syrian, maybe?

There's also a single key on one of those floating key rings that fishermen use. The key is the normal size for a house key, and darkened with age.

I pick up the cigar box and give it a little shake to see if there's anything else hiding amid the receipts. Two cuff links slide into view. They must be silver, because tarnish has blackened them. But I can see the *M* inscribed on them easily enough.

M for *Miller*?

I never saw Drew wear cuff links.

When I shake the box again, one more lumpy object thunks against the side. I push the receipts out of the way and find a small felt pouch, the kind that's meant to be used as a shoe-polishing mitt.

My stomach drops the moment I lift it out, because the weight of glass is so familiar in my hand. And when I tip it out onto the bedspread, my heart breaks right in half.

It's the shot glass Drew made in the studio with me. *My artisan lump*, he called it when I gave it back to him the following weekend.

We'd had a magical night when this was made. I'll never forget it. But he left it behind, too.

I don't know why that makes everything worse. It just does.

14

On Friday morning I feel sad and dull. Like I have a hangover, even though all I did last night was obsess about Drew's belongings and then stare at the printout Zain gave me.

The more I read, the more irritated I became. I'm not equipped to understand the techy jargon in that file. It gave me flashbacks to my childhood—my father shaming me for getting A's in art and English and C's in math.

At ten o'clock I follow Zain to the coffee maker for a whispered conversation, and I fill him in on the strange box I recovered from Drew's apartment.

Zain is so riveted by this that he forgets to brew his coffee. "What guy leaves behind his razor? That's just *weird*."

I reach past him and press the button.

"Thanks. What if he was running from something other than you?"

"Like *who*?"

"Like the *police*." Zain's expressive eyebrows furrow together. "I've never broken up with a girl. But a guy doesn't run out on his whole life just to get out of a relationship. He must have had bigger problems, and he didn't want to admit it to you."

"Yeah, I'm not sure that makes me feel better. Any news for me?"

He shakes his head. "Not until my buddy looks into the, uh, data we gave him. And not until I can spend some more time with that tape. I fell asleep on my keyboard last night." He pulls his coffee out from under the machine the second it beeps.

"I almost fell asleep on that printout you gave me. Did you actually think I could read that thing?"

"Not easily," he admits. "But there are patterns."

"That thing broke my brain. But I kept seeing one word everywhere, but I need you to explain it to me. What is LiveMatch?"

His coffee cup halts halfway to his mouth. And then he glances shiftily away from me. "You saw that, huh?"

"It's on, like, fifty different pages. But what is it?"

"I don't know."

"What do you mean you don't know?"

"Exactly what I said." He's irritated now. "He used that query a lot, but I don't know any applications by that name. I googled it, too, and all I could find is some kind of app for watching cricket games."

I'd done exactly the same thing. "I thought the whole network was your responsibility, though. How can you not know what it is?"

"Calm down. Back then, I was working on video compression. I didn't get the cybersecurity job until after your father died and Bryan quit. But there's nothing called LiveMatch on the network anymore."

"You're sure?"

"I searched the live network. If it was ever there, it's gone now."

I hope he's not bullshitting me, because it's not like I can check. "What do you think it was, though? He searched for it a lot."

Zain's comical eyebrows dip. "Seems like he was looking for some kind of AI program."

"That's . . . artificial intelligence? Is that something we do at Chime Co.?"

"No, it isn't. Because feeding our customers' videos into an AI engine would be shady as fuck."

His tone makes it impossible for me to decide if he believes that or if he's just spouting off the company rules. "Why is it shady?"

"Think about it—we capture millions of faces every day. If you had a neural network of linked video cameras, you could track people wherever they went, all across the network."

"*Oh.*" That does sound shady. "But that's what Drew was looking for? Why?"

His shrug is grumpy. "Maybe he was a corporate spy, hoping we had some cutting-edge AI tech he could steal."

A *spy*. I slept with a spy. "Call me if you get any updates from your friend. Day or night."

"You know it. Let's find out who this guy really was."

When I head home in the afternoon, I find Buzz and my mother reading in her den. Frog and Toad, of course. My mother even has her own copy of the book.

"Mama!" Buzz shouts when I put my head into the room. Then he slides out from under my mother's arm and scoots off the sofa. "You're home." He collides with my hip and squeezes me around the waist.

"Hi, baby." I drop my hand to the soft hair at the nape of his neck and run my fingers through it. "I thought you might want to come grocery shopping with me. If Grandma doesn't need her car for an hour."

My mother closes the book and rises. "Of course you can have the car." She's dressed impeccably, as always, in pressed khaki pants and a floral top. The pearls in her earrings match the warmest silver tones in her hair. But I'm startled by how tired she looks.

She's a little pale, and her carefully applied makeup can't conceal the circles under her eyes.

Maybe insomnia is contagious.

She goes to the kitchen for her car keys, and Buzz and I follow. I don't own a car, because keeping my expenses low is how I perpetuate the myth that I'm an independent adult.

"Can we get fruit pops? And a chicken pot pie for dinner?" Buzz asks as my mother hands me the keys.

"Okay." And now I won't even have to cook. "Mom—what's on your shopping list?" I always shop for both of us when I use her car.

She shakes her head. "I was all set to cook, but Ray decided he wants to go out. Oh, and, Ariel? I want to take you and Buzz to brunch on Sunday. There's an inn on Cape Elizabeth that might make a good wedding venue."

My plan for the weekend was to spend all my time googling older men named Andrew Miller and checking my phone for updates from Zain. So I guess I can fit her in. "Sure. Sounds fun."

"Let's go," Buzz says. "Can we get frozen waffles?"

"We'll see."

My mother chuckles as we head for the door. "Good luck to you both. And don't forget about Sunday."

"I won't."

On Sunday, we climb into the car with Mom for brunch at the inn. She's clutching her wedding planning notebook.

"You look . . . frazzled, Mom," I say. I was going to say *tired*, but she might have taken it as a criticism. My father used to make comments about our clothes, our hair, our taste.

That's how your father controls people, my therapist taught me in college. *It's a tool he uses to keep you and your mother on your toes. You can't change him, but you can change the way you respond to him.*

"I'm not *frazzled*." She sighs. "Maybe just a little, I guess."

"Is it the wedding?"

"Planning the wedding is fun," she insists. "I'm fine."

So I drop it. And it's possible that I'm only projecting my own stress onto her. Tomorrow it will be a week since I got the text that upended my life. That's seven days of fitful sleep and self-doubt.

I hope they're generous with the coffee at brunch.

Half an hour later, we're seated in the oceanfront dining room of a very pretty inn. The place is grander than I expected. Half elegance, half sturdy New England fishing lodge.

But it works somehow. We're given a comfortable table by the window with a view of the ocean. The beach is a fat, sandy stripe surrounded by craggy gray rocks. White sailboats dot the dark blue water.

And there's coffee, served in pristine white cups with matching saucers.

Buzz eats pancakes with a silver fork that's as long as his forearm, while I pick at my omelet.

"Is something wrong with your eggs?" my mother whispers. "My smoked salmon is delicious."

"They're perfect," I promise, trying to meet her gaze. "This place is great. Is it at the top of your list?"

"I think so." She adjusts the silver sugar bowl on the linen tablecloth. "Ray told me to go ahead and book it if I want to. This room can hold forty-five guests. They have an opening in October."

"That's lucky," I say, trying to sound like I'm paying attention. But my head is fuzzy with stress and exhaustion.

Last night I dreamed about Drew. He was standing in my father's office, talking to me through the glass wall. But I couldn't hear him. "*What?*" I shouted.

Meet me at the candelabra tree, he mouthed.

I turned around and headed for the office door, per his instructions. But when I looked back to make sure he was following me, he was just gone. Vanished.

Then I woke up in Buzz's bed, sweating, the Frog and Toad book still open on my chest, my little boy sleeping soundly beside me.

"Does this place say *classy, casual second wedding* to you?" my mother asks. She gives the room a stern glance over her shoulder.

"Absolutely." I strain for something supportive to say. "It's nice without being fussy. Just like you."

The smile she gives me is more manic than amused.

Luckily, I'm saved from further small talk by the event planner, who pours refills in our coffee cups and then pulls up a chair to talk to Mom.

Buzz gets a little fidgety after he's done eating. "Draw me something," he demands. "How about those boats?" He points out the window.

"Sure. Good idea." I pull out the sketchbook that I keep in my bag, and a travel tin with twenty-four Prismacolor pencils inside.

Buzz climbs into my lap, because that's our ritual. He unlatches the pencil case with careful fingers.

With his warm weight in my lap, I tap the blank sheet of paper. "What do I draw first?"

"The horizon," he says dutifully.

"Good man."

Buzz's preschool doesn't teach drawing. They value "free expression over form," whatever that means.

To be fair, a four-year-old's dexterity isn't sufficient for form drawing. But he likes to hear how I approach a drawing. And he *loves* to stage-manage. So I take the dark blue pencil and rough in a horizon line.

"Four boats," he says.

"What shape are the sails?"

He squints out the window. "Triangles. Two of them."

"Are the boats all the same size?" I ask, adding a triangular sail in the center of the picture.

He squints out the window. "Yes."

"But I shouldn't draw them all the same size," I point out. "Measure the closest one with your fingers. Like this." I hold up my hand and pinch the sailboat in my view. Buzzy copies me. "Now measure a farther one. See?"

He holds his fingers barely a centimeter apart. "They're not the same size. Except they really are."

"Yep."

"Why?" he asks, in the way of four-year-olds everywhere.

"Because your eyes show you one thing, but your brain changes the picture." I sketch in another boat, this one smaller and closer to the horizon. "You're a big boy who has some experience looking at things. And you're smart, so you've already figured out that distant things look small, and close-up things look big. If you remember that when you're drawing, it makes your pictures better."

"That boat is mine," he says, pointing at one that has red sails. "Make one for you, too, Mama. And one for Grandma."

"Yessir." I pick up a red pencil and write BUZZ on the stern.

"We work with a wonderful florist," the event planner is telling my mother. "Do you know what you want in terms of flowers? Some things need to be ordered with a healthy lead time."

My mother frowns, as if tasked with negotiating an international peace treaty. "Nothing exotic," she says. "Mums would be a nice seasonal choice, I think."

"Oh, I can tell you are going to be good at this," the planner says, jotting something into her own notebook. "It's easier to have a stress-free day if you aren't reinventing the wheel with every detail."

My mother smiles, but she looks a little unnerved.

I've drawn an entire regatta by the time she gets out her checkbook and puts down a deposit for her wedding.

"Can we take a stroll on the beach?" I ask as she pays the brunch check. "Buzz needs to walk off some of his maple syrup before we get back in that car."

"Of course."

After a few minutes of wrestling sunscreen onto my squirmy child, we set off together. I carry Buzz's shoes and socks so he can wade into the surf. The water will be freezing cold in May. The only people near it are young children and a couple of hopeful surfers bobbing around in wet suits.

I keep my eyes locked on Buzz, as I do anytime he's near the water. Our progress is slow, since he needs to look at every shell and rock in his path. My mother is quiet, and I'm basically a zombie. So our conversation is stalled.

"The event planner asked if this was my first marriage," my mother says suddenly. "And I told her no—that I was widowed five years ago."

"She wasn't prying," I point out. "She was just taking your temperature on what kind of event this will be."

"I know." My mother laughs. "But I felt like I just had to give her the timeline, so she wouldn't judge me. Then she said it was *brave* of me to get married again."

"Well, isn't it?"

"Marriage is always a big leap of faith," she says quietly. "But I'm a very different person than I was when I married your father. So there's no way things can turn out the same."

"That must be a relief," I say. "Seeing what a bastard he was."

She actually lets out a gasp, because we never do this. We never talk about him. "Ariel, I have no regrets about marrying your father."

"None?" I challenge. *Seriously?*

"Of course not. Edward gave me you, and then you gave me Buzz. So of *course* I don't regret it."

I don't even know what to say to that. Because regrets aren't an all-or-nothing proposition. My gaze sharpens on Buzz, who's leaning over in the wet sand, picking up shells and turning them over.

It's possible to love my little boy, but to still wish I'd paid more attention to Drew's evasions and lies.

I don't regret Buzz, but I do regret letting Drew break me in half.

We walk a little farther.

"Your father was a difficult man," my mother says.

"Yeah? I hadn't noticed."

She flinches instead of laughing. "You're still angry at him? After all this time?"

"You're not?" I counter. "He wasn't *nice* to us. Ever. And when things went wrong, he took a coward's way out."

"You *assume* he did," she says. "But you don't actually know what happened. None of us do."

I stop walking. "What do you mean by *that*?" When I turn to my mother, she has tears in her eyes. And I'm so confused right now. My mother doesn't get emotional. She's not a sharer, either. I'm pretty sure I learned it from her.

"He wasn't the kind of man to overdose," she says quietly. "He just wasn't."

"Okay," I say slowly. "But the medical examiner told you he was full of painkillers. So he overdosed—either accidentally or on purpose."

"The official cause was heart failure," my mother says crisply. "*Probably* caused by painkillers. But only God knows how that happened."

"Right." *Whatever makes you feel better, Mom.*

"Did he seem odd to you?" she asks. "That last summer—you were working with him. Was he different? Did he do anything strange?" She dabs her eyes daintily with the knuckle of her index finger.

"Mom," I say carefully. "He seemed strange to me my whole life. That summer was just the same song, different verse. I did a half-assed job in the office. He told me I was a failure at every opportunity, and I vacillated between trying to do a good job and trying to piss him off."

She looks away. "Did you know he was struggling with pain pills?"

"Nope." I give my head a firm shake. "But he'd never confide in me, and he hated to look weak. So I'd be the last person to know."

"Well, *I* knew it," she says in a low voice. "I saw how often he took them. But I didn't speak up. He would have taken it poorly."

I barely hold back another snarky comment, because that's a vast understatement. My father never valued my mother's opinion on anything more pressing than cocktail party catering. It's laughable to think he'd listen to her about something like a drug habit.

"... But I don't think he would have ended his life on purpose. Did you ever imagine your father was capable of that?"

"No," I say immediately. "But I never understood him at all. Not for one minute. So why should that moment be any different?"

She shakes her head. We walk on. Buzz bounces around in the sand like a happy little bird, oblivious to our crazy conversation and to my mother's unusual mood.

"Whatever happened, I'm sure it wasn't your fault. It wasn't *anyone's* fault. He set impossibly high standards for everyone, and then lost his shit every time someone let him down. Maybe . . ." I take a deep breath. "Maybe Dad let himself down for once. And he couldn't take it."

My mother shakes her head. "I wasn't always a good wife to him."

"*What?*" I stop walking and stare at her. "If your therapist lets you say that—fire her. I'm not kidding." The whole point of therapy is to help you separate other people's poor behaviors from your own.

"I couldn't give your father what he needed," my mother says.

"Mom, nobody could. *Jesus.*" Now I want to shake her. "Is this about the wedding? Maybe you and Ray shouldn't rush into planning the big day—if it's going to make you second-guess yourself like this. I'm sure Ray didn't mean to put you into a tailspin."

"He didn't," she insists.

"Then who did?"

My mother seals her lips into a flat line, schools her features and lifts her chin.

And now we're back on familiar ground. My mother spent her

entire marriage pretending that everything was okay. I know this because I spent my entire teenage years doing the same.

Buzz calls to me, his voice high with excitement. "Mama! I found a dead crab! Look! I can see his guts."

My mother makes a face. But I run over to admire the dead crab with Buzzy.

Crab guts are far less stressful to think about than my father. That's for damn sure.

15

By Sunday night I'm so exhausted that I go to bed at nine o'clock and sleep like the dead.

When my alarm goes off on Monday morning, I hit the snooze button and spend my extra ten minutes just staring at Drew's snapshot in its new place on my wall. I've hung it in a spot where the sunlight can't fade it.

The only real home I ever had. Was that true? Or just another lie? Maybe he cut the picture out of a magazine. Maybe he was never a foster kid at all. Grifters are excellent liars, right?

Exactly one week ago I was still living comfortably inside the cozy little myth I'd told myself about Drew: Once upon a time I fell in love with a man. It was summertime, and he was kind to me when I needed someone to be. We had lobster rolls on the dock with the tourists, we sat under a big tree in the park and we went to outdoor concerts together. I loved him, but he couldn't stay. And then he died before I could ever see him again.

That is more or less the exact speech I planned to give to Buzz someday. And maybe I still will. Any kid who grows up in Maine understands the concept of summer people. My myth about Drew cast him in the same light as a good beach day—they're great while they last.

I finally get up and shower. I make Buzz a scrambled egg to go along with the frozen waffles he conned me into buying. And then we walk to the preschool hand in hand.

Once again, Buzz takes a few minutes to join the preschool melee. This time, the patient Miss Betty lures him in with a fresh pile of oversized blocks to play with.

On my way out of the building, Maddy stops me to remind me of the upcoming picnic, and of my watermelon obligation.

"I'll remember," I promise her.

"Don't forget the knife!" she says with a catlike smile. "You can wrap the blade in—"

"—Cardboard," I say. "Got it."

I head for my favorite bakery and get into line. When I arrive at the front, I buy pastries and coffee for me and my uncle. And also Zain, so I'll feel less guilty when I badger him again about Drew's Social Security number.

Then I walk to the office. And my phone doesn't ping with any strange texts from dead men.

At the office, I drop off my uncle's breakfast at his desk. He's on the phone, but he mouths *Thank you* and gives me a wink.

Then I drop another bakery bag on Zain's desk. But Zain isn't there.

I sit down and start my day, but Zain does not appear. And as the morning wears on, it makes me increasingly anxious. Zain doesn't strike me as the kind of guy who's ever late for work. Maybe his buddy found something and Zain doesn't want to tell me.

Or maybe he's at the dentist and I've completely lost my sense of perspective.

By ten a.m. I'm just about to send out a search party when he heaves himself into his chair with a sigh and peeks into the bakery bag. "Any chance this is for me?"

"It is," I say, sounding irked. "But the coffee is cold. Since when are you late for work?"

"Since I had to go to the Portland PD and fill out a lengthy report of all the shit that was stolen from my home this weekend."

"What? Seriously?"

He nods, miserable. "Last night I went out to play D&D—don't judge—and when I came home at twelve thirty, the place was trashed."

A chill runs up my spine. "What did they take?"

"Computers. Five of them, all expensive. Including my, uh, air gap."

"You mean the one you used . . . ?"

He gives a jerky nod, like he's embarrassed.

Then I have a truly awful thought. "What about the . . ." My eyes dart toward Ray's office, where the tapes live.

"No, no," he says quickly. "I had it in my pack. Still have it."

I almost melt with relief.

"The data was still on that machine. But it wouldn't look interesting to a thief."

This doesn't make me feel much better. "Have you ever gotten robbed before?"

"No." Zain pauses to pop the top on his cold coffee and take a gulp. "But my stuff is worth some serious money, and anyone could see my setup through the basement windows. That's how they got in—breaking a window and jumping down. Then they just carried my stuff out the door."

"I'm sorry." That's what I should have led with. Oops. "Are you out a lot of money?"

"I do some crypto mining, and I have a lot of gear. But I also have good insurance. And they didn't take my monitors, which seems weird to me. Those are spendy. But they're also big and bulky." He shrugs. "The cops think they went out through the backyard. My mom heard them, actually. But my place has a separate entrance, and she just thought it was me."

"Oh man."

He shakes his mouse and turns his attention to his two giant computer monitors. There's a hierarchy in this room—the more important the programmer, the more square feet of monitor space. Zain doesn't want to talk about his theft anymore, I guess. "Did some work on our project, though," he says.

"Yeah? Any news?" I try not to sound as desperate as I feel.

He stares up at his screen and starts typing in that manic way he has. "His computer password was Harrietta. Does that mean anything to you?"

"Not a thing," I whisper. "That's it? Just one word?"

"Well, the *I* was the number one, and there's a period at the end. Because he wasn't born yesterday. But yeah, just that word. Maybe it was his great-aunt's name or something?"

I make a mental note to look it up later. "What else?"

"He spent a lot of time opening search warrants and reading them. He looked at every search warrant in Maine in 2016. Then he stopped when he got to, like, May or June, and started over at the beginning."

I pinch the bridge of my nose, where a headache is forming. "Any idea why?"

Zain shakes his head. And then his foot nudges mine. Hard.

I look up to see my uncle approaching my desk. "Morning!" he says. "Thanks for breakfast. Could I ask you to get out the projector for the Monday meeting? We're giving a presentation."

"Sure," I say, rising from my chair. "Of course."

"One last thing," Zain says after he passes by. "I just paid two hundred bucks to my friend for your search. So we should have a report this morning."

"Thank you." And now I know the price for complicating my own life—two hundred dollars. "Venmo okay?"

He gives his head a little shake. "Cash is better. No paper trail."

"Yeah, okay. I'll hit the bank machine at lunch."

"No rush," he says, biting into the sticky bun I brought him. "I know where you live."

The meeting lasts forever. Every three minutes I look over at Zain, wondering if his hacker friend's report has landed on his phone yet.

When it's my turn, I give a quick rundown on the layout of our new executive floor upstairs. "The movers are coming a week from tomorrow . . ."

Across the table from me, Zain is surreptitiously scrolling on his phone. I see him stop and stare at something. Then he lifts his gaze and looks right at me.

I rush through the rest of my announcement, finishing just as a text message buzzes my phone.

And the minute everyone's attention moves on, I unlock my phone in my lap.

Zain has sent me a screenshot.

SSN issued to Andrew Ernest Miller
DOB November 1, 1948, Maine
DOD May 6, 2016, Maine

I take a slow breath and read it again. The real Drew Miller is a *dead man*? In fact, he died a year before I met him.

Legally, I fell in love with a ghost.

Clammy sweat collects on my skin. For a couple of minutes I hear nothing of the meeting. My mind churns through these new facts, rearranging my understanding of the situation yet again.

Drew's birthday was listed in his employee file as November 1, 1988. That's precisely one digit off from the real Andrew Miller's date of birth.

Perhaps that was intentional, the date chosen in the hopes that nobody would notice that errant digit.

Supposedly Drew was twenty-eight when he and I were together—four years older than I was. He even told me that his birthday was in November. "You're a Scorpio?" I asked. "They're smart but vindictive."

He gave me a little secretive smile and said that he didn't follow astrology.

I wonder if anything he ever told me was true. Who knows if he was even twenty-eight?

At least he never said *I love you*. At least he didn't lie about that.

Across the room, Zain's eyes are trained on the sales manager, but his fingers are worrying the edges of his phone, like he can't wait to look at it again.

But nobody expects me to pay attention to the sales update. Concealing my phone beneath the table, I search *Andrew Ernest Miller death 2016 Maine*.

This is maybe the millionth time I've searched Andrew Millers in Maine. But now that I have a date to work with, it doesn't even take five minutes to find a news headline from the *Lowden Sentinel* that I'd probably rejected before: "Shawmut Street Tragedy."

The very first sentence sends chills down my spine: *Army vet, beloved neighbor to all and foster father to many, Andrew "Ernie" Miller dead at 67.*

The words *army vet* and *foster father* leap off the screen and lodge in my throat. I skim the first few paragraphs. Mr. Miller died suddenly of a heart attack, just a few weeks after a tragedy in his home. In the third paragraph, I read in glowing terms how Ernie raised foster teens in Lowden, Maine, for decades.

. . . in the sprawling house on Shawmut Street with the hand-painted plaque above the door.

16

Brainz watches out of the corner of his eye as Drew Miller enters the room from the stairwell, carrying a paper bag from the deli on the next block. Mr. Army Hero walks with a slight limp, which he tries to hide.

His rhythms are familiar by now—Drew likes to fetch his lunch early. He eats at his desk. And he only takes a coffee break when there's someone else lurking around the coffee maker to talk to.

And when he passes Ariel Cafferty, he doesn't glance at her.

Back at his own desk, he pulls a sandwich out of the bag and unwraps it. He props his phone up on the edge of his monitor and reads something on the screen while he chews.

Then he turns his head sharply in this direction, like a man who knows he's being watched.

Brainz stands up, tucks his wallet into his pocket, and carries his phone past Drew, giving the guy a nod. "Looks good. Time for lunch."

He heads into the stairwell but climbs up, not down.

The third floor is a mishmash of Chime Co. functions—accounting, billing, etc. But there's a server closet in the back corner, and that's where he heads now.

After closing the door behind himself, he sits down and logs into the terminal that's hidden inside. Then he taps in a status request for Drew Miller's terminal ID.

God, this asshole is predictable. Thirty seconds ago Drew had logged in as Nebowitz, a database manager.

That's the sixth stolen log-in, and counting.

It would be so satisfying to lock him out and then rat him out. But he's not going to do that until he figures out what this punk is up to. Only then can he get Drew's ass fired. Or—even better—scare the shit out of him and *then* fire him.

Drew Miller sends another query to the database while Brainz follows every keystroke. It's hard to watch. *Who are you really, fucker? You'd better hope I never find out.*

Then his phone beeps. An encrypted message from TheBoss to Brainz.

TheBoss: Lunch meeting? Thai place?
  Brainz: Sure.
TheBoss: Where'd you go?
  Brainz: Upstairs. Men's room.

There's no need to let TheBoss know about Drew Miller. Not yet anyway.

  Brainz: Meet you there in fifteen.

He needs a few extra minutes to watch Drew take his lunchtime stroll around the network.

Lately Mr. Army Hero has two obsessions: he looks at police warrants for videos in Lowden, Maine, and then he pokes around the edges of the LiveMatch software.

Good luck, sucker. The guts of LiveMatch are safe behind the wall he's built around it. His secrets are well protected. Army boy can query the network from now until doomsday, and he still won't be able to untangle the details of his side hustle.

But *Lowden*. That location can't be a coincidence. It's definitely something to watch.

He pulls up the corporate security system, and the tap of a few keystrokes brings up a video feed of Drew Miller at his desk. There he is—tapping away, his too-handsome face in a thoughtful frown. Now that Brainz is out of his peripheral vision, Drew thinks nobody's watching.

That's the thing about cameras—people always forget about them. Even the smart ones. (Smart*ish*, in Drew's case.) The human attention span is like a flashlight shining in the dark. It's built to focus on the most important thing in front of you.

Brainz pulls up a couple of feeds from different angles, zooming in and snapping still shots. He saves them to a thumb drive.

Then he unlocks the LiveMatch system and uploads Drew's photos one by one. **Imaging**, the software says. **Target identification: no result.**

Huh. Looks like Drew Miller isn't known to the Lowden Police Department. But there has to be some connection to that town.

He'll find it.

17

ARIEL

"I really appreciate this," I tell Larri as she merges onto 295 North. "I wasn't sure who else to ask."

"Don't thank me until we get there," she says over the growl of her ancient Subaru. "This car hasn't been so far from home in months. But I think she can make it. What did you bring for lunch?"

I bribed Larri with food so she'd agree to drive me to Lowden. "We're having curried chicken salad with grapes on a croissant. Vinegar chips and a soda. You won't regret this."

"Dessert?" she presses.

"Whoopie pies and iced coffee with that caramel crap in it that you like."

"My queen." She grins. "But you know I'd drive you anyway, even without the fancy lunch? You've asked me for something maybe once in eight years, and I ask you favors, like, daily. You are shit at taking help from other people."

"Not true. I take help from my mom every single day."

"Good," she grunts. "That woman owes you on a karmic scale for being a shit mother."

"You've met her *twice*."

"Twice was enough," Larri says.

I'm sure she's referring to the night of a group show our studio put on the year before I met Drew. My parents had shown up, which surprised me. My mother was all smiles. But I watched my father stroll across the gallery with a scowl on his face.

He stood in front of my display and said something snide about how he'd paid a quarter million dollars for my college education so that I could make a few bowls. And instead of arguing with him, my mother only smiled harder.

But I didn't really blame her. Picking a fight would only have made it uglier.

"Swear to God you and Tara had the same set of parents," Larri says. "But yours had money, so it was easier to hide how fucked up they were."

"Money hides many sins. How are things with Tara?"

Larri's face drops. "A little less tense? The dealer hasn't made any new threats for a couple of days. Either that or she hasn't told me."

Ouch.

"We need her to know that Tara's *done* being intimidated by her. Except we're really fucking intimidated by her."

"Is there anyone you can call? Would the police get involved?"

Larri shakes her head violently. "The police won't just cart her off to jail because Tara says she's bad news, right? They might pick her up and question her. Ten minutes later she'd be banging down our door scaring the shit out of us."

"Right. That was a super naive suggestion, huh?"

She laughs. "A little. But you wear it well. And don't forget that Tara is no angel. The woman has dirt on her. She did some favors for her back in the day—made some deliveries. It was years ago, but she'd throw Tara under the bus in a heartbeat. You can go to prison just for helping out."

"I did watch *Orange Is the New Black*."

Larri hoots. Then she shakes her head. "I'm not a violent person, but I would kill this woman if I thought I could get away with it. She's terrifying—but not like you'd expect a drug dealer to be, you know? She looks normal, but the threats that come out of her mouth are fucking scary."

"Yikes."

"I offered to take Tara for a weekend up in Acadia, just the two of us. I think a getaway will do us some good. We'll turn our phones off for two days and forget about the world."

"Sounds perfect," I say, although I'm not exactly the poster child for relaxation.

"So are you going to tell me why we're driving to Lowden?" she asks. "Is this about your guy?" She taps the GPS she's installed on the dash. "And what's on Shawmut Street?"

"That's a lot of questions."

"It's a forty-five-minute drive."

I lean back into my seat and close my eyes. "There are a lot of things I don't know about 'my guy.'" I make my fingers into air quotes. "His real name, for example. He told me he was born in Maine and he grew up in the foster care system. When I met him, he went by the name Drew Miller. I've just found out the name was a fake—but someone named Andrew Miller lived on Shawmut Street in Lowden."

"And their connection is . . . ?"

"Unclear. He died the year before I met Drew, but I think he might have been one of my Drew's foster parents. Drew—or who-ever he was—used this guy's Social Security number when he came to work at Chime Co."

"Aw shit." She's quiet for a moment. "And now you want to know what's up with that. So we're going to Lowden to do . . . what?"

"I don't even *know* what. Part of me thinks we should turn off at the next exit and bail. But I've been dragging this guy around with me for five years, and I can't help wanting answers. So I'm going to knock on the door of this Lowden house and ask for Drew Miller. See what they say. It might be a huge waste of time. The house was probably sold."

"You could check Zillow."

"I don't have the exact address," I admit. "But I know the street and I know what the house looks like. I'm sorry in advance if this is a total waste of time."

"Don't be sorry. I'm the queen of lost causes. What will you say if you knock on this door and somebody answers?"

"I'll tell them I was a fan of Ernie's—that's the name the older Andrew Miller went by—and that I want to pay my respects. Maybe they know something about him."

We ride in silence for a moment. Then Larri says, "That's one of those phrases that never made sense to me. *Pay your respects*. It's a meaningless phrase for a gesture the living make to the dead."

"Yeah, I guess. Do you know a better phrase, though?"

She shakes her head. "Visiting graves never made any sense to me, either. My mother puts flowers on my father's grave every year on his birthday."

"It's for her sake, really," I point out. "Not his."

"No kidding. The weird thing is? She likes him more now that he's dead than she did when he was alive. They used to drive each other batshit."

I turn to stare out the window at the highway. Drew and I never had the chance to drive each other crazy. I've always assumed we would have been happy together forever.

There was no wife or girlfriend listed in that obituary, either. I noticed that early and often.

Left to cherish his memory are his army teammates and his beloved dog, Coby, the obituary says. I wonder what happened to Coby.

I wonder a lot of things.

As we approach Lowden, my phone vibrates with several incoming messages. All from Zain.

> Zain: Anything on Shawmut Street?
> Zain: Did you find the house?
> Zain: Dying here.

I reply to shut him up.

> Ariel: We're not even there yet.

I'm pretty sure he's miffed at me for not letting him tag along. He has a stock of unused vacation days, and he was ready to use one of them for this.

But if I learn anything important about Drew, maybe I won't want to share it.

Larri slows way down as we approach Lowden, where antiquated redbrick buildings line the banks of the Androscoggin River. It's the kind of old mill town that fell into a slump after the textile factories died off a century ago.

We pass two halal butchers and the Mogadishu Variety Store. A pair of Black women in African dress and colorful headscarves push strollers down the street. A white man on a bicycle rides past us, a live chicken in the bike basket in front of him.

"Huh," Larri says, glancing at her GPS. "This town is interesting.

But the farther we go, the seedier it gets. It looks like the street where I grew up in Mass—all these triple-deckers."

She's right—the apartment buildings loom close to the sidewalk. There's barely a six-foot strip of lawn in front of each one. None of them has a garage at the side; they're too crowded together. And each one has a panel of doorbells, indicating a multitude of small apartments above.

Larri makes the last turn onto Shawmut Street.

This is it. "Go slow, okay?"

"Of course."

But as we creep down two blocks in a row, my heart sinks. We're almost to the end of the street, and none of these buildings is dark red, like the house in Drew's photo. And the roof shapes are all wrong. Unless . . . "Stop," I say suddenly.

Larri stomps on the brake.

And there it is—the only house on Shawmut Street with a peaked roofline against the sky. It's painted slate blue now, but there's a round plaque on the triangular peak, depicting a circular arc of clasped hands.

"Is that the place?" Larri whispers.

"Yep," I say with forced nonchalance, even as my skin tingles.

Drew lived here. After all the lies he told, I don't know why I feel so certain. But I do.

"Am I coming with you?" Larri asks as she parks at the curb.

"Sure." I'm already climbing out of the car, taking in the house. There's a porch, with kids' toys spread out on it. There's no car in the driveway, but some of the upstairs windows are open.

Maybe one of those was Drew's bedroom. Did he sit up there dreaming of the future?

I have chills as I cross the street and climb the porch. There's a doorbell camera, because they're everywhere. I press the little button and wait. *Whoever you are, please come out and talk to me. I need answers.*

I'm standing maybe fifteen feet below that plaque from Drew's photo, in front of Drew's front door. I can hear my heartbeat in my ears.

Footsteps echo inside, and then the front door swings open to reveal a young woman. She's in her late twenties, I think. White, a baby on her hip. Her T-shirt reads LOWDEN COOPERATIVE PRESCHOOL. "Hi?" she says, looking mildly confused.

"Hi, I'm Ariel. I think my old friend Ernie Miller used to live here . . ."

"Oh." Her face falls. "Yes, I think you're right, except . . ." She hesitates.

"He died. I know that, but I wanted to pay my respects." And now I realize I should have brought some flowers as a prop. "Except I don't know where he's buried. Did you know Ernie?"

She looks relieved. "I'm sorry for your loss, but I didn't know him. We bought this house from his estate. He was well loved on this block. I don't know where he's buried, though."

"Do you know who else we should ask?" Larri presses.

The woman's gaze moves past us and lands on a three-decker across the street. "Knock on Mr. Ossman's door? The bottom floor right there—" She points. "I'm sure he and Ernie were close. They were both active at the community center."

"Thank you for your help," I say quickly. "We won't keep you any longer."

Larri and I say goodbye and then hurry off the porch to cross the street.

"This just might work," Larri says under her breath as we walk away. "And you're good at this. You've got that whole rich-girl, non-threatening vibe."

"I'm very threatening," I tease, but my heart is galloping. I feel close to Drew, which makes no sense. But he was here. He probably crossed this same street dozens of times to approach this same neighbor's door.

I don't know why I feel so certain. But I do.

Before I can climb the three steps to knock on the door, a man appears around the side of the building. He's Black, wearing a Hawaiian-style shirt and creased khaki trousers. And he gives us a wide smile. "Hello, friends," he says. "Can I help you?"

"We're looking for Mr. Ossman," Larri says. "Would that be you?"

"That *is* me." He spreads his hands in a gentle way. "Come around back, ladies. I will pour some tea, and you can explain your business."

Larri squeezes my hand and nudges me toward the backyard. And I follow the man who might have known the real Drew.

18

The backyard is a little urban oasis, with a modest patch of grass. But much of the space is given over to a patio with a metal table and four chairs. There's a shiny library book on the table, plus a teapot, steam rising gently from its spout.

"Let me just get two more cups," he says in a lilting accent that I can't quite place. He starts for the back door.

"Oh, don't go to any trouble," I say quickly.

He laughs, ducking inside anyway. When he returns with two more mugs, he gives me another big smile. "That is almost like a Somali refusal," he says. "We refuse the tea twice, though, and accept on the third offering. Or you can save me the time and just have a seat."

Larri chooses a chair and plops right down. I take the seat beside her, and Mr. Ossman begins to pour.

The tea smells spicy. "Is that cardamom?" Larri asks, sniffing the air.

"Good nose," he says. "Also ginger, cinnamon and cloves. Here you go." He places a cup in front of her. "Now tell me how I can help you."

It's time for my command performance. I take a breath and hope that my expression is as innocent as Larri claims. "I'm here about Ernie from across the street. I met him once. And I recently learned that he passed away. I wanted to pay my respects, but I don't know where he's buried."

"Ah." His dark eyes drop to his mug. "That was a sad business, the kind of thing you never quite forget. I still miss him."

"He was a lovely man," I say, and the sour feeling in the pit of my stomach tells me that I'm the worst kind of fraud.

"How did you know Ernie?" the man asks.

Larri raises her eyes to me. She doesn't smile, but I know her well enough to feel her amusement. She's wondering how the hell I'm going to answer the question.

I consider who this man was to Drew, and my lie forms easily. "I was studying social work in college. And I had an externship— just a couple of weeks—with the county social workers' office. I met Ernie at a meeting, and he taught me more than any of the social workers I met there."

Mr. Ossman tilts his head to the side, as if allowing himself a memory. "That sounds like Ernie. He had so much wisdom, and a big heart. He brought up many difficult boys in that house. Not all of them made it. I know of one who is in jail. But they all got a real chance with him."

I nod slowly, as if in agreement. "Can you tell me what happened? The newspaper article was short on details."

His eyes drop. "The paper did not *listen* to the things we told them after Ernie died. Nobody listened. There was trouble with the police, and it ruined the block for me. I don't trust people like I used to."

"I'm so sorry." It's hard to get the words out, because I'm sitting here lying to him, too. So I take a sip of the tea and let him keep talking.

"Ernie filed a complaint against a policeman. For harassment. That is how it started."

"Oh no," Larri says softly. "What kind of harassment?"

Mr. Ossman waves a hand in the direction of Ernie's house. "Those boys they placed with him—they were difficult. There were incidents—shoplifting, vandalism. One boy—Omar—he was a tough case. Ernie used to say that all his new wrinkles were from Omar. But they were really from hiking in the sunshine."

He smiles to himself before continuing. "The year before he died, he had his hands full. For the first time in twenty years, they placed a girl in his home. Amina. She was sixteen. He said— *Ossman, I don't know how to raise a girl. Send help.*"

He laughs, so we laugh, too.

"But Amina was a good girl. Quiet. I thought maybe they sent her because Ernie was getting older, and the social workers thought he deserved a break, you know? And Omar ran wild. One of the police—he had a lot of hate inside him. Lowden has changed a lot in twenty years."

He pats his chest. "I was one of the first Somalis to come, twenty years ago now. I was new to America. It was winter, and they put me in this apartment with another family." He points at the first floor of his house. "Ten years ago I bought the whole building. But back then I was a scared young man in a strange place. I was the only one in our group who had some English, but it didn't help much. I didn't know how to dress for the cold, and we did not even know how to light the stove in the kitchen. It was Ernie who knocked on the door our second day here. He brought a vegetable casserole—because he said he didn't know what we liked to eat. And he showed me how to use the burners on the stove, so I could make my first pot of tea." He looks down at the mug in his hands and swallows hard.

Neither Larri nor I so much as breathe while he masters himself.

"Lowden has lots of refugees now. It changed the city, and some of the people who lived here before us don't like it. Officer Ward—he was the worst. And Ernie's boy Omar was his favorite target. He hounded that boy. He busted him for anything and everything—underage drinking, vandalism, even litter. The kid missed the trash can at the high school and Ward gave him a summons."

"Sounds like a real treat," Larri says wryly.

Ossman shakes his head. "Everywhere that kid turned around, Ward was there. The kid said it was uncanny, but I am not sure Ernie understood it until . . ." He clears his throat. "Ward started in on Amina. He would show up wherever she was and just . . . watch her. He made comments, too, about her clothes, her body."

My skin crawls, and Larri lets out a low groan.

"He kept showing up, like his whole job was following that girl around. Omar couldn't stand it. He'd get in the cop's face. Then he'd get arrested again." He gives his head a shake. "Ernie was out of his mind worrying. He filed a complaint about harassment. But they didn't do anything. The cop was a superstar. His arrest record was the best in the department. Then Omar said the cop was using cameras to find Amina wherever she went."

A new chill runs down my spine. "Cameras?"

"Yeah, they're everywhere now. But they were a new thing back then. Police put 'em up on the street corners. Got some on the high school, and on the bus stops. Ward even put a camera on the telephone pole in front of Ernie's place. And it seemed like they were always watching, you know? Those kids would walk out of the house and the cops would do a drive-by minutes later."

"Weird," Larri whispers.

"Yeah, it was. That's how Omar ended up doing a stint in

juvie—there was a video of him holding another kid's beer. Whole bunch of boys drinking in a parking lot, but they only pull a shot of Omar, and he's the only one who ends up in handcuffs. Ernie about lost his mind. He wanted to file *another* complaint, but Amina talked him out of it. She was afraid of Ward, and Ernie was at the end of his rope."

"Wow," Larri says softly. "So what did he do?"

"Got some cameras of his own," Ossman says. "His boy Jay's idea. You hear about Jay? Nice kid. Ernie's greatest success story."

I stop breathing. "Was he involved?"

"No. Jay was away in Syria when the trouble went down."

Syria. My blood stops circulating.

"Jay sent Ernie two cameras that he bought with his savings. To fight back, you know? Ernie put one on the front door and one on the back—to cover the alley back there. He was going to prove that police action on our street was damn strange."

"Did it work?" Larri asks.

"At first." Ossman drops his eyes. "Ward stops coming around all the time. Couple of weeks go by and Omar doesn't get picked on by the cops. Ernie relaxed some. He went hiking with his friends again. Couple weekends in a row." He stops talking for a second. Puts his mug down.

I take a sip of my tea as the old man struggles to go on. I'm listening to this story with every fiber of my being.

". . . But then Amina starts acting strange. She's sad. Stops eating. Won't come out of her room. Ernie doesn't understand it, and she won't talk. He tries to get the school involved. She needs help, and he's looking for a counselor to talk to her. But there's a waiting list. Two months go by, and she seems a little better." He takes a deep breath. "Then one day Ernie comes home and finds her in her room. Hanged."

"Oh God," I whisper, and I feel myself blanch.

Ossman nods miserably. "Poor lamb. The cop was blackmailing her. Omar was the only one she told."

"*Blackmail?* For what?" Larri demands.

"One of Ernie's hiking weekends, Amina has a boy over. They spent some time on the back porch together." He clears his throat meaningfully. "Omar says the cop had a video of them from Ernie's own camera. He saw Ward show it to Amina. Told her she had to meet with him in private." He clears his throat again. "Told her that if she didn't do as he said, he'd post that video everywhere on the internet. He'd send it to her friends at school."

Larri makes an anguished noise, but I can hardly draw a breath. There are way too many cameras in this story.

But how would a cop get footage from Ernie's private camera? That's impossible without a warrant.

"After the girl's funeral, Ernie makes a big noise at the police station. He gets the whole block talking. Turns out other people in town are having some weird experiences with the cops, too. But nobody can prove anything. Omar didn't even see the video—he just heard about it from Amina."

I'm clammy with sweat. If "Jay" is my Drew, he definitely didn't end up at Chime Co. by accident.

". . . Ernie took it all real hard. Omar was beside himself, too. Ernie called the newspaper in Portland. Reporter drove up here to talk to him, and . . ." The old man takes a deep breath. "Ernie died right on his front porch, in front of the reporter. Massive heart attack."

"Oh God," Larri says.

". . . And his news story?" I press. The article I read only mentioned a recent foster child's death. It didn't say a thing about cameras or a suicide.

Ossman shakes his head. "Without Amina, and then without Ernie, the story just died. He never got justice for that girl. That cop retired with full benefits the next year."

"Jesus Christ," Larri barks. "Why am I not surprised? The old white man gets away with it."

Ossman makes a noise that's half-laugh, half-mournful. "If you believe in karma, you should know that Ward died in a boating accident. It only took him a year after his retirement."

Larri is still not satisfied. "But what happened to the other foster kid—Omar?"

I'm glad she's still asking questions, because I can't speak at all.

"He was already eighteen, so he had aged out of the system. He stayed in that house a couple more months until Jay Marker got discharged from the army. Poor kid got hurt over there right after Ernie died. Lost a foot."

I gasp, and Larri gives me a sideways glance and puts her hand on my knee under the table. And I have to clasp my hands together, because they're shaking.

"Jay Marker," Larri repeats. "Sounds like a great guy."

And now I have a last name.

"He handled Ernie's will, and selling the house. He helped Omar get a job at the community center." Ossman makes a gesture toward the center of town. "I see him from time to time playing hoops with the younger boys. I pray for Omar."

"And Jay?" I croak, trying to keep it together. "Maybe he knows where Ernie is buried?"

"Ah, I haven't seen Jay in a few years. Not since he sold the house. But I know where you will find Ernie's grave. I have been there myself many times. Do you have a pen? I will draw you a map."

Larri fumbles into her own handbag and pulls out her sketch-book and a pen. She and Ossman talk quietly for a few moments as Ossman explains where to go. "You've been so helpful," Larri says. "We appreciate it. And thank you for the tea."

I make some noises of agreement and rise to leave.

"It is a sad story," Ossman says, pressing my hand between his. "Ernie had a big heart. And then it plain broke."

"Yes, I'm so sorry," I mutter. "Thank you."

I am a robot as we walk to Larri's car. I climb in and fasten my seat belt, just like always.

But my heart is slamming against my rib cage, beating with a strange new tune. *Jay Marker. Jay Marker. Who are you?*

19

FIVE YEARS AGO, JUNE

Drew holds Ariel in bed while both of their heart rates descend back into the normal range. The window is open to the cool Maine breeze. It's perfect.

For now, he reminds himself. Because he'll be gone before the leaves turn color.

He shoves that thought out of his head as her fingers stroke his chest. Somehow they've already become one of those couples who are always touching each other. He loves the taste of her skin, and the brush of her hair against his face. Half the time they're alone, he's pressing his nose into the nape of her neck and inhaling her lemon scent.

It's easier to be honest in silence. His hands say *I need you*, even if he won't let his mouth.

Ariel is the same, though. She pretends to be someone who doesn't care that much about anything other than her art—except when she's in his arms.

They are frighteningly similar to each other—two souls quietly wading through circumstances beyond their control. Both wary of most everyone else.

She trusts him, but only up to a point. She doesn't always speak her mind, even when he wishes she would. He wants to know what she's thinking right this minute, as her hands grow still, and her breathing slows. He wants to know what images sail past her eyes when her thoughts begin to drift.

Loving her hurts. It's like phantom limb pain—inexplicable but real nonetheless.

Ariel's breath evens out into sleep. But he lies awake. Again. Staring at the ceiling. Leg aching. Heart aching even worse. He's the loneliest at moments like this—when Ariel is asleep at his side.

She rolls onto her stomach and sighs, face in the pillow, sleeping with the same dedication she brings to all the other things she loves—glassmaking and heated discussions. Drinking. Sex.

Now he knows what people mean when they talk about chemistry. The connection between them is like a living, breathing thing. They don't even make eye contact in the office, because they can't exchange a glance that's not preloaded with heat and meaning.

He keeps promising himself that he'll break it off. And he *will*. It's only a matter of time before it's out of his hands. He can't be Drew Miller much longer. Settling the estate means reporting Ernie's death to Social Security. But if he doesn't settle it soon, the law will notice.

Ernie. Thinking of him hurts, too. His voice is still easy enough to conjure—those flat Maine vowels. His patient rasp.

Ernie, standing in the kitchen in a worn flannel shirt, teaching him how to cook fried eggs and bacon.

Ernie in the rowboat, demonstrating the right way to bait a hook.

Ernie shooting hoops in the alley, wearing combat boots and Nike shorts, tattoos fading on his fuzzy barrel chest.

Ernie grinning at his report card. *You're going places, kid. You watch and see.*

He owes that man everything, and he means to pay up. That's the point to all this mess. He'll get vengeance for Amina and Ernie.

The dirty cop will get what's coming to him. And the whole world will know that Chime Co. has never made the world a safer place. It's a company that helps gun-wielding stalkers intimidate young girls.

It will make a nice headline on the front page of the *Boston Globe*. Eventually. But so far the scoreboard is looking grim. He can't find the LiveMatch system on the network. There's exactly one directory with that name, and it's empty. At least as far as he can tell.

After Ernie's death—and before his accident—he nearly went crazy in Syria. He Skyped everyone he ever knew in Lowden, trying to find someone who could verify all the ugly things Ernie had told him about Omar's and Amina's trouble with the cops. There had to be somebody with direct knowledge of the abuse.

The best clue he got came from a high school buddy—Jerome— who was now a Lowden paramedic. Jerome knows some of the younger guys on the force, and he'd heard them talking about a surveillance system called LiveMatch. It let the cops follow anyone around town, from camera to camera.

"They brag about it," he said. "And they don't just follow the drug dealers. It's kinda gross."

Those same cops had told Jerome they were deep in bed with the Chime Co. law enforcement tools, too. It couldn't be a coincidence.

But he can't prove a thing. Yet. Nobody ever brings it up, and none of the log-ins he's stolen have access. And he can't tie anything dirty back to Officer Ward. That's the ultimate goal—to nail that guy.

First he has to figure out how a cop got access to a private citizen's home video feed.

The evidence has to be on the network somewhere. There must be a *reason* why someone at Chime Co. was willing to give private footage to a cop.

Slowly he sits up in bed. Sleep won't come for him when his head is spinning like this.

He grabs his boxers, and then his leg off Ariel's floor. At home he'd use crutches in the middle of the night. But Ariel's roommate went away for the weekend, so they're staying at her place this time.

He puts the prosthesis on, careful not to wake her. She doesn't stir as he quietly crosses the room. He stops in the doorway to watch her smooth back rise and fall as she sleeps.

There's a chasm opening inside his chest, and it gets a little deeper every time he pictures leaving Portland for good. But it's going to happen. Pretty soon.

He heads to the kitchen for a drink of water, but it doesn't do much to make him feel better. He sits down at Ariel's kitchen table. The only light in the room is from the blue glow of her laptop. He can see a reflection of the log-in screen in the window.

Earlier tonight—when she logged on to order dinner—he saw her fingers dance over the keyboard. Stealing log-ins is just a reflex now. He can't shut it off. That's how he came to notice that her password starts with the word *glory*.

He eyes the computer the same way he might look at a rattle-snake in his bed. There's almost no chance this ends well. Ariel wouldn't have access to any high-level privileges.

Probably.

He is disgusted with himself as he drags the computer toward himself anyway. *G-l-o-r-y-h-0-l-e*, he tries—the *o* a zero.

Password incorrect.

He tries one more variation. And when it fails to work, he is ridiculously relieved.

Since arriving in Portland, he's broken all his own rules. He's lied, he's invaded others' privacy in the name of research. He's manipulated innocent (if clueless) coworkers.

For good reason. But still. Ariel is his personal Waterloo. That river he can't cross. She's one of the good guys. She's the only bright light in his whole damn life right now.

He snaps her computer shut and then buries his face in his hands.

What the hell is wrong with him? Besides everything. He started this mess with a clear mission, one that would make Ernie proud: Identify those who prey on the weak. Force them to own their sins, and then get out.

It seemed so simple. And now it's anything but. He's committed fraud, with nothing to show for it. He's already running out of time.

20

ARIEL

That evening, after Larri drops me off at home, I order in pizza and then declare a movie night.

We put on *Toy Story*—Buzz's favorite, naturally. I prop my laptop up on the dresser where I used to change his diapers, and we hole up on his bed with a bowl of popcorn.

In his pj's, my son reclines against my body like Cleopatra on a chaise longue. The solid warmth of him is a balm on my soul. And I've left my phone downstairs, because I can't let myself obsess. I can't stay up late texting Zain or googling *Jay Marker*. I know myself—I might sit up until four a.m. putting his name into the search bar and getting the same results.

Not to mention that I already tried, searching his name seventy-five ways till Sunday all the way back from Lowden. But I barely turned up anything. It only made me feel more desperate.

I feel like a boat in the harbor on a windy day—rising and falling repeatedly, bumping against the choppy waves. Going nowhere fast. After all this time, that man can still throw me off my game. Even as a dead man.

A *likely* dead man.

On some level it's helpful to know that Drew—I can't think of him as Jay—might have had a soul-deep reason to show up at Chime Co. looking for answers. That maybe he wasn't a lifelong con man.

Still, he used me. He showed up in Portland with a mission and promptly got cozy with the boss's daughter. I was an easy mark, too. He probably thought I'd overheard a lifetime of secrets at the family dinner table.

Or maybe I was just a pleasant way to stick it to the man he hated—by literally sticking it to that man's daughter.

I was so gone for him that I couldn't even see it.

Buzz laughs, and I force myself to focus on the screen, where Woody is shouting at Buzz Lightyear. "*YOU ARE A TOY! A CHILD'S PLAYTHING!*" And Buzz stubbornly insists that he's much more important than that.

Dude, I know the feeling.

Memories are slippery things. It's been five years since I heard Drew's voice, or saw his smile. But it's hard to let go of the soft glances he used to give me. Or the steady sound of his breathing in the dark.

Lying next to Drew, I finally understood where people found the optimism to make lifelong vows to each other. Every time he rolled over in the morning and smiled at me, I thought I'd stumbled upon a life-changing secret. Every time he sleepily ran his fingers through my hair, I thought, *This man is different*.

And I carried that belief with me for all this time. I wrote off his betrayal as a grave mistake, not a moral failing. But I was so, so wrong.

It's hard to process. Was he an exceptional actor? Or did I only see what I wanted?

My only satisfaction now is knowing that he couldn't possibly have learned anything useful about the company from me. I was the least knowledgeable person in the room, and proud of it.

The sick thing is that I'd probably make all those same mistakes again. Even now, I'd sell my soul for another carefree day with him at the beach, or at the donut shop.

I thought it was love.

He let me think so, too. It must have been so obvious how bad I had it for him.

The movie rolls on as Buzz and Woody learn to trust each other and then work together as a team. I could probably recite all the lines of dialogue by now.

Buzz's head gets heavy on my chest. I run his soft hair through my fingers and pat his sleepy back.

"I'm still awake," he murmurs.

"I know, baby. And you still have to brush your teeth."

"Not a baby," he slurs.

I pause the movie, scoop him up into my arms and bury my nose in his smooth neck. Then I blow a raspberry, and he giggles.

Jay Marker thought he got the best of me. He thought he was so smart.

But he never got this.

Thursday is unseasonably hot and muggy. It's also a busy day at work, which helps me stay focused for a few hours. I'm working with a moving company for our upcoming office reorganization, and they require hand-holding.

The only thing I've shared with Zain so far is a one-line text:

Ariel: Found someone who knew Drew.

Zain is busy, too, though. He's been in meetings all morning. Although his texts are piling up on my phone.

Zain: How well did they know him?

Zain: Did you find the house in the photograph?

Zain: You ARE going to tell me what happened, right?

When three o'clock arrives, Ray asks me to make a coffee run. And on my way back, I hear my name called.

It's Zain, and he's literally chasing me down the sidewalk.

"Okay, spill," he says breathlessly when he catches up. "Tell me everything."

I give him a quick download of yesterday's events—including the scary description of Amina's interactions with a cop.

Zain's outrageous eyebrows rise farther with each grim detail I learned in Mr. Ossman's backyard. "Jesus Christ," he gasps. "Drew wasn't a corporate spy. He was on a *revenge* mission." I can tell how much he loves this idea. Like he's mentally casting Drew in the next Jason Bourne movie. "This changes everything."

"It doesn't," I argue. And now we're drawing close to the office building, so I slow my stride.

"It does. There was something rotten at Chime Co. I need to know what."

"Wait." I stop outside the door to the building. "Don't forget that he *failed*. The cop retired with full benefits, and the company is still thriving. There was no scandal."

Zain looks away. "Hmm."

"And if you think it will be easier to find a Jay Marker on social media than it was to find Drew Miller, think again. I already tried."

"Doesn't matter," Zain insists. "Meet me somewhere later."

I feel a prickle of unease about his involvement. Like I've lost control of the conversation. On the other hand, Zain has access to

information that I may want. "Buzz and I will be in the park at six thirty. But only for an hour."

"Fine," he insists. "Text me the spot."

That's how I find myself seated on the edge of the splash pool in Deering Oaks Park in the early evening. It's shaped like a river, winding through a ravine. I've already removed my sandals to let my feet dangle in the water.

Buzz—in swim trunks with turtles on them—is just a few yards away, kneeling beside a rock that's supposed to make the poured concrete stream look more realistic. He's got a Playmobil boat with two fishermen and a toy shark.

He's in his happy place.

Zain texts me right at six thirty.

Zain: Where are you exactly? I can't find this ravine.

Not that I blame him—the wading pool is one of those places that was invisible to me until I had a toddler to entertain. Before Buzz, all I knew of Deering Oaks Park were the walking paths and the candelabra tree, where Drew and I used to eat ice cream after bike rides.

Now I can barely think about that spot.

I send Zain my location from the Maps app—a blue dot in the green park. He walks up a few minutes later. He's still wearing the khakis and button-down shirt he wore to work, and he's carrying a backpack. "Huh. This is nice," he says, taking in the preschool mayhem in the water and wearing the expression of someone who's stumbled onto an alien culture.

"Roll up those pants and stick your feet in," I say. "Or else you'll melt."

He sets the backpack down and gets busy removing his work shoes and his socks. Then he rolls up his khakis all the way to the knee, exposing pale legs and feet that have possibly never seen daylight before.

Zain steps into the water with the caution of someone who's worried about alligators. Then he finally seats himself beside me. "All right. I can see why you chose this spot. Look at him."

We both glance at Buzz, who's sailing his boat in a circle around the shark, his lips pursed in a whistle. The tune is "Yankee Doodle."

"God, he looks a lot like Drew," Zain says.

"Really? I hadn't noticed."

A beat goes by. "That's a joke, right?"

"Yup."

Zain huffs out a laugh. "Sorry. The resemblance is just wild."

What's wild is that I've literally never had this conversation before. "It's the blue eyes that get me. Just like Drew's."

"Yeah," Zain says in a hushed voice. "He's still Drew in my head. He didn't look like a Jay."

"If Jay was even his name. I googled *Jay Marker* in a million different ways and barely found anything. I tried *Jason*, too, but that didn't work any better."

"Same," Zain says. "Who knew there were so many Jason Markers in the world?"

It's true. In Maine I found a dentist and an attorney, but neither was right. So I started looking at specifics: *Jay Marker US Army. Jason Marker computer programmer.* None of it got me anywhere.

"I found a Lowden high school football roster, but that's all," Zain says.

"Found that, too," I admit. "It was the only real hit." But the roster was just a list of names, proving that the whole conversation with Ossman wasn't some fever dream.

Jay Marker was a wide receiver. That's literally all I know about him now.

"We'll get to the bottom of it," he says confidently.

I really hate the *we* in that sentence. "Zain—you need to tread carefully. You can't tell *anyone* that Drew was an impostor without affecting me and Buzz. If you start asking a lot of questions . . ."

"Hey, I'm careful. I won't mention him at all. But today I asked your uncle about LiveMatch."

"What?" I gasp as my blood pressure spikes. "Why did you do that without asking me first?"

"Hey, it wasn't a big deal. All I said was that I'd found a reference to it in some decommissioned code. That's not a stretch. And it's literally my job to know how all of our platforms mesh. That's what security engineers do."

It takes me a moment of stunned silence to absorb this betrayal. "But you don't even know that LiveMatch is important."

"Actually, I do." He kicks the surface of the water with one pale foot. "Up until now I'd been tracking Drew around the network on those tapes we stole. But last night I stopped looking for Drew and just started looking for LiveMatch. And I found some things."

"What things?"

"Weird things. We were sending video feeds to an external server in another country. That's bad engineering. There must have been a reason."

I take a deep breath and try to stay calm. "Who did it?"

Zain looks suddenly grumpy. "I can't tell. A log-in I'd never seen before, with full admin privileges. Hey—that woman is staring at us."

I glance up and spot Maddy and two other preschool moms sitting on the opposite side of the pool together. "Ignore them.

They're just looking for gossip." My tone is pure ice. "What did Ray *say* when you asked him?"

He doesn't even seem to register my irritation. "Not much? I asked why we'd run video to foreign servers, and he said it was a pet project of your father's, and he didn't know much about it. *Just some beta test for cheaper video compression. Edward was always looking for ways to save money.* Those were his exact words."

"So . . ." I try to think, but irritation is making my blood boil. "Either he didn't know anything about it, or he lied. Those are the two possibilities."

"Basically. Yeah. Or he didn't want to explain it to me and didn't believe it was still relevant." Zain shrugs. "LiveMatch isn't on the server anymore, though, so it must have come down after your father's death."

"So maybe it *was* his pet project?"

"Maybe. I wish I could be sure what it did. My favorite theory is still that it was an AI engine for video recognition. Those were just getting started five years ago, but they're highly controversial."

"And possibly illegal?" I ask.

Zain snorts. "No way. Technology evolves faster than the law. You can build something that everyone agrees is creepy as fuck, but there's no law against it."

"Lovely." I kick my feet, splashing water onto our legs.

"Drew was focused on two things—LiveMatch and the warrant system. I couldn't figure out how those two things went together. But now that you heard that girl's story, it makes more sense."

"Does it?"

"Yeah. Both of those things involved transferring video *outside* the company's secure network. And that's what happened to his foster sister, yeah? A video ended up in the wrong hands."

"I guess," I mutter. "But slow your roll. I need you to *promise* me you won't ask more questions without discussing it with me first."

He shrugs. "It's easy for me to ask people, though. It's my job to be nosy. Nobody is going to think anything of it. Why aren't you happier about this? Buzz's daddy was a stand-up guy."

"He was a stand-up guy *who used me*," I sputter. "He got close to the boss's daughter. He pretended I was important to him. He let me think that I really knew him. But pretty much everything he told me was a lie."

"Oh." Zain blinks. "I hadn't thought of it like that."

"Obviously," I mutter. It kills me that Drew didn't trust me enough to tell me who he really was. I trusted him with my whole soul. "And you're still giving him too much credit," I add. "Think about it—he takes this job to prove that someone at Chime Co. was responsible for the death of a teenage girl. And then he disappears without a word. Nothing came of it."

"Hmm," Zain says. "Maybe."

"What does *that* mean?"

"LiveMatch got scuttled, didn't it? And then there's your father's, uh . . ." He clears his throat. "His overdose. Drew disappeared right afterward."

"Wait." That shuts me up for a second. "There's no connection, Zain. That's ridiculous."

He rubs the back of his neck. "Maybe this is way out of line, but your dad was a super-ambitious man. Maybe he did something wrong and Drew was going to expose him. And he couldn't take it."

"That is a fucked-up theory." *Although* . . . A sweaty chill rolls down my spine as I realize it has some merit.

"I know. Okay. I'm sorry." He shakes his head. "I'll stick to the facts. Want a cookie?" He opens his backpack and pulls out a package of chocolate shortbread cookies.

"No thank you."

He tears open the package. "Is it okay if I give some of these to Buzz?"

"He can have two," I say automatically, because they're small. But my mind is stalled. My father didn't leave a suicide note. His death was ruled an accidental overdose.

But I've always wondered how that happened. He'd been taking those pills for years. And suddenly he takes too many? But suicide never made any sense, either. He had everything he wanted and more.

Didn't he?

All kids have a sixth sense for sugar, and Buzz magically appears in front of us, eyes hungry as Zain extends the cookie package toward him. "Can I have one?"

"Your mom said you could have two," Zain says.

"Cool." He takes two cookies with wet fingers.

"Say—"

"—Thank you," Buzz says quickly.

"No problem, little man." Zain gives him a funny smile.

Buzz eats the first cookie so fast that he probably doesn't even taste it. Then he nibbles the second one more thoughtfully, wading back toward the rock where he's been playing.

The sunlight glints off the short hairs at the back of his smooth neck, where his hairline dips a little to the left, just like Drew's did.

Sometimes when I look at him, I feel Drew's presence like a physical thing. Like he's here beside me, watching Buzz. "I still don't get it," I whisper. "It's one thing to want answers. But creating a false persona and infiltrating a company . . . Who does that?"

"A real badass," Zain says. "It couldn't have been easy. He must have felt responsible for buying those cameras. He must have been so angry."

Angry. I sit with that for a second. He must have been. But I just didn't see it. In fact, I would have said that *I* was the angry one in that relationship.

"This Amina video," I say. "What are all the ways that it could land in a cop's hands?"

"Four ways," Zain says, counting off on his fingers. "The cop requested it from a homeowner, who said yes. The cop got a warrant for it. Or someone inside Chime Co. mishandled it somehow. Or else Chime Co. got hacked."

"So maybe the cop just hacked the system?"

Zain lets out a bark of laughter. "Nice try. But a beat cop wouldn't have the chops to break into our system. Hacking isn't magic. Most data breaches require poor human behavior. Like maybe this cop had a friend who worked at Chime Co."

"Now, there's a gross idea. Can you imagine asking a buddy for a clip of a teenager in a compromising position? Bros before hos . . ."

"That *better* not be what happened," Zain growls. "This company is my whole fucking life. I work eighty-hour weeks. I need to know the place is worth it."

Okay. Well. At least I'm not the only one who might feel used. I take a cookie out of the package and eat it, even after I said I didn't want one.

That's on-brand for me, too, I guess.

Then I check the time, and it's getting late. "Buzzy! Five-minute warning!"

My son looks up and gives me the puppy-dog eyes of a kid who doesn't want to go home.

"I'm going to finish with the second tape," Zain says. "Then I'll need one more, I think."

"Okay," I say, even if I'm privately unsure that I'll steal another one.

"I'll make you a printout again," he offers.

"Thanks." But I probably won't be reading it. My interests lie elsewhere. "Hey—can we ask your friend to figure out who Jay Marker was? Can he learn anything without his real Social Security number?"

"He can try. Sure."

"I still don't know why he had to be Drew Miller at all. Why not just take the job as Jay?"

"I've been thinking about that . . ."

Of course he has.

". . . If he was a pissed-off customer, maybe he already threatened to sue Chime Co. Maybe he was known to the firm already."

That's actually a great theory. Lawsuits pop up at Chime Co. all the time. Cheating husbands caught on camera bringing their girlfriends home, for example. They threaten to sue, but rarely go through with it. Chime Co. has multiple law firms on retainer for the purposes of discouraging them.

And my father wondered why I never wanted to run Chime Co.

"Buzzy!" I call. "Let's go! Bring your toys!"

My son hangs his head and shuffles slowly toward me in a perfect pantomime of Unhappiest Child Ever.

"Hey—do you think Buzz would like sword fighting?"

"Probably. But I'd like him to survive until kindergarten, so we'll probably stick to peewee soccer."

He blinks. "I meant *watching* it. Plus there's food involved. Will you go somewhere with me on Sunday night? It's a fair. You'll both need costumes."

"Costumes?"

Zain gives me the biggest smile I've ever seen on his face. "Trust me. It's going to be awesome."

Trust me are the two worst words in the English language. "I'm going to need more information."

21

FIVE YEARS AGO, JULY

Drew watches a caterer in a white chef's coat push a cart carefully across the lawn.

"Here comes the dessert," Zain says. "The miniature cheese-cakes are always amazing."

"Good tip." Drew pastes on a smile and shifts his weight for the hundredth time. Standing in place for any length of time makes his leg stiff and his lower back ache. He'd like to sit down, but nobody else is sitting down, except for one person.

Edward Cafferty is still recovering from knee surgery. So they've brought him a single bar stool, placing it in front of the backyard bar. There he sits, holding court for a bunch of programmers, who are very busy kissing his ass.

It's the Friday before the Fourth of July, and this is Drew's very first company picnic. It's also probably his last. Every day it's becoming more obvious that he isn't cut out for the corporate lifestyle. Even if he'd gotten a job at a company that wasn't quite so evil, he'd have a hard time feeling motivated to fatten the boss's bottom line.

Mostly he avoids thinking about where he might be a year from now. A guy can only solve so many problems at once. It's hard enough doing a job he hates while also carrying on an undercover mission.

He scans the backyard of Edward's stately home. It's beautifully landscaped, but a little crowded today. According to watercooler gossip, this party—an annual tradition—is usually held at a country club. But Edward's two knee surgeries made the planning difficult.

The boss is sporting an ice pack on his post-surgical knee. Something went wrong with his first surgery. Ariel said Edward blew a gasket at his specialists when they told him he needed it redone. Since then he's been working from home, and driving his underlings crazy. At least once a day he demands in-person meetings with various members of his staff, who drive over here to see him.

Drew hasn't missed his snarling face around the office, though. Not coincidentally, Ariel has been happier at work than he's ever seen her.

She's here somewhere. Not that they can acknowledge each other. That's probably why he's in such a piss-poor mood. He can't wait to leave, although the food is great. He's already eaten a lobster roll, an avocado cheeseburger, and crab cakes. An endless supply of Maine craft beers is being offered in metal tubs full of ice. The catering must have cost a fortune.

Still, it's not a *fun* party. Everyone else looks a little stiff. It's really just another day at the office. A command performance. Plus, it's Friday, so he's missing date night with Ariel for the first time since they got together.

As if summoned, she emerges in the corner of his field of vision, joining her mother near the door. They're chatting with Reggie, the firm's general counsel. Ariel's wearing a red polo dress and white sneakers. And she looks bored.

He has a strong urge to march across the lawn and say something to make her laugh. But that's not happening. He hasn't said a single word to her in the hour he's been here, and he doesn't plan to start now.

The only one having fun might be Ray, who's currently undefeated in an ongoing tournament of cornhole on the back property line. "Who's next?" he calls out. "Who dares to challenge me?"

"Hey, Drew should do it! Throw down, man!" says Trevor, the programmer. He parks a hand at Drew's ribs and gives him a shove that's meant to be playful.

Or maybe it isn't. In either case, Drew's balance isn't what it used to be, and he ends up taking an ungainly sidestep to avoid falling.

"Whoops, sorry." Trevor chuckles. "That's why I always lose to Ray. Too clumsy. But maybe you can do better."

Ray tosses him a beanbag, which Drew catches. "Come on, kid. Break my streak? What have you got to lose—besides your manhood."

A smile forms on Drew's face against his will. "That's some big talk, sir. I'll take you on."

The older man tosses him three more beanbags, and Drew tests their weight in his hands.

"You go first," Ray says magnanimously.

"I'm probably rusty," he says. "But you should know I spent a lot of the last five years in various deserts, throwing cornhole and playing poker to pass the time."

"Oh hell." Ray chuckles. "Remind me not to invite you to poker night, then. Practice shot?"

"Sure."

The evening sunlight slants over the yard as Drew's first bag arcs toward the board. It lands with a satisfying thud and skates toward the hole. It goes in.

Ray hoots. Then he throws and misses. "Uh-oh, kids. I might be in trouble." Laughing, he collects the bags.

Drew forgets about his aching back and focuses on the game.

He sets up a block with his first shot. Then he throws three airmails in a row.

Meanwhile, Ray manages a single bag and a whole lot of colorful, nonserious cursing. It's a rout, in Drew's favor. Ray asks for a chance to redeem himself, and so Drew repeats the performance. By the time he's won for a second time, the whole company is watching.

Whoops. So much for remaining mostly invisible.

"Nothing to see here," Ray grumbles cheerfully to the other programmers. "Have some more cheesecake, and look away from my humiliation."

Drew accepts some good-natured congratulations. Then he excuses himself and heads for the bathroom, inside the house. Except there's a line for the downstairs half bath.

"Try upstairs," a caterer prompts. "First door on the right."

It's excellent advice. He finds the upstairs bathroom unoccupied. He's zipping his fly up again when the bathroom door opens and Ariel slips inside. "Hey, soldier."

"Whoa, baby! Awkward timing."

"Nobody noticed me coming up here," she whispers. Then she wraps her arms around him as he washes his hands. "This party has lasted a thousand years. Except for the part where you crushed Uncle Ray at cornhole."

"That was fun. I noticed your father didn't challenge him."

She snorts. "The full range of the Cafferty family dynamics are on display today, aren't they? Ray and my dad don't even speak to each other if they can help it."

"How did it end up like that?" he whispers to her face in the mirror.

She shakes her head. "I don't really know if they always hated each other, or if it's a recent development. But you've met my father. Would you want to own half of a business with him? And now that they're successful, there's no way out."

He turns around and pulls her against his chest, and then changes the subject. "There's a cute picture of you in pigtails in the upstairs hallway. Looks like you won a tennis trophy."

"I won a lot of them." She kisses his neck. "And then I quit during high school."

"Because . . . you hate winning?" He rubs her back, because he can't help himself. "Or did you inherit the bad Cafferty knees?"

She shakes her head. "Because I realized my dad *loved* me winning tennis tournaments. He loved bragging about me. And I didn't want to give him the pleasure."

His hands go still on her back. "Oh, sweetheart. That's kind of . . ."

"Self-defeating? You think I don't know that?" She plants her chin sharply on his shoulder.

"Sorry." It's so confusing to be constantly humbled by a fierce artist whose hair smells like lemons. "I would love to get out of here. Another hour, maybe? I heard something about fireworks. You could come over later."

"How about now?" she counters. "I prefer our own kind of fireworks."

She doesn't have to twist his arm. He's already tasting the underside of her smooth jaw and breathing in the scent of her skin. Kissing her in her father's bathroom is stupid and risky and goddamn inevitable.

But he's incapable of saying no to Ariel. The pull he feels toward her is like an affliction.

She makes a soft sound and melts against him, lifting her face to his. And then they're kissing for real. It's been a few days, and he's hungry for it.

Until they hear a distant voice calling her name. "Ariel! Where are you, honey?"

It's her mother's voice, and Ariel groans. She opens the door and yells. "Give me two minutes, Mom."

"Bring out the sparklers!" is the response.

Ariel closes the door and glares up at Drew. "I guess you're not getting a tour of my old bedroom."

"Shame," he says, kissing her neck. "I'd like to witness your embarrassing taste in music posters."

"Oh, I had *excellent* taste as a teenager. The Cranberries. Sisters of Mercy. I dyed my hair black specifically to piss off my dad. And I was very good at sneaking out after curfew."

"You? No way." He laughs, because that is so easy to picture. "How'd you get back in? Your dad literally *invented* a thing that stops girls from doing that anymore."

"Uncle Ray invented it," she corrects. "My dad just made himself rich on it. Besides, the older models weren't as wide-angled. If I climbed onto the front porch from the side, I could usually avoid the camera." She glances toward the bathroom door. "Give me a two-minute head start?"

"Oh, at least. I'm not coming out of the bathroom with the boss's daughter."

Ariel snickers. "Seriously, we're done here. I can't take much more of this, and you need to get off your feet. I'll buy a tub of ice cream and bring it to your place. We'll put on a movie and then ignore it."

"Sounds like a plan." He kisses her forehead one more time. "Go on, before somebody comes."

When she goes, he misses her immediately. He's left staring at his tired face in the ornate mirror, wondering what the hell he's doing with his life. This party perfectly illustrates the problem—he came to Portland for justice and ended up stuffed with lobster rolls and having an affair with the boss's daughter.

And he isn't nearly as sorry as he should be. Two hours from now he'll be holding her in bed, spent, the oscillating fan the only sound in his room. He'll stroke her hair until she falls asleep, wishing the moment could last forever.

That's when the guilt will settle in. Ernie raised him to make a difference, and it's not going according to plan. He hasn't exposed Chime Co. for what it's done. And all he craves are small comforts, like Ariel's arms wrapped around him at the end of the day. The sound of her laughter when they watch a movie on his laptop.

But the clock is ticking.

He waits a couple of crucial minutes before emerging from the bathroom. There isn't anyone in the hallway, thankfully. Mindful of the thick, prosthetic-snagging carpet, he leans heavily on the banister all the way down the stairs. When he gets to the bottom, though, the terrain is unfamiliar. He's come down a different staircase from the one he went up.

Mansions, though. Must be nice.

He's arrived in a corridor with three doors to choose from. Two of them are shut—probably to discourage people from wandering the house. The third leads down a narrow hallway toward the kitchen. But the caterers have blocked it off with a deep, three-tiered cart where they're stacking dirty dishes.

Drew is not about to climb those stairs again. But there are still two means of egress. One of the doors is ajar, so he pokes it with his fingertip. The door is heavier than he'd anticipated, and it barely swings an inch into some kind of parlor.

But he's instantly relieved he didn't push it open farther. There are two people standing together in that room, and they're kissing, much like he and Ariel were doing only minutes earlier.

Except those two people are Ray Cafferty and Ariel's mother.

He's so startled, he doesn't move a muscle for a long moment. And then, gathering his wits, he takes a slow step backward.

Seriously? The Cafferty family is even more fucked up than he'd thought.

"Mom?" Ariel's voice calls out from somewhere at the other end of the house. "Where'd you go?"

Her mother answers a beat later. "Just a second!" And then there's a frantic, whispered conversation in the parlor.

Shit.

Drew backs up toward the third door and turns the knob. The door swings silently open into an elegant home office with floor-to-ceiling bookshelves and a big walnut desk.

It will have to do. Any second now, Ray is going to come out of that parlor and catch him standing here like an eavesdropper. So Drew goes into the home office and sits down in the only chair—which happens to be at Edward's desk.

It's another untenable situation, of course. If anyone sees him sitting here, he'll look exactly like the snoop he really is. Unless . . .

He hastily yanks his trouser leg up and over his prosthetic. Then he leans forward, digging his fingers into the tired flesh of his stump. Massaging his leg through the barrier of the liner isn't very effective. But Ray won't know that.

And sure enough, Ariel's uncle appears in the doorway seconds later. He does a literal double take when he glimpses Drew in the chair. His eyes widen comically, and he sputters. "Jesus, are you okay?"

Who knew the shock value of a missing limb could actually be useful? "Yessir. It didn't happen at the picnic." Drew throws him a grin. "I won't file for workers' comp."

"Sorry." Ray chuckles nervously. "You just took me by surprise. I had no idea. Is that . . . You're a vet, right?"

"Army. I got good at cornhole in the same country where I lost a leg. Win some, lose some."

He blinks. "You need anything? Ice?"

"Nah, just needed a break. The kitchen was full of caterers, so I ended up in here. Sorry. Door was open."

"It's no problem," he says quickly. "I could bring a folding chair outside for you."

Drew shakes his head. "Probably time for me to head home and take a painkiller anyway. Unless you want a rematch?"

Ray snorts with laughter. "I'd better throw some practice shots first. But rest up, okay? I think we could set up the board in the office. Maybe between the design guys and the devo team." He makes a show of cracking his knuckles. "I'll get you yet."

"Sure, sure. Don't take the loss too hard. You could probably take me on the tennis court." He pats his artificial limb.

"Likely story. You're probably a ringer there, too." Ray taps the doorjamb. "See you Monday, kid."

"Later." He watches Ray disappear. Then he closes his eyes for a moment and slows down his breathing.

Christ. So much for being the guy that nobody notices. He should never have come inside the house. Hell, he shouldn't have come to this party at all.

Get it together, Marker. You used to be better at running a mission.

He stands gingerly. A glance out the window confirms that Edward is still seated outside at the makeshift bar, his post-surgical leg propped up on an overturned milk crate.

Drew's knee gives a sympathetic throb. It may be the first time he's ever felt any sympathy for that bastard. He knows how it feels to be the least mobile guy in the crowd. He's been that guy.

And Edward's wife is banging Ray? *Jesus*. He wonders if Ariel knows. Would she even want to? It's hard to say.

Another moral quandary. *Yay*. But he'll have to worry about that later. Right now, he needs to make like a rabbit and get the fuck out of here.

He reaches over and grasps the edge of the hulking desk for support, because his leg really *does* ache. As he levers Edward's ostentatious chair back toward the desk, his hand brushes the cord of the computer mouse.

The screen blinks to life, revealing a spreadsheet. Not a lock screen.

Holy shit. The CEO doesn't keep a password on his home computer?

Holy. Shit.

He drops back into the chair and reaches for the mouse. Another quick glance out the window shows him that Edward hasn't moved. And Ray is heading across the yard, beer in hand, another smile on his face.

So he doesn't waste time. He minimizes the spreadsheet and zeroes in on the boss man's network connection, launching it onto the screen. Then he heads right over to the LiveMatch directory and double-clicks on the folder.

A menu he's never seen before resolves on the screen.

Lowden Beta Program is the first thing on offer. He opens that menu and blinks as a lengthy list of camera feeds and usernames fills the page.

Reaching for the phone in his pocket, he unlocks it and starts snapping pictures of the screen.

22

ARIEL

"This is so exciting," Tara says as she riffles through her closet. "Look at you going on a date!"

"It's *not* a date," I insist. "Definitely not. Just a little excursion with my coworker."

She pulls out a . . . Actually, I have no idea what that thing on the hanger is. "I'm *not* wearing a leather corset, Tara. Absolutely not."

Larri laughs from the bed where she's reclining. "I would give all the cash in my wallet to see Ariel in a leather corset. Not that five dollars would be sufficiently motivating."

"Do you have maybe just a cape? I'd put it over regular clothes and call it good. Where did you even find . . . that?"

Tara puts the corset back into the closet. "At another fair, during my wild years. My asshole ex was a big fan. Some of the ren-faire crew really like their substances."

"So I'm taking my child to a drug den?" I ask in a voice pitched low enough to escape Buzz, who's in the living room. "Is this a bad idea?"

"You'll be fine," Tara assures me. "Most of it is family friendly. That's probably why your date suggested it."

"It's not a date," I remind her. "It's just an outing. There's a guy who will be there who used to work with Drew. We want to ask him some questions."

"Couldn't it also be a date?" Larri presses. "Any guy who's willing to take your kid on an outing can't be all bad."

"He's not my type." And, lord, I *really* hope Zain doesn't see this as a date. "And a man is the last thing I need. Especially with Buzz in the picture. He's already been abandoned once."

Larri sits up and squints at me. "Not really. That guy didn't even know he was abandoning you both."

"But he would have," I point out.

"You don't know that," Tara says, pulling a midnight blue cloak out of her closet. "Did you even tell what's-his-name that you loved him? That you wanted him to stay?"

I try to imagine saying that to Drew, and find that I can't. I'm not into saying pointless things. And he'd already said *I'm not the kind of guy who sticks around.* Those may have been the only true words he ever spoke to me.

"You know she didn't," Larri says softly. "Some of us are just excellent at self sabotage, aren't we?"

Those sound like fighting words to me. But Tara turns to her girlfriend with soft eyes. "One hundred percent," she says. "But I'm trying."

"Baby, I know it." Larri sits up and opens her arms, and Tara steps into them.

I slip the cape around my shoulders while they whisper to each other. I hope those two can make it.

And I admire them for trying.

A few hours later I'm standing beside Zain in the waning light of evening. A bonfire rages on our left, and a battle rages on our right. Two "knights" are engaged in a fierce exhibit of swordsmanship, while a couple hundred people look on.

"Okay, this is kind of cool," I admit. "But also weird."

"Which is the best kind of cool," Zain says with obvious glee. He's wearing slim-fitting black pants and a white linen shirt that laces at the neckline.

And he looks surprisingly dignified in that getup. Who knew?

"Want some more popcorn?" Zain asks Buzz, who's wearing a wool vest and a felted helmet that we borrowed from Miss Betty's dress-up box.

My son doesn't answer. He's too busy staring wide-eyed at the two men—in full body armor—who are circling each other with swords on the lawn in front of us.

In many ways, the Renaissance fair is like any other. There's a pony ride, deep-fried Oreos, cotton candy and vendors. But some of the costumes are wild. Tara's leather corset has friends here. I've also seen chain mail and leather jerkins.

I notice that men between the ages of eighteen and thirty are *very* well represented. If I had a kink for nerdy guys who usually stay home to play video games and D&D, I'd be in heaven.

One of the fighters parries and then lunges. Their swords clash, and Buzzy jumps. "Are they gonna die?" he asks me with real fear in his voice.

"No," Zain and I say in unison.

"They're actors," Zain adds. "They're good at this."

"We can watch something else, though," I offer. "If this makes you nervous, we could go on to the pony ride."

My son slowly shakes his head, his eyes unblinking.

"If he has nightmares, I'm blaming you," I whisper. "Remind me why we're doing this?"

"Because sword fighting is cool, duh," he whispers back. "And every time I've come to one of these, I see Bryan Zarkey. He has booth selling weapons."

"Really? What kind of weapons?" I can barely remember Bryan from his Chime Co. days. But Zain has that guy's job now. And Zain thinks he might be honest about LiveMatch. Because he doesn't work there anymore.

"He makes daggers. They're cool—like something out of *The Hobbit*."

"Does this crowd have a lot of use for daggers?" I ask.

"Well, duh. You can use them as a letter opener—and you'll look like a badass while you do it."

"I will never understand boys."

Even as I say this, the fighters clash swords again, and the guy with the blue chest plate forces the red guy to stumble backward. And Buzz lets out a surprisingly bloodthirsty roar.

I give Zain a sideways glance, and he laughs. "It's innocent fun, I swear. Here—have the last cheese puff. You know you want it."

He isn't wrong. I've already polished off a startling number of them, along with a tasty sausage.

The swordsmen pick up the pace of their fight until they're whirling and lunging at a furious pitch. Buzz watches with an unhinged jaw, and Zain watches with a boyish smile on his face.

Until one knight finally loses his footing and falls with a crash to the dirt, his sword sliding out of reach.

The other knight looms over him, sword poised, and Buzz's hand tightens in mine.

"Shall I show you mercy, knave?" the victor demands.

"Mercy," the other knight begs.

The victor steps back and takes a bow, and Buzz's small shoulders relax.

"That was very exciting," I say, patting his head. "Now let's go meet some armorers."

"Cool," Buzz says. "Can we get a fried Oreo?"

"No," I say at the exact moment that Zain says "Yes."

Buzz is just finishing his Oreo when we stroll down a double row of vendors. Their wares are hung in a zigzag path, and barkers stand on wooden crates, calling out to potential customers. "Ribbons! Fine lace! Silk from the other side of the world!"

There's also a stall selling full-sized armor "for battle or for show," and Buzz stops to admire it. "Mama, can you take my picture?" he asks, touching the chest plate.

"She can't, because you're not allowed to carry a phone here," Zain says.

"Why not?" Buzz demands.

"There weren't any phones during the Renaissance," Zain explains. "People had to just experience things in real time. Instead of a picture, you have your memory."

Buzz looks unconvinced. "But what if you need to call somebody? What if we get lost?"

"We won't," Zain says. "And your mom's phone is just in the car."

It's actually in my pocket, because I am not a rule follower. But I keep that to myself. "I don't see any daggers," I say as we continue down the row.

"Patience," Zain says. "He'll be here. Or else I'm going to have to invite you to a D&D event next week."

"Jesus Christ."

He laughs, and that's when I spot a familiar face. Familiar*ish*. Like so many of the young men who work for Chime Co., I never had much interaction with Bryan Zarkey. But he was one of the more charming guys in the room. He tried, anyway, and that's more than I can say for a lot of them.

He has a beard now, and it makes him look older. And the purple velvet cape he's wearing over a leather chest plate makes him appear as though he's stumbled in from another era.

Honestly, he's pretty easy on the eyes.

"There," Zain says, stopping just outside the booth. "And you doubted me."

"What's your plan?" I ask. Bryan hasn't spotted us yet. He's talking to an older man who's looking at a set of daggers laid out on turquoise velvet.

"I don't need a plan. He's chatty—I can just slip my question into the conversation."

"Huh. Okay." Zain is not a subtle person. This will probably be a disaster.

"Come on." He wraps an arm around me as we step into the booth. There's a long table full of sharp-looking knives of various lengths. The ornate handles are stained in assorted colors.

"*Cool*," Buzz says, and his voice is full of awe.

"We can't touch *anything*," I caution, locking his hand into mine.

"Bryan, wow. Good spread this year!" Zain says in an enthusiastic voice.

Two people look up. There's Bryan, who gives Zain an automatic smile.

There's also a woman. *Girlfriend*, is my first thought, since their purple capes match. But the capes aren't the only resemblance. She has the same pale blue eyes that Bryan has.

My eyes are drawn to her hands as she repositions one of the daggers on the table. The handle is made of wood in a deep purple hue. And I notice that her fingers are stained various different shades.

She's the artisan here, I realize. I can always spot them. It would be fun to ask her some questions about metalwork, but I don't want to miss out on Zain's conversation.

Bryan steps around the table, still smiling. His eyes travel from Zain to me and then to Buzz. His smile takes on a little bit of a smirk as he notes the three of us together. "Hey, old friends," he says slowly. "Taking in the fair?"

"You know it," Zain says. "We just watched a sword fight. How've you been since I saw you last?"

Zarkey shrugs. "Chained to my keyboard. You know how it is. How's the job treating you?"

"Got promoted. Can't complain." Zain rocks back on his heels. "Although, since you asked, I do have one question for you. Were you ever familiar with a piece of software called LiveMatch?"

Lord. That wasn't very subtle. I watch Zarkey's reaction closely as his eyes widen slightly. But it's the reaction of someone who wasn't expecting to think about his old job while dressed like a medieval squire. "Maybe? The name is familiar." He looks up at the ceiling of the tent, as if thinking about it. "Why? Is something broken?"

"Nah. It's a relic on the network," Zain says. "And I wondered what it was. Looks like some kind of software running on overseas servers. And I couldn't think why that made any sense."

"Oh!" Bryan glances at me. And suddenly his expression is less cheerful. "*That* thing. Some kind of beta program." He shrugs. "Honestly, it was frustrating. Like, it's my job to keep things secure, but I can't do that if you're sending a feed to someone else's server."

"But what was it *for*?" Zain presses. "There's nothing left of it except for some old comment lines."

Bryan's forehead wrinkles. "If I ever knew, I don't remember. Some kind of joint venture with another company."

"Huh," Zain says. "So it never launched?"

Bryan spreads out his hands. "No idea, man. Not my circus anymore. Not my monkeys. And I doubt you'll find anyone to tell you, because it was, uh . . ." His eyes flicker to me again. "It was Edward's project. Sorry for your loss."

"Thank you," I say softly.

Edward's project. That lines up with what Ray told Zain, too.

"Now, if you'll excuse me." He gestures toward two men who've appeared to fondle daggers at the far end of the table. "I have customers."

"Right," Zain says. "Sorry."

We retreat, with Zain chewing on his lip in a gesture that I now know means he's annoyed with how that went.

I'm not, though, because my expectations were already low. I've had five years to get used to the idea that Drew will always be just out of reach. "Let's find the pony ride," I say. "We must be getting closer. I smell manure."

And I'm not wrong. Buzz and I get in line, and after ten minutes or so, it's his turn to amble around the ring on a small horse, with a woman in a milkmaid costume holding the lead.

He's beaming, and I really want to pull out my damn phone right now for this photo. Is that really too much to ask?

When Buzz is finished, I realize I've lost track of Zain. And now it's grown dark, so he isn't as easy to spot in the crowd.

It takes me a couple minutes of looking over my shoulders to finally spot him. He's standing at the edge of the crowd. And Bryan stands beside him, gesturing to Zain.

Who's clenching his fists.

23

"What was that all about?" I ask as we make our way back to the car.

"Later," he grumbles.

On the ride back into town, Zain sits in a silence that's almost sullen.

Buzz is quiet, too, although it's probably because he's fallen asleep. I lift myself in my seat to try to glimpse him in the back, but I can't see him.

Zain catches on and twists his body around to peek. "He's out like a light. It's so cute."

As soon as I stop at a traffic light, I turn around to see. Sure enough, my little knight is slumped over in his car seat, his helmet askew, mouth open. But he's still clutching his felt sword tightly.

"I love the way little kids can fall asleep anywhere," Zain whispers. "So much trust."

"Yeah," I agree softly. "He knows he'll wake up in his bed tomorrow. Where am I dropping you?"

"I can walk home from your place," Zain says. "You need to get him into bed. Want a beer? I brought a few bottles of Corona, in a cooler." He jerks his thumb toward his pack on the back seat. "That's your favorite, right?"

Shit. Am I the only one who doesn't think we're on a date?

"Ariel," he says in a low voice. "It's just a friendly beer. Nothing more."

"Sure." Now I feel foolish. "Just let me get him upstairs first."

Five minutes later I ease the car into our garage. It's a tight fit, because this garage is a hundred years old, and my carriage house apartment takes up half the building.

"You need a hand?" Zain asks as I open Buzz's door and unstrap him from the car seat.

"I've got a system," I tell him. Although carrying a sleeping four-year-old gets a little more unwieldy with every inch he grows.

"At least let me unlock the door," he says as I stagger out of the garage with Buzz in my arms. "Where are your keys?"

He unlocks my kitchen door and opens it. Then he steps inside and puts the keys on the counter, beside his padded cooler.

"I'll be right down," I promise.

When I return ten minutes later, Zain is sitting at my kitchen table drinking a Corona. Another one waits for me, uncapped in the cooler.

I extract a lime from my refrigerator and cut it into wedges, pushing one of them into my bottle and then offering Zain the dish. "Corona with lime was Drew's bar order. He called it his summer drink. I don't know what he drank any other time of year. I only knew him for one season."

Zain takes a wedge and pushes it into his bottle. The beer fizzes as the lime falls in. "I bet Drew was a whiskey guy. Just have a feeling."

I try to picture it, but he feels very far away tonight. And I realize I've been drinking Drew's brand of beer for five years in a pathetic bid to hold on to him. "What did Bryan say to you?"

Zain takes a slow sip of his beer. "Nothing too useful. He said he didn't want to badmouth your dad in front of you. But he agreed with me—that shipping video to another server was a security nightmare. Your father didn't listen to him, and he refused to explain his actions."

I snort. "Well, *that* sounds plausible."

"I know. He said the whole thing left a bad taste in his mouth. And that it was one of the reasons he left Chime Co."

"Yikes."

"Disclaimer"—Zain props his chin in his hand—"I'm not that good at reading people."

"I got that."

"But he seemed *nervous*. He told me to drop it. He also made a point to say that there's ten more employers for every guy with our training. *There's no need to work for assholes*—his words."

"Huh. Well, that's kind of eerie. But also a dead end."

"Unfortunately." Zain rubs his hands together. "So now I need another big idea."

"Don't we all."

He rolls his beer bottle between his hands. "How about this—we figure out whether Drew found anything weird in those warrants he was looking at. I bought a new air gap machine, and I'll back up the second tape onto it. But I think Drew's final days at Chime Co. will be on the *next* one. Maybe he got caught. And that's why he sent you that weird message."

That damn text. *There's trouble. I need to see you.* "Right. For at least thirty seconds, he wanted me to know the truth."

Zain laughs. "Harsh."

"Is it? I didn't show up in the park, so he obviously just shrugged and then skipped town. Then he broke up with me by email, like a chump."

He sits up a little straighter in his chair. "Wait, I forgot about that email. I could probably trace the machine he sent it from."

"What does it matter?" I ask, even as my heart flips over. The email makes less sense now than it used to. I always found it cold. But now that I know Drew tried to send me a desperate-sounding text before he split town, the tone of the email seems weird.

"I need that third tape," he says. "Monday we'll do the swap. That should take us all the way up until his exit date."

"Okay," I say immediately. And I already know I'll steal the next one when Zain asks me to. Just one more rule to break for Drew, who'll never appreciate it.

"Thanks for going to the fair, Ariel." He pushes back his chair. "I'd better go."

"It was actually fun," I admit. Zain isn't so bad.

He carefully works the lime out of his empty beer bottle, then rinses the bottle before depositing it into my recycling bin. "I hope you've figured out that I'm not hitting on you. Although I've had real crushes on people at work before."

When he turns around, he's wearing a funny little smile that invites me to ask the obvious question. "On who, then?"

"Drew," he says quietly. "And, yeah, I know I'm not his type. He was never going to stand in line at Holy Donut with me on a Saturday in sweats and sex hair to buy *me* a Holy Cannoli Ginger Glazed. But I'm still going to be really pissed off if we don't find out what happened to him."

I watch him walk out then, my jaw on the floor as he tosses me a wave on his way through the door.

And here I'd thought Zain wasn't great at reading people. But I'm just as bad. Or maybe worse.

Chastened, I carry Tara's cape upstairs and hang it up. Then I tidy the kitchen. When I open the door to take out the trash, my mom's lights are still on. So I grab the car keys. I might as well return them to her now, in case she needs the car tomorrow morning.

Ray's car wasn't out front, so I'm not very worried about intruding on a private moment. I tap on the kitchen door and then open it.

I hear my mother's voice, but she stops speaking abruptly. "Ariel? Is that you?"

There's nobody in the kitchen, so I track her down in the dining room. She's sitting there with a man I recognize but can't place.

Oh wait—I can. Even in his business casual clothes, he has that cop look—the short hair and authoritative posture. "Hi, Officer . . ." I say, trying to dredge up his name from my memory.

He was the first person to arrive at the scene when my panicked mother found my father slumped over his desk five years ago. He stayed with her after the paramedics took him away. Then he became her liaison to the police during the brief investigation of his death.

"Todd Barski," he says, rising to shake my hand. "It's a pleasure to see you again, Ariel." He's a white guy, probably a few years older than I am. Sandy hair, square jaw. Probably gets a lot of female attention.

Not from me, though. I mumble a half-polite reply, but I'm trying to figure out why he's here. "Is there a problem?"

They exchange a glance that makes the whole moment even more awkward. "I asked him to stop by," my mother says eventually. "I had a question about the day your father died. Remember that story Ray told us the other night? About the five-year-old texts?"

Gosh, Mom, you have no idea. "Sure."

"Well, I got one of those, too," she says quietly. "It was a doorbell notification with a man on it that I didn't recognize."

"Really? You didn't say anything." And I'm still not sure where this is going. "You get those all the time, though. Delivery person, maybe?"

"Maybe. But he wasn't in uniform." She picks at her manicure. "I just wanted Officer Barski to see it, in case it was meaningful."

"In what way?" I ask.

"Your father's death was investigated," the cop says gently. "And ruled to be an accidental overdose. But the dose he took was pretty large, and we did wonder where he got it."

"*Oh.*" I'm trying to read between the lines here, and it isn't easy. "So the photo might be his *dealer*?"

When I say that word, my mother recoils. Officer Barski doesn't flinch at all, though. "The man in the photo is not familiar to me," he says carefully. "It's not a great photo."

Interesting. And yet he's still sitting here.

Although my family has a long history with Portland law enforcement. My grandfather was a captain back in the day. These days the Portland PD is a Chime Co. partner force. And my family has donated equipment to the department, and money to their charitable causes.

In other words, if my mother calls the station with a question, Officer Barski is going to drive right over here and kiss the dowager's ring.

"Let me see this photo," I demand, because it's the only way I'm going to figure out what has my mom so spooked.

The policeman reaches for his phone and unlocks it before offering it to me.

I look down, and the floor drops out from under me. It's not even a good photo—just a dark shot of a man in a baseball cap. One of his hands is presumably on the doorknob, while the other shields much of his face from the camera.

But holy shit. It's enough. And I nearly sway on my feet.

The photo is Drew.

"I was at the butcher's when I got this," my mother says. "He looks so *menacing*, and I panicked, thinking this man was letting himself into my house. But then I noticed the flowers. I haven't put mums on the porch in years."

"Mums," I repeat stupidly. Sure enough, there are flowerpots visible in the frame.

"So I knew the photo was a glitch. But then when we learned the date . . . from the radio." She shakes her head. "This man was in our home on the morning your father died. And I don't know who he is."

I fight to keep my expression neutral, and then I make myself hand the phone back to the cop, as if I haven't just seen a ghost.

Even though his eyes were hidden by the baseball cap, I'd know that rugged chin anywhere. And the set of his shoulders. That's *Drew*. Or Jay Marker. Take your pick. And he was *here* on the day my father died?

Holy. Shit.

"Do you recognize him?" the officer asks.

"Nope." I look him square in the eyes, hoping I don't look as rattled as I feel. "Sorry. I didn't live on the property back then, though. So I'm probably not the right person to ask. And I have to get back—my son is asleep upstairs."

"Did he have fun at the fair?" my mother asks.

"Absolutely," I say, setting the keys down on the table. "Thanks for letting me take the car. Good night."

Then I turn my back and get the hell out of there.

24

Zain stares at me from across a table at the coffee shop where I'd demanded that he meet me, even though it's Memorial Day and he doesn't have to go to work. "Are you *sure* it was him in the picture?"

"Of course I'm sure. I'd know that body anywhere. Those muscular shoulders. That strong jaw. Am I right?"

He gives me a feeble grin. "I don't *want* it to be him. Why was he at your house on a weekday morning? Unless he was there to see you."

I shake my head. "I didn't live on Chadwick Street then. He'd have no business there."

Zain swallows. "So . . . during the same sixty-minute period when you got a text from Drew, he was letting himself into your father's house? And then your father dies the same morning?"

"Something like that."

He props his head in one hand. "What the hell did Drew say to him?"

"I don't know. And I don't see how we'll ever know. The cop seemed to think he was bringing street drugs to my father."

"What?" Zain looks incredulous. "There's no chance."

"That was my reaction, too."

"Do you, uh, have a copy of this photo?"

I shake my head. "I know you doubt me, but I'm telling you it was him."

"Okay." Zain lets out a heavy breath. "So this took a turn for the weird."

"Didn't it just?"

We sit there in silence for a second, until the barista calls my name. Zain pops up out of his chair. "I'll get it." He returns a minute later with two cups of coffee.

Not that I need caffeine right now. I'm already jumpy. "You might be right, Zain."

"God, I love hearing that." He gives me a rueful smile. "But what about?"

"Your pet theory about Drew finding something bad. And sending my father over the edge."

He flinches. "Keep the trophy. I don't want to be right about that."

"But what the hell did he *find*?"

Zain shakes his head. "Get me the third tape, and I'll figure it out. Here, I brought the second one back." He leans over and unzips his backpack. Then he awkwardly passes me the tape under the table.

"We would make awful spies," I mutter, tucking it into my bag. "Tomorrow is our office move, though. So I know I can swap it in all the chaos."

"Yeah, but . . ." He takes a thoughtful sip of his coffee. "I'm sorry this got so complicated. I feel bad for pushing you to look into it."

"You didn't really push me. I need to know what happened."

I owe it to Buzz to know everything. Although it's anyone's guess how much I'll end up telling him.

When I carry the tape into work the next morning, it occurs to me that I should have bought Uncle Ray a cup of coffee—it would give me an easy excuse to walk into his office even if he isn't there.

He is, though. In fact, it looks like he's spent some quality time in his office over the long weekend. The whole place is a shambles. There are moving boxes everywhere. All the pictures are off the walls. And all the shelves behind him are barren.

I approach the open door and stop on the threshold. "Wow. I love what you've done with the place."

"What a mess, yeah?" he says, straightening and pointing at an overflowing garbage bag in the corner. "Who knew how much junk I could accumulate in ten years? That's not even the first bag."

"You could have had help," I point out.

"Not really. Lots of tricky decisions were made. For example— how many issues of *Wired* magazine dating back to 2014 does a guy need?" He points to an overflowing box against the wall.

"Please tell me you pitched them."

In answer, he steps over and slaps a bright orange sticky note on the pile. RECYCLE, it reads. "Promise me you won't lift that box yourself? Maybe the moving guys can help us haul it away."

"I'll ask," I promise. "They're due in an hour."

"Good. I have meetings out of the office for most of the next two days. Just put things where you think they should go, and I'll sort the rest out later."

"No problem," I say.

Except there is a problem. A big one. When I leisurely unpack Ray's boxes in the new space that afternoon, something important is missing—the tapes aren't in any of the boxes. By four p.m., I've unpacked every single one.

The tapes are just gone.

"They have to be in the building somewhere," Zain says during our whispered conversation in front of the new coffee station upstairs.

"You'd think," I hiss. "But every box has been emptied. I went back downstairs to look for the stuff he decided to throw away, but it's already gone."

Zain's eyes widen. "You think he threw them *away*?"

"I don't know!" I yelp. "But they aren't here. On the off chance that he moved them into a storage closet, I checked all of those, too. On both floors."

"Fuck." Zain rubs his temples. "That's so odd. Especially since there's a backup set at our server farm in Westbrook."

"Really?"

"Yeah. They're important enough that we don't keep our only backups here. Still, I can't believe he'd take them out of easy reach. What do you think he's up to?"

"No idea. But you always could ask," I point out. "Can't you dream up some reason for needing one of them?"

He chews his lip. "Eventually. But swiping a backup copy would draw less attention."

"That's your call."

"I find it suspicious that he hid them somewhere. Now I *really* want to know what's on that next one."

I glance over both shoulders to make sure nobody else is nearby. But the new office space is quieter than the old one, and we're the only people in sight. "You think he hid them intentionally? That doesn't sound like Ray."

"Yeah, that's what I used to think, too," Zain says darkly. "But this thing gets shittier with every rock we turn over. I want to know why. I'll go to Westbrook tonight."

I can't decide if that sounds wise, or melodramatic. "What if you get caught?"

Zain shrugs. "If anyone asks me why I made a trip to the server farm, I'll just say I was trying to investigate a backup anomaly."

"All right," I say slowly. "Is there anything I can do?"

"Keep looking for those tapes," he says, his face clouding over. "If he's hidden them for a reason, I'd say that looks bad."

When I arrive home from work, my mother invites Buzzy and me to stay for dinner. "I got the most beautiful tomatoes at the farmers market, so I'm making bruschetta and a bean salad, and I thought we could grill some chicken."

"That sounds nice, Mom. Thanks. What can I do to help?"

"Peel that cucumber?" She hands me a peeler.

While we're side by side at matching cutting boards, I size her up, wondering how she's doing. Her anxious behavior makes more sense to me now that I know she got a rogue text, too.

"How was your day?" I ask, because in this family we don't ever get straight to the point.

"Fine," she says, predictably. "Buzz has been whistling the same tune over and over again. It's a tune I know and couldn't name. He—" She breaks off and holds up a hand.

And I hear whistling from two rooms away. It's the same tune he was whistling on the way to preschool today. "That's . . ." I listen a little harder. "What is that tune?"

She laughs. "Welcome to my world. I've spent the whole day trying to figure it out."

Buzz whistles again, and I try to supply the lyrics in my head. But I can't.

"Ray will be joining us for dinner," my mother says. "Oh, and I might have found a wedding dress this morning. What do you think of this?" She sets down her chef's knife and pulls her phone out of her apron. She opens it up to a photo of herself in a dress shop, smiling at the camera.

"Oh, wow, Mom. That's a *great* pick." The dress is white, but not a traditional wedding dress. The length is above-the-knee. The fabric has big round flowers embroidered onto it. Like giant white-on-white polka dots. It has blousy elbow-length sleeves that lend it a casual whimsy. "You look great in that."

"Is it too short?" she demands. "Do I look like I'm trying to be twenty-five again?"

"No!" I insist. "You look fashionable but not silly. The neckline is super modest." Boring, even. "But that only makes those sleeves stand out. And you have great legs for someone so ancient."

"*Young lady.*" She plucks a wooden spoon from the ceramic utensil holder and pretends to swat my backside with it. "*That* was uncalled for."

"Oh, come on. There was a compliment in there, too."

She smiles as she puts down the wooden spoon and picks up the knife again. "I do like the dress. I think I'll buy it."

"Still planning for October?" I ask.

"Absolutely," she says firmly. "I can't wait."

I peel the rest of the cucumber without comment, until my phone starts to ring in my pocket. I pull it out and see an unfamiliar number with a 910 area code. "Spam, probably." But something tickles my subconscious about that area code. So I answer it. "Hello?"

"Hello, have I reached Miss Ariel Cafferty?"

The accent is Southern and genteel, and it makes me answer with an uncharacteristic formality. "Yes, this is she."

"My name is Elizabeth Carter, and I'm calling from the Cedarwood Cemetery. You called recently looking for a friend's grave?"

My stomach does a loop-de-loop, and I walk immediately toward the back door, where I let myself out onto the driveway. "Yes ma'am, I did."

"I'm sorry it took me so long to return your call," the woman says. "We don't have lengthy office hours, and I was away on vacation last week."

"That's all right," I say numbly. But my heart is beginning to pound, and I lean against the shingled exterior wall of the house, because I feel suddenly light-headed. "Did you find Andrew Miller?"

When this woman gives me a plot number, it will be like losing him all over again.

There's a beat of silence. "No, I'm afraid I was unable to locate anyone with the surname of Miller who was interred here in the last decade. In fact, we were largely closed to new interments after 2015. The only burials we have now are in existing family mausoleums, or plots sold before 2005."

"Oh." I gasp, and replay that in my head as best I can. "And nobody named Miller owns one of those?" I need her to say it again.

"We have only one Miller family in the cemetery," she says. "And their last interment was more than fifteen years ago."

"Oh," I say again. I prop myself up against the house and try to remember how to breathe. "So his obituary was wrong."

"I'm sorry to say that seems likely," she says quietly. Somewhere in the depths of my confusion I recognize that Ms. Elizabeth Carter has the kind of gentle delivery you'd need if your job was speaking to bereaved family members. "Perhaps I could help you get in touch with another cemetery in the area? Many of them are still open, and you're more likely to find a burial from 2018 at one of those."

"All right, thank you," I say with forced calm. As if I weren't screaming inside. "Who should I call first?"

She rattles off a couple of names, which I probably won't remember as soon as I hang up the phone.

Because Drew is not buried in that cemetery in North Carolina. And I feel a hundred different ways about it. I'm so confused. But I also feel weirdly elated, like a death row prisoner who just got a temporary stay of execution.

What if he never died? I haven't really allowed myself to consider that possibility before now. Not really.

I stumble through a polite dismount from that phone call. And then I stand there by the back door, clutching my phone, feeling shaky.

After a moment, a shiny BMW pulls into the driveway. It's Ray's car. And whether I'm ready or not, he climbs out, his tie loose at the neck, his jacket slung over his arm. He looks tired. But when he sees me, he straightens up and smiles. "Hey, Ariel! How'd moving day go?"

It takes me a long beat to process the question. "Fine," I say, shoving my phone in my pocket and straightening my spine. "Everything is done. Your phone line is transferred to your new desk. I tested it. And they moved your computer and plugged it in, but I didn't try to boot it up."

"Excellent work, as always. Let me change out of this suit, and I'll fire up the grill."

I watch him go and then sag against the house. Pulling my phone out, I hit Zain's number and wait until he picks up.

"Hey," he says. "I'm heading over to the server farm now. Is there a problem?"

"No," I say hoarsely. "Well, not about that. I, uh, just got a call from the cemetery in North Carolina."

"And?"

I swallow hard. "He's not there."

For a second I think the call has dropped, because he doesn't say anything. Then, "Holy shit."

That's pretty much how I feel about it, too.

"I *knew* there was something weird about that obituary. Okay, I didn't *know*. It was more of a hunch."

"Good hunch," I mutter. "What other hunches do you have for me? Because I'm spiraling right now."

"God, Ariel. What if they printed the wrong cemetery name?"

"That's the first thing I'll check," I tell him. "But what if he's . . ." My voice cracks before I finish that sentence.

"Alive?"

I make a noise of disbelief. Zain just said it. Out loud. The thing I haven't been willing to contemplate until now.

"Then I'd assume he's been hiding," Zain says. "But not from you."

Of course from me. Because I never mattered.

"Ariel? You still there?"

"Yeah," I grind out.

"What if he found something dangerous? Maybe leaving wasn't enough distance. Maybe he had to fake his own death."

"Who does that?" I whisper.

"Someone who has no other choice."

"Or maybe they just put the wrong cemetery in the obit." I rub my temple with my free hand. "Now I have to go have dinner with Ray and my mother and Buzz and pretend that everything is fine."

"Good luck with that," Zain says. "I'll call my friend and ask him to get on that search for Jay Marker."

"Thanks," I say, even though I'm shaking.

"Hang in there. We'll know more soon."

That's what I'm afraid of.

25

FIVE YEARS AGO, JULY

It's already late July. The summer is flying by.

Drew is spreading a blanket on the grass in the park while Ariel waits, holding the cooler.

This date was his idea. There is a symphony orchestra playing in the band shell. The article he read promised music by Mozart.

Or, wait. Beethoven?

It doesn't matter. He's never going to be a classical music buff. The point of coming here was to feed Ariel picnic food and lie on the blanket under the sky.

She settles onto the blanket as he opens the cooler he bought for this occasion. "There's wine, and it looks like that's allowed." He sees other picnickers with alcoholic beverages, which is reassuring. He absolutely cannot get arrested. His fake driver's license would not hold up to scrutiny. Weeks ago he took the real one out of his wallet, right after he and Ariel became a couple.

He's broken all of his rules for her. Every single one.

But now is not the time to worry about that. From the cooler he pulls paper plates, napkins, and a fresh baguette. There are also three different cheeses, knives to spread them with, assorted olives, and even pâté. Plus dessert.

Maybe he's overshot, though. When he pulls out the prosecco—

and two plastic champagne flutes he purchased to serve it in—Ariel's eyes widen with surprise.

He braces himself to be teased for going that extra mile, but that's not what happens. Instead, Ariel's face takes on a stunned, unguarded expression. "This is the nicest picnic anyone ever made for me."

And, yup, now he feels like he's just unpacked his heart instead, and laid it bleeding on the blanket between them. He can feel their summer slipping away. Every night they spend together is another day closer to his departure.

It feels shitty that he's the only one who knows it.

A moment later, though, she tries to recover her characteristic snark. "To be fair, this is the *only* picnic anyone ever made me."

"That is a damn shame, then." He holds her eyes, and for a moment they get trapped right there, tangled up in the things that neither of them is willing to say.

Ariel drops her gaze. "I'll hold the glasses while you pour."

"Great idea."

It's a beautiful night, and the orchestra starts up while they're busy filling up on cheese and French bread.

He's never had pâté before, and he's not sure he's a fan. It's like salty meat that's been put through a blender. But the cheeses are buttery and delicious. And the blueberry shortcake he also brought—two generous portions—is a real winner.

After they've eaten their fill, he props himself up on the soft-sided cooler, and Ariel fits herself under one of his arms, reclining on his chest. The musicians—dozens of them—are crammed onto the stage a hundred yards away. Their shiny instruments glow under yellow stage lighting, while a million moths and fireflies dart in confused circles near the bright beams.

Drew knows how they feel—dizzy. The classical music carries his drifting thoughts in a thousand directions. Falling for Ariel was never part of his plan.

But his worry cycle is interrupted when an older man plops a metal lawn chair down beside their blanket. His Bud tallboy opens with a metallic scrape, and then the man takes a loud gulp.

Ariel's eyes flip up to find his, and they share an implicit eye roll.

When he'd set out the blanket, it was just the two of them alone at the edge of the crowd. But the place has really filled up by now. It's wall-to-wall picnic blankets. So they can't move away from their neighbor, even if they weren't too comfortable and lazy to take action.

When the guy lets out a loud belch, though, they both shake with laughter.

It's all fun and games until Drew glances up to see him eyeing Ariel. Tonight she's wearing a cute little red sundress and strappy sandals. Her bare legs are tanned from the summer sun, and he has the inappropriate urge to punch the guy just for checking her out.

He even has to clamp his jaw together to avoid saying something. Drew gives him a dirty look, just to make the guy aware that he's being watched.

The geezer opens his yap and talks right over the music. "Nice night, yeah?"

"Indeed," Ariel replies at a whisper that suggests she'd rather listen than talk.

But the guy can't take a hint. "Young women become old women, you know," he says, as if they're already having a conversation. "I bet that tattoo seemed fun, yeah? But no man wants that on a forty-year-old."

Drew unclenches his jaw and prepares to tell this asshole where he can shove it.

But Ariel beats him to it. "Oh dear," she says with loud, uncharacteristic sweetness. "You've got that a little wrong, sir. You see—I never wanted a tattoo. I got this one to cover up my medical tattoo—I had to get one right here, for my cancer treatment." She places a hand on the side of her calf, where a butterfly spreads its wings. "Bone cancer. Treated with radiation. I beat it for now, but it could come back."

She lifts serious eyes toward the old man and blinks away imagined tears. "I hope you're right that young women become old women."

The old man's jaw drops so low it grazes the gray chest hair puffing out of his threadbare T-shirt. Then—with more agility than he ought to have—he stands suddenly. He grabs his chair and hightails it through the patchwork of picnic blankets, making tracks for the other side of the grassy lawn.

A couple on an adjacent picnic blanket starts clapping avidly. "Well done! I hope that story isn't true, though?"

Ariel smirks. "Not a word of it. But he won't pull that shit again, will he?"

Drew almost can't breathe for laughing so hard. He buries his face in one hand and tries to quiet himself. They are, after all, at a concert. But it's just so damn funny. "God, you're so evil. I love it."

And I love you, too, he manages not to say.

"He had it coming," she whispers, settling against him again.

Eventually he stops laughing. He closes his eyes and listens to the singsong of the violins on the breeze. As the orchestra transitions from a fast movement to a slower one, she kisses the underside of his jaw, and he plays with her hair.

If he could bottle tonight, he would. He loves the weight of her on his body, and the way her fingers tease his chest. He's never been in a real relationship before. He didn't know a woman's hands could feel both familiar and arousing at the same time. He didn't know you could glance across a busy street and instantly find her in the crowd because your senses are tuned to her, like a radio station that comes in louder than others on the dial.

Lately, he finds himself cataloging all the little things she does. He doesn't want to forget any of them. The particular tilt of her head while she considers a drawing in her sketchbook. And the way she catches her top lip in her teeth when she's uncertain.

She's not uncertain right now, though. She's kissing her way across his neck to his throat. Then she snakes a knee across his thighs and moves even closer.

He catches her smooth knee in one hand and sighs as she props herself up on one arm and meets his mouth with her own. Unbidden, his fingers thread into her hair and hold her there so he can do the job right—taking over the kiss until they're both panting.

When she finally pulls back, they're still nose to nose, wearing matching expressions of naked longing. "Baby, you make it hard to concentrate on Beethoven-Mozart."

Her laugh comes quickly. "Which one is it again?"

"Both, I think. This song's a banger."

She touches her smile to his. "Take me home. My plans to thank you for this picnic aren't very family friendly."

He sits up and starts packing away their plates, because a guy can't really turn that down.

Not this guy, anyway.

Four hours later, though, he's lying awake staring at the ceiling.

This happens a lot. He has a lot on his mind.

Guilt, mostly.

He thought that revenge would taste sweet. Some progress on his mission should have been gratifying. And it's been a fruitful couple of weeks.

Yet the weight of it all feels heavier, not lighter.

From Edward Cafferty's computer, he gave himself access to the LiveMatch beta. And he did it in such a way that he can access the network from his personal laptop at home. So now he has a treasure trove of evidence that Chime Co. has been testing an incredibly dangerous piece of surveillance software in Lowden.

LiveMatch has turned out to be exactly what his buddy hinted at—a tool that allows law enforcement to tag and track citizens via facial recognition software. If a person walks past the camera at Kennedy Park and then walks past another one on Canal Street, the system will note their movements and save the data, whether that person is known to the police or not.

It's problematic even when used with good intentions. But the things the cops are doing with it are downright disgusting. Each officer can create his own watch list. Most cops are tagging known suspects with police files, which was the system's intention.

A few cops, though, have found grosser uses for LiveMatch. One cop has tagged a woman *wifey*, and he checks her whereabouts several times a day. Hopefully she's his actual wife. But still. And then there's a cop with a watch list called *MILFs*. Every face on the list is a different brunette captured outside a public school.

The cop checks it every night at ten or eleven p.m. Drew feels sick thinking about why.

The effect is that LiveMatch is equally useful for finding criminals as it is for stalking.

Last evening Drew began composing a letter that he'll eventually send to a handpicked list of journalists who cover technology and privacy. He's including screenshots, dates and technical specifications.

But he's not done yet. He still has to nail Officer Ward for stalking Amina, and for accessing Ernie's private camera.

That footage could only have landed in the cop's hands one of two ways—if someone at Chime Co. gave it to him or if he had a judge's warrant for it.

If it was an inside job, Drew will probably never find it. It would be a proverbial needle in a haystack. And since the camera is already offline, the haystack will have been deleted.

But if the cop used a bogus warrant, Drew can still find it. He's taken the risky step of downloading all the Chime Co. police warrants for the weeks leading up to Amina's death.

They aren't sorted by geography, so he's had to slog through hundreds of warrants on pdfs from judges all over the country, one by one.

Quietly, he sits up in bed. Sleep isn't happening. So he swings his legs over the side and reaches for his crutches on the floor.

His small living room is lit by moonlight as he opens his laptop on the sofa. He has about two hundred more warrants to read before he's finished. But tonight could be the night.

After reading the first twenty-five, he gets up and fetches himself a soda from the fridge. It's past midnight, and before he settles back in to read, he closes his eyes to listen to the soft sound of Ariel sleeping in the next room.

Every good moment is a gift, Ernie used to say. And he finally understands how true that is.

Opening his eyes, he refocuses on the task at hand. The cold soda fizzes on his tongue, and he says a silent prayer of thanks to Ernie. *Thank you. I've got this. I won't let you down.*

With his free hand, Drew opens the next file on his hard drive and double-clicks the document.

As it resolves on the screen, the first words he sees are **Shawmut Street.**

26

ARIEL

I don't sleep at all the night after I hear from the cemetery. The next morning, I call in sick to work. I text my uncle.

Ariel: Woke up with a sore throat.

The office manager shouldn't disappear the day after a move. This is not cool.

But I can't function. Not really. It takes all my energy just to smile my way through the preschool drop-off. After that I climb back into my bed and hug the pillow. And that is where I stay for another hour or two, drifting in and out of sleep.

Drew comes to me in my dreams. He invites me on another picnic in the park. But this time when he opens the cooler, there's nothing inside it at all. "I can't stay," he says. "I have to go. You know that. I warned you."

I wake up sweating and agitated. It took me years to deal with Drew's death. I'm not equipped to handle the idea that he might be alive.

Or maybe he's not. Round and around we go. My uncle had responded within minutes:

Ray: So sorry! You did look tired last night. Get some rest and don't worry about a thing!

I drag myself out of bed and google the hell out of Fayetteville cemeteries. There are dozens, it seems. But some of them have been shut down for years. And then I hit on the idea of calling a funeral home and asking a helpful person's opinion of where my friend might have been buried in late 2017.

That narrows down the list quite fast, and I end up making five calls. And each time I reach another cemetery, I brace myself.

"I do apologize, but we do not show an interment for Andrew Miller or Jay Marker during that year or the next."

That's what I hear five times in a row.

Nobody asks me why my friend had two names. They are all unfailingly polite to the anxious woman with the strange request.

But nobody has ever heard of him.

My next move is to try to find a death certificate for Jay Marker in North Carolina. But you need to know which county they died in. And the precise spelling of their first name.

Frustrated, I nudge my phone off the bed, hug my pillow tightly, and sleep again.

That afternoon, Buzz has a friend over. But I've forgotten all about it until I wake up at two o'clock to the sound of two kids' voices instead of one.

"Ariel?" my mother is calling. "We're here!"

Hell. I stagger off the bed, still half-asleep. "Coming!" I croak. I swipe a brush through my hair and smooth out my wrinkled T-shirt.

But I catch my reflection in the bathroom mirror as I pass down the hall, and there's really no way to disguise the pillow crease down my face.

Still, I lift my chin and descend the stairs as if everything is fine. "Hi, guys!"

My mother gives me a head-to-toe inspection and then frowns. "Are you all right?"

"Sure, just a little tired. Took the morning off from work to catch up on some sleep."

Her frown deepens. "They wanted chicken fingers for lunch," she says in a way that conveys disapproval. I can't tell if it's the fried food or the fact that I look hungover.

"Thank you for that," I say as graciously as I can.

"What are we going to do?" Buzz chirps. "Can we go to the museum?"

He means the Children's Museum, which is always throbbing with people. The floor is sticky and the din is overbearing. Picture a rave, but with preschoolers drunk on juice and freedom instead of intoxicants.

But his eyes are full of hope, and we don't host that many playdates. "Maybe," I say quickly. "Let me just talk to Grandma . . ."

My mother is already holding out her car keys. "Go ahead. I was going to spend the afternoon in the garden. It's time to transplant my tomato seedlings."

Buzz and Kaden, his friend, let out whoops of joy.

So I guess I'd better find some juice boxes and hand sanitizer.

The afternoon is survived by not really having to interact with anybody. I trail Buzz and Kaden from the water play area to an arts and crafts station, and then I watch while they climb and slide through a vertical structure that reminds me of those tubular hamster homes advertised on the pet channel.

But Buzz is happy. He makes me a picture frame by gluing dried flowers onto a wooden rectangle. I offer to carry it while it dries, treating it like a delicate treasure.

"This one is for my mom," Kaden says, handing me a similar frame. "And this one is for my daddy. I put rocks on his."

Buzz leans over and studies Kaden's work, and I wonder what he's thinking. Everyone else seems to have a daddy. Except him.

It's hard to miss something you never had, my mother says sometimes.

But she's wrong. I wanted a dad even when I had one. And the older he gets, the more questions he'll have.

I used to know exactly how I'd answer them.

Worn out from all the excitement, Buzz falls asleep early tonight. That leaves me sitting in front of the TV sipping wine and feeling wobbly and alone.

I hear a car pull into the driveway. My windows are open, so I also hear Ray tap on my mother's kitchen door and then let himself in. One day soon I'm sure they'll announce that he's moving in. Her house is nicer than his, and closer to the office.

Plus, if she sold this house, we'd be uprooted. And I just can't see my mother doing that to us.

Another sip of wine down the gullet. I flip bleakly through the Netflix offerings, looking for something to distract me from my troubles. But nothing appeals.

It's maybe ten minutes later when I think I hear my mother's raised voice. I mute the TV and listen closely. She must have her windows open, too, because I can hear her and Ray arguing.

Anxiety rears its familiar head, and I tiptoe to my kitchen window.

"Why wouldn't you *say* something?" she demands.

"This is why!" Ray shouts back. "Because it doesn't matter. And you're making a big deal about it!"

Eventually I realize I'm holding my breath. When I was a little girl and my mother and my father fought, I used to cower behind my bedroom door.

She rarely had the courage to stand up to him. And when she did, it always ended with a sharp slap. And then sobbing, behind a bathroom door.

He didn't hit her, I told my therapist in college. *But he would say* anything. *And the slap was, like, punctuation.*

A slap is hitting, *Ariel. Men who strike their wives are abusers. And men who try to use* shame *and belittlement as weapons against their daughters are also abusers.*

I open my door and step outside to listen for the slap.

"Why is that police report here in this house?" Ray demands. "It's just going to upset you." He sounds aggrieved, but he waits to hear what she has to say.

"I want to know what happened!" she yells back. "It never made any sense. And now you tell me you saw him that morning?"

"We both saw him! He was *fine* when I was here. He wanted some files from the office, and he wanted his meds delivered. So he treated me like his gopher. It was just another day of dealing with his bullshit, until it wasn't anymore. I brought him his things, he didn't say *thank you*, and I never saw him again."

My mother says something too low for me to hear, and I take another few steps closer to the backyard. Their voices are coming from the second-floor den.

"I'm *sorry*, Imogen. I know you have questions. But we'll never know who rang the doorbell, and we can't ask Edward why he did the things he did. You're making yourself crazy with this."

Their voices drop to a level I can't make out anymore, and I finally remember to breathe. It takes me a few beats to realize that my mom is having a different kind of fight with Ray than she had with my father.

They're arguing, but it's a fair exchange. Just two people with some things to get off their chests.

It's not like the old days. I can unclench.

Or I would have, if I didn't see movement out of the corner of my eye. I whirl around, peering into the backyard shadows. And my heart seizes as I see a man walking toward me in the gloom.

He takes another step closer, and I finally recognize Zain's skinny form and wild hair.

"Jesus Christ," I hiss as he gets close to me. "Are you trying to give me a heart attack?"

"Sorry," he whispers.

I wave him toward my kitchen door, let him in and then close the door behind us.

"I came up Pine Street and crossed the yard as a shortcut. But then you were standing there, eavesdropping, so I held still, like a criminal." His expression is sheepish.

Well, I haven't exactly cornered the market on rational behavior myself this week. "What's up? Did something happen?"

"Yeah, you didn't show up for work today." He leans against the counter and takes me in. "Everything okay?"

"Not really." I move to the cabinet and grab another wineglass out of the cabinet. Then I take the bottle out of the fridge. "Want some?"

"Sure."

I pour him a glass and then retreat to the little sofa and flop down on it.

Zain follows me, choosing the chair and setting his backpack down next to it. "Do they fight like that a lot?"

I shake my head.

"It sounded like they're arguing about the day your father died."

"Yeah, I noticed that. My mom is having some kind of . . ." I don't even know what to call it. ". . . Attack of conscience. Like she could have done more for the man who abused her. And Ray doesn't want to hear it. I mean—I wouldn't, either."

Zain cringes. Then he pats the top of the bag. "I got the third tape last night and made myself a copy. Been waiting all day to tell you about it."

"Sorry. Was it easy to find?"

He nods. "Nobody had touched the copies at the server farm facility. Now I'm wondering if Ray's moving them was just a random thing he decided to do."

"Must be," I agree. "He went through everything in his office—ten years' worth of junk—and did a lot of clearing out."

Zain looks thoughtful as he props his feet up on my coffee table next to mine. "Are you actually sick with something?"

"No." I sip my wine. "Just feeling wrecked by life. And freaked out. I made a lot of calls to cemeteries today."

Those wild eyebrows lift. "And?"

I shake my head.

Zain blows out a breath. "So that entire obituary is possibly . . . made up?"

"Possibly," I say with gritted teeth. I once lived in a world where Drew was alive. And then I learned to exist in a world where he's dead. But I don't know how to navigate this halfway place.

It's like standing with one foot on either side of a fault line. During an earthquake.

"Okay, okay," he says softly, the way you'd speak to a feral animal. "My guy will do some digging. And I'm going to spend some quality time with this third tape. But let's also do this—let's make a list of every fact we know about Drew." He opens his backpack and pulls out a legal pad and a pen. "Real name, Marker. Jay or Jason. He's an army vet . . ."

"Probably," I grumble.

"Probably," he concedes. "Maybe I need three columns—things we know for sure, things we believe, and things that could be lies."

"Plenty of entries in that last column."

Zain ignores me and starts listing off items for his worksheet. ". . . Lived on Shawmut Street in Lowden. That's a fact. Played high school football. Blue eyes, brown hair. Hot body—never skips chest day."

I snort. He's working hard to lighten me up, but there aren't enough jokes in the world.

And most of the things I remember about Drew aren't useful. Like the scent of his skin, and the way he shakes his head like a dog right after a shower.

"Programming languages he knows . . . are facts." Zain keeps scribbling. "In the *probably* column we've got a college degree from UMass."

"Probably injured in Syria," I add. "Probably has a best friend named Woody," I add. "From Wisconsin. No—Michigan."

"Ah—that's a good one. Maybe we can find Woody."

"Oh, I've tried. Five years ago I googled the shit out of Woody. It's probably a nickname. He had a foster brother named Omar. I think."

He jots that down. "Okay, next. His computer password was Harrietta. Any new clues about what that means?"

I shake my head. "A search brought up a lot of elderly women's obituaries. I'll look again, though."

"Definitely do that." He clicks the pen on and off a few times. "In the fact column we can also add that he was the executor of the estate of Andrew Ernest Miller. Then he hired a lawyer . . ."

I sit up straighter on the sofa. "*Zain.*"

He looks up. "Yeah?"

"Wills are public record."

"Really? Are you sure?"

"Positive." After my father died, there was a newspaper article about his estate. That's how I learned that anyone can read a dead man's will. And it's also how I learned that he owned more than half of Chime Co. when he died. Fifty-nine percent, to be exact.

I grab my laptop off the coffee table and open it. "Jay Marker will be listed as the executor."

Zain gets up to circle the coffee table and plunk himself beside me.

I've already googled *Maine probate filings*. "Okay—the documents are organized by county. Lowden is in . . . Androscoggin County?"

"Probably? Yeah."

Hastily, I search *Miller*, and the screen lights up with a whole page of results. I start scrolling, until Zain jabs at the screen. "Right there!" he practically yells. "Andrew Ernest Miller, died in May of 2016."

I click, and four document links pop up.

Zain whistles as I choose a document at random. We both lean closer as a court filing resolves on the screen. "The court accepted the deceased's personal representative in August—three months after Miller died," Zain says. "And look—his signature."

In a terse cursive that I definitely recognize, he's signed: *Jacob L. Marker.*

Jacob. I say it a few times in my head, but it sounds like a stranger's name.

I wonder if he thought so, too, whenever I called him Drew. Or maybe lying to everyone you meet just gets easier after a week or so.

"*Jacob!*" Zain repeats. "We're going to google the shit out of that." He laughs like a child who's winning a scavenger hunt.

Meanwhile, my stomach clenches.

"But first . . . there are more documents. Click on the next one?"

Instead, I just hand him the computer.

Zain's hands race over the trackpad. "Okay . . . it looks like he didn't complete the probate process himself. He missed some deadlines during the summer he was here in Portland. And then Jacob L. Marker assigned a law firm to complete the probate process in 2017."

I take a deep breath and ask the scariest question of all. "What is the *last* document with Marker's signature on it, though?"

"Uh . . ." He scrolls and taps, while I start to sweat. "November first, 2017."

I exhale. That date is a couple of months after he ghosted me. But it's still a few months before his obituary appeared in that North Carolina paper.

In other words, it doesn't prove that he lived. And yet it doesn't prove that he died.

I know nothing, and it might drive me insane.

Zain is still talking, oblivious to my anguish. "Look—I think I understand now how he used Miller's social on his employment records at Chime Co."

"How?"

"Google says that the executor of a will is the one responsible for reporting a death to the Social Security Administration. If he didn't report it, they wouldn't flag Mr. Miller's Social Security number as deceased."

"That makes sense," I say. But in my head I'm repeating *Jacob Marker* like a mantra.

Where are you, Jacob? What happened to you? *Who are you?*

"This lawyer he hired . . ." Zain points at the screen. "The guy is right here in Portland, Ariel. You could call him and ask for a forwarding address for Jacob Marker. See what he says."

"No lawyer will give up his client like that," I point out.

"True, but . . ." Zain thinks for a moment. "Try writing Drew a letter, and send it to his lawyer with a request to forward it. If the lawyer is still in contact with his client, he'll have to pass it on."

The idea makes my heart race. "The lawyer is the last person we can name who interacted with him."

"*Yes.* He should be at the top of your to-do list. Let me just jot down his address . . ." Zain scribbles on his pad.

My head is spinning, and my next sip of wine tastes like acid.

Could it really be as simple as writing a letter?

Dear Drew, I don't know how to reach you, so I'm forwarding this letter via your lawyer. I still don't know why you faked your own death to get away from me, my family and Chime Co. But you should know that our son turned four in March . . .

God. And then what? If the letter reaches him, he might still ignore me.

Or the phone could ring, and it might be him on the other end of the line.

"Ariel," Zain says quietly. "You don't *have* to write the letter."

"No, I do."

"Okay." Zain gets up and moves back to the armchair. He pulls his own laptop out of his bag. But he hesitates before opening it. "I was going to dive into tape number three. Should I go home and do that? Or should I sit right here?"

I open my mouth to tell him to go. But then I hear myself say, "You can work here." As if I'm doing him a favor.

The truth is I just don't want to be alone right now.

Zain doesn't comment. He opens the laptop and plugs the tape into a port on the side. Then he leans back in the chair, making himself comfortable.

Feeling a little foolish, I get up to forage for snacks. It's really the least I can do.

Then I tuck myself back onto the couch with Zain's legal pad and a pen. And I try to imagine what kind of letter I'll write to Drew—and how much anger I'll let bleed into it.

I start scribbling.

Dear Drew, or Jacob, or whoever you are. If you're reading this, then you lied to me. You let me think you were dead, and I've been busy trying to make my peace, without ever really understanding why.

But there's one thing you need to know. Together we made a child. Buzz is a bright and kind four-year-old boy with your eyes. He looks a little more like you every day.

He is my greatest joy, and my only real priority.

If you are in the position to have a relationship with the best little boy in the world, then please reach out to me. If you can't do that or aren't sure, then maybe it's best if you don't respond.

Honestly, life was easier for me when I thought you were dead. I didn't have to wonder why you seemed to care about me and then stopped. And I didn't have to wonder why you would never be a parent to your child.

This isn't about money. We don't need you. I just want to do right by you and by Buzz, to the extent that I can figure out what that means. You have a choice about whether or not we're in touch, which is a lot more than you gave me.

That sums it up pretty well.

I contemplate the sign-off. *Sincerely, Ariel*, maybe. The letter is certainly sincere, even if I've left a few other sincere ideas out. Like—*How could you?* And *I thought you loved me.*

Or maybe: *Bite me, Ariel*. That has a nice ring to it.

When I send this letter, it will open me up to a whole new world of hurt. I might get a quick reply from the lawyer—accompanied by a death certificate. Or maybe the lawyer will reply that he doesn't know the whereabouts of his client.

Or I could just hear nothing, and spend the rest of my life wondering if he's out there somewhere, regretting me.

27

FIVE YEARS AGO, JULY

Fishing is very popular in Maine. There are literally thousands of unspoiled lakes and ponds. Summertime brings tourists flocking to the state with their Orvis vests and their tackle boxes.

That's why nobody will notice Brainz—in a beat-up canvas fishing hat—rolling to a stop in the quiet gravel turnaround of a public boat launch on the outskirts of Auburn. Even if his luxury car is a little shiny for this part of Maine.

He waits, air-conditioning blasting, until a familiar Ford truck with a canoe on the roof pulls in beside him ten minutes later. Then he kills the engine and steps out of the car.

The off-duty cop gets out of his truck and walks around to shake his hand. "Nice day, yeah?"

"Yeah," he agrees. "Hope the fish have been biting."

The cop snorts. "Oh, they're biting. That's the stupid thing about fish. They never learn."

"I hear that. How's work, otherwise?" He parks his ass against the car and assesses the cop. His name is Chuck Ward, but they never use names when they meet up. That was one of Ward's many conditions. He also picked this meeting place, a remote spot outside his jurisdiction.

"Work is good. Almost too good. Chief said that if my conviction rate goes up any more I'm going to get an award from the governor."

"Whoa, now. Let's not get carried away."

Ward laughs. "Don't worry. I'll step it back a notch. Can't help it if your new product makes my job a lot easier. Saves gas, too— don't even have to drive around looking for the perps. I always know where they are. When are you gonna roll it out statewide?"

"Not sure. Could be a while." His answer is a dodge, because LiveMatch isn't meant to become a regular feature at Chime Co. anytime soon. It's too edgy. And frankly too valuable.

He and TheBoss have bigger plans for it. A spin-off company. As a matter of fact, these fishing trips to meet Ward are funding his half of the start-up investment.

But Ward doesn't need to know any of that.

"I'm out of town next weekend," the cop says. "Training mission at the state barracks."

"Cool. No bragging about our little collaboration. *Either* of our collaborations."

He chuckles. "Not born yesterday, man. I read my NDA. Not looking to get sued by your asshole partner."

"Corporate spies are everywhere," he says, sounding like a nag. He often reminds the cops on the beta program about the threat of corporate spies. The irony being that it was just a convenient lie until Drew Miller turned up at Chime Co.

But Brainz and TheBoss have other reasons for keeping Live-Match quiet. They don't want to get blasted by the right-to-privacy crowd, for starters.

And there's also the delicate matter of moonlighting. It's not cool to use one successful corporation's private database to beta test your new start-up's tech.

"Help me with the canoe?" Ward says.

"Of course." He hops up onto the tailgate to lift the boat off its custom rack. He helps Ward maneuver it off the back of the truck and over to the little beach.

There's nobody in sight except a couple of kayakers out on the water.

Perfect.

They walk back to the vehicles. Brainz opens the back door of his Mercedes and pulls out his yellow tackle box. "Let's do this."

"Good plan." Ward pulls an identical yellow tackle box out of his truck's cab and carries it around to the truck's tailgate.

They trade positions. Brainz pops open the top of Ward's tackle box and peeks inside. It's lined with baggies, some containing powder and some containing pills. "Anything I need to know?"

"Naw. It's exactly like I said." Ward pops the top of the other box, which is full of bundles of cash in small bills. "Looks good." He riffles one of the packs with his thumb, but he doesn't need to count the money. They've been doing this for a year, and it's mutually beneficial to both their health and their safety if nobody gets fucked over.

"One more thing," Ward says. "I'm retiring at the end of the year. You're gonna have to find someone else to fish with."

"What?" He snaps the box closed. "You're pulling my chain." Ward is in his early fifties. Too young to retire.

"Nah, I'm past my twenty years. And the fishing has been so good this year that I don't need to chase assholes forever."

Fuckity fuck. Is this guy even real? Who walks away from the best side hustle ever?

"I'm sorry to hear that," he says in a low voice that doesn't betray his rage. This fucking cop is taking home a hundred grand a year in drug money. And he wants to take his ball and go home?

"It's time. I promised the wife."

Poor wife. She has no idea that her husband likes handcuffing teenage girls on their knees and then shoving his dick down their throats. "Won't you go stir-crazy? A man of action like yourself?"

Ward smirks. "I've got some new plans. Going in with some buddies to start our own private security firm. I'll get my pension, and now I also got a nice nest egg, thanks to you."

That's just plain infuriating. Even if it's basically the same plan that Brainz has—using ill-gotten resources to buy even more freedom.

The problem is that Ward is a dirty cop already, and he'll be an even dirtier PI. And if the guy ever decides to brag about their little business arrangement, he'll be a huge liability.

But that's a problem for another day. "I'll toast you on your retirement day," he says. "Better yet—I can get you some cheap cameras for your start-up."

"Sweet deal," Ward says, and Brainz smiles. *They'll be hacked, motherfucker. Keep your nose clean.*

"Hey, one more thing?" he says as Ward collects his actual tackle box. Fishing isn't just a ruse for him.

"Yeah?" The cop waits.

"You know this guy?" On his phone, he pulls up a photo of Drew Miller and enlarges it on the screen.

Ward snorts. "Sure I do. That's Jay Marker. Punk-ass foster kid who grew up in Lowden. Thinks his shit don't stink."

Jay Marker. Now I've got you. "Cool. Thanks. Have a good day on the water."

"I always do."

He shakes that asshole's hand and gets back into his ride. On the highway, he mentally counts his cash. This arrangement has been lucrative, but he'd been counting on another year's earnings.

It was low-risk, too—picking up product whenever Ward could skim it from a bust and passing it on to someone close to him who deals.

Easy money. And he needs it. Server time doesn't come cheaply. They'll need a lot of horsepower to scale LiveMatch up from its beta program to a thriving business.

Then the real payoff happens—he'll own half of a start-up in the fastest-growing tech on the planet.

28

ARIEL

When Zain shakes me awake, my eyes spring open. I sit up fast but I'm utterly disoriented.

"Sorry," he whispers. "But I found it."

"What?" I rub my eyes. I'm on my sofa, where I seem to have fallen asleep after writing and rewriting my letter several times.

"I found it," he repeats. "The warrant Drew was after."

"How do you know?"

Zain launches into an explanation, and I do my best to follow. "The second week of July, he downloaded every Chime Co. warrant request—with their video files—between two dates in 2016. He saved hundreds of documents to an external drive. And yet nobody flagged him. It should have triggered a notification to the security account at the very least."

As he talks, my gaze swims over to the clock on the TV. It reads 4:14. There's an empty coffee cup on the table in front of Zain, and the wrappers from several granola bars.

He's been pulling an all-nighter and watching me sleep.

I am a terrible friend.

". . . After that, he stopped logging in as other people, presumably because he didn't need to anymore. He was busy reviewing all these files on his own time. So I went in and downloaded the same set of files."

I blink. "From the live network? Isn't that going to leave a trail?"

Zain flicks his bloodshot eyes in my direction. "I've been doing that all along, Ariel. But I'm careful. I always expunge my activity from the log."

"Will anybody notice?"

He gives a guilty shrug. "Probably not. In the first place, I'm the one who'd notice. But I also know some tricks. Anyway, it took Drew two weeks to open the files one by one and find the right warrant. But I've found it already."

"How?"

"Optical Character Recognition." He flashes me a rare smile. "I ran all the pdfs through a scanner script, with *Shawmut* as the search term. And I found it. See?"

He stands up and plops his computer onto my lap, and then I'm blinking at a pdf of a judge's warrant. The Lowden Police Department requested video of Andrew Ernest Miller's home covering a four-hour period in the early morning hours of an April date in 2016.

The probable cause listed on it is "the sale of narcotics," and the suspect is Omar Isak.

Omar. Of course. "And are there drugs on the video?"

He pushes a thumb drive toward me on the coffee table. "I didn't play it. I thought you should do it."

"Good idea," I say immediately. "I don't want you to break the law for me."

He shakes his head. "I'm not scared, Ariel. But if this video badly violates a young woman's privacy, it should only be viewed once. And probably not by me."

"Oh."

Oh.

"I'm gonna go now," he says, taking his laptop back and closing it. "There's a folder for all the warrants on the thumb drive, too. Disconnect your computer from the internet before you look at anything, yeah? Just being paranoid."

"Okay." I close my hand around the drive. "You're sure Drew found this?"

"I'm sure," he says, zipping his pack closed. Then he grabs his granola bar wrappers and shoves them in his pocket. He crosses to the door and pauses with his hand on the knob. "Let me know what you find?"

"You know I will. Go home and take a nap."

"I'll sleep when I'm dead," he says. And then he goes out into the predawn gray, closing the door behind him.

It's four thirty now. I lock the door and turn off the lights. I tiptoe upstairs with the thumb drive in my hand.

After changing into a sleep shirt and brushing my sticky teeth, I bring my laptop into bed with me and shut off its Wi-Fi connection. I plug Zain's drive into the port and open it up.

He's given me the warrant document. There's also a file with basic metadata that shows when the warrant was processed by Chime Co.

And then there's the video file itself. I mute the volume on my laptop and double-click on the video.

Doorbell videos have a certain look to them, and it's a little creepy. The lens is curved into a fish-eye shape for breadth of field, which causes visual distortions. The straight lines of the Shawmut Street porch railing are rendered as curves, like a fun-house mirror. And since it's nighttime, the camera's straining light sensors wash the color out of the scene, rendering it in shades of gray.

The frame contains a back porch, lit by a fixture on its wooden ceiling. The corners darken into shadows, and there's a small lawn beyond. That's where the young people gather—on the grass. There are probably a dozen teenagers milling about, most of them holding beer cans. One kid has a soccer ball under his foot that he keeps kicking into his friends' shins.

If there are drugs at this party, I can't see where. Nobody is even smoking.

I advance the video with a nudge of the mouse. And then I do it several more times. Nothing much changes, but eventually the crowd drifts into the house, one by one.

A skinny guy in baggy shorts—probably Omar—gathers up all the beer cans in a trash bag and then disappears around the side of the house.

Just when I think the whole show is over, the back door opens. Two young people emerge from the house—a boy and a girl. He's tall and lanky, with a basketball player's build and a Celtics jersey. She has a heart-shaped face, beautiful big eyes, and closely cropped hair.

The two of them linger on the porch talking. It's like they can't quite stand to separate, until eventually the young man puts his hands on the girl's hips.

She lifts her chin, and the camera catches the shape of her shy smile. When he leans in for the kiss, it's tender and sweet.

Tentatively, she closes her eyes and slides her arms around him.

He goes stock-still for a moment. I hold my breath, and then he kisses her again.

I slap the space bar and remember to take in oxygen. On the screen, a young couple is frozen in time, caught inside a moment where nothing exists in the world but each other.

Everything is still fine. But I'm afraid for them.

Once upon a time I was just like that girl. There's magic in trusting someone. Letting another person near you is the hardest thing there is.

And if she died because of this video? I don't even know what to do with that.

With a grim determination, I tap the space bar again. I speed up the video to triple time, because it feels less voyeuristic to watch them make out in fast-forward.

They stand there for a while, their hands wandering while they try every sort of kiss that it's possible for the human body to accomplish. I look away from the screen, taking only periodic glances while I wait to know how this ends.

At my next glance, they've made it over to a rattan-like sofa with cushions on it. The boy lies on his back, the girl spread out on top of him, her hands on his cheekbones, their mouths fused together.

I nudge the video forward and see a split second of a blow job in progress. *Yikes.* Then I nudge it again and . . . cringe when I see a lot of full-on nudity. With a swift click to the X in the upper corner, I kill off the whole window.

My little carriage house is completely still, except for the drumming of my heart. It's tempting to delete the poor girl's video right off the thumb drive. Nobody should have their privacy invaded like this.

There are those who would blame the girl for forgetting about the camera. And sex on one's back porch is just a terrible idea. These teens weren't careful. They didn't think.

But they're *teenagers.* At that age, I did stupid things by the dozen, and mostly got away with them. Just lucky. Really lucky. It's hard to live in a world where cameras are always watching.

It's not just a teenage problem, either. Maybe we're not wired to think like this—as if the whole world is our stalker.

I tab over to Drew's obituary and gaze at the photo again. Once again I have the eerie sensation that I'm following him around, looking over his shoulder.

He needed to know why this girl died. And now I do, too.

Okay. I get it. You tried to do what you thought you had to do.

Did it work? Did you fix the broken things?

Or did you just accidentally break me, instead?

"Mama?"

I startle violently at the sound of Buzz's voice. He's standing beside my bed in his pj's, his small face in a frown. I glance at the clock, which reads 5:04. "Are you okay? It's not morning yet."

He scrambles up onto my bed. "Who's that man?"

"What?" I turn back to my screen, as if somehow it has changed. My heart begins to pound. "This man?" I point at Drew's face.

"Yes. With the line here." He reaches out and traces a finger down Drew's facial scar.

Oh God. Buzz is staring at his father's face. And I don't know what to say. I never wanted to lie to him. But I'm not ready to try to explain his father while caught off guard in the predawn hours. "He was a very good friend," I whisper.

And I'm a horrible mother. I'm sorry.

Buzz pauses, his short finger still on the screen. "He was Uncle Ray's friend."

"Hmm?" I remove Buzz's hand, holding it in my own, as if I can erase this moment. And how badly I'm fucking this up.

"Uncle Ray has that man on his computer, too."

"*What?*" My blood stops circulating. "Where? When?"

Buzz looks up at me with solemn eyes. Then he raises his short arm and points in the direction of my mother's house. "On the screen. In the kitchen."

My pulse throbs at my throat. "The *same* man? When was this?"

"It was soon." He yawns.

Chills climb up my neck, and I close the laptop with a snap. Then I reach down and stash it on the floor. "Come here, baby." I shut off the bedside lamp and flatten myself onto the bed. "Let's have a nap before it's time to get up for school."

He plops down on my pillow, rolling immediately onto his side and snugging his little butt up against me.

But my eyes are wired open, my heart thudding. Why would my uncle have Drew's photo on his laptop? Maybe he recognized the doorbell text my mother got. She's probably been nattering about it all week.

If that's the case, though, then he lied to her about recognizing Drew. He said he didn't know who it was.

Unless he's uncertain. I recognized Drew in that photo immediately. But my visual memory bank of Drew has a lot more to go on than Ray's would.

And when did Buzz see this photo? *Soon* makes no sense, but little kids aren't good with time. At all. Even if Buzz had said *yesterday* or *a long time ago*, it could mean anything.

Buzz lets out a sleepy sigh, and the sound turns my heart rate down, as if on a dial. I close my eyes and try to match my breathing to his. There are few things more relaxing than a sleepy four-year-old in turtle pajamas.

But my mind still churns.

29

FIVE YEARS AGO, AUGUST

The week after he's seen the video, Drew isn't great company.

He takes Ariel to a movie the next Friday night and spends much of it deep inside his own rage. They eat dinner at a loud seafood restaurant, and he does his best to keep up his end of the conversation.

She doesn't seem to mind that he's quiet and moody. If anything, she holds him a little tighter while they make love.

But he can feel himself slipping away from her already. Some of the distance is his own distraction, and some of it is him pulling back intentionally.

He needs to finish his mission. Amina and Ernie are waiting for justice.

The following weekend, Ariel heads to Boston for a big art fair with her friend Larri, and he is almost relieved. On Friday night he kisses her goodbye in the stairwell of Chime Co. and watches her walk away.

On Saturday, he spends the day as Jay Marker, renting a car with his real driver's license and heading north on the highway. When he gets to the Lowden exit, he feels Ernie's absence in the pit of his stomach.

The streets are the same. But *nothing* is the same.

He finds Omar working a kids' summer day camp at the same youth center where Ernie pushed teenaged Jay to take a job.

"You got any news?" Omar asks immediately when he spots Jay at the fence.

"What, no greeting? What would Ernie say?"

Omar rolls his eyes in his skinny face. "Hey, Jay, how's it hanging?"

That isn't much better, but he lets it slide. "I'm well. And I have a couple questions for you. When are you done here?"

"Gimme half an hour. You can shoot with us." He hooks a thumb toward the net. "If your leg can take it."

Well, now he *has* to shoot hoops, just to prove that he can. And it works pretty well, possibly because all the other players are four feet tall and he doesn't have to do a lot of pivoting on his prosthetic.

"Old man's still got it!" Omar calls when he sinks a three-pointer.

He smiles in spite of himself, because that sounds like something he would have said to Ernie back in the day.

When Omar is done, they get into the rental car and Jay drives them to a fish-and-chips shack one town over.

"Why we all the way out here, Jay?" Omar asks as they sit down at a weathered picnic table.

"There really are eyes all over the fucking place in Lowden," he says. He took a chance already that LiveMatch would ID him playing basketball with the kids. "You weren't wrong about that. It creeps me out."

Omar's dark eyes narrow. "How do you know?"

"Research," he says. He hasn't told Omar where he's working in Portland. Nobody can know.

"Any word on selling the house?" is the kid's next question. Omar knows that he'll get a little money from Ernie's estate. The will divided it up among all the former inhabitants of Shawmut Street.

It's Jay's job to sell off the place and determine how many of Ernie's foster kids are eligible to receive a share. The will gives him full discretion to hold the payment back—either temporarily or permanently—from anyone "whose lifestyle would not be made healthier by a sudden cash windfall."

It's a lot of responsibility. For his trouble, he's supposed to receive a double share—the extra as payment for settling the estate. But he doesn't plan to keep that extra money. He doesn't feel he's earned it.

Not yet, anyway.

"The sale can't go through until Halloween at the earliest," he tells Omar. "You don't need to look for a new place yet. Did you get the front hall painted?"

"Yeah, and I got proof. Hang on." Omar shoves a fry in his mouth. Then he pulls out his phone and shows off some photos of the entryway.

"Nice. And you used a drop cloth, right?"

"Of course. Wasn't born yesterday."

He was, though. Practically. Omar is only nineteen. And when Jay leaves Maine behind in a few weeks, he's leaving Omar, too.

Shit.

Pulling his wallet out, Jay hands him two hundred dollars in twenties. "Your next job is deep cleaning the kitchen. Start with the backsplash."

"The . . . what?"

"The tiles on the wall behind the stove and the sink. They've built up grease over the years. Use Soft Scrub and a toothbrush. Then use a sponge on the underside of the wall cabinets."

"Okay, sure." He pockets the money.

"There'll be dust on the light fixtures. It has to go. Just be very careful if you take any of them down to clean. Maybe kill the breaker first."

"What, I shouldn't stick my finger in the socket?" Omar grins. He's going to miss this little asshole. He really is.

"That all?" He takes a big bite of fish. "Thought you had something to ask me."

"Yeah." It's just that he's been avoiding it. "Tell me again about the video that upset Amina. Ernie told me some things, but I want to hear it from you. Tell me everything you remember."

Omar puts his piece of fish down and looks immediately ill. "Why?"

"Maybe I can prove that video exists. And now I want to figure out how the cop got it."

"How?" Omar demands. "Cop would never tell you."

"I know some hackers" is his answer. "Guys I went to school with."

"They can hack the *cops*?" His eyes go round.

"Maybe," he hedges. "Tell me what Amina said about it."

Omar starts wiping his fingers individually with the napkin. "I don't like talking about it."

"I'm sure you don't. But what if Amina needs you to?"

The kid looks three years younger when he glances up. And scared, too. "Don't know what good it will do."

"Let that be my problem. Come on. Tell me."

Omar drops his head. "It was after school when he showed it to her. Maybe a week after the party."

"When was the party?"

"Uh, April? And it was muggy for April. That's why we hung out outside. Seemed fun. We lit a fire in the barbecue. Odie brought some marshmallows. There was beer, too."

He nods, trying to keep his face neutral. But his neck is tingling with foreboding. He knows how this story ends, and he knows he won't enjoy hearing it.

"Amina and the girls stayed inside, mostly. But her girls left first, and her boyfriend went inside to hang with her."

"Hang with her?" he repeats.

"Yeah, Netflix and chill. But then me an' Cedric went in to watch TV, and I guess they wanted their privacy, because they went outside. I thought he was leaving, but he didn't. And Amina didn't come back inside." Omar swallows.

"Where were they?"

"On the, uh, porch. On that couch. She forgot about the camera." His eyes are cast downward.

"When did she remember it?" he asks gently.

"A week later the cop calls her over to his car window. On our own street. He did that a lot. She always tried to ignore him, but he didn't give up."

"What did he say to her when this happened?"

He swallows hard. "'Come here, pretty girl. I got something to show you.'" Omar averts his eyes. "She probably knew he could make a scene. So she went over to talk to him."

"And then what?"

Omar sighs. "I shoulda done something. Anything. Way before that."

"Hey, no way. This is not Blame Omar Day. Just tell me what happened."

"Ward talks to her. With that evil smile of his. Then he holds his phone out the window to show her the screen."

"Is that something he'd done before?"

Omar shakes his head. "Nah. He just used to talk to her and

smile like a creeper. This was different. And she had a real bad reaction. She freaked, but quiet like. Then she turned her back on his
ass and came right back to the sidewalk."

"You ask her what happened?"

"Of course I did." Omar shakes his head. "I said—*What did he
show you?* And she said—*Something nasty.* But she was really shook
up after that, you know? After that, she stopped coming out of her
room except for school. Then she stopped going to school. It was
bad. Ernie was so freaked. He asked me to try to talk to her. Figure
out what happened."

Omar takes a slow breath. It's mean to ask him to relive this,
but it could be important.

"So I knock on her door, and I sit down on her bed, and I ask
her why she's so upset." He puts his head in his hands. "She said—*I
did what Ward asked me to, because I thought I had to.* And I asked what
did she mean? And she told me—" Omar swallows hard. "He asked
her to get into the back seat of his car with him. To, uh, blow him.
And she did it."

Jay's stomach drops. "Holy shit. You didn't tell Ernie that, did
you?"

He shakes his head. "She made me promise. And it's, like, the
last thing she ever asked me to do, you know?" His dark eyes are
glossy with unshed tears. "And then she said—*Now he'll never leave
me alone. He has a video of me and my boyfriend. From the back door camera. And if I don't do what he says, he's going to send it to everyone in school.*
Then she started crying real hard and told me to leave her room. So
I did." His voice cracks on the last word.

"Aw, man. I'm sorry." Jay puts a hand on Omar's shoulder and
squeezes.

"She was dead a few days later. I didn't know she was going to do that."

"Of course you didn't. It's not your fault."

It can't be, because it's Jay's fault. He's the one who sent the cameras to Ernie. *Here—fight fire with fire. You can keep a log of how often he cruises slowly by your house.*

All that did was give Ward ammunition. He got a goddamn *judge* to give him the video, and then he used it to blackmail the girl.

"Where did the cop get that video?" Omar asks.

"I'm going to find out," he says, dodging.

This thing could blow up in his face, and this time he's not taking anyone else down with him.

30

ARIEL

"Now, this is living," Ray says, spinning around in his new leather chair. "I even have a *view*." He spins one more time and then gazes out his new fifth-floor window, where the harbor is visible in the distance. But when he turns back around to face me, he looks tired. "How's your new desk?"

"Fine," I say automatically. "Nice." Although I've barely sat down there yet.

I'm not seated next to Zain anymore, either. He's sharing an actual office with another programming manager.

"Do you think the Kittery PD will find us up here?" Ray asks, looking at his watch. "Hester wondered if we need a sign on the old conference room door. *Friday law enforcement meetings are now held on the fifth floor.*"

"Already done. Plus there's a new sign in the elevator." Even in my anxious, exhausted state, I have anticipated this problem.

"Good, good," he says distractedly. "And the coffee service . . ."

"On its way up."

"Thanks, Ariel."

"No problem."

On my way out of his office, I take another assessing look at Uncle Ray. Did he really have Drew's picture up on a monitor in my mother's kitchen? The question is going to torture me. And I can't think of any way to find out.

Swinging by the printer, I remove a stack of Ray's presentation materials, properly collated and stapled. The title: "Top Ten Reasons to Join the Law Enforcement Support Program at Chime Co." I carry them into the new conference room, with its slick wood table and big round window. Then it's time to meet the delivery person who's brought coffee and pastries for our guests.

The food is beautiful. The room is beautiful. And I just want to flip all the tables.

A girl *died*, and nobody at Chime Co. gave two fucks about it. Oldest story ever.

I head back to my grand new desk and leather chair. It has that new-chair smell, but I don't really care.

Since I saw Amina's video, nothing gives me joy.

When the client arrives a half hour later, most everyone on the fifth floor heads into the meeting, the door closed behind them. Only then do I sag into my new chair and check my phone for messages.

Nothing from Zain, or his PI.

I don't know what to do with myself. The workweek ends in just a couple of hours, and I'm no closer to finding any answers.

My eyes flick toward the conference room, where Ray is holding court. He's always been the family charmer—the nice boss—the fun guy. When I look at him, it's still hard to imagine him as a liar.

And yet there's no good reason he would suddenly move the backup tapes, or have Drew's picture on his monitor.

A girl could drive herself crazy like this.

From my pocket, I pull a printout of the warrant Zain gave

me. I've nearly memorized every word on the page. It's signed by a judge named Arnold Kerry. The name tickles my memory, but I've read this warrant a thousand times, which could easily be the root of its familiarity.

What I need is another look at the warrant system. I need to know if there's anything weird about the pattern of this judge's activity.

The warrant desk is downstairs, though, and undoubtedly staffed by some junior person who drew the short straw to work the busy Friday evening shift. There's no logical reason for me to butt in and ask to look something up.

But Ray's computer would have access to that system. The CEO can see literally anything from his terminal. Zain told me that.

A quick glance at the conference room shows that Ray's meeting is in full swing. So I pick up a couple of file folders and stroll with them into Ray's office. Once there, I pause to move a potted plant closer to the window, where it can get better light.

Then I sit down at Ray's terminal and nudge the mouse, waking up the monitor. I tap in his password—remembered from the time he called me from a remote meeting with an urgent need to access a file. That was three months ago, at least.

But *boom*. I'm in.

My stomach fizzes with anxiety as I reach for the mouse. The first thing I do is locate the icon for the warrant system. That takes me a couple of sweaty minutes. But once I find it, the search for Judge Arnold Kerry is quick. The screen lights up with a string of warrant requests.

A *lot* of requests. Judge Kerry signed warrants fifty-three different times in a period that spans just over two years. But it ends abruptly after summer of 2017. In fact, the last warrant the judge signed was August tenth of that year. That's six days before Drew disappeared.

A chill climbs up my spine.

Fifty-three warrants sounds like a lot, but I have nothing to compare it to. I don't have the names of any other judges handy, either. And I don't have a lot of time to snoop. In fact, when I turn my chin to check the progress of the meeting, someone is staring at me from right outside the glass.

I nearly have a heart attack until I realize it's Zain. *What are you doing?* he mouths.

Go away, I say, and then make a shooing motion. Even if I'm a clumsy snoop, his standing there staring at me isn't really helping.

He beckons urgently, and I close the window on Ray's computer. I pop out of Ray's chair, pick up my file folders and then leave the office.

Zain waits for me at our new, deluxe coffee counter, stabbing the buttons on the espresso machine as if they've offended him.

"Seriously," he whispers when I reach him. "What the hell are you doing?"

"The judge," I whisper back. "Arnold Kerry. He requested video fifty-three times in two years. But then he stopped *right* before Drew went away."

"Is fifty-three a lot?" Zain asks, removing the steaming cup from the machine.

"I don't *know*. But aren't you curious?"

"Yes," he whispers. "But you're leaving a trail, Ariel. You're going to get caught."

"Got a better idea?"

He nods. Then he glances toward the conference room before

speaking. "We need to see the warrants for the five years *after* that judge disappeared. Then we'll know if the pattern was strange. Let me do it. I know tricks."

I simmer inside, because I don't like the way he's taking over.

But nobody knows the system like Zain.

"Your job is to google Judge Kerry," he says. "Figure out if he retired or died in the summer of 2017. Why does he go off-grid?"

"Fine."

"And, Ariel? There's a reason I was looking for you." His eyes dip, and my pulse quickens.

"Yeah?"

"Yeah. My PI friend isn't going to send us a bill this time. He, um, couldn't find any evidence of our Jacob Marker's existence after 2017."

My stomach takes a dive.

"He said that either he's dead or he's really good at staying hidden."

"Oh." I make myself inhale. "Is that . . . Can people just disappear?"

Zain fiddles with his coffee cup. "It's possible. But you'd need to be really smart about it. You could never have a bank account or a credit card in your own name. Or a driver's license."

But he faked his identity before. My impulse is to argue like a child who doesn't want to hear that Santa isn't real.

"Did you send your letter to the lawyer?" Zain asks.

I shake my head. "Not yet." I typed it up, but haven't been able to bring myself to mail it.

Zain sets his coffee down. Then he actually pulls me into a hug.

My surprise is overridden by how badly I need a hug. Zain smells like coffee and cinnamon gum. And my eyes feel unexpectedly hot.

But then I look up and see Hester watching us through the conference room window.

I step back, and Zain gives me a soft look. "Take it easy this weekend."

"You too," I choke out.

Then I go back to my desk and google the judge. But it doesn't go well. There's a lawyer named Arnold Kerry in Ireland. And a judge named Armand Kerry in Arizona.

But I can't find an Arnold Kerry in Maine.

Of course I can't. Because nothing about this is ever going to be easy.

On Saturday, I leave Buzz with my mom for a couple of hours and head over to the studio. After another night of wine, Google, and sleeplessness, I'm going stir-crazy.

"So now I know everything about judges and warrants. Some judges are elected, and some are appointed." I pause after I tell Larri this and puff more air into the glass bubble on the end of my pipe. I blow until my lungs burn, and then I swing the pipe in a slow arc to let gravity exert some force on the shape. "But either way," I pant, "it leaves a paper trail. This Judge Kerry? Nothing on Google. Don't you think that's weird?"

Without waiting for Larri's answer, I hustle back to the glory hole and heat my piece again.

She watches me from the worktable in the corner, where she's sorting a pile of colored glass chips. "Honey, I'm tired just looking at you. And you lost me with this judge stuff about a half an hour ago. Now I'm just nodding and smiling."

"Whatever. But I'm telling you it's *weird*. You'd think if a judge was busted for taking bribes, he couldn't just vanish. There would have been a news story."

"What if he just retired?" Larri asks. "Why are you so sure that the judge was taking bribes?"

I carry my piece over to the marver and gently flatten one side against the steel. "It turns out that fifty warrants for one small police force is a *lot*. He only wrote three warrants outside of Lowden. And there aren't any judges in the system with as many warrants as he had, and in such a short period of time."

"Hmm" is all Larri says.

I carry my piece back to the flame, then repeat my steps, once again pressing a flat plane into its curved surface. Glass hates to be square, so it's a lot of work keeping the material just soft enough to get the square shape that I'm looking for, but firm enough to hold the edges.

"You know . . . I've met judges," Larri says. "I've stood in their courtrooms with Tara, holding my breath while they made their arrogant decisions. Those people aren't easily intimidated."

"Fair. But what if he was greedy?"

"Cops don't have a lot of money to pay out bribes."

"I've thought of that," I grumble, crossing the studio again to warm my piece. And she's right—how many bribes could a dirty cop really afford? Unless the cop had something dirty on the *judge*. "It could be a blackmail situation."

This time she only lifts her eyebrows at me.

"That sounds like a bad *CSI* episode, huh?"

"You said it, not me."

Her skepticism only drives home the fact that I don't really know a damn thing about law enforcement. Or, as my father used to put it, *You don't know a damn thing about anything*. He lived to point out my ignorance about the world. Bruising my self-esteem was his favorite sport.

The studio is the only place I feel truly competent.

"You're not going to give this up, are you?"

I look down at the bottle I'm making. "The shape is coming together."

She cackles. "I meant the thing with Drew. You're going to keep picking it until it bleeds."

"Probably." I've already dug into the rest of the warrants that Drew initially downloaded. Other judges' names appeared with far less frequency than Kerry's. And they were all googleable, too.

"Look, there are really only three reasons that people screw up their lives," Larri says. Then she ticks them off on her fingers. "Money, drugs or sex. It's always one of those three things."

"Not always," I grumble. "What about burning curiosity and deep-seated neediness? Those are my issues."

"Nah," Larri clucks. "You haven't actually screwed up your life yet. You're just making yourself a little bit obsessed. Besides, I like this new version of you—the one who shares things, and admits that she's just as messy as the rest of us."

I trot back to the glory hole without dignifying that with a response.

"Don't give up, Ariel. You won't feel satisfied until you get some answers. And that bottle is going to break if you thin those walls any further."

"Just doing things the hard way. Like I always do."

She laughs, but I'm dead serious.

Drew's obsession is now my obsession. I want to know what he found.

And I want to know if lying to me turned out to be worth it for him.

———————

Three hours later I'm walking to the grocery store, sweaty and tired, but in a good way. I always feel better after some time in the studio. The furnace just burns the frustration right out of me.

It didn't help me find Arnold Kerry, though. It's like he doesn't exist.

Wait . . .

I stop walking so suddenly that a jogger curses and has to swerve around me.

"Sorry!" I'm already pulling out my phone and hitting Zain's number, though.

"Good afternoon, this is Zain," he says when he answers.

The formality is confusing. "Wait—are you in the office? On a Saturday?"

"Yes, and how can I help you?"

Hmm. "I just had a big idea about the elusive judge Arnold Kerry. What if you were a dirty cop, and you wanted to put warrants through the system whenever you felt like it, what do you need?"

Zain doesn't answer me at all for a moment. But the background noise changes, and I hear a door click closed. "A judge. You need a really friendly judge."

"Right. So what if you just created one? Wouldn't that be handy?"

"I don't get it."

"Hear me out. What if we can't find him because *he didn't exist*? If the dirty cop *invented* a judge, he could get access to any video he wanted."

"Whoa," he says, sounding a little breathless. "You think Judge Kerry didn't *exist*? But what good is that? The warrants wouldn't stand up in court. What would be the goal?"

"Oh, that's easy—the godlike power to do whatever the fuck you want. Like stalking high school girls, or violating people's privacy. And inventing a judge is cheaper than buying a judge. You could just cheat your way into the information you need, and then figure out how to get a *real* judge to give you a warrant for it. If you even need one. If you're just getting videos for your own personal bullshit, court doesn't matter."

"Jesus, that's an evil idea," Zain says. "Which probably means you're onto something. Do you think it was an inside job at Chime Co.? Setting up a judge in the system is kind of a pain in the ass."

"Think about it—we don't exactly train our people on the ins and outs of the judicial system. It's just a form on a screen. You've worked a shift or two on the warrant desk, right? If someone gave you a bunch of faked paperwork, would you actually be able to tell?"

"Probably not," he says quietly.

"That's why it's the perfect scam. You could fake that shit pretty easily if you knew how the warrant system at Chime Co. worked."

"Okay . . ." he says slowly. "I see what you mean. You'd just copy another judge's documents . . . And fake a notary's stamp. The more I think about it, the better this theory gets."

"At Chime Co., we'll put anyone with a pulse on the warrant desk. Even me. Whoever set this up would be someone who understood that."

He grunts his agreement.

"Zain, can you find the *first* warrant for this judge? Wouldn't we be able to see who set it up in the system originally?"

"Of course," he says. "But not right now."

"Really? Lot of people around the office on a Saturday?"

"Actually, yes. We're in the middle of a messy intrusion. I got a three a.m. call about a denial-of-service attack. We're still trying to get back to a hundred percent."

"Oh shit. Sorry."

"Yeah, it's been a long day already. And also . . ." He drops his voice another decibel. "I think someone else in the system is watching all my database requests. They're being mirrored to a dummy account."

"Wait, what?" I don't speak geek, but that sounds bad. "Are you saying that someone is spying on you?"

"Feels like it."

"*Who?* Is it Ray?" Zain is already suspicious of my uncle.

"I don't know if it's him," he whispers. "Some of the time stamps don't add up."

"What do you mean?"

"It's complicated." He sighs. "But it also doesn't matter. I need to see this thing through. I like your theory about the judge, but that's a *huge* system vulnerability. What if there's more of them?"

"Oh shit."

"Exactly. This is officially my problem. I'm responsible for ensuring the integrity of the database. And if I get fired for doing that, my next employer wouldn't hold it against me."

"God, don't get fired," I whine. "Who would I complain to?"

He laughs. "Let me go. I've got a network to fix before I try to verify your evil theory."

"Okay, later."

He hangs up.

31

Drew is hunched over his laptop in the living room, his crutches on the floor beneath him. Again.

He's so close. He's *this* close to nailing down the whole scam, and shutting down Chime Co., too. His notebook is open in front of him—the one Ariel can never see. It's filled almost completely now with notes about the so-called warrants signed by Judge Kerry.

When he figured out that the judge who signed the warrant was fake, his first reaction was awe. So simple. So smart. And so revolting.

Unfortunately, there's a further twist—every single warrant request is signed by a Captain Whitman. Who also does not exist.

The *balls* on these guys.

He still doesn't know who's at fault, though. Someone smart enough to exploit the system.

Someone who knows a lot about both Chime Co. *and* law enforcement. Edward, probably. He has a God complex. And arrogant people make stupid decisions. Just ask any soldier or sailor who's had the misfortune of serving under an officer like that.

But Edward doesn't have the programming chops to create LiveMatch by himself. So there must be someone else, too.

Like Ray. But they'd never conspire together. They'd kill each other first.

He keeps digging. Hell, he barely sleeps anymore. Instead, he sits here on his secondhand sofa, pawing through his notes. Looking for the trail of bread crumbs.

He yawns so hard that his jaw cracks. Maybe sleep will finally come now that he's exhausted himself. He slides the notebook between the futon mattress and the frame. Then he closes the browser on his computer.

His email inbox comes into view. Two a.m. is the wrong time to check emails, but his eye snags on the subject line of the most recent message. **ID Verification Request.**

Everything goes still inside him as he reads those words a second time. It's the message he's been dreading since his first day in the office.

He opens the email.

Dear Mr. Miller,

Our payroll service has identified a discrepancy in your employment record. We've entered 11/1/88 as your date of birth. But a routine reconciliation has returned a DOB of 11/1/48 from the SSA.

Please bring your Social Security card into work on Monday so that we can copy it and send it back to the payroll company as proof of your DOB. Your next paycheck will unfortunately be held up until we can straighten this out.

Thank you very much,
Shiela Banks
Assistant Manager of Human Resources

He closes the lid of his laptop. As if that will make the message disappear. He knows better, though.

It's over. His time here is nearly up.

His pulse thumps in his ears as he leans down and plucks his crutches off the floor. He rises to cross the darkened room to the bedroom doorway.

There's just enough moonlight filtering in through the windows to illuminate Ariel's sleeping face. Her brow is furrowed, as if sleeping requires great concentration.

And maybe it does. She hasn't shared her nightmares with him, as he hasn't shared his own.

He regrets everything they haven't done yet.

Easing himself down on his side of the bed, he lowers the crutches to the floor without making a sound. Then he stretches out beside her. He isn't sleepy at all now. Not when there's still time to gaze at her in the darkness.

After a moment, though, gazing is not enough. He palms her bare shoulder and runs a hand down her arm. He needs to memorize the shape of her body curled under the sheet, and the softness of her moonlit skin.

She stirs, rolling toward him. And it's all the invitation he needs to pull her against his chest.

"Are you okay?" she asks groggily.

He doesn't want to lie again. So he dodges the question by kissing her neck instead. And then her shoulder. And then her breast.

Her fingers wake up and begin to weave through his hair. He closes his eyes and soaks it in. He'll miss this so much that it already hurts. Even as he kisses his way up her body to claim her mouth, he keeps his eyes slammed shut. If he looks at her, she'll ask again if something is wrong.

Just everything.

He doesn't want to talk, so he kisses her hungrily instead. This is the only way he can be truthful—with his questing hands and his tongue and his knee nudging her legs apart.

Her body softens beneath him, as it always does. Her arms tighten around him. Their kisses are bottomless as he slides inside.

The room is quiet, but his thoughts are loud. Even his heart beats out a rhythmic plea. *Love you, miss you, need you.*

And a new thought, too.

I'll come back for you.

Wait for me.

32

ARIEL

That night Buzz and I make pizza together.

He slathers his dough with an unreasonable amount of sauce. And then he covers every square centimeter with pepperoni and olive halves.

I'm not a fan of olives. But when Buzz was two, he ate an entire dish of them that my mother had set out for her book club.

Look at him go! she'd said. *You never know what kids will like.*

But Drew loved olives.

My pie has onion jam, serrano ham, feta and arugula. And last time Buzz tasted the arugula and made a face that accused me of child abuse.

"Let's go, pal," I say when they're ready to bake. "We're borrowing Grandma's oven. You don't even have to put on your shoes."

He perks up. "Can I watch a movie on the big TV?"

"Sure."

I let myself into Mom's kitchen, because she's off to an art film with her friends, and because her Wolf oven gets a lot hotter than mine, which makes for a crispier crust.

Buzz is in front of her TV before I can even set the oven to preheat. But that's how we roll on a Saturday night.

While I wait for the oven to reach five hundred degrees, I wander around the main floor of my mother's immaculate house trying to keep my mind occupied. Then I climb the stairs to scope out her bedroom bookshelf. She always gets one or two hardbacks from Book of the Month, and I am free to help myself after she's finished reading.

As I peruse the new offerings, my eye snags on a gray file folder on the bedside table. It's unlabeled, but even as I reach for it I know what I'm going to find. *Incident report: August 16th 2017.*

Opening it up makes me feel queasy. But this doesn't belong to my mother. The police shared it when she asked. They'd probably give it to me as well.

I listen to make sure that Buzz is still in front of his movie, and then I flip to the first page.

It's grim reading. My mother's 911 call was logged at a few minutes before one p.m. The transcript is brief. *It's my husband! He's died. He's dead. At his desk. Oh my God, he's gone.*

The dispatcher asks her the obvious questions and summons the first responders to the house. They arrive only seven minutes later.

When I flip the page, I find Officer Barski's report.

Fifty-nine-year-old man found slumped over his desk. Declared dead at the scene. Entered into evidence: one prescription pill bottle found on the desktop, prescribed for the deceased. Dated the day before his death. Pill count listed as thirty. Twenty-six remained in the bottle. Also found: a yellow index card with times and dosages listed on it. The last entry is "2 pills 10a."

Behind this, I find a photo. I wasn't ready for that. But there he is, head down on the desk, cradled in his arms. And I feel sorry for him, maybe for the first time ever.

God. I flip the page again and find a photo of my dad's index card, where he recorded what he'd taken. It was probably the last note he ever made on one of those cards.

Beyond that, I find the coroner's report. I skim like crazy, because I don't need to know how much his heart weighed. And the notes at the bottom sum everything up. *Cause of death: heart failure due to opioid overdose.* Then there's a bunch of technical jargon about the drugs. I have to read it three times before it makes sense.

But the gist of it is this—the two half-dissolved pills in his stomach don't seem to match the dosage listed on the pill bottle. If I've understood it correctly, there are two possibilities—either he took too many doses in a short period of time, or he took different, stronger pills than the ones found on the desk.

> *In either case, the overdose could easily be accidental. The lack of a suicide note raises the odds against intentional self-harm.*

That's diplomatic.

I replace the file at her bedside. And on my way back to the kitchen I pause in the door to my father's office, a room I've avoided my whole life. The place is untouched, basically. The computer is gone, but the books on the shelves and the diplomas on the wall are unchanged.

My eyes land on the desk, where my father died on the same day that Drew came to this house.

Perhaps Drew stood right where I am now. And said what, though?

It's hard to picture my father ending that conversation with a handful of painkillers. The man had an ego the size of New England. Whatever Drew had on him, he would have gone down swinging.

The office is so tidy that I feel as if I'm on the threshold of a shrine. My mother must have asked Maria to keep it clean, in spite of its emptiness.

I wonder if Uncle Ray will reclaim this space if he moves in. Or maybe that's too much like *Hamlet* even for him.

The oven beeps to tell me it's reached 500 degrees, and I hustle off to put our pizzas in.

After dinner and a lengthy story time, I put Buzz to bed. Fifteen minutes later he's still whistling to himself up there.

Meanwhile, I'm on my hands and knees, cleaning my kitchen and wondering where Drew would go to start his life over if he had the choice.

The obituary said North Carolina. There's a big army base down there. It's certainly plausible. But if the death notice was meant as a misdirection . . . ?

Above me, my phone buzzes with an incoming call. I sit back on my heels and grab it off the counter. **Zain Calling**. "Hey," I say a little breathlessly. "Find anything?"

"No, but I thought we might try something," he says. "What are you doing right now?"

"Trying to get cookie crumbs out from under my dishwasher."

"Why are there—? Never mind. Can you come into the office?"

"*Now?*"

"Yeah. I know it's late, but we had to take some systems down to restart and refresh. So there's a lot of unusual traffic on the network. It's a perfect time to"—he drops his voice—"find an old video of the warrant desk. Nobody will notice it in the logs."

Oh. "You mean, like a needle in a haystack moment?"

"Exactly," he says. "Let's do this."

"I can't leave. Buzz is in bed upstairs. I'm not going anywhere."

"Oh shit," he says. "I didn't think."

I shake my head and ball up the paper towel I've been using. "You go ahead and watch it. If it's really that interesting, take a video of the monitor."

"Oh, genius! I'll put you on FaceTime. Maybe in, like, ten minutes? It will take me a while to find the archive and then sort through the video files. Actually, I need the date . . ."

"It's November sixth, 2015."

Zain cackles. "Look who's been sitting in the front row of class."

"Shut up."

"I'll call you back in ten, on a video call."

But then he doesn't. I'm waiting on my couch, TV off, just listening to the silence. Buzz's whistling has stopped, too.

Fifteen minutes pass, and then thirty. My mind wanders to the last day I saw Drew.

And, to be accurate, I barely saw him at all. I was asleep in his bed, naked, because he'd woken me up in the middle of the night for sex.

My phone alarm went off while he was drying himself after a shower. I squinted sleepy eyes in his direction, and he sat down on the bed and played with my hair for a minute. It had the unfortunate effect of making me drowsy. And I dozed off when I should have been getting up for work.

He kissed me on the hair, though, before he left. Still, I didn't get up. I don't know why. I'll always regret it. That was my last chance to talk to him, and I had no idea.

And now I'm sitting here mooning over it like a dummy.

I pick up my phone and text Zain a GIF of an old woman in a rocking chair.

Ariel: This is me, waiting for you. Did you find it?

Zain: Actually let's not do this right now. I'll see you in
the morning.

Ariel: Why?

But he doesn't answer.

I'm so frustrated I could spit. But I head upstairs, where I'll undoubtedly waste another hour googling judges and Jacob Markers all over the interwebs.

33

FIVE YEARS AGO, AUGUST

On the morning it's all going down, Brainz makes sure to go into the office bright and early.

If anyone ever checks the log, they'll see he tagged into the building around eight and logged into his terminal shortly after.

But he's not getting any ordinary work done. Not with The-Boss messaging him every five minutes.

TheBoss: Is the kid at work yet?

Brainz lifts his eyes and scans the room. Drew Miller's chair is empty.

Brainz: Not yet. But it's early. You make the drop yet?
TheBoss: Going in now.
Brainz: Keep me posted.

Brainz hopes TheBoss doesn't chicken out. He's been a solid partner so far. But you can never know for sure. Some people talk big but then panic when shit gets real.

Today's mission is twofold—get rid of Drew Miller, and clear out all the evidence that little asshole discovered on the network.

Actually, the mission is threefold. Brainz has an extra little surprise planned. But TheBoss doesn't know that yet.

Everything is on a need-to-know basis. And TheBoss nearly lost his mind when Brainz finally laid out all the dirt on Drew Miller. "A spy? We have a fucking spy? I'll fucking kill him."

That's pretty much what Brainz had expected. So he was ready with a plan. "It's personal with this kid, so we're going to shut down the LiveMatch beta ahead of schedule. If he was just a corporate spy, we could fry his ass. But this isn't going to go away."

TheBoss fumed some more. But in the end, he agreed. They'd sit on LiveMatch for a while, until the dust settled. After all, it will be just as valuable six months from now.

Then he laid out a very specific plan for removing the evidence from the Chime Co. network. Just to cover their tracks.

"You are a goddamn genius," TheBoss said when he'd heard the whole thing.

That's true, of course. But he's also a nervous genius at the moment. Because ten long minutes tick by before he gets another response from TheBoss.

TheBoss: Done. Went even better than I expected. Visual confirmation that it's going to work.

Brainz keeps his expression impassive, but inside he's pumping his fist.

Brainz: Well done. So you're on your way downtown now?
TheBoss: Yes. ETA 5 minutes. 10 with parking.
Brainz: Got it.
TheBoss: Just hope that was necessary. It's a little too cloak-and-dagger for me.

Ah, there it is—a moment of uncertainty. But that's okay. What's done is done.

Brainz: It won't blow back on us. You wanted insurance, right? This is the only way to buy it. And I know you're going to enjoy this next part.

TheBoss: You bet I am. Lock the kid out now. I'm OMW.

Brainz: Roger.

He pulls Drew Miller's profile up on his terminal and edits his permissions.

Brainz: Kid's profile locked. Get into position.

TheBoss: Will do.

TheBoss: This will be very satisfying.

Brainz: Not as satisfying as punching the guy in the throat. But it's something.

TheBoss: LOL. Pretty violent for a nerd.

He has no idea. But it's better this way.

34

ARIEL

Monday morning again. Tension headache. Clingy Buzz. And Maddy in a blinding white skirt, reminding me once again to buy the watermelons.

"Got it," I insist.

"Good work!" The pitch of her voice is like a knife through my head. "We'll gather at eleven tomorrow to set up."

Tomorrow? *Hell.*

"See you then," I say with a tight smile. Then I open my phone and set a reminder for tomorrow. *Borrow the car, buy ten watermelons! Set up @11.*

This is Buzz's last week of preschool until September. My schedule is about to shift into summer mode, when I work even fewer hours and spend more time with Buzz. Lazy days at the wading pool and ice cream cones.

If I don't crawl out of my skin first.

Everyone at the office is grumpy. The network is still laggy, and there are a lot of closed-door meetings about the weekend attack.

Zain has barely come out of his office at all. When I text him for a coffee break, he replies that he is too busy. I press him.

Ariel: Are you sure? I went downstairs and fetched your favorite coffee mug. The round one with the stupid joke about binary.

Zain's only response is:

Zain: Thanks.

Impatience bubbles up inside me.

Ariel: Zain! Did you watch the video? Who was on it?

He doesn't answer me. At all. Even at lunchtime, he doesn't emerge. He's avoiding me.

I'm going to burst. So I keep myself busy hauling away empty boxes from our move. It's about as emotionally fulfilling as rearranging the deck chairs on the *Titanic*, but I have a good view of Zain's office door so I can pounce when he emerges.

Still, I'm full of nervous energy. On one hand, nothing has changed for me. My job is the same as it ever was, making regular deposits in my checking account. My child is happy. Tomorrow we'll be serving watermelon to the preschool-aged population of Portland, Maine.

On the other hand, I'm not the same person at all. One text—a single burst of electrons lighting up my phone—and nothing will ever be the same. And I can't stand it anymore. The unknowns are killing me.

Leaving my work behind, I grab my handbag and trot down the stairs of the building. I hoof it a block or so until I find a mailbox.

From the depths of my bag, I pull the letter I wrote to Drew's lawyer. It's already addressed and stamped, so all I have to do is open the mailbox's hinged door and fling it inside. When I let go of the handle, the mailbox closes with a metallic thump.

There. It's done. Whatever the fallout, I'll survive it.

I retrace my steps toward the office building. And out walks Zain, punching the crosswalk button before glancing guiltily up and down the street.

When he spots me, he flinches.

"Zain!" I hustle over there before he can step off the curb.

"Hey. I was just running out to pick up my Bagel Tree order."

"*Seriously?* You waited for me to leave the office. You're ducking me. What happened to the video?"

He crosses his arms and scowls. "It's just a really bad day, Ariel."

"Answer this question to my face—did you watch that video this weekend? Who was on it?"

"Ariel, Jesus," he says with a red-faced scowl. "It's not about that. I haven't slept more than four hours in three nights."

"Uh-huh. Note the lack of a denial. I've had a lot of practice being lied to by men. I know what it looks like. So let's try again—did you watch that video?"

"You're not listening," he growls. "This network attack is bad, and it seems *personal*, okay? So I have to fix my shit before I can fix your shit."

At that, he steps off the curb and stomps across the street.

I watch him go. Either I'm a bitch, or he's a liar.

Actually, both could be true.

I look up at the office building, and the rage I feel for that place is so red-hot that I can't walk back inside. So I turn around and head for the only place where I still feel like myself.

I let myself into the empty studio. I change into an old T-shirt and check all the temperature gauges before grabbing a pipe and propping it into the warmer.

When I step on the pneumatic pedal that opens the furnace door, molten glass greets me with its orange glow. I dip the pipe into the blazing liquid and twist, forming a tidy ball of burning hot glass.

It's tempting to hurl it across the room, like a fire-breathing javelin. Right now I'd rather break things than make things.

Breaking things is so much easier. Just ask Officer Ward.

I put my mouth on the tube and blow. This is where I need to be—right here with the pipe in my hands. I'm going to stand here forever, blowing piece after piece. And never, ever think.

This works fine for about fifteen minutes, until Larri breezes through the door. "Look who's early!" she shrieks. "Great to see you, even if you look like hell. Did someone or something keep you up last night? Or are we just going for the strung-out look today?"

"That second thing," I mutter.

"You ready for a punty?"

I squint at the piece on the end of my pipe. "Sure. Thanks."

She puts the tool into the warmer and changes my playlist without asking.

But it's fine. I don't care.

I don't care. I don't care. It's my goddamn mantra.

"You want to talk about it?" she asks, fitting the punty onto the bottom of my piece.

"Nope. It won't change a thing."

She quirks an eyebrow at me. "It's been three weeks of hell over this guy, hasn't it? What would it take to get you to let him go?"

"I've already let him go."

Larri lets the lie pass. We fall into our usual rhythm. It's comfortable, and I imagine myself off the hook.

Until the damn door opens once again, and the person who steps through it is Zain. "There you are!" he says in a voice that assumes I'm not still mad at him. "You aren't answering my texts, and I have news."

"Kinda busy here," I grumble.

"No you're not," Larri argues. "That piece is ready to come off, and you've been hogging the glory hole anyway."

Zain squints at the glowing flames visible in the circular cutout. "Do you seriously call that thing a glory hole? Because, I gotta tell you—"

"We know!" Larri says cheerfully. "But feel free to make your jokes—you'll only owe a dollar to the dick joke jar." She points to the jar on the ledge. "What's your name? I love meeting Ariel's friends."

"I'm Zain," he says. "Ariel and I have been working on a little project . . ."

"Chasing down Drew?" Larri demands. "Or whatever the fuck his real name was? I'm gonna need you to work a little faster. The girl is a mess."

Zain blinks. "Uh, okay. Ariel? Can we talk?"

"Take her," Larri insists, waving a hand at me. "She's no good to me like this—all broody and dramatic."

I remove my goggles and grudgingly join Zain near the door. He opens it, as if to usher me outside, but I shake my head. "Here's fine. Larri is my best friend. She can't hear us anyway over that music."

"Can't hear a thing," Larri says unhelpfully. Then she cackles.

Zain gives her a nervous glance, then he turns back to me and drops his voice. "Look, I'm sorry, okay? I didn't want to admit it. But it was me on the video."

"Wait, *what*?" Shocked, I meet his sad eyes, and he looks away. "*You're* the one who set up Judge Kerry in the system?"

He nods, a contrite look on his face. "Obviously I had no idea."

Did you, though? I take a deep breath, wondering if Zain is playing me for a fool. But why tell me now? Unless he just assumes I'll never stop asking for that damned video. "So . . ." My mind spins. "If there was ever an investigation, they'd come after you?"

"Maybe." He shifts his weight. "But think about it. If you wanted to set up a dirty judge in the system, you'd let some rando do it for you, right? That's what I plan to say in court."

"Jesus." I rub my temples. "Do you remember who asked you to take that shift?"

He shakes his head. "I sat on the warrant desk maybe three times ever, and I don't even remember which time that was. So I can't say for sure who asked me to do it. Maybe Evan. Maybe someone else."

I take a deep breath. "So the video's a dead end."

"Yup." He clears his throat. "Sorry I snapped at you. But I saw it, and I felt so paranoid. Especially after the break-in at my apartment. And now this network attack seems personal, too."

"Why?" I demand.

His eyebrows knit. "Because of the way they got in. It would take me a half hour to explain . . ."

"Right." I sigh. "But you think someone is fucking with you on purpose?"

"Either that or I'm paranoid." He winces. "Listen—there was another thing you wanted me to look at—the breakup email. And I just did that as a peace offering."

"Oh." *Oh.* "Well?"

"Took me a while to find it. But I don't think Drew sent it. That email was spoofed from outside the network to look like a Chime Co. mail. There'd be no reason for him to do that."

"Maybe someone cut off his access," I point out.

"But so what? Spoofing is a pain in the ass," Zain says. "If they cut off your email access at work, and you still wanted to email a girl, you'd just break up with your gmail account."

"Oh, you sweet summer child," Larri says from the bench. "It's cute that you think that. But a guy breaking up with a woman in his personal email is just asking for a truckload of ARE YOU FUCKING KIDDING ME blowing back on him."

"Huh," Zain says. "I hadn't thought of that."

"You must never get dumped," Larri says. "Lucky."

"Whatever," he says with a sigh. "You'd have to *have* a boyfriend to get dumped."

Larri cackles. Then she points at Zain. "Do you like tacos?"

"Me?"

"Yes, you. I'm making tacos for Ariel tonight. You're invited."

I shoot her a look, because I don't remember agreeing to dinner. But she ignores me.

"I like tacos," he says. "If I can get my work done, I'll come."

"Cool," Larri says.

Zain turns back to me with an apologetic shrug. "I also spent some more time looking at our favorite fifty-three warrants. Every one of them was routed through a single cop's name—a Captain Whitman."

"Let me guess—he doesn't exist?"

"Yup." Zain shakes his head. "So that's another weakness—our system doesn't store the name of the *cop* in the database—only the judge. So we can't spot strange patterns. We've been too reliant on having the judges set up correctly."

"And we know how well *that* worked out."

"Honestly, this has been humbling. I thought I ran a nice, tight system. Now I'm worried I'll find more fake judges. It's the next thing I'm looking at before I can make a recommendation to overhaul the whole system."

"*Don't* take this to Ray. Not yet."

"Not yet," he agrees. "But eventually I'll have to. After I get a chance to pick through the whole system and document any and all fraud. But I'd never blindside you. You'll see everything I have, okay?"

"*Everything?*" I demand. "Promise me."

"I promise," he says firmly.

"We can't talk to Ray until we figure out why he'd let this happen. This judge thing could blow up the company. It wouldn't make sense for either Ray or my father to risk it. Unless we're missing something."

"I know," Zain says with a frown. "That's bothering me, too."

"There's only three things that men fuck up their lives for," Larri says from the bench. "Money, drugs or pussy. It's *always* one of those three things."

"Hey, that's awfully heteronormative of you," Zain says.

Larri snorts. "I like him! We're keeping him," she declares. "Tacos at seven. My place. Ariel will text you the address."

I sigh.

Zain puts his hand on the door, but doesn't push it open. Not yet. "Look," he whispers. "I know you're freaked out. And we're going to be careful. But don't forget why this matters—someday you're going to inherit Chime Co.—you and Buzz."

"Now, that's a dark thought," I grumble. "I thought you weren't trying to depress me."

He gives me that crooked smile. "Only you would say that about inheriting a potentially billion-dollar company. Don't ever change."

And then he's gone.

35

FIVE YEARS AGO, AUGUST

For Drew, walking into the office building that morning is a surreal experience. It's the beginning of the end.

He opens his desk drawer and drops his wallet and keys inside, the same way he does every morning. Then he takes his seat in his ergonomic chair. Even though he's planned for this, it's still weird.

What the hell does it mean that he might actually miss this place?

On that disconcerting thought, he shakes his mouse, and the screen blinks to life. But an unfamiliar text box appears on his screen where the log-in should be.

> Please report to HR at 69 Cross Street. You will need to
> provide the requested documentation before you can
> log back in to the system.

Well, fuck. He'd planned to stall. *The card is at my family home in Lowden. I can go there this weekend . . .* etc. But that's not going to work now, is it?

Okay. He takes a slow breath. Sometimes missions go sideways. Time to move to plan B.

Casually, he switches off his monitor so nobody will see that red flag on his screen. Then he slides the desk drawer open again, retrieving his wallet and keys.

He has no other possessions in this drawer, or anywhere on the desk. He glances around just to be sure there's not so much as a coffee shop receipt. But no, it's clean.

Like he was never here.

Pocketing his things, he stands up and moseys over to the project manager. "Dec, I'm sorry. I was just called to fill out a missing form in HR. They need me to run over to Cross Street. Should take me about an hour."

The guy makes a face. "Hurry, okay? We're starting on the new avatars today."

"Okay. I'll be back when I can."

He leaves the office, walking a couple of blocks to the nondescript brick building on Cross Street where the HR company is located. Inside, a balding guard asks his name.

"Drew Miller," he says easily. He's used to it now.

"Third floor. Room 306."

"Thanks." When the elevator comes, he presses the button for the third floor. The fact that Chime Co. outsources its human resources department is probably the reason he was able to pass himself off as Drew Miller in the first place. He's never been here before. His hiring was done by passing scanned images back and forth via email.

He pats his pocket, where his forged Social Security card waits. *Relax*, he tells himself. *It's just a bunch of HR nerds. Not the KGB.*

If they don't like his documents, he'll just play dumb. People don't expect someone who looks like him to use a fraudulent identity. White guys with blue eyes and a close shave can get away with a lot in the world.

The elevator doors open on three. There's a frosted glass door at one end of the hall with the name of the HR company on it, so he starts in that direction. But room 306 comes up first—it's a wooden door right off the hallway. He hesitates in front of it, and then raps once on the door.

"Come in," says a muffled voice.

He opens the door and steps into the room. It only takes a nanosecond to register the absence of a person behind the desk. Those battlefield reflexes kick in, and he's already sidestepping to get clear of the man who's hiding behind the door.

Time slows down. The door slams shut as Drew squares his body to his opponent.

It's Ray Cafferty.

Holy fuck.

"You're finished," Ray says with a sneer. "Hand over your ID and go home. If you do exactly as I ask, maybe you won't get arrested today."

It takes a colossal effort to keep his expression neutral while his mind whirls. Ray Cafferty is behind the warrant fraud? And Live-Match? He'd seemed far more interested in banging his brother's wife than colluding with dirty cops.

But now he's visibly angry. And that's good. An angry opponent is easier to outmaneuver than a calm one.

"Arrested for what?" he asks with an arrogant shrug. "I thought this was a paperwork problem."

"Fraud, for starters. And identity theft. Industrial espionage. Theft of digital property." Ray's practically spitting out the words.

"Uh-huh," he replies in a slow, monotonous tone that's guaranteed to irritate Ray. "If I were you, I wouldn't send the police to my door. And certainly not the FBI. If you accuse me of identity theft, the feds will get in on the action. I'll have some stories to tell them about you."

Ray's gaze is shooting bullets at him. "You're a young punk with no money and no job. I have a team of lawyers ready to shoot down whatever bullshit theories you're spinning. You think an overworked public defender would stand a chance against us? Is that a bet you're willing to take?"

It's a battle to stay calm. He's so fucking sick of bullies. "Tell you what," he says in the same slow cadence that ought to make Ray twitch. "You shut down LiveMatch by five p.m., and then delete Judge Kerry's profile. Do that and I won't email any of the thirty technology journalists on my list. There's a guy at the *New York Times* who I think would be particularly interested. Although CNN might make a bigger splash."

He watches Ray's expression carefully. There is no confusion flickering on his face. No surprise, either. Only rage. "Social Security fraud will put you in jail, Mr. *Marker*."

Ouch. It's very unlucky that Ray knows his real name. But it's not fatal. "I admit nothing. But if I'm in jail, I'll have lots of time on my hands to talk to journalists about Chime Co. And by the way, does your brother know that you're banging his wife?"

That's what finally sends Ray Cafferty over the edge. He steps into Drew's personal space and reaches out, as if to grab him by the shirt. Just like a junior high bully.

Dumbass.

Drew catches his hands and shoves him roughly against the wall, pinning him there. "Never grab a guy who's trained to kill you. Didn't the cops in your family teach you anything? Now I have to frisk your ass."

Then, before Ray has time to counterattack, he quickly pats him down.

No weapons.

"Get your *hands* off me."

"Look." Drew steps back from the glowering man, putting a safe distance between them. "You don't want to tangle with me. But I don't want to tangle with your lawyers, either. You want me to leave town? I'll do it. By tonight I'll be halfway to a buddy's place in another state."

"I don't ever want to see your face again. If you come back to Maine, I'll have you jailed," Ray growls. "And don't go *near* the office. Just leave."

"But I have to clean out my desk. And you asked me for my ID."

"*No*," Ray snarls. "Just get gone. Don't say goodbye to Ariel, either. You're going to ghost her just like the asshole you really are. No explanation."

That blow lands, but he tries not to show it. "Okay. But there's two more things you need to know." He holds up a single finger. "One, I already sent my buddy a thumb drive with everything on it. If I don't make it to the army base, he's been instructed on what to do."

He adds a finger. "Two, my leaving is conditional on one thing—Ariel is untouchable. If any harm ever comes to her, I'll be back before you can *blink*, fucker."

"Nothing will happen to her," he says through a clenched jaw. "She knows nothing."

"Keep it that way," Drew says. And since the conversation is over, he exits the little office without turning his back on the worst of the two Cafferty brothers.

He heads for the elevator, his mind spinning.

Ray is more dangerous than Edward. He's smarter.

This is bad.

As the elevator doors part in the lobby, he slips his hand into his pocket. There are two IDs in there now. His—because he lied about leaving it in his desk. And Ray's—because he unclipped it from the man's belt loop when he frisked him.

He has an hour, maybe two, before Ray realizes it's gone.

He'd better make the most of it.

36

ARIEL

I love my friends, but I'm not in the mood to hang out with Larri, Tara and Zain tonight.

On the other hand, I'm not in the mood to cook dinner. So I'm still weighing my options when I pick up Buzz from a playdate in our neighborhood.

His friend's mom greets me with a precise retelling of everything the kids did and ate since she picked them up from preschool at noon. It's a struggle to keep my focus on her earnest description of organic cheese and crackers and an art project involving homemade play dough.

"That sounds lovely. Thank you so much for having him," I say when she's done.

"He can come back anytime." She gives me a smile. "He always says thank you and helps clean up. Buzz is a delight."

"I'm so happy to hear that." And it's true. He's all the best parts of me and none of the ugly ones, and I certainly don't deserve him.

I would never say that out loud, but I'm privately, guiltily delighted anytime anyone praises my child.

"Tomorrow is the picnic," Buzz says on our short walk home. "You're bringing the watermelons, right?"

"Yep. Hang on—did Dicey's mom ask you to tell me that?"

He looks up. "She said you needed a reminder."

Oh, for fuck's sake. I don't know if I'm more angry that she recruited my four-year-old or that she's probably right. "Okay, Buzz. Thank you." We turn up the driveway. I'm just about to ask him how he feels about tacos at Larri's when I notice the door to my apartment is ajar.

I stop walking. It's not my imagination. That door is standing open a few inches. "Mom?" I call.

"Ariel?" Her voice comes from inside her own house, though, not mine.

Taking Buzz's hand, I open her door and stick my head inside the kitchen. "Hi! I had a question about borrowing the car tomorrow. But can Buzz visit with you a sec? There's something I need to do."

My mother steps into view. She's wearing a red linen dress and carrying her handbag. "I was just headed out to meet Ray for a cocktail and dinner."

"Just for a minute," I say firmly, looking her directly in the eye. "*Please.*"

"Sure, honey." Her expression is confused, but she goes along with it. She sets her bag on the counter. "Tell me about Dicey's house, Buzzy. What did you do?"

He starts talking, and I slip outside and head for my door. I give it a nudge with one knuckle. The door swings open, and I take a sharp breath when I see the mess inside.

My eye lands on the tipped-over trash can, and my first thought is *Raccoons?* That's who thrashed garbage all around our garage once when I was a kid.

But no. Raccoons don't open every single kitchen cabinet. And every drawer.

"Hello?" I call, like a fool. But the silence inside my place has the weighty quality of abandonment. And flies have already found the garbage. I think it's been this way for a while.

I step through to our little living room, which has also been tossed. The sofa cushions are helter-skelter, as if someone wanted to be sure there was nothing concealed beneath them. The books are toppled on the shelves, with some on the floor.

My gaze drops to the coffee table, where my laptop usually lives.

It's gone.

Shit.

Maybe a smarter girl would turn around and walk out. But anger rises inside me as I climb the stairs. This is so . . . *violating*. And the second level is much the same. All my bathroom cabinets are plundered.

And then I see Buzz's room. His toys have all been tossed out of their baskets. The mattress is askew on the bed. My little boy's stuffed animals are mashed into his rug.

Buzz will freak out if he sees this. I want to howl at the sky.

Pulling my phone from my pocket, I dial my mom. And when she answers a second later, I keep my voice low and calm. "Mom—don't scare Buzz. But someone has broken into our apartment and made a huge mess."

I hear a sharp intake of breath.

"Easy," I say quietly. "Can you give Buzz a video to watch? I'm going to have to call the cops."

"Of course," she murmurs. "Are you safe?"

"Yes, I promise. See you in a few minutes." I hang up.

Before I call the police, though, I take a deep breath and walk into my bedroom. And it's bad. Every drawer is ripped out of the dresser and dumped on the floor, along with the contents of my nightstand.

Hell. My vibrator is right there beside the bed, yanked from its case and *cracked*. Like someone beat it over a rock, or stomped on it with steel-toed boots.

I yank it off the floor and toss it back into the open drawer. Then I have to force myself to breathe. The violence is getting to me. A petty thief wouldn't bother with destruction. This just looks *mean*.

My gaze snags on my open closet door. With growing dread, I tiptoe over heaps of my clothing to peer into the closet, mindful not to touch the handle. Even in my terrified haze, I know better than to ruin any fingerprints.

The first thing I see is Drew's army uniform mangled on the floor. Several buttons have been torn off it. They are scattered on the closet floor, their threads tangled.

The jacket looks trampled. I'm on my hands and knees without thinking, gathering the buttons into the torn satin lining of the jacket. I fold it into a ball and gather it to my chest. Shaking, I stagger to my feet and back out into the bedroom again. My overturned laundry hamper is still more or less in place in the corner. I cross to it and place Drew's uniform in the bottom, for safekeeping. Then I gather a wad of my dirty clothes and drop them on top, concealing the dark blue fabric.

Think, Ariel. Who did this? What else did they take?

In the closet, the cardboard box of Drew's belongings is among the detritus on the floor. I lean over and place his copy of *The Hobbit* back into the box. Then I add the cigar box, the cuff links, the leather tray and all the other bits and bots.

My breaths are coming in gasps now. I shove the box back onto the high shelf where it had been before.

Then I walk out of the closet, pull out my phone and dial the police.

37

After leaving the HR office, Jay gets a cab at one of the hotels. He pays cash for the trip to Chime Co.'s brand-new server farm in a renovated mill building in Westbrook.

When he waves Ray's ID past the reader at the door, the light flashes immediately to green.

He's in. That was simple.

And then it's shockingly easy to convince the bored young man working alone here—a kid named Jed—that downloading some network data onto a thumb drive isn't that weird of an errand. "It's a sensitive matter, Jed," he says gravely. "Ray sent me here so I could review it privately."

When Jed frowns, he pulls out his ID and also Ray's, side by side. "He's hoping I'll be back inside of an hour, though, so if you're going to call him, make it quick."

Instead, Jed waves him toward an admin terminal and logs it in. "You know what you're looking for? My job is server maintenance—I don't really touch the archive."

"I'm good," he says. "Thanks."

First things first. He opens up the warrant archive and downloads every single warrant from 2010 onward. If there's anything more illegal in there, he can study it later. That takes fifteen minutes, and most of the free space on his thumb drive.

Then he finds the LiveMatch directory, but he can't open it. This terminal has no access.

Okay, that's a disappointment. But not much of a surprise. Edward's terminal is the only access point he's found so far.

Ray's machine will also have it, of course. He'd expected it to be either one brother or the other. Not both. That's where he really fucked up.

But he can't worry about that now. He's running out of time, with one more important task to complete.

Luckily, he finds the in-house security system in the first place he looks. He skims the directory for the camera feed that's trained on the warrant desk. Hopefully the videos are archived by date, or he could be here all day.

It takes a stress-inducing amount of time, but he locates the feeds from 2015.

Another glance at Jed. The kid is on the phone.

Shit. He has to get out of here. On the off chance that Jed called Ray just to check things out, it won't be long before the cops show up.

The moment he spots the file for November sixth, he copies it onto his thumb drive. There's no time to watch it now.

Later he'll put it all together in one incriminating package, wrapped up in a fucking bow. Ray is a fool to think he'd give up after one single threat.

As soon as the file is saved, he ejects the drive. Then he walks out of the server center without a word to Jed. The sun is shining. It's a glorious midmorning in Maine.

Yet everything about this moment is disorienting. He's unemployed, and a fugitive. He's standing on an unfamiliar block in Westbrook, Maine, his mission in tatters. Time to leave town and regroup.

He crosses a bridge over the river and turns onto Main Street.

He's uncertain of the direction he's headed, but he has to get away from the company property, in case Ray knows where he's gone.

He pulls out his phone and gets his bearings. His product manager—Declan—has peppered him with texts wondering where he is. The last one was only ten minutes ago.

That's odd, actually. You'd think Ray would have pulled him aside and made up a story explaining his sudden disappearance. Embezzlement. Security violations. Something that would make Declan blanch.

But Ray hasn't done that yet.

Head down, he trudges toward town, counting up all the different ways that Ray kept their meeting quiet. He'd called him over to the HR Center, for starters. It makes sense, though, to fire someone off-site if you'd like to prevent a scene in front of the other employees.

But maybe there's a better reason.

Maybe Edward doesn't know anything about this.

That stops him in his tracks for a second, literally. Because the idea requires another adjustment to his thinking. He's assumed that Edward—Mr. Law and Order—had been the one to give the Lowden cops their illegal advantage. And he found the LiveMatch gateway on *Edward's* computer.

But what if Edward isn't in this thing at all?

Walking again, he tries on that idea. The two brothers seem to genuinely hate each other. And LiveMatch was so buttoned down that most employees can't even see it. Crouching in a corner of the network like a dirty secret.

Ray is the programmer, though, not Edward. Edward probably never touches the majority of the network. He wouldn't even see it on his machine.

Yeah, okay. *Wow.* The whole damn thing might be Ray's doing. That might even be the point—to undermine his brother.

Oh my God. That is totally the point.

He might have even said that out loud. But every time he thinks he's seen the worst of the Cafferty brothers, there's always farther to fall. One of them is a giant asshole. And the other one is a pathological liar and a cheat.

That's beyond twisted. But it means that Drew has one more chance to set things right.

He pulls out his phone again and pulls up Edward's personal cell phone number. It's the only piece of data he ever took from Ariel, and now he's finally going to use it.

The phone rings only twice before a gruff voice answers. "Yes? Who is this?"

"Sir, my name is Drew Miller. I'm a programmer on the customer-facing app."

"The ex-military kid?"

"Yeah, that's me." And how fascinating that Edward knows his name—yet doesn't seem to know that he's just been fired. "Mr. Cafferty, I found a really egregious security problem in the warrant system. And it's already resulted in a crime."

"*Jesus.*" Edward lets out a breath of pure surprise. "You'd better explain."

"Sir, it's bad. And furthermore, it's an inside job. Can I come and show it to you? But not in the office."

"Christ." Edward clears his throat. "Does Ray know?"

He hesitates, because he made this call before he had time to decide how to play it. "Well . . . it's hard to say. There are reasons I haven't asked him."

"Fuck. *Really?*" he barks. "You think he has something to do with this?"

Tread carefully. "I can't say for sure, sir. But I'd like to explain it to you alone. If that's okay."

The ensuing silence is nerve-racking. But finally Edward speaks. "I'm working from home today. I live on Chadwick Street—"

"Yessir. I came to the party on the Fourth."

"Of course. I have a conference call in a minute. But meet me here in ninety minutes."

"All right," he says, checking the time. "So I'll see you at eleven fifteen."

"Miller—" he says gruffly. "This had better not be a waste of my time."

"It's not," he says firmly. "And I can prove it. Actually—while you wait for me, try to remember if you know a Captain Whitman on the Lowden police force."

"There's no Captain Whitman in Lowden," he says immediately. "I know all the brass up there."

Bingo. "I was afraid of that. Because Captain Whitman submitted fifty-three affidavits for warrants to the Chime Co. system. And that's just the tip of this iceberg. I'll be there in ninety minutes." Then he hangs up.

A sudden adrenaline spike propels him up the sidewalk, because a lot of things are about to happen really fast.

He needs to be ready.

38

ARIEL

We have a nice meal of tacos at Larri and Tara's kitchen table, and I do a remarkable job of staying calm in front of Buzz. I drink one of Tara's nonalcoholic beers and do my best to smile.

And it must be working. Buzz is shoveling chips into his mouth like it's his job, while Larri hums along to Joni Mitchell.

When Buzz finally gets up from the table, I fill my friends in as quickly as I can, with a quick, whispered conversation.

"God, honey," Tara says. "That's terrifying."

"Tell me about it," I whisper back.

"What does Zain think?" Larri asks. "And where is he? I thought he was coming tonight."

That is a very good question. "I texted him on the way over here, but I haven't heard back." And now I'm paranoid about that, too. "He's going to freak out when he hears they got my laptop."

Buzz materializes at my side. "Can I see Tara's guitar?"

"Wash those hands," I say, setting my fork down and preparing to supervise. "And only if she says it's okay."

"Sure, let's play some music," Tara says, getting up from the table. "I'm down."

After they head for the living room, Larri covers my hand. "Are you okay? You look rattled."

"I *am* rattled. This doesn't feel like an ordinary break-in. And I need to call Zain."

Larri gives me a pat. "You are really bringing the drama tonight."

"No kidding. Bet you're sorry about that speech you gave me a week ago—that I needed to learn how to ask for help. I'll do the dishes right after I call him."

"Go," she says, waving me off. "He needs to hear what happened."

I slip out the kitchen door and lean against the wood cladding of Larri's little old house. My phone is clutched in my hand, but I need a moment to just calm down.

At home, I called 911. But my mother called Ray, who immediately phoned the police on my behalf.

Less than ten minutes later, two detectives pulled up outside, at the same time as Ray. I was treated to VIP service by Portland's finest, all while Buzz stayed glued to *Moana* in his grandma's den.

I showed the cops around my little apartment. I pointed out the missing laptop, and the mess.

But I didn't mention the army uniform, because I wasn't about to explain it to Ray. And I wasn't forthcoming about the files on my laptop, either. Not until I can do some more thinking. And maybe talk to Zain.

After taking some photos, they allowed me to pack a few things I need for an overnight escape to Larri's house and for the picnic tomorrow.

"I'd rather you stay with us," Ray argued. He looked worried, too—the kind of worry that looked real.

"We already had this plan for tonight," I told him. "I'll see you in the morning. Actually—I might come in late. I'll need to clean my place up while Buzz is at school."

"I'll help," he said. "Your mother and I will work on it tonight."

"That's okay, I'd rather do it myself." The idea of even more people in my space made me shiver with dread.

He gave me a tight hug, and then I called an Uber to get us to Larri's.

I dial Zain, half expecting that he won't answer. But he does. "Hey," I squeak. "I thought you were coming for tacos."

"Oh, shit," he says with a laugh. "I got distracted. You didn't seem all that into it, either."

"I changed my mind after something happened at home. Are you sitting down? And don't freak out . . ."

"Great opener. I'm fucking terrified already."

"You should be. My apartment was searched and my laptop stolen."

"*Holy* fuck," he says before lapsing into a deep silence. And then, "Holy. Fuck."

"I know. This is bad, right?"

"They're gonna crack your laptop open in about seven seconds, Ariel. How much did you have on there? The warrants, right? *Fuck fuck fuck.*"

"But Zain, who's *they*?"

And a voice inside my head adds: *Is it you?* I think of that night after the renfaire when I handed him my keys to unlock my door. Could he have made an imprint of my key?

I can't tell if this idea is sharp or paranoid. I don't trust *anyone* right now. "If you think you know who did this, you need to level with me."

"We're making somebody uncomfortable, but I don't know who.

A Lowden cop? A Chime Co. employee? Someone is pissed at us. I just hope it's not your uncle."

That shuts me up for a second. But the mess in my bedroom—the torn uniform. It felt like an emotional cavity search. "I just don't think Ray did this. Not to my apartment. The destruction was . . ." I picture Buzz's toys scattered on the floor and shiver. "It was gross. If Ray wanted my laptop, he wouldn't trash his nephew's bedroom. He'd just steal it."

"Unless he was covering his tracks," Zain says. "Or he paid someone else to do it. Maybe to scare you."

The idea makes me feel ill. "Well, it worked. I'm scared."

He's quiet for a long moment. "If you need me to stop digging, I will. But somebody has to be told about the fake judge. What if there are more fakes? What if they're still active in the system?"

"But *who* in law enforcement?"

"Um . . . ?" Zain says. "I'll have to do some research. The FBI is in charge of cybercrime. Where are you right now, anyway? At Larri and Tara's? Are you safe?"

"I'm safe," I say, dodging the first question. I'm not in the mood to tell anyone my whereabouts.

"Do you need anything?" he asks softly.

"No. But thank you for asking," I say quietly. I *want* to trust Zain. But there's a reason I don't make friends easily.

Sometimes they lie.

"Let me know if the cops find anything. Are you going to change your locks?"

"Of course. Tomorrow, first thing. I'm sorry about the laptop."

"Don't be," he says immediately. "I just hate it that they got to both of us. Two robberies? It *has* to be connected. Be careful, okay?"

"You know it."

After we hang up, I go back inside and do the dishes with Larri. Then I draw a bath for Buzzy in Tara and Larri's clawfoot tub. The house is creaky and old, every appliance ancient. But it has big old windows and prewar charm.

There's a collection of candles on a table beside the tub, and when Buzz points them out, I light them.

"That's pretty," Buzz says, flattening his body into the water like an otter. "It makes the ceiling flicker."

I take a seat on the wood plank floor and prop an arm on the lip of the tub. Then I tilt my head up to see the spectacle on the ceiling. The candlelight is reflected in the water, so the ceiling ripples with light and motion.

Maybe Buzz will be an artist, too.

Or an astronaut, or a dinosaur hunter—those were the career ambitions he gave the preschool teacher on career day.

"It's almost time to wash your hair," I tell him.

Predictably, he wrinkles his little nose. "Five more minutes."

"Okay." I lean my cheek on my arm and watch him swim around Larri's tub.

Buzz is my first and only real priority. I will never let anything happen to him. And Drew—whoever he was and wherever he went—would never want his child to be snarled up in the Chime Co. mess.

Maybe I didn't know him as well as I thought. But I knew him well enough to know that.

There's trouble, he'd said. My heart aches to know how much he would have told me if I'd met him under the tree that day.

Will I ever know?

Do I even deserve to?

I put Buzz to bed in the guest room.

"Where are you going to be?" he demands after I read him some poems from a Shel Silverstein book that Tara says she used to enjoy more when she was stoned.

"I'll be right here." I pat the other side of the bed. "Next to you. But first I'm going to sit up with Tara and Larri for a little while."

"Are you going to watch a movie?" he demands, because FOMO is real.

"Nope. Just grown-up talk, and then I'll brush my teeth and come to bed."

"Okay," he says grudgingly. "Am I going to school tomorrow?"

"Of course. It's picnic day." And I will show up with ten watermelons if it kills me. "Good night, my baby."

"I'm not a baby."

"But you're *my* baby."

He grins.

Out in the living room, Larri is pouring out a pot of chamomile tea. I drape myself on the beanbag chair.

"What can we do for you?" Larri asks.

"You've already done it," I insist. "But I need to talk to the detective before I collapse into a heap of exhaustion." I glance at my phone. The last text from the detective was a half hour ago. He said he'd stop by soon.

"I can't believe you invited the cops to my house," Tara groans from the sofa.

"She didn't do it to trigger you, sweetums," Larri says.

Although I do feel like an ass for forgetting that Tara is afraid of cops.

Officer Barski knocks on the door not five minutes later, and I jump up and greet him on the porch. "We have to stop meeting like this," I say as I slip outside.

He chuckles in response.

"Can we talk out here? My friend would prefer it."

"Of course." He steps aside and takes a seat on one of the rocking chairs on the rickety front porch. "Nobody likes law enforcement anymore. And yet we're the first people to be called when anyone has a problem."

He offers this with an easy smile, though. And I'm really glad I don't have his job. "Did you find anything significant at my apartment?"

"We took some fingerprints, but they might turn out to be yours. Can you come down to the station tomorrow and supply your prints?"

"Later in the day?" I hedge. "I have to take my son to his preschool picnic."

"Of course." He smiles again. "Whenever you're ready."

I wonder how different this experience would be if I *weren't* the heir to a tech CEO who plays golf with the chief of police. "What else do you need from me?"

"Just a couple more questions." He flips through a small notebook. "It looks like your lock was picked. But do you know why anyone would want to break into your apartment?"

"No," I say immediately.

"Any guys bothering you lately? Do you have any exes who might not have gotten the message? Or maybe your child's father is upset with you?"

"My child's father is dead. And I haven't had a boyfriend for a good five years. I can't even remember how to *spell* boyfriend. That is not what's happening here."

His grin grows wider. "Okay. Good to know. Any other enemies? Trouble at work?"

"Nope." I shake my head. If I told him that my stolen laptop held a bunch of warrants from a fake cop and a fake judge in Lowden, Maine, it would probably pique his interest. But then what?

He's probably a good cop. I bet most of them are. It would probably never occur to him to use police technology to cyber-stalk teenage girls.

But bad apples are real. Some guys used my family's technology for terrible things. I have no way of knowing who those guys are.

And I'm too afraid of them to tell this one the truth.

39

FIVE YEARS AGO, AUGUST

The walk home from the bus stop to his apartment takes longer than he expects. His leg is throbbing.

The place is quiet when he unlocks the door for the last time. Ariel is long gone. He left her asleep in the bed this morning when he headed for the gym.

Now he wished he'd skipped the workout to wake up with her one last time.

He pushes that thought away and looks around at his meager belongings. This part of his mission will be depressingly quick.

From the tiny coat closet he extracts his go bag. It's an ordinary-looking backpack, secured by a crappy little luggage lock. It wouldn't hold off a pro, but it means that if anyone—namely Ariel—ever stumbled on this bag, she couldn't easily open it to look inside.

The pack contains two thousand dollars in cash, a prepaid debit card for another two thousand, a change of clothes. His real IDs. His gun and some ammo. Plus a bus schedule—every route to Fayetteville, North Carolina.

He adds his computer, and then a prepaid mailer addressed to a friend from the army—with his notebook inside it.

He grabs his toothbrush from the bathroom. Then he limps to the doorway of the bedroom and stops at the threshold. It's probably better if he doesn't even step inside. He can't take anything of

Ariel's with him. If Edward double-crosses him and has him arrested, he'll be asked to explain why he has that blob of glass he blew that night they first made love.

The sheets on the bed are still rumpled. If he crossed the room to lift her pillow, it would still smell like her.

He doesn't, because that will just make it worse. He turns his back on the bedroom, and every one of those memories. For now, anyway.

Sitting down on the futon couch for the last time, he unlocks his phone. He sends a text to the landlord.

> **Drew:** A buddy needs my help. I have to leave Portland in a hurry and I won't be back. The key is on the coffee table. Apologies for the things I left behind. So sorry for the inconvenience.

He takes the key off the key ring and places it exactly where he said he would.

Then he writes one last text. To Ariel.

> **Drew:** There's trouble. I need to see you. Meet me in one hour under the candelabra tree. Don't tell anyone where you're going.

He hits *send*.

With his go bag over one shoulder, he leaves it all behind. The key, his clothes, his life.

The door locks behind him as he goes.

40

ARIEL

I wake up in the guest bed with Buzz's heels pressed firmly into my kidneys. He's what you'd politely call an "active sleeper." He nailed me in the head with his elbow at one point in the night, too.

But as I roll over and look at him, I don't really mind. His dark lashes lie neatly against his baby-smooth skin. He won't be four forever. All the cuddles I am freely given will dry up like raisins when he hits puberty.

That's what the parenting books tell me, anyway. Which is why I rarely bother to read them.

He opens his eyes and blinks at me.

"It's seven thirty already," I whisper. "I'm taking a shower."

"Okay," he says sleepily.

When I return, Buzz has dressed himself in yesterday's clothes, not the clean ones I brought for him. "Good work," I say, unwilling to burst his bubble. "You're ready."

"We have the picnic today," he says. "I don't want to do the sack race. It's not fun. You just fall over."

"Okay. You don't have to do the sack race."

He smiles.

I pack his pj's into his backpack alongside his clean clothes, and I wonder where we're going to sleep tonight. Maybe in my mother's house? I'll need upgraded locks before I'm willing to go back home.

I wonder how I'll explain that to Buzz.

"Does Tara have cereal?" he asks hopefully as I walk him into the kitchen. "The one with marshmallows in it? She had that last time."

"Let's see," I say, although what I really mean is *Let's hope not*. Because ick.

"Do you mean this?" Tara shakes a box of Lucky Charms. "I already got it out for you, Buzzy boy. But we're adding some Cheerios to the bowl so your mother doesn't freak out about the sugar."

"Cool," he says, showing me all his baby teeth when he smiles. There's an older kid in his class who's already lost a tooth. It's only a matter of time.

"It's shopping day, though, so we don't have much else," Tara says, opening her refrigerator to peer inside. "Eggs, but no bacon."

"Don't cook," I insist. "We'll have brunch after I drop Buzz at school. My treat. As a thank-you."

So that's what we do. We drop Buzz off at school and then get a booth at Becky's Diner.

We order, and I pounce on the coffee as soon as the waitress brings my cup. I feel hungover, even though we drank nothing stronger than tea last night.

Stress is exhausting.

My phone rings, and it's my mother's ringtone. It's rude to take a call in a restaurant, but given yesterday's break-in, I'm afraid to let it go to voice mail. "Hello? Mom, I'm just at Becky's. Is everything okay?"

"Everything is fine," she says quickly. "Take your time. I was just calling to tell you that I called in a favor with Maria." That's her twice-a-week housekeeper. "She's in your apartment right now doing her best to make it look like nothing ever went wrong in there."

"Oh wow." I take a grateful gulp of my coffee. "Mom, thank you both. I had assumed I would spend the afternoon doing exactly that."

"You shouldn't have to," she says. "I want you to put this behind you. I have a locksmith coming, too. Ray and I think you should have your locks changed."

"Thank you," I repeat. "Although locks are pickable, apparently. The detective thinks that's how they got in."

"That scares me," she says. "I'll ask the locksmith about a security bar for when you're alone at night. And isn't Officer Barski rather cute?"

"*Mama.*" I let out a startled laugh. "Are we discussing my personal safety? Or are you trying to set me up with a cop?"

"No *way*," Tara grumbles. "*God.*"

"It was just an idea," my mother insists. "If you and Buzz were with a policeman, I'd know you were always safe."

Tell that to a girl named Amina. "Thank you for all you've done. I'd better hang up now."

"Take care, sweetheart."

Larri rolls her eyes as I end the call. "Not a fan of that woman."

"I know." I set my phone down, but then think better of it. I open up my texts and find a message from Zain. "I don't think Zain ever sleeps. He messaged me at one thirty in the morning." And it's a voice note, which isn't like him.

I press *play* and hold it up to my ear. It's Zain's voice, but he sounds high-pitched and weird. "Ariel. Take bussan run." Then there's a loud thunk before the sound cuts out.

Wait. What? I play it three more times, each time with rising anxiety. But that doesn't help it make sense. So I pass the phone to Larri. "What do you think he's saying?"

Her eyes widen when she listens. She puts it on speaker and plays it for the table. But it doesn't make any more sense that way.

"Um . . ." Tara says. "Sounds like he's saying—take Buzz and run."

"What the hell?" I demand. "Why would he scare me like that and then hang up?"

Larri cringes. "I don't know, sweetie. Maybe check on him?"

I take my phone back and text:

Ariel: Zain, you okay?

"Okay, new rule," Tara says, slapping the table. "No more eerie messages. Ever. Not even as a joke."

Larri laughs. "Seriously. Anything that hits our phones better contain puppies or rainbows. Preferably with pictures."

"Good rule," I say, but my next sip of coffee tastes like acid. Maybe I should ask the waitress for my breakfast to go. I need to find Zain.

"And no more doorbell camera texts," Tara says. "None."

"Not even with puppies or rainbows?" I ask.

"Even then," she insists. "They are just inherently creepy. Apologies to your family, Ariel, but a doorbell camera could make even a puppy look like Marilyn Manson after a bender."

I snort. "Noted." And then I eye my phone, hoping for a response from Zain.

Nothing.

". . . And if you're just *naturally* a creep, you don't stand a chance," Tara says. She slides her phone my way. "Look. This is the photo that almost broke us up."

I glance at the screen. She's right about fish-eye lenses on Chime Co. cameras. They all have the bent lines and harsh lighting.

Then my gaze snags on the shadowed face of Tara's former drug dealer. And I've seen her before, although it takes me a second to realize where. "Wait. Is she . . ." I hesitate, because I might be totally wrong. "Is her last name Zarkey?"

"Um . . ." Larri and Tara share a glance. "Yeah, babe," Larri says slowly. "Her street name is *Weezer*. But how do you know her name?"

"She's—" I swallow against a suddenly dry mouth. "Her brother used to work for Chime Co. At least I *assume* they're siblings."

"That's wild," Larri says.

Our food comes, and the waitress puts a steaming plate in front of me. I pick up my fork like a robot and take a bite. But my mind is elsewhere.

Money, drugs or pussy, Larri said. *It's always one of those.*

I assumed the fake judge scam was about money, and maybe sexual harassment. But I haven't considered drugs. "Do you think it could be a family business?"

Tara seems to shrink a little at the question.

"Baby," Larri says heavily. She puts a hand on Tara's arm. "What do you know?"

Tara drops her eyes to the table. "I tried not to ask too many questions," she says quietly. "I was afraid of her. I still am. But I did meet the brother once. I got the feeling that he sourced the product and she was in charge of distribution."

My fork lands on the table with a clatter. "Sorry. I think I'd better go. I've got to find Zain." I lift a hand in the air and look around for our waitress. "Check?" I call when I spot her taking an order a few tables away.

She gives me a look of irritation, and I guess I can't blame her. But I'm suddenly terrified for Zain.

41

Brainz pulls up in the empty driveway of the mansion on Chadwick Street and kills the engine. Then he pulls out his laptop and piggybacks a signal off his cell phone.

It only takes a few keystrokes to pause the Chime Co. camera feeds at this address for fifteen minutes.

From his bag, he removes a pair of latex gloves and puts them on. Then he removes a plastic baggie of Edward's pain pills and shoves it into the pocket of his khakis before getting out of the car.

He walks casually around to the front door and opens it. "Hello, Edward!" he calls out cheerfully.

When no one responds, he isn't surprised.

He walks quickly toward the office at the back of the house, finding Edward slumped over the desk.

"What are we giving him?" Ray had asked when he hatched this plan.

"Just homemade Rohypnol," he'd said. "The pills will look identical to his regular meds, except they'll knock him right out. All I need is a half hour to do some work on his terminal. He'll never know I was there."

He won't, either. Because it *wasn't* roofies in the bottle Ray gave his brother this morning. And when Brainz slips two fingers to the side of Edward's neck, there's no pulse at all.

All right then.

He pulls the medication from his pocket and carefully swaps the prescription pills for the fakes. He sets the bottle—which has Ray's fingerprints on it—back down on the desk and pockets the fakes.

Then he stands behind the dead man's desk and makes a few adjustments to the network. The connection to LiveMatch is quickly eliminated. He'll have to field a couple of calls from bummed-out cops in Lowden later when they realize their free toy is toast.

Then he flips over to the warrant system and does some more tidying up. The whole thing takes nine minutes. So he spends a few more writing pointless commands to the network—renaming directories and reorganizing cells in the spreadsheet that's open on his screen.

It's like packing peanuts—if someone wants to reconstruct Edward's last moments on the Chime Co. network, they'll have to dig.

But they probably won't bother. His death will look like an accident or a suicide.

And if Drew fucking Miller ever tries to go public with Live-Match and the fake judges, the cover-up will look like Edward's. Not Ray's. And certainly not his.

He leaves the Cafferty home thirteen minutes after he arrived.

At a traffic light in downtown Portland, he sends a single text, directly from his real number to Ray's. It's just incriminating enough to make Ray keep his damn jaw locked shut once he realizes what he's actually done.

Ray won't appreciate the breach of protocol. Their communications are supposed to go strictly through the encrypted app. So he doesn't expect a reply.

When none comes, he thinks nothing of it.

42

ARIEL

Zain isn't at the office when I arrive. It's already after nine thirty, too. He's *always* here by now. I send him another message.

Ariel: Hey! Call me. We need to talk ASAP.

"Ariel?"

Jumpy, I glance up so fast that my neck cracks. My uncle watches me from the doorway of his office with an unusually stern expression on his face. "Yes?"

"Can you come here, please?"

I get up and follow him into the office like a good girl. But I'm in full panic mode. "Have you seen Zain?" I ask in lieu of a greeting. "He sent me a weird text. And he's not here."

My uncle's forehead wrinkles. He looks haggard today. "No, I haven't. Why is he texting you anyway?"

"We're friends. We used to sit next to each other. What's so weird about that?" It comes out a little shrill.

Ray's forehead furrows as he studies me. And I stare back at this man I've known all my life. He's the gentle one. The guy who wants to tell stories, and jokes that take five minutes to set up.

Or am I wrong? Are Ray and I at war in a game of cat and mouse that I never signed up to play?

Did you break into my apartment to scare me?

"Close the door, would you?" he says, tossing a pen onto the desk. I do it. And then I sit, hoping he'll finally tell me something useful.

"We have to take this break-in seriously."

"You think I'm *not*?"

He gives me a stern look. "I tried to pull up your doorbell camera footage, only to discover that there is none."

I blink. "You tried to look at it? But I canceled my account."

And maybe I should have worried more about my own safety, but I'm still struck by his casual disregard for the company's rules. *Nobody* at Chime Co. is supposed to access private video without permission. Ray clearly doesn't think this applies to him.

What other rules don't apply to you? I want to shriek. *And did you know that Bryan Zarkey was a drug dealer?*

Did my father know?

There are too many variables now. And I can't ask Ray about it. I don't trust anyone in this building. Except maybe Zain.

Where is Zain?

"Why would you *ever* cancel your account?" my uncle demands. "With that data, we could have this guy already."

"Because I'm cheap, and I live for free on the nicest block in Portland? Buzz and I were the only people who ever appeared on camera. We don't even get packages delivered at home. It was a waste of twenty bucks."

"*Jesus Christ!*" His voice rises to a level that I didn't even know Ray possessed. "And how are you feeling about that decision now? The twenty bucks would have caught this guy!"

My heart thumps against my ribs. And I'm so confused. Zain wondered if Ray was behind my break-in, but my uncle is as angry at me as I've ever seen him.

Although Dad would have called me a *stupid little twat* by now. His anger was always tuned to the *total annihilation* setting.

Ray is different, even in anger. And he actually sounds scared.

This moment of family drama is interrupted by a tap on the door. Hester pokes her beak-like nose into the room. "Your breakfast is here." She gives me a dour look as she steps inside to put a paper bag from Bagel Tree on the desk. Then she retreats.

"Look," Ray sighs, grabbing the bag. "I'm sorry I yelled. Want half a bagel? I'll even make us coffee as a peace offering."

"Sure. Thanks," I say quietly. But now I'm staring at the Bagel Tree bag, because something bothers me about it.

Way back when Ray explained the mystery of all our five-year-old texts, he said his came from the Bagel Tree, which is right across the street from our office building. It sounded perfectly plausible at the time.

But now I realize that place didn't open until after Buzz was born. Five years ago it was a convenience store. During my pregnancy, I was a regular customer of the slushies they served.

It wasn't until later that the new place moved in, to the delight of our office staff, bringing wood-fired bagels and bagel sandwiches into the neighborhood.

There *was* no Bagel Tree five years ago. And I'm not even sure we were ordering food on apps back then.

"Ariel?" Ray asks, nudging a napkin with half a bagel toward me. "Want a cup of coffee?"

"Sure, thanks." I lift my half of the bagel. Then I wait until he's on his feet before I make another request. "Mind if I check the weather on your phone? Buzz wants me to take him to the beach this weekend."

Ray pauses mid-stride. He looks down at the desk, where his phone is resting, idle.

The question just sits there between us for a long couple of seconds. But it feels like a year. Our eyes meet. His are the same light brown shade as mine. It's the Cafferty family color. And I can see confusion in them.

I've never asked Ray for his phone before. It's a pushy thing to do. He can't decide whether to just hand it over or to make it weird by telling me to get my own damn phone from my desk.

"Please?" I say, and then I summon a sweet smile. The kind my father never would have fallen for in a hundred million years.

My heartbeat glugs two more times at least. It's awkward now. But I don't back down.

"Sure," he finally says. He grabs the phone and unlocks it. He taps something and hands it to me—the weather app is already loading. "Be right back."

"Thanks," I say lightly. And a half second later—as his backside clears the door frame—I'm swiping up to look at his texts. I scroll through them as fast as I dare, hoping I'll know what I'm looking for when I see it.

In the first place, I can't find anything from the Bagel Tree. It's Hester who usually orders his lunch there two or three times a week.

But Ray loves a good story. If he wanted to tell us the story of a five-year-old text without revealing who it was actually from, it might have been the first thing that came to mind.

My uncle has corresponded with dozens of people in the three weeks since that text, though. I'm scrolling as fast as I can.

Come on, come on.

When Bryan Zarkey's face slides into view, I nearly jump. It takes me two tries to open up the thread, because my hand is shaking. But there it is, and the text is terse and even more ominous than I'd expected. **The job is done just the way you wanted.**

The job. What job were they discussing on the morning my father died?

I scroll up to see texts prior to that, and they're all old, and mostly automated updates. **Network report August 12 2017: 0 minutes downtime.** Etc.

The seconds tick by, and I'm sweating. It doesn't take very long to brew two cups of coffee in the new machine. And if Ray decides to take a couple of steps back from the coffee bar, he can probably see me in his office.

The job is done just the way you wanted. I shiver. Then I close the texts and reopen the weather app. It's going to be a gorgeous week in Portland, Maine. A high of 74 tomorrow.

I place Ray's phone on his blotter, like a good girl. And when he returns a minute later, I'm taking a bite of bagel and looking as bored as a girl can look when she's just realized her uncle is hiding something. Possibly something terrible.

He could have told us that he got a text from an employee who doesn't work with us anymore. The story would have been just as interesting. But he didn't want to mention Zarkey.

What the hell did they *do*?

My bagel tastes like wet cardboard. I need a sip of coffee just to choke it down. Then I stand up just as my uncle sits down. "Look, I'm sorry about the dead camera. I promise to hook it back up again tonight. But I'm afraid I have to get a move on. Mom said something about a locksmith."

He rubs his temples. "Yeah. And your picnic today."

"Right." That damn picnic. "In the next ninety minutes, I need to find ten watermelons."

Ray opens his desk drawer and pulls out a set of keys. "Take my car, honey. I drove because I had another off-site meeting later. But then I canceled it."

I take the keys, feeling like a teenager asking her daddy for the car. That's how he must think of me. At the moment, though, I need him to. "Thanks for breakfast."

He attempts a smile. "Don't mention it."

I loop my finger in the key ring and turn toward the door. "If you see Zain, will you tell him I really need a call?"

"Sure," he says.

"Okay. Hope he's not sick or something. It was a rough week on the network."

I leave his office and my eyes go right to Zain's desk. His chair is still empty.

Hell.

At my own desk, I grab my shoulder bag and toss in Ray's keys. I drain the coffee but drop the bagel into the trash. Then I walk out of the office and head up the street, toward the nearby parking lot where Ray pays for a monthly spot.

Meanwhile, I'm also tapping Zain's phone number and listening to it ring. "Leave a message," his voice says into my ear. Then I hear a beep.

Nope. Not good enough. I hang up and redial him a second later.

This time, the ring is cut off as the call is answered. For a hot second I'm flooded with relief, until an unfamiliar voice—a woman's—answers the call. "Hello? Who am I speaking to?"

I stop walking. "This is Zain's friend Ariel. Is he okay? I need to speak to him."

"Can I ask your relationship to Zain?" she asks, not unkindly. "My name is Angela Block, and I'm a Portland police officer."

My stomach lurches, and my voice comes out high and thready. "Did something happen? I'm a friend. I've been trying to reach him all morning."

Her brief silence fills me with dread. "Ariel, are you somewhere you can talk for a moment? And not driving?"

"I'm . . . I'm just standing on the sidewalk. Tell me what's wrong."

"I'm afraid that Zain has overdosed, and he didn't make it. His mother is quite distraught, and I'm wondering if you know her. We've been unable to locate any other family members, and she's housebound. We're not sure who to call for her, and she had to be sedated."

Speech fails me completely. *Overdosed.* It's all too familiar. *He didn't make it.*

"Ariel?" she asks gently. "Are you there?"

"He didn't use drugs," I choke out. Although I don't actually know that. "Overdosed on *what*?"

"Opioids, we believe," she says softly. "I'm sorry. You can be sure that we'll try to figure out how he died. Often the people closest to a user don't know about their habit. Maybe he wasn't an experienced user."

"Of course he wasn't!" I snap. This doesn't make sense. Nothing makes sense. "When did this happen? He texted me last night. Where was he . . . ?" *Found.* I can't even say it.

"It happened in the middle of the night," she says in a voice so soothing that they must teach it at the police academy. "He was at his desk. Maybe he thought the drug could keep him on task. There was nothing you could have done."

It's like a recurring bad dream. *Your father passed, Ariel. I still don't understand it. They say he took too many pills.*

What is happening?

"I know this is shocking," the police officer says in that trippy voice. "Do you know any friends of his family? We're worried about his mother."

"No," I croak. "Can I see him?" Maybe then it will make sense.

"I'm sorry, but no. The body has been removed from the premises."

The body. I shiver. "He *didn't* overdose. Did someone break in? I'm telling you he wouldn't do this. And he had a break-in last month."

When it comes again, her soothing voice makes me inexplicably angry. "I promise we'll do what we can to investigate this tragedy."

I yank my phone away from my ear and hang up.

A jogger passes me on the sidewalk. I feel dizzy. *Zain is dead of a drug overdose.* It wouldn't sound any more real if I repeated it all day long.

The past twenty-four hours are like a wave crashing over my head. The break-in. Zain's weird message on my phone. Four seconds. *Take Buzz and run.*

I hurry toward Ray's BMW and climb in.

43

FIVE YEARS AGO, AUGUST

Drew makes his final approach toward the Cafferty home.

Portland, Maine, with its brick buildings and its painted shutters, looks more beautiful today than any city has a right to. Seagulls cry overhead, reminding him how close he is to the water.

As he crosses into the West End, he spies a sushi restaurant that he and Ariel always meant to try, but never did.

He pulls out his phone and checks for an acknowledgment from Ariel. They don't ever text, but he broke that rule today because it's crucial that he gets the opportunity to say goodbye in person. He's rehearsing his speech as he walks. *I've stirred up some trouble. I'm sorry to complicate your life, but I can't explain. It's better if you don't know the details. I'm going to stay with an army buddy for a little while. I hope you can forgive me. But it's not over between us. It will never be over.*

Leaving her is going to tear him apart.

She hasn't replied, though, so he taps her number, dialing her. She doesn't answer. And when it goes to voice mail, he hangs up and powers down the phone.

He's confident she'll see the missed call. She'll check her texts. She always takes a lunch break, and he's still got almost an hour to meet her in the park. There's still time.

The farther west he walks, the more beautiful the buildings

get. Stately old homes with bay windows and slate-tiled roofs. The Chadwick Street house has a corner lot, and he can already see the second story. He studies the windows and wonders which of them was Ariel's.

He never got the chance to find out.

Rein it in, he reminds himself. He needs to stay alert now. He slows his steps as he approaches the Cafferty property from Pine Street, at the rear of the house. He hears a screen door slam, but a tall hedgerow of lilacs hides both doors from view.

The sound might not even have come from the Caffertys' house.

A car's engine cranks to life. And then the glint of a rearview mirror penetrates the hedgerow for a split second. He pauses on the sidewalk as he picks up the sound of tires rolling slowly down a driveway.

Well, shit. If the driver is another Chime Co. employee, he could be spotted, depending on which route the driver takes after he pulls out onto Chadwick. He leans down, sliding his backpack onto the sidewalk, and kneels down to tie a shoe that doesn't need tying.

It's not the most brilliant disguise, but it doesn't even matter. When the car—a very shiny Mercedes with darkly tinted windows—comes into view, it doesn't turn onto Pine. It heads straight up Chadwick and quickly disappears.

He rises again, shouldering his pack beside a row of lilac bushes—the same one Ariel described to him when she explained her method for approaching the house off camera. *It was easy. I came through at the break in the hedgerow, ducked under the window of my father's office—in case he was up late—and hopped onto the front porch from the side.*

Sure enough, he arrives at the break in the hedgerow and steps through. He doesn't duck, though, as he's not trying to avoid Edward. Instead, he glances up at the window to the office—the same one he invaded on the Fourth of July.

In spite of the sunlight's glare on the window, he can see the collar of Edward's crisp white shirt. But something about the angle of the boss's head is strange. As if Edward is bowing to his desk.

Curiosity brings him two paces toward that window for a better look.

44

ARIEL

I'm at Hannaford supermarket pushing a cart through the produce section. Like a zombie, I stack ten watermelons in my cart. Because I will not fail Buzz.

But inside I'm screaming.

"Hey." I look up to see a handsome, bearded man aiming a lazy grin at me. He glances into my cart. "Nice melons."

On any other day, I'd give him either a smile or the finger, at my whim. But I do neither. Instead, I push the cart a little farther into the store, toward the dairy aisle.

Take Buzz and run. My senses jangle every time I think of that four-second message. Whatever happened to Zain, he somehow took a moment from his last night on earth to leave that message.

Did he know Zarkey was a killer? Had he figured it out? There had to be some reason he left that message.

If I'd told Officer Barski a long, weird tale about a five-year-old cybercrime last night, could I have prevented this somehow?

Did he hear them coming? Or did he fall asleep at his desk, and feel nothing?

I blink, and I'm still at Hannaford with ten watermelons. But my senses are dialed up into the red zone. Because my gut says I need to heed Zain's warning. I know too much. I need to take Buzz and run.

The *whys* will have to be sorted out later.

I grip the cart's handle and let out a breath. I feel only two per-cent calmer.

Pushing the cart toward the premade foods, I pick out some sandwiches. Then I hit the snack section and grab a box of Buzz's favorite granola bars.

A big bottle of water.

A travel-sized toothpaste.

A coloring book in the checkout lane.

"Would you like help out to your car, ma'am?" the bagger asks.

"No thank you," I manage. My head feels like a thunderstorm gathering—odd pressure and noise. Nonetheless, I'm forming a haphazard plan. Buzz and I are getting out of town, and I'm not going to tell *anybody* where.

Maybe when I feel safer, I'll be able to think clearly.

I doubt my uncle would hurt me. But sometimes the only per-son you can trust is yourself.

After loading the watermelons into Ray's trunk, I drive over to the park, near the picnic tables. The other parents have already gathered on the lawn. Maddy has laid out tablecloths in complementary colors. When I open the trunk of Ray's car, her husband tromps dutifully over to help me carry the melons. I accept his assistance in silence.

On one of my trips to the table, I see Maddy remove a chef's knife from her own purse—wrapped in cardboard—for the slicing. She didn't trust me to bring one.

Any other day, I'd be annoyed. Lucky for her, I've got bigger problems.

"Excuse me, Leeza?" I walk up to another mom who has always been friendly to me. "My phone has died. Could I possibly borrow yours for a second? I need to look something up."

"Of course," she says immediately. She pulls a phone out of her pocket, unlocks it and hands it to me without any further questions.

If someone means to harm me, I won't leave a trail of bread crumbs for him to follow. I open Leeza's browser and search for Amtrak trains out of Portland.

The next one is in sixty minutes. We can just make it.

The children are approaching us now. They're following behind Miss Betty in a line. Each one holds a loop of the "magic rope" they use to walk the children anywhere. Another teacher brings up the rear.

Buzz is near the front, and he's laughing at something his pal across the rope is saying. When he sees me, he drops the loop and runs. They all do, and seconds later, the teachers are left holding an empty rope.

"Mama!" he yells, arriving at my side. "I don't want to do the sack race."

I take his hand firmly in mine. "No sack race. What is your favorite picnic food?"

"The watermelon. Did you bring it?"

"I did. You should have seen my shopping cart. Full of watermelons."

He grins.

"Let me talk to Miss Betty for a second? Then I'm going to get you a slice of watermelon."

"Okay!"

I drop his hand and hightail it over to his teacher, who shoots me a smile. "Hello, Ariel! Lovely to see you."

My own smile is a reflex. "I'm afraid there's been a bit of a family emergency, and we're not going to be able to stay."

"Oh dear." Her face turns grave. "I hope it's not too serious."

"Everyone will be fine," I lie. "But thank you."

My mind offers up an image of Zain slumped over his desk, and a shudder runs through me.

The sun is shining brightly, and the grass is green. It's hard to make sense of my fear and Zain's tragedy and the deep blue sky. Nothing seems real. I walk like a robot to the food table, where Maddy and her husband are setting out all the sandwiches and treats. I pluck a piece of watermelon off the tray.

Maddy's expression turns to shock. "We're not ready to serve!"

"Oops. My bad." I turn around and walk away. "Buzz!" I call.

My son looks up from a mesh bag full of balls that someone has brought for the children to play with.

"Come here, sweetie." He trots over immediately. "Listen, this is for you." I hand him the wedge of melon. "I'm sorry, but we have to leave the picnic."

"Why?" He looks alarmed.

"You and I are going on a little adventure on a train. But it leaves soon."

"A train?" That perks him up.

"Right. But we're not going to tell anyone. It's a secret."

He blinks. Then he takes a bite of the watermelon.

"Come on." I put a hand on his head. "Let's go now. Try not to drip that in Uncle Ray's car. Where's your backpack?"

He points to a pile of the kids' things under a tree, and we march over to collect the bag. Then I steer him toward the car. A couple of people are watching our untimely exit, but it can't be helped.

There's no car seat in Ray's BMW, but I buckle Buzz in the back seat for the one-mile trip home. My hands are practically shaking with adrenaline as I make a small detour to the drive-in window at the bank. It's the kind with a speaker, a pneumatic tube, and a human two yards away on the other side of the glass. "How can I help you?" asks an older white woman through the speaker.

"I'd like to withdraw two thousand dollars. The girls and I are going to the casino this weekend." I fashion my face into a smile while my heart jackhammers against my ribs.

Two thousand dollars is almost my entire checking account balance. But it will easily cover a few days' journey.

"Cash card and ID, please," the teller says, and the tube descends through its tunnel toward my open car window.

"Cool," Buzz says from the back seat. "It's like an elevator."

I place my ATM card and my driver's license into the tube, which is sucked back toward the bank.

Buzz makes a noise of delight.

A couple of long minutes later, the tube returns, and I pull out my cards and a thick envelope of cash. "Thank you," I say, shoving that envelope into a zip pocket of my bag.

Then I drive the rest of the way to Chadwick Street. There's a locksmith's van just pulling away from the curb when I reach the house. But my mother's car isn't in the driveway. I'm taking it as a blessing, as well as a sign to move quickly.

When Buzz and I disappear, she's going to freak out.

I stop in the driveway, pulling a wet wipe out of my bag and tackling Buzz's sticky hands. I swipe it across the leather armrest of my uncle's car, too. This morning is full of cognitive dissonance. Zain is dead, and I'm wiping up melon juice, because it's crucial to tidy up the BMW while I run for my life.

I leave the key in the cup holder.

Buzz unbuckles himself and follows me up the driveway to our apartment, where there's a shiny new key taped to the door. I use it to let myself in. Then I leave it on the countertop. I whip out my phone and summon an Uber, which will arrive in six minutes.

"Hey, Buzz? Wait here, okay? We have to go soon to get our train." Without waiting for an answer, I dash upstairs with both our bags.

The place is immaculate. You'd never know it was ransacked yesterday.

To Buzz's bag, I add a couple pairs of underwear, socks and three Matchbox cars. Then I head into my room, where I open my backpack. My dirty clothes get tossed into the hamper. I grab another T-shirt and clean underwear. Deodorant. I dash into the closet and choose a cardigan. What color does a stylish single mom wear when she's running for her life? Navy blue.

Finishing up, I zip my cash and wallet into the front pocket of the backpack. My phone buzzes with a text from Uber. The car is outside.

I trot downstairs. "Buzz! Let's go!"

On a three-by-three sticky note on the counter, I leave a harried message.

> *Buzz and I are still staying with some friends!*
>   *—A*

That might keep Mom from worrying for, oh, an hour.

Buzz follows me outside, and I pull the door shut without locking it. Then I buckle Buzz into yet another car with no booster seat. The driver heads for the Amtrak station.

My phone buzzes two times in quick succession.

> Ray: Ariel, honey, can you come back to the office?
> Ray: Something terrible has happened. It's about Zain.

Then my phone rings. **Ray Calling.**

I decline the call. Then I power the phone all the way down.

But that's not really enough, is it? Phones are trackable even when they're off.

I slip the phone into the pocket on the back of the driver's seat.

It cost me eight hundred dollars when I upgraded. But I'm going to leave it there.

That's either smart or crazy. Like everything else I've done in the past twenty-four hours.

"Can we go to the museum?" Buzz asks as we pass the sign for it.

"Another day," I whisper. "This is a different adventure."

Buzz loves the train ride. He spends it on his knees, peering out the window, even when there's nothing to see.

When we arrive in Boston, though, the station is chaos. I have to clamp my hand onto his arm as we dodge commuters at South Station.

"Where are we going?" he wants to know.

"On a bus," I say. "But first we have to buy some tickets."

Everything I know about long-haul buses I learned from listening to Larri and Tara complain about them. Buses take forever, and they always take the longest routes.

But they don't usually check IDs. So that's how we're going to travel.

So I brace myself for the conversation with the woman at Boston's South Station. "Where would you like to go?" asks the woman at the Greyhound counter.

It's time for another round of *Smart, or crazy?*

My college roommate lives in Evanston, Illinois. She's pregnant with her first child, between jobs and recently invited me and Buzz to come and visit. So I should head for Chicago. We know each other well enough from drunken nights in college that if I turned up on her doorstep, she'd take it in stride.

Door number two is a wild little theory I've been nursing about where Jay Marker might be. It's so outlandish that I didn't even mention it to Zain. "There's a tiny town in Michigan that probably doesn't have a bus stop. It's near Cadillac, though."

She starts typing. "We have Cadillac. What's the other town's name?"

"Harrietta." It was Drew's password.

More typing, and then she shakes her head. "Cadillac, then?"

"Two please. One adult and one child."

"The next bus leaves at seven p.m."

Ouch. It's only four thirty now.

"And it arrives in Cadillac at five fifty a.m. . . . ."

For one glorious second this sounds like a reasonable plan.

". . . the day after tomorrow. You transfer buses four times. Total cost is four hundred and ninety-six dollars."

A day and a half on a bus with a four-year-old, for five hundred bucks. That's the cost of chasing a ghost.

I unzip my pack and dig into my envelope of cash.

45

I spend another hundred dollars at the Boston aquarium, pretending for Buzz that our sudden trip is just a fun outing with Mommy.

He picks out a fuzzy tiger shark stuffy in the gift shop, which I dutifully buy, in spite of the fact that I'm carrying two full backpacks already.

We eat an early dinner, then I make him brush his teeth in the bathroom of Legal Sea Foods.

"Can we just go home?" he whines when I have to remind him again not to touch the toilet seat and the trash can and every other surface he encounters.

"No, buddy, I'm sorry. We're not done with our trip."

We walk back through the crowded bus station, and I wonder how many cameras there are in the terminal.

Zain told me that LiveMatch was gone from the Chime Co. network. But once a technology exists, it doesn't just disappear. LiveMatch probably found its way to a competitor. My presence in this station may be lighting up with my full name and address on a network right this second.

Before now, I wouldn't have worried. But nothing wakes a girl up to privacy issues like running for her life.

"When can we get on the bus?" Buzzy whines.

"Any minute now," I say, holding his hand a little more tightly.

I hope it's true.

When they finally call our bus, I have another moment of anxiety. I approach the driver with our tickets in my hand. The name on my ticket is Allie Grant, and Buzz is listed as Billy Grant.

Please don't say our names aloud, I privately beg the driver as I hand them over. Who knows what Buzz would say if the guy called us by the wrong names?

And please, God, don't ask for ID.

But the man just glances at the tickets, hands them back, and waves us on.

"Let's find you a window seat," I say magnanimously to Buzz as we climb aboard. He picks one out and settles in. I hand him the coloring book and the box of crayons.

We're probably still within Boston city limits when he gives up on the coloring book. Within a half hour, he's bored and squirming. There isn't any good scenery to distract us. Just the gray interstate, and my terror.

"Can I have a granola bar?" he asks.

I stun him by giving him two. Then he has to go to the bathroom, so I carry my backpack with us down the aisle and discover that a long-haul bus bathroom is even dirtier than I had the capacity to imagine.

Yikes.

Back in our seats, Buzz starts fidgeting almost immediately.

"Can I play with your phone?" he asks.

"I don't have it, baby. I'm sorry."

He gives me a disbelieving look, and I don't blame him. When he asks the same question again a half hour later, though, he gets the same answer.

Eventually he falls asleep in my lap, the shark wedged under his arm, and I fight my own drowsiness. Our itinerary requires us to change buses in New York at eleven p.m., in Scranton at four in the morning, in Harrisburg at seven a.m. and Detroit sometime tomorrow night. If I fall asleep, I could miss a transfer.

Unfortunately, that leaves hours of empty time for my mind to spin. The bus darkens, and so do my thoughts.

I think one of the Zarkeys killed Zain for digging too deep.

I think Ray and Bryan Zarkey were responsible for the wrong-doings at Chime Co. And maybe my dad, but maybe not.

I think Drew turned up asking too many questions, too. He found some things he wasn't meant to find.

Then I came along and kicked over the barrel of secrets again. Zain and I dug for the truth, and now he's dead. I feel responsible. The least I can do is listen to the last piece of advice he gave me. *Run*.

We arrive in New York more or less on time, and most everyone on the bus stands up to depart.

I ease my sleeping child off my lap and onto the seat. Instead of waking up, he screws his eyes shut and curls up like a potato bug. So I unzip the pocket where my valuables are, removing the tickets and stuffing them into the pocket of my jeans, where I'll be able to reach them. Then I put on my backpack.

Buzz sleeps through it all.

I ease the fuzzy shark out of his sleeping arms and stuff it, tail first, inside his backpack. Then I lean down and lift my sleeping child off the seat.

He whimpers in protest. But then he wraps his arms around my neck as his head sinks onto my shoulder.

Okay. That works. If I can prop one arm under his butt and use the other to carry his backpack, then I've got this. Except I didn't plan ahead, and his backpack is still on the floor.

Shit.

I bend over very slowly, trying not to let my own pack and Buzz's weight destabilize me. I close my fingers around the strap and start to straighten up.

My pack collides with someone in the aisle, and the bump almost sends me toppling. "Hey, watch it," someone snarls.

"Sorry," I murmur as Buzz's arms tighten around my neck like a hungry anaconda.

"Relax, man," another male voice says. A pair of hands stabilize my pack. "She don't mean nothin'. Take your time, miss. You okay now?"

"Yes. Thank you." I get a grip on my various burdens and maneuver into the aisle. The three steps off the bus feel like a cliff descent, and I stumble at the bottom, breathing in diesel fumes. Then I follow the other passengers into Port Authority.

The place is gross, not to put too fine a point on it. I'm glad our layover is only a half hour.

A giant monitor provides the departure location of our next bus—Gate 204. An escalator delivers me up one level, which is no more appealing than the one I just left.

I approach our gate, and it occurs to me to wonder if Drew passed through this very same place after he left Portland.

Sleepy passengers gather in clusters, some of them seated on the drab tile floor. There's only one bench in the rough vicinity of the gate. I linger near it for a moment, but none of the five lucky seated people makes eye contact with me, and nobody offers me a seat.

Hard to blame them.

But I still do.

Rolling on through the night, my head lolls from side to side whenever the bus takes a turn. I wake up with a start at every stop, listening for Scranton.

This time, Buzz wakes up for the transfer, but I have to carry him again nonetheless. He's groggy and unhappy with me.

We take a trip to the dingy bathroom. "Want to put on your pj's?" I ask Buzz.

He shakes his head, giving me a look that implies I'm insane.

Under the flickering fluorescent lights, I look like the worst, most exhausted version of myself. I wash my hands and my face and take a swipe at Buzz's while he fights me off.

We troop back onto the bus. I can't believe there's another twenty-six hours of this to endure.

Buzz settles on me again and sleeps until our next transfer in Harrisburg, at seven a.m., where we have an hour to wait.

"They have food here?" Buzz says, pointing at a darkened fast-food counter.

"It's closed," I say gently. "It's too early for hamburgers anyway. Hey—want a granola bar?" I dig into his pack where I've hidden them and produce the box.

He eats one like he's starving and then asks for another one. And I've already broken all my rules, so I hand it right over. I eat the last one and throw away the box.

We brush our teeth in another public bathroom and get back on the bus.

The next stretch feels long. Longer than being in labor for ten hours. I haven't slept in more than twenty-four hours, and I'm tired all the way down to the bone.

Buzz is done with the bus ride. He's done with me. I read him both the picture books I managed to bring. Twice. But then he's done with those, too. He kicks the seat in front of ours. I tell him not to.

Rinse. Repeat.

"Can I have your phone?" he asks suddenly.

"No, baby. I don't have it. I mean it."

"WHY?" he yells. "That's so stupid."

"It's broken, so I left it in . . ." I almost say *Maine*. But of course I don't want anyone to know where we're from. "I left it at home. Want to play a game?"

"Okay."

"We have to find something out the window from every single color on the wheel. In order. What color comes first?"

"Red," he announces.

"That's my boy. Let's find something red."

This keeps his interest for, oh, four minutes. But after green and blue are just too easy, he says "I don't like this game. Can I have another granola bar?"

"We ate them all. But at lunchtime we'll get off the bus and find you a burger."

"Okay. Cool."

He asks me every five minutes after that if we're there yet.

Eighty-seven years later, the bus pulls into Pittsburgh. We don't have to transfer buses, but there's a three-hour stopover. *Hallelujah.* "We're going to walk around," I announce. "We'll go to the bathroom, too. Brush our teeth. Get some lunch."

"Can't we just go home? We could go to the splash pool."

There's a pain right behind my breastbone as I picture Zain sitting carefully down at my side and rolling up his pants like he'd never seen water before. That was about two weeks ago. It feels like a lifetime.

I shake my head.

"*Why*, Mama? I want to go *home*."

I swallow thickly and pull my pack off the floor and into my lap. "I'm sorry. Let's see what there is to see in Pittsburgh." We're going to need some funds, so I unzip the slim pocket of my backpack where I've kept my valuables.

And it's empty.

I draw back and look at the backpack again, in case I'm in the wrong pocket. But no. There's just nothing here. Tasting bile, I plunge my hand into the pocket, all the way to the bottom. Nothing.

"Let's go," Buzz says as people file past us off the bus.

"One second!" Frantic now, I open the main compartment and fish around. No envelope. No wallet.

Oh my god. I've kept this bag in my sight the entire time. Except when it was on my back.

Then I think back to New York, where I was jostled in the aisle. To the man who stabilized my pack, pretending to help me. He stole it all. He and the other guy, who pretended to get mad.

They must have glimpsed my cash when I retrieved my tickets. They were working together.

A wave of horror rushes through my body. I've been so, so stupid.

I *thanked* that man who robbed me.

"Mama!"

"Just a *minute*!" I'm frantically searching my pack one more time. As if I could have moved that money and my wallet and somehow let it slip my mind.

I search Buzz's pack, too. In the bottom, I find a small bag of raisins, which he hates. It's probably been there for months. But I also find four dollar bills and some change that I crammed into an outside pocket one day at the Children's Museum when someone gave us change at the snack bar.

Four dollars and thirty-seven cents. That's all the money we have.

46

I buy Buzz a Happy Meal with the last of my money. Then we board another bus.

The afternoon passes in a haze. My stomach is so empty it feels like it's folding in on itself. And in spite of my nerves, I can't keep my eyes open. But every time I hear Buzz's voice, or the driver's, I snap awake, heart pounding.

Around six p.m., Buzz tells me he's hungry again. I fish out that bag of raisins, expecting him to turn them down.

But he eats every single one.

I wad up the bag and shove it in the same pocket where my money used to be.

Buzz flops around in his seat. "Mama, *pleeeeeease*? I want to go home."

"I know, baby." The guilt I'm choking on makes it hard to get the words out. "But I'm looking for a friend."

"Can we just *go*?"

I shake my head. There's no way I can make this make sense for him.

He kicks the seat in front of him, and a gray-haired woman turns around and gives us a glare.

"Buzzy," I say, my voice dripping with exhaustion. "Want to read one of our books again?"

"NO."

I catch his leg as he tries to kick it again. "Okay. What if I told you a story about your daddy?"

He goes immediately still. "Really?"

"Yeah." I take a big breath. "You're not a baby anymore. I bet you'd like to hear about him."

His mouth falls open, and he nods immediately.

"Okay. I met him at work—at the office where I still go every day."

"Before he died?" Buzz clarifies.

"Right. And before you were born."

He waits for me to go on.

"One day, someone was very mean to me at work. The manager yelled at me in front of everyone."

His eyes are like saucers. "Was it my daddy?"

"No!" I say quickly. "No, of course not. The manager was a different man." *Your grandfather.* Of course I leave that detail out. "It was embarrassing to be yelled at, and most everyone stared at me. But not your daddy."

Buzz gets up on his knees, kneeling in his seat, listening with his whole body. "He was nice?"

"He was *so* nice. He took me out to dinner after work. He told me jokes, and he made me laugh. He was kind to me."

"What else did my daddy do?"

It's hard to know where to start. And I'm so tired. But Buzz is hanging on every word. "We used to go to the park. You know that big tree where they hang those lanterns? We would meet there sometimes. Then we'd go for a walk together."

"What else?"

"I took him to the glass studio. He wasn't very good at it, though."

Buzz grins. "You let him try the pipe?" Buzz is desperate to try glass, but the studio isn't safe for a four-year-old.

"I did. He was terrible at it."

He giggles.

"Your daddy was good at so many things, though. He was a soldier before I met him. He helped other soldiers get rid of explosives that could hurt people. And one time he got hurt, too."

"Where?" Buzz demands.

"Syria," I say, before I realize he means where on his body. "That's a country far away. He got a scar right here." I reach out and trace a line down his cheek, under his eye. But I stop short of mentioning his limb difference, because Buzz will ask me a thousand questions about it, and I won't know the answers.

Besides, Drew is so much more than his scars.

"He loved dogs," I say. "Do you know what a German shepherd is?"

Buzz shakes his head.

"It's a big, furry dog with black and brown fur. Looks like a wolf. When he was a soldier, some of his friends used dogs to sniff for bombs. So at the end of the day, your daddy got to pet all the dogs. His favorite one was named Coby."

"What else?" Buzz breathes. He slides a little lower in the seat and then leans against me.

"He was a great swimmer. I took him to the beach, and we jumped in the waves together." He'd told me he hadn't been in the ocean since his amputation, so I borrowed my roommate's car for a day trip. "One night he made me the nicest picnic."

"What happened to my daddy when he died?" Buzz asks eventually. "Was it an accident?"

I finger his hair and consider my answer. "I'm just not sure, baby. But I'd like to find out. Maybe someday we'll find out together."

Night falls, and the bus heads northward. Buzz sleeps.

My stomach is empty and my mind can't hold on to a thought for longer than a few fuzzy seconds. I ride through the Midwest in a dreamy state of unreality. I've made it this far, almost to Michigan, where the bus is scheduled to make a million little stops.

Buzz is tipped to the side, his head pillowed on my lap. My child has never known real pain or fear.

I'm afraid to take my eyes off him. Losing the money is scary, but losing Buzz would end me.

We roll on. It's the middle of the night when the Greyhound pulls into another station. Passengers file off the bus after the driver announces a forty-minute meal break.

I sit as still as a statue, willing my child to remain asleep.

Miraculously, he does.

Our trip won't end for another twelve or fifteen hours. Then we'll get off the bus in a strange town with no money and only the faintest clue about where to go next. Just a thin, fragile hope that I've made the right assumptions. That there's a miracle waiting for us.

Three weeks ago, my biggest problem was which summer day camps Buzz might enjoy—would he prefer Mad Science? Or the one at the arts center?

Then a text message from a dead man blew our lives apart with the force of a grenade. Now I know what it means to be scared.

A bearded man looms in the aisle beside me. My heart falters as he gives me a squinty stare. But then I feel his gaze shift away from me. And then he slides into the seat opposite us, letting out a sigh.

As my heart rate descends, I realize he was probably only

questioning the wisdom of taking the empty seat across from a preschool-aged kid. A quick glance over my shoulder confirms that ours was the last row with two open seats.

Breathe. I've managed to keep my wits for six states and counting.

Buzz shifts in his sleep as the bus begins to move again. "Shh," I whisper, a hand on his hip. He twitches, but his eyes remain closed.

Then the man across the aisle opens a paper bag and pulls out a fast-food hamburger in its cardboard container. When he pops it open, the pleasantly greasy smell hits me right away. Buzz sits up suddenly. "Mama? I'm hungry."

My heart clenches, but I keep my tone even. "It's not mealtime. It's time to sleep."

He peers out the window. "I want a Happy Meal. They have that?" He points.

Sure enough, the Golden Arches are gliding by as the driver accelerates toward the on-ramp.

"Not tonight," I say quickly. "Do you want to hear a story? How about Frog and Toad?"

"You have the book?"

I shake my head. "But I remember how it goes."

"But, Mama," he says, "I'm *hungry.*"

Fear rises inside my chest. "You had the raisins for a snack." *Hours ago.* "How about a sip of water?" I still have half a bottle, but that's it. I already fed him the mints from my purse.

Dread fills me up as I try to think of another way to distract him. We're hundreds of miles from the only home he's ever known, with no food and no money. For the first time in my child's life, he's gone without dinner.

And I have no idea how I'm going to feed him tomorrow, either. I can't even think about that right now. "Buzzy," I whisper. "Let me tell you about the time Frog and Toad were afraid." Because I need that story right now like I need my next breath.

"Okay," he says, and I could faint with relief.

I'm just settling into the story when the man across the aisle pulls out a bag of French fries and starts eating them. The scent clobbers me, and my empty stomach gurgles.

"Mama, I want French fries," Buzz announces immediately.

"I'm sorry, Buzz," I whisper. "We don't have any."

He starts to cry. "I'm so hungry!" He presses his face against my ribs and sobs.

And that's when I finally break. My eyes flood, and my chest shakes and I bite my lip until I draw blood. *I'm sorry. I'm sorry. I'm so sorry.*

"Miss. Here." The man seated across from us is holding out the sack of fries. And even though I know what I'm going to do, I still hesitate.

He extends the packet a little farther. "I don't need them."

My hand closes around the bag and Buzz makes a little whimper as I pass it to him. The first fry is in his mouth a fractional second later.

"Say thank you," I choke out.

"Thank you," Buzz says immediately.

"Thank you," I repeat, but I'm too embarrassed to look the guy in the eye. Buzz gobbles down the fries inside of three minutes, while I try not to cry anymore. I pull a wet wipe out of the bag to mop my face, and then degrease his fingers. The wipes are lavender-scented, from an organic shop my mother loves. Last month, my most pressing worry was germs from the playground equipment.

I tuck the empty bag and the spent wipe into the seat pocket. Then I start whispering to Buzz again about Frog and Toad. My little boy lolls against me, falling asleep with his head in my lap. I try to slow my breathing, but fear crashes through me like waves on a rocky beach at high tide.

The bus grows very quiet as we ride on through the night. And then the man across the aisle speaks so softly that I almost miss it. "Is there someone who will help you after you get off this bus?"

I turn my chin a fraction and consider my answer. "I hope so. I've bet everything on it."

The bus rolls on as I leak silent tears. I'm practically drowning in them. It's the first time I've cried in years.

I keep picturing Zain's lopsided smile, and his caterpillar eyebrows.

He's *gone*. And I know it's partly my fault.

My breathing is ragged, and my cheeks become chapped from repeated swipes from the back of my hand. The man across the aisle shifts uncomfortably in his seat, and I don't blame him. I'm like a broken dam. If I were him, I'd steer clear, too.

At some point I drift off, waking only when the driver calls out a stop. *Howard City. Morley. Stanwood.*

When we hit Reed City I wake up for good, because we're almost there. The bus is lit by gray morning light that washes the color from everything, like a Chime Co. video. My eyes are swollen and tender, and my nose is clogged.

The bus is emptier now. And the man across the aisle is gone. I never heard him leave.

Careful not to wake Buzz, I shift my stiff legs. Something scratchy rubs my ankle. And when I look down, there's a white thing sticking out of the mesh water bottle pocket of my backpack. A piece of paper.

I pluck it out. It's a sheet torn from a magazine that's been folded several times to conceal a small window envelope—the kind you'd use to pay a bill. I gasp when I find a hundred dollars in twenties inside.

There's also a note in chicken-scratch handwriting on the envelope.

Be well and use this to get a nice meal for yourself and your boy. My sister works in social services at the hospital in Cedar Springs. If you are in real trouble call this number and ask for Kelsy. Take care and God bless.

My eyes fill. *No no no,* I can't start crying all over again. I breathe slowly and focus on the spindly pines passing by out the window. At least I can pay that man back. When this is all over, I'll find him through his sister and send him a fat check.

He needs to know how much I appreciate it.

I breathe deeply until the urge to cry passes. Buzz stirs, and I tell him the glorious truth. "We're almost there, buddy," I say, stroking his back. "We're finally getting off this bus."

47

The first thing I do after we stagger off the bus is lead Buzz across the street to a diner. The place is a little shabby, with worn linoleum floors and faded vinyl booths.

But we're shabbier. And so hungry. I have never been happier to be anywhere.

Breathing in the scent of coffee and bacon, I feel almost optimistic. "Let's eat a big breakfast," I say to Buzz as we slide into a booth. "Want a booster seat?"

He shakes his head. "I want pancakes. And bacon?"

"You got it."

Buzz smiles at me, his face barely visible above the table, and my heart breaks a little more.

After a good breakfast, I lead Buzz for a lengthy walk toward the heart of Cadillac. It's an ugly little town on the shore of a lake. But I find a house with a hand-lettered sign in the yard reading FURNISHED APARTMENT FOR RENT.

I knock on the door, and an old woman answers. "Help you?" she demands.

"Hello, ma'am." I hold Buzz's hand and try to appear harmless. "We just got off a long bus ride, and I haven't found a motel yet. Is there any way we could pay for a few hours' use of your furnished apartment to get a little rest before we meet up with my cousin? I have twenty-five dollars. It would really help me out."

She squints at me, and I can already hear her refusal forming. And Buzz is looking up at me like I must be crazy.

"Sure, honey," she says. "Just this once."

The tepid shower in her creaky over-the-garage apartment is the best one I've ever had. After I change into clean clothes and brush my teeth, I scrub Buzz up, too.

Then I set the alarm on the unfamiliar clock radio for three hours and take a much-needed nap.

We wake up groggy when the alarm blares around noon.

After I pay the homeowner, I'll still have more than fifty dollars left. My biggest problems are now: finding a ride to Harrietta, which is about eighteen miles away, and finding Woody.

And possibly Drew.

I give a silent prayer. *Please, God, let one or both of them be here.* I hope I didn't drag my child across the country for nothing.

"I really appreciate this," I say for the tenth time as Mrs. Jonas—the landlady—pulls into Harrietta in her aging Ford Explorer.

"It's no big thing. I hope you find your cousin."

"I'm sure I will," I lie.

"Where do you want me to drop you?"

I take quick stock of the tiny post office and the shuttered library that comprise the downtown of Harrietta. Then my eyes land on the best choice. "Right there, if you don't mind," I say, pointing at Red's Hardware and Lumber. If Woody or Drew lives here, they'll be known at the hardware store.

Hopefully.

She pulls over and wishes me well.

"Let me give you some gas money," I say, reaching for my bag.

"You've given me enough," she says, holding up a hand. "Good luck and God bless you."

It's the second time someone has said that to me. And I guess I need all the help I can get.

"What is this store?" Buzz asks as we step inside the big space.

"They sell tools, and wood to build things. But we're not really shopping today."

"Okay," he says. But as we approach the counter, Buzz drops my hand and darts down an aisle. I watch as he kneels down in front of a rack of die-cast metal work vehicles.

Well, crap. He's going to ask me for one, and I'm going to have to say no. But in the meantime, I use this moment of freedom to approach the big, bearded man behind the counter.

"Can I help you, miss?" he asks.

"Hope so," I say, giving him a smile. "I'm in town to visit friends, but I misplaced the address. You probably know Woody—he's an army vet. And maybe his friend Jay? Blue eyes. He's got a scar right here." I trace a line under my eye and pray that Buzz isn't listening right now.

The big man is already shaking his head, though. "Haven't heard of 'em. Sorry."

My heart plummets. "You haven't? I'm sure they'd come in here."

"Nah, sorry." He crosses his burly arms. But then his phone rings. "'Scuse me." He answers his phone.

Crushed, I turn my back on him so he won't see the gutted look on my face. I go back to Buzz, where I left him in the aisle. I crouch down and watch him play, one truck in each hand.

What the hell am I going to do now?

I hear the big man behind the counter hang up his phone call. He can't be the only one working here, though. Maybe someone else in the store has heard of Woody and Jay. I can't give up yet.

"Hey . . . Pete?" I hear the guy calling to someone else. "You going anywhere near Pine Pitch Road today?"

"Oh, yah," answers another voice. "Heading out now. Got some lumber for Buzz."

My son lifts his head at the sound of his own name. "He said . . ."

I clamp a hand over his little mouth. "Shh."

". . . Would you take a note to him?" the cashier asks. "Gimme a sec to write it."

"'Course. I'll go there first."

My heart pounds, like I've just committed a crime. Carefully, I take the trucks out of Buzz's hands. Then I hold a finger to my lips.

He nods solemnly.

Stooped low, I take his hand and scuttle toward the far aisle by the wall.

I hope they don't have security cameras in here, because I *look* guilty as hell right now. But we manage to slither out the front door without notice.

With a firm grip on Buzz's hand, I head across the street, toward the tiny public library. The sign on the door says CLOSED, but I need somewhere to stand, so I pretend to inspect the hours taped up inside the door.

"Mama, can we play in that park?" Buzz points at a little square where there's a patch of grass.

"Maybe," I hedge. "But I need to wait and see something first."

"Is it lunchtime yet? I'm hungry."

"Soon," I say vaguely.

He squirms. But a minute later I hear an engine roar to life. It's out of sight, but I have high hopes.

Sure enough, an ugly red flatbed truck rolls out from behind the lumberyard a couple of minutes later. It's laden with plywood and what must be somebody's new front door.

After making a slow left turn onto the empty street, it heads up the road, away from us.

I clasp Buzz's hand. "Come on. We're following that truck."

"Why?"

"See those boards on the back? I think they're for my friend. We can find him."

We set off together, my eyes pasted to that truck. Although the truck is slow, we're a lot slower. The road curves in the distance, too, which means I'm going to lose sight of it. But just before the bend in the road, the truck slows all the way down and turns right.

I pick up my pace, following with dogged determination, and Buzz is happy to trot along beside me for maybe ten minutes.

But his legs are short, and I'm going too fast for him. He slows down, tugging on my hand. And he starts to complain well before we reach the turn. "Can't we go to the park now?"

"No, baby. Sorry. I'm hoping we can stay with my friend tonight. If he says yes, then we'll talk about the park."

Buzz lets out a sigh and drags his feet. He's probably exhausted from poor sleep and the change in our routine. He's underfed, too.

Yet I'm vibrating with nervous energy and burning up with curiosity. For the first time since I was brave enough to wonder if Drew is alive, I'm mere miles away from either heart-stopping success or soul-crushing failure. "How about a piggyback ride?"

"Okay," he mumbles.

I rotate my bag so it hangs in front of my body. Then I crouch down for Buzz to climb onto my back.

And it's fine, for maybe five minutes. But he weighs forty pounds, and it's a muggy June day. I'm already sweating and thirsty as I put one foot in front of the other.

"I want Grandma," Buzz says from my back.

Oh, hell. I've been trying not to think about her. She's probably frantic. I wonder what Ray is saying to her right now. What lies he's invented to explain why I'm gone.

He'll just play dumb, maybe. File a missing person report.

But she's probably hysterical, imagining Buzz and me dead in a ditch.

I can't think about her yet. Soon, but not yet. And I've finally reached the turnoff, which is signed for Pitch Pine Road, just as the man in the hardware store said.

It's a narrow road, with tall pines on either side. Truth in advertising. After a hundred exhausting paces, it levels out a little, and the road turns to dirt.

This is it. He has to be up here somewhere.

Then I hear a truck engine, and it's the most beautiful sound. I step into the trees and wait for it to pass.

"Mama? Are you hiding?"

Yes. I hitch him up a little higher and then lie. "The road is narrow," I say over my shoulder. "No sidewalk. I want to stay safe."

Someday I'll stop lying to my child.

The hardware store truck rumbles slowly past us. There isn't as much lumber in the back now. I wish I knew how long it's been since he turned up this road. It couldn't be more than fifteen or twenty minutes. He couldn't have driven that far.

"Mama, I can walk now," Buzz says as soon as we're back on the road.

"Oh glory be," I say, and he laughs as he slides down my back.

We walk ten more minutes before we come to the first driveway. But there's a very elaborate sign on the tree: THE WILSONS, with a lucky horseshoe hammered below their name.

That can't be it. And I know I haven't gone far enough. We press on.

48

Later, I won't remember these last few miles. It probably takes us two hours in the heat, the hill growing steeper again as we climb. We pass maybe a dozen driveways. Not a single one of them beckons to me. Some are so quiet and buttoned-up that it's clear nobody is home.

From one, arguing voices rise up. We hurry past without discussion.

And then, just up ahead, the road suddenly forks into two final driveways, with two last mailboxes on display. One has CARTER scrawled onto the metal.

The other mailbox is newer. Plain white metal. "*That one*," I whisper. But I'm not feeling confident. And we can't see the house from the road. "Stick close," I say to Buzz.

He holds my hand as if it were a Monday morning at preschool. We creep along the curving gravel driveway. The corner of a tidy log cabin comes into view. There's a single folding chair on the porch, a water bottle beside it. A red Jeep sits in the driveway.

I feel dizzy with expectation. But I could still be wrong. This is probably a stranger's house.

There's no name on the house, no ornamentation of any kind, unless we're counting a sign that says BEWARE OF THE DOG.

But I don't even see a dog.

"Buzz, can you wait behind that big tree?" I ask quietly, pointing at a thick trunk. "I'm going to knock on the door."

I haven't even thought about what I might say if his face appears in front of me. I haven't allowed myself to plan for that.

And now I realize I'm terrified. I don't know what I'll do if he's not here. And I don't even know what I'll do if he is.

"Okay," Buzz says, going along with the millionth weird thing I've asked him to do.

I nudge him into the shadows, behind a fat oak. "I won't leave your sight, I promise. Watch me."

He nods.

With a deep breath, I turn to face the house. I feel a bone-deep certainty that he's here. But I don't trust myself anymore. Maybe it's just the desperation talking. I take maybe three slow steps toward the porch.

But then I hear it—the clear trill of a man whistling. It's coming around the side of the house.

Goose bumps rise up on my skin. I change direction, crossing in front of Buzz's tree, inching toward the corner of the house for a glimpse. The lumber comes into view first—it's lying on a sawhorse or a table.

Then I see a man, bent over a workbench. And all the air leaves my body. Because I know the familiar angle of his neck as he inspects his work. And the flex of his hand as he tests the smoothness of a piece of wood.

A dog's low growl startles both of us.

The man straightens up quickly, turning toward me, his eyes finding me where I'm half-hidden behind the corner of his house. "Who's—"

I take another step, revealing myself fully. But I don't say a word. I can't. I'm too busy cataloging all the tiny, familiar things. That ARMY T-shirt stretched across his chest. Those blue eyes. I'd know him anywhere, in spite of the unfamiliar beard on his face. And the deep tan of a man who doesn't work in an office anymore.

And I still can't speak. Not even a squeak. I can't move, either. I'm afraid to ask my questions. I'm afraid he'll send me away.

But I don't want to stop looking at him. Not ever.

"Ariel?" he whispers as clear blue eyes take me in from head to toe. "Holy shit."

My thoughts exactly.

The German shepherd is also surprised. He lets out a single bark, stalking toward me.

Drew holds up one hand, palm down, moving as if the gesture is automatic. "Buster, sit. Stay."

The dog drops his butt on the grass, and I gasp. *Buster.* The dog from *Toy Story*. My face is wet with tears, and I don't know how they got there.

Drew advances slowly, like I might be a mirage. And I know the feeling. It's impossible that he's walking toward me. And yet he is.

"You're the one asking for me at the hardware store?" he asks.

I give him a jerky nod, but that's all. I didn't plan this part. I never thought I would see him again. My throat threatens to close up, and my tears make me angry all of a sudden. "I don't even know what to call you," I croak. "You didn't even tell me your real name."

"God, I'm sorry." He's still coming closer. And I'm fighting dueling urges—to step back, or maybe to launch myself at him and never let go.

". . . I only left because I had to. Not because I didn't love you. I miss you every damn day."

I feel a jolt of heartache. And then he's *right* there, pulling me into his arms. He smells like sunshine and cotton and skin. I push my face against the collar of his T-shirt and try not to shake.

"Sweetheart," he whispers. "How did you get here?"

I don't answer right away, because I can't process the question until I force myself to take a step backward, out of his embrace. "That . . . that's a very long story," I stammer. "But first, there's someone—"

Before I can get the sentence out, the dog barks. Loudly. His dark nose points toward the woods. Toward my little boy.

Drew's whole demeanor changes. He steps back and squares himself toward the tree line. "*Who's there?*" he demands.

Then he draws a handgun out of his pocket and aims it toward the big oak.

Cold, naked fear rolls through me so fast that I feel my insides collapse. "Drew, *NO!*" I shriek.

He drops his arm immediately, the gun pointed at the grass.

And then Buzz steps out from behind the tree, terror in his eyes.

"*Holy . . .*" Drew whispers.

My whole body is shaking. But I raise my arms, offering them to Buzz.

He runs toward me like a lost soul, colliding with my hips, grabbing me around the waist, burying his face at my hip. I palm his head and try to remember how to breathe.

Drew stands a few feet away, gun holstered, body locked tight. His face all shock as he takes in my child. "Ariel . . . ?"

"This is Buzz," I say in a wobbly voice.

"Buzz," he repeats slowly. He licks his lips and takes a slow breath. His blue eyes are trained on both of us. So steady. So serious. "Is he . . . ?"

I nod slowly.

A gasp whooshes out of his chest.

We stand there, nobody speaking, while I try to get over the memory of a gun pointed toward my baby.

Only Buzz seems to relax. After a moment I catch him looking behind me, and I see that he's waving at the dog.

"Buster, come," Drew says quietly.

The dog weaves his sleek body between us, ears up, tail wagging. "Lie down."

He plops down on the grass, tongue lolling.

"Let him smell your hands," Drew says softly. "You can pet him."

Buzz is on his knees in a heartbeat, hands out. The dog shoves his wet nose into his small palm, looking for treats. Then my little boy reaches out and ruffles the fur between his ears.

"Give him this," Drew says, fishing a dog treat out of his pocket.

Buzz looks up, and their fingers touch as he takes the dog treat from Drew and offers it to the shepherd, who takes it politely, tail wagging.

Then Buzz looks up at Drew. "Do you have any food for people?"

Drew's face flips through about seventeen emotions in quick succession, ending with the corners of his mouth turning up. But his eyes are sad. "Yeah I do, little buddy. Do you like ham sandwiches?"

"Sure." Buzz hops to his feet.

"Go into the house." Drew points toward the steps at the end of his porch. "There's a plate right inside the refrigerator. Your mom and I will be there in a minute. Buster will go with you, but don't feed him any of the sandwich."

"Okay!" He leaps toward the stairs.

"Wash your hands!" I call after the back of Buzz, who's already on the porch, stretching up for the screen door handle.

Buster follows him, and the screen door slams just seconds later.

Then it's just me and the man I still think of as Drew.

"Holy shit, Ariel." His eyes are suddenly red. "I had no idea."

"I know," I say, my throat like sand.

"No idea," he repeats. Then he bends over and braces his hands above his knees. "He's not on your Instagram."

I let out a shocked laugh. "You look at my *Instagram*?"

"All the time," he says, straightening up, his eyes searching my face again. "But it's all glass. I love the new stuff—those bottles with flattened sides, like gemstones."

"Thanks?" In my wildest dreams, I never imagined having this conversation.

He shakes his head. "You never even show your face, and I decided that was a good thing. So long as you kept making art, I knew you were doing okay. But I didn't ever have to look at selfies of you with some other guy."

As if. I swallow down my fear and confusion. "Well, I thought you were *dead*, Drew. Or—not Drew. Jay. I don't even know what to call you."

"Yeah, I bet." He puts a hand to the back of his neck and rubs, and the familiar gesture makes me want to cry. "I'll answer to anything you call me."

"Anything?" I grumble, and he grins.

But then his smile fades. "Sweetheart, are you in trouble? Is that why you're here?"

I manage to nod. "So much trouble. But can we go inside? I need to be near Buzz."

"*Buzz.*" He gives me a watery smile. "I can't stand it. You know I didn't leave you because I wanted to, right? On your way to getting in trouble, did you figure that out?"

"Sort of," I whisper.

He moves fast then, wrapping his arms around me again. The feel of his body against mine is so familiar I almost can't bear it—except for the beard, which tickles my neck. "Christ, Ariel," he says to my jaw. "I'm probably saying all the wrong things. I can't believe you're here."

I shudder out a breath, and my eyes feel hot. But I make myself pull away, while I'm still capable of it. "Do you have any more guns in your house?"

"Why?" He glances toward the house, looking confused. But then his eyes widen. "Oh, shit. It's okay—they're locked in a safe in the cellar. This is the only key." He pulls a chain out from the inside of his T-shirt.

I swallow hard. "I've never been so scared as I have these past four days. I can't even think straight."

"Come on." He takes my hand. "Come inside. You're going to be okay. And so is"—his eyes redden—"our little boy."

"He doesn't know," I whisper. "I told him we were going to see a friend. I didn't know if we would find you."

He blows out a breath. "I'm so glad you did. But that means someone else could, too." He squeezes my hand and leads me toward the door.

49

The main floor of the log cabin is one big room—a kitchen at the back, fronted by a cozy seating area and a fireplace.

Buzz is already seated at the kitchen counter, as if this were his own house. He's eating a sandwich while the dog waits patiently at his feet, probably hoping for scraps.

"How's the food, little guy?" Drew asks, his voice husky with emotion.

Buzz just nods and takes a huge bite. I don't even think he's tasting it.

Drew stands stock-still and watches him for a long beat. Then he sort of shakes himself and turns to me. "Are you hungry?"

"I don't know" is my truthful answer. My mind is swirling too fast to think about my stomach.

Drew moves into the kitchen and starts opening cabinets. He makes two more sandwiches and pushes one toward me. He takes out three glasses and begins filling them with water. But then he stops before he gets to the third one. "Do you drink milk?" he asks Buzz. "I used to like milk with my sandwiches."

"Yep," Buzz says, swinging his feet.

Drew goes to the fridge and grabs a gallon of milk.

"How about a thank-you?" I say automatically.

"Thank you," Buzz chirps.

Drew puts the glass in front of him and then watches with wide eyes as Buzz lifts the glass with both hands and gulps from it.

"*Jesus Christ*," he whispers, his voice full of wonder.

Not that I blame him. Sometimes I feel just the same way when I look at Buzz.

I manage to eat a few bites of food, while Drew pulls out a phone and taps on a number. "Hey, Woody," he says. "I got a situation. Ariel is here, and we're going to need to tighten up security. Yes, *that* Ariel. She walked up the road and . . ." His eyes cut to Buzz. "There are complications. Come over later and you'll see for yourself."

Buzz chases his sandwich with a handful of chips.

When he's done, Drew grabs a tennis ball and asks him if he wants to play fetch with Buster. "His favorite thing in the world is having somebody throw the ball for him in the yard."

Buster wags his tail in agreement, and Buzz climbs down from the stool. "'Kay. Let's go."

That's how I end up outside, sitting on the porch in whispered conversation while Buzz throws a slobbery tennis ball for the dog.

I'm trying to provide a quick accounting of my last three weeks, but it's such a wild tale that he keeps stopping to ask questions. "You got my text *when*?" And "Zarkey's sister is a *drug dealer*? Fuck." He grips his coffee mug like he'd rather strangle something.

I know I'm blowing his mind, but we have a lot of catching up to do.

"How did they kill Zain, do you think?" he asks.

"The cop just said opiates. I don't have the details."

He's silent for a long moment. "Let me ask you if you remember something—five years ago, did anyone in your family drive a gray Mercedes with darkly tinted windows? Like maybe Ray?"

I shake my head. "He's a BMW guy."

"I wonder what Zarkey drives. On the morning your father died, I saw a car pulling away from your parents' house when I arrived there."

"Why did you go over there, anyway?"

He watches Buzz for a moment before answering. As if he's trying to decide what to say. "I had a lot of information about Live-Match and the fraudulent warrants. I knew Ray was guilty, but I didn't have enough evidence to pin it on him. Then I figured out your dad wasn't part of it. I was going to rat Ray out to Edward."

"Oh."

"I was going to explain what a huge liability it was. That he could lose the whole company in the scandal. I called, and he told me to come to the house."

"And you told him?"

Slowly, he shakes his head. "I snuck up to his office window to make sure he was alone, right? And he was . . ." He swallows hard. "He was slumped over his desk. So I hopped up onto the front porch—just like you told me you did in high school. The front door was open. I went in and felt his pulse. Nothing. He was gone, honey."

Chills climb down my body. "It was ruled an accidental overdose. But it wasn't, was it?"

Another shake of his head. "I don't know how it happened. But I could tell that someone was in his office just before I got there. The computer was all lit up—a spreadsheet on the screen. But I tabbed over to the command window and started scrolling. Guess what was purged a few minutes earlier from your dad's terminal?"

"What?" I whisper.

"*Everything*. LiveMatch and two judges."

"*Two* judges?"

"The other one was Amelia Brown. I didn't document it, though. I was not willing to get caught scrolling through a dead man's computer. I needed to get out of there."

"So . . ." I try to piece together what happened that day. "My father takes his pills, and then he dies. Then somebody does a little work on his computer, probably after he's dead. And then you show up."

"Right. Although I'd spoken to him ninety minutes beforehand. He was his usual grumpy self."

"What time was that?"

Drew rubs the back of his neck. "A few minutes to ten? That's my best guess."

"Ray told my mother that he'd stopped by to see my father that morning." I wish I could remember his exact words, but the details of their argument didn't seem very important at the time. "I think Ray dropped off his medication. Do you think Ray could have . . . ?" I can't even say it out loud.

Drew covers my hand with his. "I really don't know. Although the car I saw driving away wasn't Ray's."

"Right," I whisper. "Maybe Zarkey's?"

He makes a face. "It burns me up that I never fingered Zarkey."

"Zain didn't, either, though. Or maybe he did, and didn't get a chance to tell me. But he must have tipped the Zarkeys off somehow. And you're *sure* my father wasn't in on it?"

"Pretty sure. He wasn't a programmer. And I'll bet Ray had big plans for LiveMatch. As a new, separate venture."

"*Oh.*" That makes sense. I think about how my father treated Ray, capturing a majority stake in the company for a tool that Ray invented. "Ray would never share another business with his brother. Not a second time."

"Right. So that was my shortcut—tell your dad, make it his problem, and then leave town for a while. I thought I could watch the heads roll from a distance."

"So you wouldn't get arrested for identity theft?"

"Yeah." He clears his throat.

I withdraw my hand from his. "That's not what happened, though. You just left. And faked your own death so you didn't have to get involved. That obituary stunt was cold."

"Whoa, there." His eyes widen. "That wasn't a stunt. That was a *threat*. I didn't publish that obituary."

I stare. "You didn't? Who did?"

"Probably Ray," he says, watching Buzz throw the ball. "It was a message to me—that he knew where I was, and what I was doing. I assume he hired a PI to find out everything he could about me. The essential facts of my life were right—they knew I had a motorcycle, they knew I was living in North Carolina. They even knew my dog's name at the time."

"So . . ." My head reels. "They published an obituary for Drew Miller. As in—here's what we'll do to you if we ever see you again?"

"Yeah." He shrugs. "It's clever, you've got to admit."

"Sure, if you're into really fucking evil humor."

He laughs suddenly. "I've missed your snark, lady. And I cannot believe you and Zain found all that stuff—the judge. Ernie's death. The video of Amina . . ."

"We got it by sort of following you around the network. Well, Zain did. Oh my God. *Poor Zain*."

He shakes his head. "I can't believe he's gone." Drew sighs. "That's fucking *awful*."

My eyes get wet again.

On the lawn, Buster drops the ball. He lifts his head and lets out a single bark. His tail begins swishing back and forth.

A bearded man crosses the lawn toward us, his hand raised in greeting.

"Woody," I guess as he approaches. "Army vet. Bowling fiend."

"That's right, and you must be Ariel." He's older than Drew. Maybe forty. "I heard we got a situation. Who's the little guy?" He jerks a thumb at Buzz.

"His name is Buzz," Drew says. "So it would be helpful if you didn't call me that for a while."

"Buzz." Woody's forehead furrows. "You mean to tell me . . . ?"

Drew nods. His lips quirk into a smile.

Woody turns to stare at Buzz, who's seated in the grass now. The dog comes over and flops down to put his head on Buzz's knee.

"*Jayzus*," Woody hoots. "Looks just like you, except handsome."

"Yeah, I noticed that."

Woody barks out a laugh, then he turns to extend a hand to me. "Unfuckingbelievable. Nice to meet you, sweetheart." I shake his hand. "Goddamn, Jay! I don't talk to you for two days, and look what happens?"

Drew shakes his head. "You have no idea. Ariel stepped in the mess I left behind on my way out of town. Turns out I missed a few things. We're going to need to make ourselves scarce for a little while."

"Oh, damn." Woody's face falls. "All right. Time for a family vacation. It's high season, but we can probably still find you a cottage in the UP. Or somewhere else remote where you can hide for a few weeks."

"But then what?" I have to ask. "We can't just hide forever." They both turn and stare at me, and I realize that's exactly what

Drew's been doing. For years. "It's no life for a child," I say slowly. "We have to end this."

Drew—no, Jay turns to me with soft eyes. "I know, baby. But Zarkey and your uncle are in bed with a lot of law enforcement. So we need a strategy that's *tight*. Which means I need some time to strategize."

"Oh."

"But we *will* end this. I thought I couldn't throw Ray under the bus, because . . ." He stops.

"Because why?" I ask. "You could have blown the whole company up from a safe distance. But you didn't."

"I didn't," he repeats, his serious gaze fixed on me. "You're right."

"Was that because you thought Ray would come for you?"

"Something like that." He rubs the back of his neck, and I wait for him to explain further.

But he doesn't. "Like what?" I press.

He shrugs. "I didn't make it out of Maine with the evidence I needed. And a halfway accusation wasn't going to be enough."

That isn't a very satisfying answer. But that's all he gives me.

There are plans to make, so we offer Buzz a movie on Jay's TV.

Tickled at meeting a man named Woody, he picks *Toy Story*. "You guys could watch it with me."

When Jay answers, his expression is as sad as I've ever seen it. "Someday we'll watch all four of them in a row," he says. "But we have some work to do now, okay?"

Buzz is asleep in front of the TV not fifteen minutes later.

Woody and Jay bring a laptop out onto the porch. "So how'd you find us?" Woody asks me. "I thought our tracks were buried pretty deep."

"They are. But I *guessed*. His old computer password was Harrietta. And I'd heard all about his best friend in Michigan."

Woody laughs, shaking his head. "You are terrifying. In a good way. I hope the bad guys don't put that together."

"I'm worried that they can," Jay says quietly. "It's possible that Ray—or Zarkey—knows exactly where I am. They might have known for years. Let's not be sitting ducks if they decide I need to be silenced. We're going to have to rig up the perimeter."

Woody nods sagely. "Let's get to it."

For two hours, I watch the two men hang motion sensors and cameras around the edges of the property. Jay owns three acres that he bought off Woody—whose real name is David Carter.

"You've done this before?" I ask, as they cooperate with nothing more than the odd word or grunt.

"Yeah," Jay says, unspooling an extension cord.

"I can't believe—after all you've seen—that *cameras* are your big solution."

"Rich, isn't it?" The beard alters his smile, but the blue eyes are exactly how I remember them. "Except I don't use cloud cameras. My data stays on my network. And usually we're only violating the privacy of a white-tailed deer."

When Buzz wakes up from his impromptu nap and comes outside to investigate, that's exactly what Jay tells him—that they're setting up wildlife cameras. "If we're lucky, we'll see a bear," he says. Then he reaches down and puts one hand on Buzz's head, stroking his soft hair.

I can't look away. Watching them together makes me ache. I never thought I'd see this. I never even dared to hope.

"Is it almost dinnertime?" Buzz asks suddenly, snapping me out of my reverie.

"Sure, baby. Soon."

Jay has defrosted some meat, and we make hamburgers, which Woody grills behind the house. We eat outside at the picnic table. I keep glancing at Jay, as if to verify that he's really here.

And he does the same to me.

After dinner, I take Buzz upstairs and make him change into his pajamas and brush his teeth. There are two bedrooms up here, but only one of them is furnished. He's working a bachelor vibe—a king-sized mattress on a blocky metal bed frame. The only other furniture is a dresser. And right in the center of it is a glass bowl. That I made.

My heart lurches as I lift the piece and cup it in my hands. It's from a series of ombré glass that I did about two years ago, for the gallery on Exchange Street. The price was probably $150.

He bought it. Somehow. It's the only decorative item in this room.

"Mama?" Buzz calls from the bed.

I set the bowl down and then tuck Buzz into one side of the bed. It's a warm, sticky night, so I only use the sheet. I switch on a box fan that's poised in the window. It makes a pleasant hum, which will probably help Buzz fall asleep.

"Where are you going to be?" he asks.

"Right there beside you." I pat the mattress. "After I talk to the grown-ups."

"I want my Frog and Toad book," he complains.

"Tomorrow I'll see if the library is open," I promise. "It's late, honey. Time to sleep."

"Stay here," he demands.

I lie down beside him, and Buzz closes his eyes. Soon he's sleeping deeply. And my eyelids feel like lead weights.

But then Jay appears in the doorway, watching us with a soft expression on his face that I've never seen before. I get up and join him on the landing outside the bedroom.

"This is for you," he whispers, pressing a clean T-shirt and a pair of boxers into my hands. "Make yourself at home. But there are a couple more things you need to know."

"Like what?" I whisper.

He draws me to the doorway, where Buzz is sleeping, and taps the heavy wood door. "This is reinforced. And it locks with a bolt," he whispers. "The closet is built the same way. It's a safe room. If there's trouble, lock yourself in this room. And keep away from the windows."

I blink. "You built a fortress?"

His frown is grim. "I have enemies, and Woody is a paranoid guy. There's a fire ladder under the bed, too. It hooks onto the window frame." He points. "If you think someone is going to breach the door, leave by the window. Or lock yourself in the closet. The lights come on automatically."

I grab his arm and pull him back to the staircase landing, where Buzz is less likely to hear us. "You think that could happen?"

"Anything could happen, baby," he says, cupping my face in one broad hand. "I just like to be prepared." Then he leans in and kisses me.

I'm not ready, either. There's no time to brace myself against the gentleness of his kiss, or the drag of his thumb across my jaw. The pain of losing him is still a raw, ugly thing inside of me. I don't know whether to grab him by the T-shirt or shove him away from me.

So I pick the second thing, pushing off his firm chest and taking a healthy step backward.

The result, I think, is that we're both confused. We just stare at each other for a long beat, while I try to figure out what to say.

Until someone clears his throat.

When I look down, Woody is grinning up at us from the sofa. "Not to interrupt, but I've got something you should see."

50

As soon as I sit down on the sofa, Woody hands me his laptop. There's a news article on the screen: **Portland homicide detectives take over the investigation of a drug overdose.**

The piece is only a couple of sentences long, and it doesn't mention Zain by name. But it does mention forced entry into a basement apartment on Grant Street. "It's him. That's where he lived."

Jay rubs my back gently. "Maybe this time they won't get away with it."

"I could call that cop back from some untraceable number." If that's a thing. "And tell her that the Zarkeys were trying to stop Zain from exposing them. And that my father's death might have been related."

"Yeah, maybe," Woody agrees. "But first I want you to log in to your email and see if anyone is trying to contact you."

The idea gives me a flare of fear. "Is there any way that could reveal where I am?"

"No, we use a VPN for absolutely everything," Jay says. "Anyone who'd hacked your email would see an IP address in Europe. You know your password?"

"Of course." I open a window and put my password into Google. And I get nowhere fast, because of two-factor authentication. Without my phone, I'm locked out. "I *hate* technology," I cry, burying my face in my hands.

"Hey, it's okay." His hand finds my lower back again, and I fight the urge to sag against his solid body and close my eyes. "You look exhausted. Go to bed, sweetheart. We'll figure this out in the morning."

"Good plan," Woody says, rising. "I'll see you at three, man."

I pick my head up. "Three? A.M.?"

"Second shift of the watch," he says, taking the laptop and flipping to another app. I see six different displays on the screen—each one a live cam of Jay's house and yard. "Lock up behind me."

He leaves, and Jay bolts the door. "Go on," he says softly. "Sleep. I'll come to bed after Woody shows up to keep watch."

I yawn so hard that it shakes me. And then I climb the stairs to sleep beside Buzz.

Hours later, I wake suddenly when the bed shifts under someone's weight. My eyes pop open, but I don't move.

I'm lying on my side in the middle of the bed. Buzz is sleeping in front of me, his limbs flung wide like a starfish, eyes slammed shut.

Jay is silent, but I can feel his gaze on us. Then his hand swims into view. He strokes his son's hair with a slow, barely-there touch before retreating again.

I hold my breath, and I couldn't even tell you why.

Jay settles behind me. But then he moves closer—his chest to my back, his arm draped over my hip. He relaxes.

My eyes close, and I try to remember how to breathe.

For years I've wanted this. *Exactly* this—a peaceful moment with the two most important people in my life. But now that it's here, I don't trust it.

Doesn't make me paranoid, either. There are people out there who would snatch it away again in a heartbeat.

My chest contracts suddenly, as if the weight of it all is more than my body can take. I make a noise that comes out like a sob.

Jay's arm tightens around me. "Baby?"

My whole body shudders, and my eyes are fountains.

Jay slides off the bed. He scoops me out from under the sheet and carries me out of the bedroom, while I cling to him with a white-knuckled grip.

In the bathroom, he sets me down on the counter. After closing the door, he grabs a towel and begins dabbing at my streaming tears.

But I don't want a towel. I push it away and lean against his chest. Burying my face in the collar of his T-shirt, I just let go and cry.

He doesn't ask me why, thank God. I don't know what I'd even say. It's just an avalanche of terror and anguish.

"Shh, shh" is all he says as I soak his shirt. "I got you." His arms close protectively around me, and it only makes me sob harder. I lean into him and practically drown us both, until finally I run out of tears.

The night is so quiet that all I can hear are my own sniffles, and the sound the borrowed cotton T-shirt makes when he rubs my back. "You should sleep," he whispers eventually. "Let me take you back to bed."

Neither of us moves, though. I'm too busy staring up at him—still stunned to be in his presence. He's so familiar, except for the beard.

I lift my hands up to his face and run my knuckles through it. "You look like a mountain man."

His smile is surprised. "You hate it?"

I swallow hard, and shake my head. "No, you're . . ." *You're ev-erything.* "I *missed* you. A lot. All the time. I'm still angry."

"Yeah, I'll bet," he whispers.

"You could have talked to me. But you didn't *trust* me." I feel so much sudden rage that tears threaten again.

"Hey, hey." He puts both hands on my shoulders. "I was trying to *protect* you. It almost worked."

"I don't want *protection*." But even as I snarl these words at him, I realize they're completely hypocritical. All I want in the world right now is protection. I want him to scoop me up in strong arms and never let go. *Fuck.* I take a deep breath and try again. "Look—I'm mad. And I want answers. But when I found that obituary I could barely get out of bed for a week. Please don't lie to me like that again. I love you."

God, what a lot of word vomit. My nose is probably red and runny. I'm a hot mess. But at least *I* finally told the truth. Even if he never did.

Jay looks back at me with clear blue eyes that don't miss a thing. He can probably hear the gears grinding in my head. "I love you, too," he whispers. "Always did. And I won't let you out of my sight. Promise."

The words sort of hang there in the air between us, after all this time. I blink back at him through watery eyes and wonder if it would be weird if I asked him to repeat that a second time.

I don't get the chance, though, because he leans in slowly, the way you'd approach a feral animal—one that might bolt. And he kisses me once, very softly.

But I don't bolt. Instead, I grab his T-shirt in both hands—the way I've wanted to since I walked into his yard—and I crush my mouth to his.

He lets out a grunt of surprise. But he's always been a smart man, so he catches up in a hurry. His fingers tangle in my hair, and he steps closer to me, extinguishing all the empty space between us.

Sliding deeper into the kiss is like sliding into a warm bath. The heat of his body against mine is like medicine, and his mouth is nourishment. For the first time in weeks, I forget to worry.

Besides, we were always good at this. We're still good at it. His hands remember the shape of me. And mine remember exactly how to make him shiver, as I slide my palm beneath his T-shirt to stroke his chest.

It's like riding a bike. He still knows just where to drag his roughened fingers up my spine, and just where to kiss my neck so that I melt further into him.

"Love you," he whispers again. Maybe he knows how much I crave those words.

I don't say it back. I'm too occupied with the button on his pants. And the zipper.

"Love you," he repeats, sliding my T-shirt up over my heated skin. Then, with the same sweet fire that always burns between us, he shows me how much.

Right there on the bathroom counter.

51

JAY

Jay wakes up alone, to the sound of birdsong coming through the window, just like he does every morning. For a split second he's filled with the heart-rending certainty that yesterday was some kind of fever dream.

But then he smells coffee and bacon. His eyes flip open. The bed is an empty mess around him, and his leg is stiff from sleeping in his prosthetic, which he never does.

When he rolls over, he spots a fuzzy tiger shark on the floor beside the bed. And a very small pair of pajamas with the Toy Story characters on them.

He's already grinning as he throws his legs over the side of the bed.

He takes a shower, trying to collect himself.

The appearance of Ariel and a child—*his son!*—is literally a dream come true. The fact that they're in danger—and it's his fault—is his most gut-churning nightmare realized.

He dresses in shorts and a T-shirt and goes downstairs. Buzz catches sight of him, and the boy's eyes grow round. "You have a metal leg!" he stage-whispers.

"That's right," he agrees, his voice hoarse from disuse. "Later I'll show you my plastic foot."

"*Cool.*" The little boy smiles, and Jay's heart threatens to explode.

So far, he's done a first-rate job of keeping his emotions in check and their interactions casual. But he's desperate to come clean. He wants to hold his little boy and promise never to leave him.

He won't make that promise, though, until he's sure he can fulfill it. If he has to trade his freedom—or even his life—for Ariel's and Buzz's, he'll do it. No question.

Downstairs, Woody is ensconced on the sofa in front of their makeshift control center—a laptop and two monitors.

"No bears in the woods?" Jay asks.

"No bears," Woody confirms. "Although we saw an eight-point buck about an hour ago." He stands up and removes his gun belt, passing it to Jay. "I'm headed home to sleep for a couple hours. Keep me apprised of your whereabouts."

"You know it."

Woody reaches over and squeezes his shoulder. "Call me if you need to strategize. This is a lot."

"I will. Thanks."

It is a lot. But it's the best kind.

Jay takes a look at the monitors and the motion sensor read-outs, but they're quiet. So he crosses to the kitchen, where Ariel is cleaning up from breakfast.

"I already fed Buzz and Woody scrambled eggs and bacon. Your fridge was well stocked," she says. "Your bacon is in the oven. Want a couple eggs? Fried or scrambled?"

"You cook? I've never seen that before."

"Don't judge." She gives him a warning look. "I had an awful little kitchen in that apartment."

"Scrambled, then. Please." He comes up behind her while she

breaks two eggs into a bowl. He wraps his arms around her and kisses the back of her neck. Given the choice, he would never let go again.

But Buzz has stopped playing with the dog to watch the two of them.

So he steps back and pours himself a cup of coffee before moving back to watch the monitors on the sofa.

After breakfast—and after a lot of grumbling—Ariel sets up a brand-new email account. Without her phone, she can't get into the other one.

The first message she sends is to her mother.

> Buzz and I are fine, but we felt the need to get out of town for a few days.

After a couple of minutes of thinking, she adds:

> I neglected to bring Frog and Toad, so I will probably have to buy another copy.

"She'll know it's me," she says quietly.

"What's Frog and Toad?" he whispers.

Ariel laughs. "A book. Buzz will train you up, you watch." Her smile fades as she addresses a fresh email message to Ray.

> Hi. I hope you saw the news item that Zain's death was suspicious. If you know anything about it, you need to come clean right now.

"That's a zinger," he says. "Short and sweet."

"Light on the details. Passive-aggressive. All my favorite things," she agrees. Then she sends it.

"Look," he tells her, pointing at the bookmarks on his browser. "Click there."

When she does, her Instagram comes up on the screen. It's a colorful display of glass objects she's made. "I check it daily," he says, "to see if there's anything new. Want to know which one is my favorite?"

She turns to him with unguarded surprise.

"Let me show you. It's down here . . ." He has to scroll down pretty far to find it and enlarge it.

"That one?" She studies the vase he's chosen. "It's kind of a clunky shape. Not my most elegant design."

"But see?" He zooms in on the photo. "You accidentally captured a reflection of your face in the glass. I look at it all the time." With his finger, he points to the screen, where the perfect curve of her cheekbone is visible in the vase's glossy surface.

"*Oh.*" Her brown eyes soften, and she presses her fingertips to her tear ducts. "That is . . . wow. Never thought to leave a comment, huh?" She takes the laptop back and scrolls to the top. "What kind of fan are you?"

"The silent kind," he says softly. "Nice job on getting your work into that gallery on Exchange Street, by the way. That must be pretty cool."

"It is. They take thirty percent, of course." She squints at the screen. "At least *somebody* is leaving me comments. Hmm." When she clicks on her latest post, there are five comments. But they're all from the same person, the last one from two days ago.

@LarriGlass: Where. Are. You.

@LarriGlass: Bitch please.

@LarriGlass: Lost your phone?

@LarriGlass: Not funny.

@LarriGlass: Scary lady / sister person looking for you and
              we are out of our minds but no big deal.

"Well, shit," Ariel says.

"Bad word, Mama," Buzz chimes in. "Can I have juice? Woody said there's juice."

Jay glances at the monitors, checking the cameras. There's still nothing there, but he feels like a sitting duck. They need a plan to end this.

He gets up to pour his little boy some juice. "Guys, I was thinking we should take a trip to Target. You probably need some things for the trip I want to take. Extra clothes."

"We need a car seat," Ariel says.

"Can we look at the toys?" Buzz asks immediately.

"You bet," Jay says before Ariel can weigh in. "I can't wait to look at the toys."

That's how he finds himself enmeshed in a discussion with Buzz two hours later regarding the pros and cons of Hot Wheels versus Tonka trucks. "Trucks are good in the sandbox, but not inside. Hot Wheels get jammed if you play outside." He adds a shrug of his narrow little shoulders.

Those are valid points, so Jay puts both the Tonka truck and the Hot Wheels collection in the cart. Ariel gives him a look he's never seen before, but recognizes instinctively. It says she doesn't approve, but she's not going to argue in front of the child.

He can work with that.

Then, while Buzz is thoroughly distracted, he puts a lot of supplies in the cart. Canned food, so they won't have to show their faces in stores near the cabin where they're headed. Boxes of that milk that you don't have to refrigerate. Cereal. Pasta.

"That's a lot," Ariel points out.

"Yup." He wants to be able to disappear. "Can you find some clothes, and bathing suits for you and Buzz? There's a lake."

While she's perusing the choices, he scans all the faces around him. There's nobody threatening. Nobody who looks like Zarkey or Ray. Nobody even skulking around in a low baseball cap. But he won't let his guard down. And he can't wait to get out of here.

At the register, Ariel begins unloading the cart. She's added some clothes, toiletries and a couple of picture books along with the car seat.

Ariel has changed. She was always fierce, and she still is. But her feisty personality has a new mama-bear quality. Buzz softens her a little. Makes her more accessible somehow.

Whenever her little boy raises his arms to be picked up by her, he *aches*.

"Your total is three forty-seven, seventy-eight," the cashier says.

Ariel flinches, but he hands over the cash without a second thought. This is what money is for.

Back at the Jeep, he moves the passenger seat forward and lifts the car seat into the back.

"Step aside. I'm a pro at this," Ariel says.

She isn't kidding. Turns out his Jeep has anchors in its seats that he didn't even know were there.

"All right, buddy," he says when Ariel clears out. He's anxious to get on the road, so he picks Buzz up off the ground, and now he's holding his little boy for the very first time. He can't help wondering what it would have been like to hold him the day he was born. "Can I strap you into your new seat?"

The boy puts a warm hand on his chest and frowns, his blue eyes holding his own. "But I can do it *myself*."

He laughs. And having no more excuses to hold him out here in the sunshine, he leans over and eases him onto the seat instead.

It's a thirty-five-mile drive back to the house. That's what you get for hiding out in the middle of nowhere. In the back seat, Buzz is chatting with both his Tonka truck and the shark stuffy.

Jay listens with one ear while keeping an eye on the other vehicles on the highway. He's watching for a tail.

"Can I ask a question?" Ariel says.

"Anything."

"How do you make a living?"

"Ah." He chuckles. "That's a boring question. I do freelance programming as an LLC registered in Delaware. Freelancing isn't the most lucrative, but my house is cheap, and my taxes are low. My bills are all in the corporate name, or in Woody's name. The VA handles my healthcare, but I use a fictitious address and drive out of state to see doctors, just in case someone hacks their records."

His phone chimes, and he puts a hand on Ariel's knee. "Check that, would you?"

She picks up the phone and unlocks it by turning it toward his face. "Okay—Woody is up, and says everything is quiet."

"Excellent. Do me a favor and check your email? There should be a signal here." It's not a given in Northern Michigan.

She taps away at the screen for a while, as his curiosity grows. "Anything?"

"Yeah. It's interesting. I'll show you when you pull over for gas."

He stops a few minutes later. She gets out of the Jeep to show him what her mother and Ray have written back.

Her mom wrote:

Ariel, could you call me? You are giving me such a scare. It's not like you to disappear. Is something wrong?

Ray's message is both vague and irritating:

Honey, this is serious. Please tell me where you are, so I can keep you safe.

He nudges Ariel. "Note the lack of detail. He's still trying to cover his ass."

"Keep reading," Ariel says. "I pushed that point."

So she did.

Safe from who?

And her cowardly uncle responded only a moment later:

There are bad people in the world.

She fired back:

Noted. But I'm not coming home until I figure out if you're one of them.

"You are so hot to me right now," he whispers.

She laughs, but he can tell she's nervous.

"Hey." The pump clicks off, but he wraps his arm around her instead of dealing with it. "I will keep you safe, or I will die trying."

"It better not come to that," she whispers.

He gives her a quick kiss on the jaw, because he doesn't like to make promises he can't keep.

52

ARIEL

I take a nap after our trip to Target, because I still haven't caught up on my sleep.

And when I come downstairs in the late afternoon, Jay and Woody have formed a plan. It involves swapping Jay's Jeep for Woody's SUV, and a fishing cabin owned by a friend of a friend.

"What's our other plan?" I press. "I want to call the police-woman I spoke to after Zain's"—I stop myself before saying *death*, in case Buzz looks up from his new toys—"and ask her to look into Zarkey's sister."

"That could work," Jay says. He's poking potatoes with a fork and placing them into the oven. "But I'm worried that the Portland PD is in your uncle's pocket."

"How far in his pocket, though? I'm sure they like free cameras and charitable support as much as the next guys, but unless the ring of fraudulent judges is a whole lot bigger than we thought, I don't know why they wouldn't care about a—" I stop myself again before saying *murder*.

"You can take their temperature on it," Woody says. "Meanwhile, you guys can send Ariel's, uh, CEO some of the evidence you guys have. If he thinks coming clean is inevitable, he'll work harder to end up on the right side of the story."

"Or he'll run for the hilltops," Jay murmurs.

"Maybe," I concede. "But I like this idea. He's probably scared. If we give him a last chance to throw the Zarkeys under the bus, he might take it."

Jay nods, but the expression on his face says he doesn't quite buy it.

I'm not sure I blame him.

"We'll leave tomorrow," he says. "First thing."

I don't argue.

Jay defrosts some steaks for dinner. I wash lettuce for a salad. Buzz covers the living room floor with die-cast cars and pieces of plastic track.

As I do laundry, I can smell the charcoal heating on the grill, and I let myself pretend that this is an ordinary summer day with the family. The only one I've ever had.

Sure, we're packing to run from killers. And Jay is monitoring the perimeter. But a girl can fantasize. As I pass his command center on the sofa, I run my knuckles gently across the back of his neck. He turns to me with a glance that's loaded with appreciation. I hold his gaze, and he gives me a secretive smile that suggests the bathroom counter might see some more action later.

When it's almost time for dinner, Woody drives over and leaves the keys in his SUV so we can drive it away in the morning.

Jay opens three beers and passes them around. Woody sits down in front of the monitors, and Jay waves me out into the yard with him.

It's a beautiful night, and the shadows are growing longer at the tree line as I follow him outside. "When are we going to tell him?" he asks as he checks the coals on the grill. "Can it be soon? I want him to know me."

The rush of love I feel is swift and fierce. "Yes. Tomorrow. When we're alone, just the three of us."

Those blue eyes flash to mine. "Waiting any longer might not work anyway. I don't know what you told him about me, but when you were in the laundry room, he asked me if I used to be a soldier, and how did I get that scar under my eye?"

"Oh God." I laugh nervously. "Tomorrow, then."

His expression turns solemn. "I'll say anything you need me to. I'll tell him I was an idiot to leave you both."

"There's no need to martyr yourself. Four is little. He accepts things, as long as you make him feel safe."

"And how do I do that?"

"By reading picture books and watching *Toy Story*."

He flashes me a smile over his shoulder. "I love that you named him Buzz."

"I guess I wasn't ready to let go of you." Another rare admission from the queen of not caring. But I'm working on it. "Nobody else knows the significance. My mom took it in stride."

"Hey—you'd better check your email." He hands me his phone. "Maybe your mom replied to you. Or Ray. The VPN is already on."

"Okay." When I open up my new account on his phone, there's a message from Officer Barski of the Portland PD. "No *way*."

"What is it?" Jay moves to read over my shoulder.

Ariel—I just went by your family's home on Chadwick Street, and you weren't there. Your mother is very worried about you and your son. She's on the verge of filing a missing person report. If you get this message, please call your mother and then me, in that order.

I'm also looking for your uncle Ray, with regard to an ongoing investigation into the death of your coworker Zain. But we can't find Ray, either. Your mother is worried about him, too. And I would like to interview him.

Please call when you receive this.

Jay lets out a low whistle. "Ray is in the wind? Or else the cop could be lying. Are you going to reply?"

"I sure am."

Dear Mr. Barski, I have no idea where my uncle Ray is. But if you can't find him, he's either running for his life or running from law enforcement. You should absolutely take it seriously.

I'm pretty sure the break-in to my apartment, and Zain's death, are the result of me asking too many questions about illegal activity at Chime Co. Hence my trip out of town.

Here's a sample of what I know: There's an ex-employee named Bryan Zarkey who I suspect is a violent criminal. He and his sister are probably drug dealers. I think Zarkey used inappropriate access to Chime Co. technology to pull off a variety of illegal activities. But now that Zain is gone, I'd have trouble proving it.

Ray is the one with all the answers, and I no longer
trust him. I have not explained any of this to my mother
because she will lose her mind. I don't think she's in
any danger, though. She doesn't know anything about
Zarkey. And Ray would never have told my mother
anything that reflects badly on himself.

If you find Ray or the Zarkeys, please let me know. Until
then, I'm staying put.

"We can rig up a VoIP call," Jay says as I tap endlessly on his
screen. "You can call him instead of writing all that."

"Next time," I grumble.

"How's your mom been, by the way?"

"Fine up until now. She's planning to marry Ray in October."

"So they're making it official."

I lift my head. "You heard about them?"

His mouth twists. "Well, remember that Fourth of July party
at your parents' pl—"

"Marker! We lost a camera," Woody calls from inside the
house. "South perimeter."

My heart leaps in fear. "Oh God."

Jay shakes his head. "Don't panic yet. Those cameras eat bat-
teries. I'll check it out. Come inside, though?"

I follow him into the house, where Woody is studying the other
camera views with a new intensity. "Better suit up," Woody says.
"Just in case."

"You know it." Jay heads upstairs.

Nervous, I follow him. He heads into the bedroom, and then
into the closet.

"Wow. This really *is* a fortress." The motion-sensitive lighting illuminates shelves of gear on the walls. He plucks some kind of vest off a hook and straps it on.

Jesus. My eyes dart around the odd little room. Some camo clothing hangs on a rack. There's camping gear, too—sleeping bags, and a duffel bag with a lock on it. I spot a filing cabinet and tug open the top drawer. It's full of file folders.

JUDGE KERRY: METADATA reads the first one. SHAWMUT STREET WARRANT reads the next.

"Hold on," I sputter. "This is a whole *trove* of evidence."

He grunts an acknowledgment. "I've got to head outside. Can we talk about this later?"

"You said you didn't make it out of Maine with the evidence! There must be a hundred file folders here."

"Baby—"

"Don't *baby* me. You had this when you left Maine? Yes or no? Do *not* lie to me."

His eyes dip. "Yeah, I did."

"And you didn't use it? Why? Because you were saving your own ass?"

Those blue eyes flash with irritation. "*Yes!* Now can you just let me save it again, please? Now is *not* the time." He steps out of the closet, and I follow, hot on his heels.

We're on the landing when Woody yells, "Intruder! Ariel—take Buzz upstairs. Now."

Even before I can process the sound of Woody's voice, Jay has bounded down the stairs and scooped Buzz off the floor.

"But I'm *playing* here!" my son protests.

I meet him at the bottom of the stairs, taking Buzz in my arms. "Come with me. Your daddy needs you to go upstairs."

"My daddy?"

I'm already climbing as Woody says, "South perimeter. White male. Camo jacket, baseball hat . . ."

Before I run into the bedroom, I turn around and glance over the banister for one last look at Jay. He's unholstering a gun and shoving something into his ear. "Keep talking," he says to Woody. Then he heads out of sight, in the direction of the kitchen door.

My stomach bottoms out. I make myself walk into the bedroom, close the door and bolt it. I set Buzz down on the bed.

But then I don't know what to do, and I don't know what to tell my child. He's already looking at me for answers. "What are they *doing*, Mama? Did Woody see a man on the screen?"

"I think so." My voice is shaky.

"Jay has the scar right here," Buzz says, pointing at his cheek beneath his left eye. "He was a soldier."

I don't say anything. I just hold him close. Until we hear the sound of a gunshot. It's so loud we both startle. "*Oh my God.*"

Buzz starts to cry.

"Baby, it's okay." I cuddle him against my body. "I'm sorry. This is scary. Jay shot the gun to scare the other man away." As I say these words, I realize they're possibly true.

Since the windows are open, I can hear the rumble of Woody's voice drifting upward. The words are indistinct. But it sounds like he's talking to Jay, keeping him up to date on the intruder's whereabouts.

Then I hear a second gunshot.

I have never been so scared.

"Mama, is my daddy okay?" Buzz babbles.

"Yes," I say, because I have no choice. "But guess what?" I pick up Buzz's stuffed shark. "Sharks don't like loud noises. Would you take him in the closet for me?"

He gives me a tearful nod. "Okay."

"Good boy. Look—the light in here is automatic." Staying low, I carry him to the closet door and open it. The light flickers on. "See? If it gets dark, all you have to do is wave your arms and it will light up again. Now, you sit down."

He plops into the center of the rug.

"If I tell you to, close the door, okay?"

He nods.

"Now whistle something for the shark. So he isn't scared."

When I turn my back, I hear him start a shaky tune.

I scurry to the bed and peer underneath. As promised, the only thing under there is a rope ladder. The top of it is strung through a steel bar that's wide enough to catch on either side of Jay's windows.

As I drag it out, we hear another gunshot.

"You have to look outside," Buzz insists.

"Only if you stay there." But he's right. I have to look. I can't stand not knowing. "Do *not* move," I say to Buzz. Then I crawl across the wood floor toward the windows, bringing the rope ladder with me. I tuck myself into the corner of the room and rise to my feet. Then I risk a glance outside.

What I see makes my heart stop. Jay has moved away from the safety of the house. He's hiding behind a wheelbarrow. As I watch, he makes a dash for a small shed thirty or forty paces from the house. There's another blast, and the wood splinters just as he ducks behind it.

Then there's *another* blast, from inside the house, and I can't see its target. But Jay's strategy seems to be drawing the intruder away from the house, while Woody tries to pick him off from inside.

He's using himself as *bait*.

I slump down into the corner, panicked. My backpack is here, though, and I plunge my arm inside, looking for my phone. And when I don't find it, I upend the bag and stare at the mess of its contents.

But of course my phone isn't here. It's a thousand miles away.

I can't dial 911.

I can't even think.

Woody's voice grows suddenly louder. "Second perp! White . . . male or female. West perimeter, just south of the driveway . . ."

I pop up again, afraid to look but also afraid not to. Something moves right below me, and my insides seize up.

It's a man. I can't see his face under the hat. But I don't miss his gun.

Then he pivots and shoots right into the first floor of the house. I hear the distant sound of glass breaking, and then an angry curse from Woody.

"Mama," Buzz gasps. "Do something!"

"It's okay," I say stupidly. Nothing is okay. I watch the shed. Jay's shadow is visible on one side. The shooter advances two steps, and I can't even breathe.

"Watch your six!" Woody yells. "Fuck!"

I hear another gunshot—a more distant one. But there's a loud thump from the shed as Jay's shadow jumps in a sickening way.

The shadow flails and then holds still.

"Talk to me, Marker!" Woody barks.

Oh my God. I bite down so hard on my lip I taste blood.

Beneath me, the first shooter advances slowly along the wall of the house in the direction of the shed. It's Bryan Zarkey. Like a snake in the grass, he's crouching low to stay clear of the windows and Woody. Then he stops and takes a position on his knees. He's reloading the gun.

"Mama?"

"Close the door and lock it," I hiss.

Miraculously, he does. I hear the bolt slide into place as I reach for the only weapon I've got—a chef's knife. With a cardboard sheath slipping off the blade.

Beneath me, Zarkey finishes reloading. He raises the gun carefully, aiming again at the corner of the shed, where Jay's shadow is now moving out of view so achingly slowly that I gag on nothing.

Oh, God. What can I do?

With a quick yank, I pop Jay's cheap screen out of the frame. Then I brace the rope ladder against the window and heave the rope outside.

Zarkey whips around at the noise.

I've bought Jay a few seconds as Zarkey advances toward the ladder instead of firing more shots at Jay. I put the knife blade on the rope and begin to saw back and forth. The first bits of rope immediately begin to fray.

The ropes go taut as Zarkey puts weight on the ladder. I keep cutting. I'm already halfway through the first rope, and I'm hoping Jay doesn't need much time to regroup.

Then my knife goes thunk against something hard. What the . . . ? I saw frantically, but the rope doesn't slice through. Instead, I see the glint of metal. There's a steel cord inside the nylon one.

And just as I'm having this realization, I can already hear Zarkey breathing. He's advancing quickly toward my open window.

I step back, horrified, and the next few seconds seem to last ten years. As Zarkey climbs, I close my fist around the handle of the knife. Holding my breath, I flatten myself against the wall as the top of his head appears.

For a terrible moment, I'm paralyzed with fear. He grasps the windowsill and begins to turn his head toward me.

That's when I come unstuck. I raise my arm overhead. And just as his gaze swings toward mine, I thrust the big knife downward toward the juncture of his neck and shoulder.

He ducks, so it's not a clean strike. Not even close. But even so, the knife digs into his shoulder through his shirt.

He shrieks, losing his grip on the windowsill and dropping out of view.

I hear his body hit the grass, and then I peer out of the window. But I don't even get a good look at him, because Woody emerges from a window below, jumping out onto Zarkey's body and punching him in the head.

Jerking back from the window, I run to the closet and knock on the door. "It's Mama. Let me in."

The bolt slides open again, and I fling the door open and crush Buzz into a hug.

"Is my daddy okay?" he whimpers.

I don't answer, because I don't want to lie anymore.

Buzz cries. And so do I.

Then I hear sirens.

53

The trauma center in Traverse City is forty miles away.

I'm in the back seat of the Jeep with Buzz, who has finally passed out after two hours of crying.

For a long time we couldn't come out of the bedroom. The cops took a while to verify that the Zarkeys—both neutralized by Jay and Woody—didn't have backup waiting in the woods.

So we were still up there when the paramedics ran Jay's stretcher to the ambulance. There was so much blood. Buzz watched from the window, crying hysterically, and fighting me whenever I tried to pull him away.

With me murmuring *I'm sorry, I'm sorry* on repeat while I tried to calm him down.

Finally, after a few questions voiced over my sobbing child, the cops let me go.

But not Woody. He's being interviewed by law enforcement. I have no idea if he'll be charged with a crime. I don't know anything about firearms, or how self-defense is supposed to work.

Zarkey was visibly responsive when they carried him off. But his sister was not. I suspect she's dead, but I wasn't willing to inquire in front of Buzz.

If she is, though, then Jay killed her.

Nobody asked me about the knife in the grass. Nobody seems to realize yet that I'm the one who used it.

Although the cops were skeptical about my complete lack of ID.

But I referred them to Officer Barski in Portland, Maine. And then I demanded to go to the hospital, while Buzz hiccupped in my arms.

Miraculously, they said yes.

Woody seems to be friendly with the cops. They agreed to call his mother, who fussed over him and then offered to drive us to the hospital.

She's a sturdy-looking woman with sun-toughened skin and frizzy hair. I don't even try to make conversation with the back of her head on the ride. All I can do is stare down at Buzz and hope he'll get past this somehow.

My baby's sleeping face is tearstained and puffy, and it's all my fault for being so selfish. I just had to know why Jay left me. I steered us here to satisfy my own curiosity. The result is either that I gave Buzz his daddy back. Or that I gave him a lifelong trauma. Or both.

Only time will tell, and time is determined to move forward at a crawl.

"You should try your mother again," Mrs. Carter says from the front seat.

"I will. Thank you." I take the phone that she hands back and redial my mother, who didn't answer the first time I called.

"Hello?" she chirps as soon as she picks up. "Who is this?"

"Mom, it's me," I say. "I'm in Michigan. There's been some trouble, but Buzz and I are okay."

She lets out a sob. "Michigan! That's where Ray was trying to go. But he was arrested at the airport."

"Really?" I ask, before I realize that I don't care. He had so many chances to do the right thing. And he didn't. Not once.

"Do you need me?" my mother asks in a shaky voice. "I'll come."

The question takes me by surprise. "Yes," I tell her. "Bring Frog and Toad."

The hospital waiting room is nicer than it should be, with blue sofas and matted prints of Michigan landscapes on the walls.

Jay is in surgery for hours. Around midnight, a doctor comes out to tell us in a droning voice that the surgery is complete. He uses phrases like *significant repair* and *internal bleeding*.

"Does he wake up?" my child asks.

Only then does the exhausted doctor seem to make eye contact. "Not yet," he says. "He's breathing on his own, but it could be a long time. You should go home and sleep."

But I don't have a home. And even if it makes me a terrible parent, we aren't leaving. They move us to a waiting room nearer to the ICU. The sofas are a different shade of blue. Buzz curls up and falls asleep, and one of the nurses brings a blanket to tuck around him.

I wait.

Woody arrives around two in the morning, looking exhausted. He gives me a wan smile. "If you want to go to a hotel, I'll wait here."

I shake my head. "Glad to see you're not in jail."

"Michigan has a stand your ground law. And my guns are legally registered. They found your knife, by the way. Your prints are probably on it, so I told them you stabbed the guy. Honey, you might have saved Jay's life."

"Might have. If he ever wakes up."

"Hey, none of that," he whispers. "He's strong. We've been here before. I tied the tourniquet on his leg last time."

"How'd that happen, anyway?" I ask. "He would never give me the details. Told me it wasn't much of a story."

Woody tips his head back and laughs so loudly that Buzz twitches in his sleep. "You are kidding me. That's hilarious."

"Why?"

He shakes his head, smiling. "He was directing a sweep—checking for mines in a Syrian neighborhood we'd just helped the locals retake. His K-9 guys are trying to clear this alley, but people are just pouring into this town. Total chaos, and we don't have enough translators. There's a kid, about that size." He points at Buzz. "He's walking into the alley at the far end. Jay tells him to stop, it's not safe. And for God's sake don't go near that stack of crates on the wall. So what does the kid do?"

"Makes a beeline for the crates?" I guess.

He nods. "Kid couldn't understand him. Jay runs down there as the kid picks up the first crate. Something starts to teeter—always a bad sign. That's how you set a trap. Jay dives to push the kid back out of the alley, and then I hear the boom." He shakes his head. "I got a nice piece of shrapnel lodged in my scalp." He points at his head. "And Jay left his foot behind. But we made it out alive. We always do."

"Well, I hope you're right." I swallow the giant lump in my throat. "Optimism doesn't come naturally to me."

He laughs again. "I heard that about you. But I also heard you come by it honestly."

I'm dozing, my head heavy on my own shoulder, when Woody shakes me. "Hey, hey. Ariel, he's asking for you."

"What?" The fluorescent light burns into my eyes as I come swiftly to consciousness. "Can I see him?" I slur.

"Sure, honey." The nurse beckons.

I look down at Buzz, who's sleeping soundly.

"Go on," Woody says. "I'll stay."

Still, I hesitate. After all Buzz has been through, I am afraid to walk away from him.

"I won't move from this spot," he says. "I promise."

Dizzy from anxiety and sleep deprivation, I sway to my feet and follow the nurse through a set of double doors.

As she walks me into Jay's room, I realize that his bed is actually visible from the windows in the waiting room. But I didn't recognize him underneath all the tubes and machinery.

He's very still, and his skin is a pasty color. When people say *he looks like death*, I'm pretty sure this is exactly what they mean.

"Five minutes," the nurse says. "You can touch him. It's okay."

I take his hand, which is warm and dry. "Hey," I whisper, my voice untrustworthy. "It's me."

When his blue eyes flip open and focus on me, the tight metal band inside my chest eases up just a little. "You okay?" His voice is shredded.

"Fine," I rasp, trying to hold myself together.

"Buzz?"

"Fine," I say more firmly. "Woody, too."

His eyes close. "That was a close one. Too close."

"I don't know," I say, trying for a joke. "You didn't lose any limbs this time."

"Too close to *you*," he says. "Unacceptable. What were you thinking? I drew him away from the house. You threw him a ladder."

I put my elbows on the bed and lift his hand up to my face, just so I can feel his skin against mine. "It didn't go exactly how I planned."

"That happens . . ." He has to pause between words. "With us."

"Yeah, it does." I push my face into the warmth of his palm and sigh.

There's a rap on the window. I lift my eyes to see Woody standing there, Buzz on his hip. My little boy is smushing his nose against the glass, trying to see.

"Can you wave?" I ask, releasing his hand. "I wouldn't ask, but Buzzy wants to know you're okay."

"Oh yeah," he says, opening his eyes. "Tell him the Toy Story marathon starts tomorrow."

He slowly waves, and Buzzy bangs on the glass in delight, which sends two nurses scurrying toward the window to shush him.

I take my first full breath in hours.

54

SEPTEMBER

"Do you see a spot?" Jay asks me as we creep past the preschool in the Jeep. "Where's a guy supposed to park around here?"

"There. She's leaving," I say, pointing at a car with its taillights illuminated.

Parking was never an issue when I used to ride the bike. But Buzz has officially outgrown the kiddie seat. And Jay wasn't about to miss the first day of school.

He zooms into the spot as soon as it's free. "Okay, kiddo. Let's do this school thing."

My son is ready. He unbuckles himself and hops out, backpack in hand.

Another little boy races up to him on the sidewalk. "You got a red car? Jeeps are cool."

"I know!" Buzz says. And then, with obvious glee, he adds, "There's a bullet hole in it!"

Oops. I should have asked Buzz not to mention that.

When I look up, about a dozen other parents are openly gawking at us. The bullet hole isn't the only reason, either. They're staring at Jay. I've never arrived at school with a man at my side. That's the kind of gossip these women live for.

Meanwhile, the Cafferty family drama has dominated Maine news coverage for three solid months, with no sign of letting up. My uncle is currently out on bail, wearing an ankle monitor and awaiting trial for multiple crimes, including corporate fraud charges and accessory to my father's murder.

There's talk he'll make a deal with the prosecutor in exchange for nailing Bryan Zarkey on multiple drug charges and murder.

Ray and I don't speak, but my mother fills me in, whether I ask her for details or not. I hear he's keeping a whole team of lawyers busy defending him. They claim he wasn't aware of the fake judges, or Ward's video stalking, or Amina's death.

Although it was Ray who swapped my father's pills for the ones that Zarkey's sister had made for him. But he says that Zarkey double-crossed him with the lethal dose, to ensure his silence. He says he was in over his head with Zarkey, the psychopath.

That's the most believable part of his whole defense. But it's still Ray's fault. He turned a blind eye because he and Zarkey had a plan to build an AI company that would dwarf the success of Chime Co.

But after Jay put a wrench in their plans, they quietly sold the LiveMatch technology to a competitor at the fire-sale price of forty million dollars, and Zarkey allegedly still consults on the product, which is how he tracked me to Michigan. So neither one of them will have trouble paying their legal bills.

They can both go to jail, for all I care. Someone should pay for Zain's death. That's the part I'll never get over.

Jay is recovering from his gunshot wound, though. And his legal troubles aren't as bad as they could have been. In exchange for his complete cooperation in the matter of Chime Co.'s corporate sins, his identity fraud charges will be downgraded.

Jay's file cabinet full of evidence is finally seeing the light of day, and our lawyer expects him to receive a sentence of probation and community service.

The unfortunate result is that our little family has become rather infamous. It's all over the papers, which is why the other parents are watching our approach to preschool like we're the latest episode to drop on some grizzly HBO crime series. I don't even blame them.

But Jay is oblivious. "Wait, wait," he says, corralling Buzz in front of the preschool building. "Don't run inside yet, I need a picture."

"We did the picture at home," Buzz argues.

"That was the *at home* picture. This will be the school picture."

Amused, I wait on the sidewalk as Jay photographs Buzz near the door.

"Now pretend you're going inside," Jay says, taking multiple photos.

"We *are* going inside. Aren't we?"

"In a minute," Jay says, snapping another shot. "Okay—now a selfie with me and Mommy. Ariel, come here a sec, would you?"

"Another one?" Buzz squirms.

I hurry over and stand beside him, because it won't take too long, and I don't want to ruin Jay's first-day-of-school vibes.

"Smile!" Jay urges. "Good job. Okay, now show me where your classroom is. I'm ready to meet Miss Betty." We all start toward the door.

"Excuse me, Ariel?" Maddy steps forward, halting my progress with her infernal clipboard. Today, the pen is disguised as a chrysanthemum. "It's time to sign up for the fall festival." She thrusts the clipboard in my direction. "Please take one slot for you and one slot for your partner."

"Baby, take *two* slots for me!" Jay calls from the steps.

As if. He has no idea how slippery that slope can be. So I check just two boxes—one for apple bobbing, and one for pumpkin carving.

"Oh, those are fun choices," Maddy gushes as she takes the clipboard back. "The apples and the pumpkins come to us at a discount from the orchard. You'll pick them up the day before, okay? I'll get you the number. We've got plastic carving tools, but you'll need a chef's knife to cut the stems out. You can wrap a piece of cardboard—"

"Around the blade," I say. "So I won't cut my bag. You gave me that tip last year. And thank you, Maddy. Really. I literally found that tip to be a *lifesaver*."

Maddy gives a slow blink. "You're welcome, Ariel."

"Now if you'll excuse me . . ."

I hurry after my family into the school while the other moms continue to stare.

Ten minutes later we're back in the Jeep. But Jay doesn't start the car. He just sits there for a second, tapping his fingers on the steering wheel.

"Everything okay?" I ask. "Aren't we going to the paint store?"

"Yeah," he says, turning to me.

I should probably be over the surprise by now. But when I see those steady blue eyes look my way, I am still a little stunned that he's here with me. For good.

"Is he really okay?" he says, his gaze flipping toward the school building. "We're just *leaving* him here with strangers? Didn't he seem a little hesitant?"

I laugh and grab his hand. "He's always a little quiet during the first half hour. That's just Buzz."

"If you're sure." He gives me the kind of smile that makes my stomach swoopy. "Paint store, then?"

"Definitely. We've got the whole morning."

Needless to say, I'm no longer an employee of Chime Co. My uncle isn't, either. My mother and the C-suite team have hired a new CEO—one who promised to make privacy and security his number one priority.

After all the bad press, I expected Chime Co. to go belly up. I'm no businessperson, but I couldn't fathom how a brand could survive all this negative coverage about privacy violations and illegal surveillance.

For a minute there, it looked like I was right. Sales of new devices and subscriptions dipped a whole ten percent. But then sales leveled off when the new CEO came onboard. Which means that ninety percent of Chime Co. customers simply shrugged at the thought of randos with bad intentions watching their private video feeds.

What's more, my mother expects to sell the company to a tech giant in the next three years, after the scandal dies down. She tells me they're already circling like seagulls on the pier.

Mom is coping. I'll give her that. She's had to step in and involve herself with Chime Co. now that her ex-fiancé is in disgrace. The wedding is off, too. For now, anyway. I have a sneaking suspicion that Ray and my mother will find their way back to each other eventually. She still talks to him all the time.

I love my mother, but I don't understand her. But I guess she'd probably say the same about me.

———————

"How about this one?" Jay asks, holding up a paint sample in a saturated yellow.

"Baby, that's a little bright. What's it called?"

He flips over the paint chip. "*Nacho cheese.*"

"Get out of town. Really?"

Laughing, he hands it to me. The color is called *Corn silk*. "You believed me, though."

I give him a playful swat with the stack of paint chips in my hand. "It's too bright, whatever it's called. How about this—we'll buy a sample of yours, and a sample of mine, and put them to the test?"

He hands me the paint chip. "Baby, you can choose all the colors. You're the artist in this relationship. I'm just the comic relief."

"Don't sell yourself short, Marker. You also look good in a tool belt."

He laughs loudly, and heads turn in our direction. I don't know if they're staring because we're rowdy or because they read about us on the internet. But I don't actually care. We have a house to paint, and it will be a little easier to work on now that Buzz is back in school.

With my mother's generous financial assistance, Jay and I have purchased a fixer-upper on Neal Street. Over the coming year, Jay's going to restore it. He's got the time—there isn't a lot of demand for programmers who have identity theft in their résumés.

Although the new CEO of Chime Co. offered him a job.

He declined.

We spent the summer playing with Buzz, walking Buster around the neighborhood and making renovation plans. There were legal appointments, and a lot of post-surgical care appointments for Jay. He's healthy enough now to sand the floors and paint the upstairs rooms. This winter, Woody will come out for a visit, and they'll renovate the kitchen together.

My role is to choose all the decor. Buzz wants a "space wall" in his room—deep blue with painted stars that glow in the dark.

I can't wait to start. But choosing colors is tricky, so I buy samples of three different yellows for the upstairs hallway and two different blues for Buzz's wall, and now I need something for the trim.

"Why are there so many shades of white?" Jay wants to know. "I thought white was just white."

"There are cool whites and warm whites. I just need five more minutes."

Jay looks at his watch. "Where do you want to have lunch after we pick Buzz up from school? I was thinking either the Black Cow or Duckfat."

The idea of eating fried food is strangely off-putting at the moment. "Let's make it a game-time decision."

"Okay. Fair."

We pay and head home again. Our new house is in the West End neighborhood close to my mother's. It's a brick-and-shingle home dating back to 1897. Three bedrooms, two bathrooms, and a driveway so narrow that the Jeep barely fits.

I love it desperately. Every creaky board, and every drafty window. And I can't wait to splash new paint on the walls. Everything upstairs is currently a murky beige.

"Uh-oh," Jay says. "Wasn't expecting to see him today."

I look up to see an FBI agent on our front porch. Jim Hickson is the lead investigator on the Chime Co. crimes. He and Jay have spent a lot of quality time together these past few months as the prosecution builds its case.

"Did you forget a meeting?" I ask. "Your lawyer will have a cow if you speak to Hickson alone."

"Maybe it's just a quick question," he says. He climbs out of the Jeep and greets the agent with a wave and an outstretched hand.

I collect our bag of tiny paint cans and head for the door.

"Hey, Ariel?" Jay calls. "Honey?"

When I turn, Hickson is approaching me. "Sorry to interrupt your morning," he says, offering his hand for a shake. "But the question I have is for you, not Jay."

"Oh." That's unusual. "Will it take much time?"

He shakes his head. "Five minutes, tops. You either remember this detail, or you don't."

"All right. Come inside." I lead him into the kitchen.

"If you wouldn't mind," Hickson says, "this question has to be asked in private. Is that your office?" He points into the room that will eventually become our den.

"That room is a *mess*. But sure." If he wants to step over the belt sander and some wallpaper samples, it's no skin off my nose.

Once we're inside, he closes the door. "I promise to be quick. Can you tell me—maybe you keep a calendar on your phone—if you know where you were on the night of November sixth, 2015?"

I pull out my phone. "Seven years ago? Why?" But even as I speak the words, I remember what happened on November sixth, 2015. "That's the date that Judge Kerry got set up in the warrant system."

He nods. "Could you just have a peek at your calendar?"

I tap the calendar app. But as my finger hovers above the screen, I pause. "Why would you care where I was that night?"

"If you could just check, please."

My stomach bottoms out. "Hold on. Do you think it was *me* who put that judge into the system? It wasn't. Zain told me it was *him*."

His face doesn't change. "If you could just check your calendar?"

Oh my God. I start scrolling. But my mind is spinning faster than the dates on the screen. How could it be *me*? I worked maybe four shifts on the warrant desk, ever.

But I have the worst sinking feeling. And then November comes up on my screen. "Oh God."

"Did you find it?" the jerk asks.

"No." But also yes. My calendar reads **First Friday party. Open Studio 6p-9p!**

My heart takes a sickening dive. And I hand the phone to Agent Hickson.

"You were at a party?" he asks, skeptical.

"I was supposed to be. Portland has First Friday parties all the time . . ." I lapse into silence for a moment, remembering how it unfolded. I'd been to dozens of these Friday night gatherings. "But that night my boss—Larissa—had decided to host a cocktail event at our studio. She never does that."

So I helped her clean the place and string fairy lights all over the windows. We bought boxed wine and fruit for a sangria punch bowl that was both generous and affordable. We went to BJ's for cheese and crackers, and hors d'oeuvres we planned to heat in the annealing oven.

". . . But that afternoon my father called and demanded that I work on the warrant desk."

"Did that happen a lot?" Hickson wants to know.

My throat is suddenly so dry that it's hard to answer. "Almost never. I tried to refuse, on the grounds that it was a big night for the studio. But he yelled at me. He reminded me that he paid my rent every month. And if I expected the arrangement to continue, I'd better show up."

I was *so* angry. But that wasn't even unusual. And I gave in, because I didn't have a choice.

"Do you remember setting up a new judge that night?" He hands me my phone back. And then he hands me a printout. It's a still shot, and it must be from the video backup they take of the warrant desk.

It's me all right. In the picture, I'm wearing a black dress. I remember that now. I wore the dress so I could run out at the stroke of eight fifteen and make the last half hour of the party.

This is the video that Zain never got around to showing me before he died. And now I realize why. He saw this. And he knew it would gut me.

So he decided to lie about it. He said *he'd* set up the judge. Because he realized I'd never know the difference.

Oh my God. I'm the guilty one. "Do I need a lawyer?" I croak. "Am I in trouble?"

"No, not at all," Hickson says immediately. "The way the warrant desk was set up, anyone could have taken this inquiry. But I needed to know who asked you to work that shift."

"My father." I feel suddenly light-headed, so I sit down in the only chair. "It has to have been a coincidence."

"Or insurance," he says quietly. "For whoever sent the inquiry through that night. If your father thought you could be implicated, he could have been persuaded to keep quiet about the crime."

"Who did this?" I demand. "Who put this first warrant into the system? Was it Zarkey? Or Ray?"

He lifts his hands in a gesture that usually means *I don't know.* But from an FBI agent, it means *I'm not going to say.*

And now I'm just angry. "We're done here. That's enough questions."

"All right, Ariel. Thank you for your cooperation. It helps a great deal." He leaves the den, and I lean over and put my head in my hands. I feel shaky.

It only gets worse a minute later when Jay arrives. "You okay?"

"*No.*" I look up fast, and it doesn't help my sudden nausea. "It was *my* fault Judge Kerry was entered into the system. *I put him in.*" The last words come out as a gasp.

And Jay's face falls. His eyes dip as his expression fills with despair.

Oh God. If I'd been more careful . . .

Suddenly, my stomach tries to climb up my throat. I shoot up out of my chair, stumble over the wallpaper samples and hurry to the little bathroom off the kitchen.

I make it just in time to hurl into the toilet.

Jay is there seconds later, kneeling beside me, reaching for a tissue and making soothing noises.

"Don't," I say, swiping at the tears on my face. "Don't be nice! I can't believe it was me. No—I *can* believe it. I was so *proud* of not giving a damn! And look what happened!"

"Shh, shh," he says. "It's okay."

Nothing is okay. A girl *died* because I sat there like an idiot and tapped that judge's name into the system.

Jay is very matter-of-fact as he puts the lid down and flushes the toilet. Then he hoists me up to stand and turns on the sink.

I grab a handful of icy water and rinse out my mouth. Then I splash some more on my face. The water is bracing, but I'm still reeling.

It's just hitting me that Zain tried to protect me, too. I didn't deserve that. "Goddamn him."

"What, honey?" Jay passes me a towel.

"Zain watched the video. He watched it, and he knew. And I think he said you . . ." I freeze.

Jay goes very still beside me.

"Wait. Didn't you . . . ?" I turn to face him. "Didn't you download it, too?"

He drops his gaze to the floor.

"Jay. Tell me."

"Yeah," he sighs. "I downloaded it on my way out of town."

I feel a fresh wave of nausea. "Oh God. You *knew*? This whole time?"

"Yeah, so? Christ, I didn't *ever* want you to know. It's not your fault. You were set up."

"Of *course* I was," I sputter. But now I have a horrible new realization. "You never told anybody about the fake judges. You could have sent that to the FBI or the *Boston Globe*. But you didn't."

He blows out a breath. "The judges had been deleted from the network. And Ray knew I was onto him. There didn't seem to be much point."

I grip his arms in both hands. "You didn't go public, though, with a whole filing cabinet full of evidence. And I've been wondering why. Was it because . . ." It's too wild of an idea to say aloud.

He takes my wet, tearstained face in both his hands and holds me still, and the warmth of his palms makes my panic ratchet down. "Because the blast zone would have been too wide," he says quietly. "I went into Chime Co. with guns blazing. I was going to take down my enemy, and I didn't care who got caught in the cross fire. But then things got complicated."

"*I'm* the reason you never went public?" My voice comes out high and hysterical.

But his gaze is so calm that I start to relax. "Amina didn't deserve what she got. But I wasn't going to let you take the fall for what your uncle did."

"But Hickson said I'm not in trouble."

"Right." His voice is quiet. "Because he has Ray trying to nail Zarkey and Zarkey trying to nail Ray. It's different now. I couldn't count on that, though. And I just wasn't willing to risk it. Not for one minute. Not if I could help it."

He leans in and kisses my forehead, and I relax against him instinctively. "Still. What went through your mind when you saw that video?" I shiver. "*There goes the worst employee of Chime Co. My dad was actually right about that.*"

"No, baby. That's not it at all. When I saw you on that video, I saw my own arrogance. I showed up in Portland to make someone *pay*. But the further I got, the more rules I broke. Just like Ray and Zarkey. And even Ward. I thought my own goals were more important than the rules."

"They were," I insist.

"My intentions were better. But when I saw that video, it didn't matter anymore. I wasn't going to take you down with me. Even a one percent chance was too much. Revenge is a shitty lifestyle, baby. I learned that from you."

"You didn't," I argue.

"I did." Jay tightens his arms around me. "You live your life on your own terms, and now you're teaching Buzz to do the same. Don't waste one minute thinking you're to blame for anything that happened at Chime Co. I don't."

I sort of sag against his body, and he holds me up.

"Is there something I can do for you? Are you sick?" he asks, rubbing my back. "Or was that just a really bad shock?"

"I . . ." Deep breath. "I might be just a tiny bit pregnant."

His hands freeze on my back. "Seriously?"

"Probably." I screw my eyes shut, because of course I didn't mean to blurt it out after an ugly moment. "It's a theory I'm working on. The timing isn't great, but . . ."

The rest of that sentence is lost when Jay lets out a whoop that's way too loud for the bathroom. "Holy fu . . . dge," he says, laughing. He's been trying to work on his language, for Buzz's sake. "I *hope* it's true. This time I want to see you get all round and wobbly."

"That is not a selling point," I say into the collar of his T-shirt.

"Says you." He picks me right up off the ground. "Come on. We have to be sure. Let's go."

"What? Where?"

"To a pharmacy. I need to know if this is true."

"Now?"

"Yes, now! We'll need to pick out another paint color, too. Do you hope it's another boy, or a girl? Which room should the baby get?"

"Put me down. I don't care."

But those are lies. I want his arms around me, and I care a great deal.

We both know it, too.

ACKNOWLEDGMENTS

First of all, thank you to my agent, Mollie Glick, for encouraging me when I said, "I think I might like to try suspense." You made the magic happen, and I'm so grateful. And thanks as well to Sarah Stein and the team at HarperCollins who said yes! I'm so excited to be making this journey with you.

It turns out, though, that switching genres is hard. Several people rescued this book at various stages, and they have no idea how grateful I am. Sarah Mayberry, Rosemary DiBattista, KJ Dell'Antonia, and Melissa Frain, thank you for your prompt, thorough, and wildly insightful edits.

Thank you to Jess Lahey, Sarah Stewart Taylor, and Jenny Bent for patting me on the back when things get hard.

Thanks to Erik Zoltan for your tech industry insights and to Michaell Kraatz for welcoming me into your glass studio to learn to blow a beautiful, shiny . . . blob. All research mistakes are my own!

Thank you Claudia F. Stahl for your sharp eyes and to Lauren Blakely (of course) for the killer insight about rogue texts.

ABOUT THE AUTHOR

Sarina Bowen is a twenty-four-time *USA Today* bestselling author and a *Wall Street Journal* bestselling author of contemporary romance novels. Formerly a derivatives trader on Wall Street, Sarina holds a BA in economics from Yale University.